To Dave~

Hope you like This adventurous
Read. Lots of action — love and
good Patriotic values —
Blessings/Peace

Author — Rod Lowry

MW01154248

The DORK OF YORK

AN ADVENTUROUS-LOVE STORY

A MAN FOR HIS TIME AND COUNTRY

A WOMAN STRONG AND TENDER

BY ROD LOWREY

COPYRIGHT © 2019 FOREST R. LOWREY
ALL RIGHTS RESERVED.

ISBN: 9781799260097
INDEPENDENTLY PUBLISHED

INTRODUCTION

Many years ago, as a 'widdo-kiddo' (as Red Skelton verbalized), I probably, typically, enjoyed comic books like many of you. And, like many of you, I had heroes I was particularly fond of and fantasized about when reading about them. Some of them could leap buildings in a single bound – others were super-fast, super-strong, and sometimes big. Sometimes they were all three.

Somewhere along the way, my fantasy crossed with my wish to be something like those heroes. You see, I was always kind of a smaller skinny kid. I was nothing like any of those heroes. Yeah, I played varsity football, basketball, and baseball – but, I was lucky not to have been 'killed'. I seemed to be an average kid, with some good coordination.

So, it was over my many years I, at age 79, took up a life equalizer called 'the pen'. I transformed my life into 'hero' lifestyle full throttle. Gotta say, it's been fun. I've found fiction a good tool to promote old 'fantasy' thoughts and insights.

The hero of this story, 'Billy,' is my alter-ego-be. He is super smart and built like a very large oak tree. I hope you read all of his story. There is treasure there. It's homey, adventurous, romantic, demanding, loving, and provides a good look at mentoring. It is full of the joy found in living-doing what you want to do in life – with your high school sweetheart by your side. You'll find sports, action, career choices, politics, dedication – all in the name of destiny – for two.

Enjoy a life from York to Iraq to Washington D.C. It's quite a trip. You'll learn something new and useful.

Thanks, and enjoy the read.

– Rod Lowrey

DEDICATION

I dedicate this book to the men of old at the morning coffee assembly at Gambrill Gardens Retirement Center and to my new 'old' ex-marine younger friend, Rich, who inspires me to storytelling and laughter. Long live his humor.

Many a good Navy, Army or Marine story has come alive in our coffee clutch times together. The stories and experiences of these people make my days retired worthwhile. We learn as we listen and read.

Hope you read my new book. There is 'stuff' to learn, laugh at, and share positive emotions with. Blessings to you, fellow morning early birds – enjoy a cup for me. AND, thank you for being my friend as we sail into the sunset together. Live, laugh and love.

– Fellow Retiree,
Rod Lowrey
4/18/17

SPECIAL THANKS TO:

Sheri Luster – Manuscript Typing

Don Francis – Computer Advisor

West Point Military College – Consulting

Internet – Research

x

BOOK 1

CHAPTER ONE

In the heyday of time, lived a young man so inclined with greatness, that though being from a little city in Illinois called 'York' his early years were spelling trouble. His life was different, especially when some mean 'peers' called him "The Dork of York." It was a label he did not like, but he was at a loss as to what he could do about it.

He was a funny, skinny twelve-year-old, at an awkward age of life. He wandered the streets, avoiding school many days and buffeted adversity with his cleverness, clowning and pretending he was dumb. He befriended most everyone, who laughed at his jokes, laughed at his looks and skinniness. Many of his mean peers thought him a perfect target for taunting and casting insults at will. He became the target by some for receiving their prejudiced superior airs in the form of physical abuse. This WAS NOT good.

So, it was that William Joseph Brewer, known as 'Billy', entered his teen age years with a bleak future life with not much but his carefree, free-swinging, clown-like image he called life. It was a buffoon image that deceived most all who had contact with him. He had a lot of his teachers fooled at school into thinking he was the class clown. Temporarily, this helped him get away with lot of things in his Middle School Years.

What testing later revealed in his 8th grade life was that he indeed possessed a super memory, photogenic quality ability. His brain was not being challenged in his schooling experience, and his truancy at school was interfering with a continuous flow of each year's academic curriculum progression. He was potentially placing himself in harm's way by not attending school regularly. He was injuring himself on a social level as his life became distanced from his normal school day experiences and relationships.

Occasionally he would do something stupid to some kid or attempt to play up to some girl and she or a boyfriend would take exception to his verbal action and would physically challenge him. Inevitably he would evade a 'slam dunker' by the other guy by laughing or joking his way out of his 'JAM'. Indeed, he might just get hurt, maimed or killed. He really abhorred violence – his body and mindset were not advanced toward violent ways.

He had seen so much of it, in his neighborhood, his city and in the news across the world! Violence was seemingly the preferred way to dealing with differences. It appeared to be a way of life to many.

In Billy's dreamland, he wanted to solve and make good the 'violent' world around him. He clearly saw that as he presently appeared and was physically and mentally attuned, that he was very inferior with abilities to deal with all the problems of the world. At 'Twelve' years old, with the body he possessed, his hope to do anything – change anything – looked negative. His present character of influence left a whole lot to be desired.

It was this condition that his buffoonery with a mean trio of his peers got him the name, "The Dork of York". Unfortunately, that name stuck with him for a while. Influence on anybody or anything would be a non-positive in results if that label hung around his neck. He dreaded his 'state of presence', it in fact frightened him. He silently said to himself, "my life can't go on like this – everyone thinking I'm such a 'wimp', a buffoon and a dumb one." He just didn't have an advantage that impressed anyone.

One day as young Billy got out of bed, he dressed in his jeans, an Old Navy 'T' shirt, Keds and dragged himself downstairs for breakfast. His mom and dad both worked, and he was left to fend for himself – and it was in his twelfth year, yet one year short of being an infamous teenager.

He'd grown a few inches that year – which boosted his height – and his skinniness. His parents were average height though his dad was of six-foot height. His dad couldn't believe that his son was so skinny and such a wimp, or so it seemed. Billy felt the tugging and urge to change – but how? For some reason at the breakfast table Billy bowed his head and folded his hands – to say a 'prayer' to God. He offered these words, "God please change me, so I can be believed as I try to change this troubled world for the better, and for Peace." He finished his Wheaties and milk cereal - "Breakfast of Champions" and then trapezed out the door to wander the streets to see what fun or trouble he might find.

It wasn't long before he ran into a trio of guys looking for 'trouble' and he realized he was vulnerable. They looked at him and decided they needed some play time – and they surrounded him and taunted him with insults and bad offensive language saying, "And what are you going to do about it?" One kid pushed him daring him to push back. He didn't, instead he made a joke about how brave they were. Picking on a skinny kid with the name of the "Dork of York". IT temporarily worked and the 'bad boys' laughed while still encircling him. No one was around that time of day to cede in his behalf. The smallest of the taunters engaged Billy by slapping him in the face to provoke a fight.

For some reason, Billy got mad and tried to sock the mean kid one in the 'chops' – which connected, and the boy staggered a few seconds. The others came to the rescue, grabbed Billy and proceeded to punch him in the gut and face, knocking him to the ground. He lay there bleeding in the mouth and out of wind from the belly punches. The kids found their fun fulfilled and gleefully headed on, leaving Billy licking his wounds.

Billy laid there a few minutes, head swirling, gut hurting, thinking there must be something I can do to prevent this victim status. As he re-assembled himself and wearily stood up and wiped off some blood from his mouth. He looked around only to see three other guys appearing and coming his direction. Now they were running towards him, discerning his condition. Unknown to Billy they 'came to help. They appeared to be some more 'toughies' of the neighborhood, but older and much bigger. They stopped and befriended him. They asked him what had happened, and Billy told them. They listened and asked him who had done this to him and said they would teach these scoundrels a lesson in politeness.

One of the 3 guys called 'Big John' said, "Hey, why don't you come with us to 'Max's Gym' while we work out. Maybe you could find something fun to do there. It'll take all this pain away and get your mind off this incident. Come on Billy – Do you good – You'll be safe with us."

Billy thought the plan sounded good – especially the 'Safe' part. So off they went. Billy thanked them for their caring friendship, saying to them, "You know, it's scary and lonely being skinny like I am." Big John, who thought Billy quite funny said to him, "Billy, why don't you work out with us while you're there. Maybe you'll find something to like – build yourself up. You know, you're young and have lots of growth ahead yet. You can come with us when we workout anytime. We can help you.

"Thanks, Big John," said Billy. "I'd like that." A ray of hope surged through him and he saw that opportunity as a real hope – and a plan jumped into his head. A vision overtook him, and he saw himself not as he was, but as he might be – it was a long shot. He was tired of being known as the 'Dork of York.' That was not him – the real self.

CHAPTER TWO

They all went to Max's Gym and went to their lockers and changed out into some athletic shorts or flannels, and a Max's Gym 'T' shirt. Billy thought this was to be cool. He stayed by his new friends and watched them change. They were all seemingly in superb shape and well-muscled, obviously having worked out for a long time. Especially 'Big John,' who at 6'4" 260 pounds was muscled on top of muscles. His six-packs latterly rippled. He was a force to be reckoned with. Billy said to himself, "I want to be like him – 'Big and Powerful' so no one would dare to mess with me – that's what I want."

He said to Big John, "Big John, how do I get to be like you – all muscled and in shape?"

Big John replied, "Watch what we do for a while, then do it, we'll help you along the way. You can change your appearance and ways. You are going to be tall – I can tell – maybe taller than I am and if you start now, if four or five years – you will be big and strong."

That was music to Billy's ears and hope in his heart. So, Billy just watched the guys work out and looked at everybody else in Max's Gym and took note of what they were doing. His eyes were opened. He realized and felt his luck was indeed changing. It appeared he was in the company of new friends by adoption. His new trio of friends, 'Little Dave' - a tiger of a guy and 'Heavy Lou' - who appeared to be on the fat side but was thick and big – and lifted very heavy weights – seemingly effortless.

Billy discovered 'Little Dave' was a boxer, in fact a 'golden glove boxer of note. He was around five foot ten and weighed in at 185. Big John and 'heavy Lou' were weight lifters – for different reasons.

Heavy Lou weighed in at about 240 pounds; he was a very strong guy and Billy found that he lifted weights that no one else at Max's could even approach: He noticed also that he was a very agile large man, very coordinated; and athletic.

Now Big John at 260 pounds and 6'4" in height was a solid block of a guy, very intimidating. He was a body builder, not a lifter. He attended to every muscle in his body to see that they pronounce themselves BIG and sculpted. Apparently, he had several titles in body building contests – wining many local and state level contests. He was an impressive kind of guy – physically and personality wise.

To Billy; he was maxed out from being around these guys for days at Max's gym. The trio of new friends had all taken an interest in him and had decided to help him become a new person. They established the importance of being physically sound and toned – mentally as well as physically in-order-to withstand the slings and arrows of the world. Sound body advanced self-confidence, assuredness as well as strength.

Billy hung out with his new friends daily and grew in confidence about and for himself. He soon found himself immersed in a plan and routine of weight training and food nutrition programs. His new friends kept at him to persevere and stick with his daily efforts. They said and promised 'his' day would come, and he would find his real grown self to his fullest liking someday. They had full confidence that under their tutelage they could make him into a fully bloomed 'Flower of Iron.' He was now a definite willing volunteer, and his friends became his new teachers and mentors. He was their 'project' and consolidated their friendship even more. They were happy and pleased that they had taken on this 'new' young friend – who was willing.

Indeed, Billy woke up every day, grew in confidence – and new outlook and determination to become that someone – a new human being. He felt differently about himself, yet he was still the twelve-year-old 5'9" 125-pound kid, skinny kid – the perceived wimp and doe-doe, comedian of his class. The teachers could not see past their perception of how he acted, how he performed and how he tested throughout his early school years. The jokester, prankster, the reprobate of 7th Grade – who seemed to be relegated to the prime seat in the headmaster or principal's office.

His parents were concerned, but not very vigilant in helping him become more 'average' in his behavior and in his academic schooling efforts. They were rarely home, working long hours.

Any improvement that Billy had would have to be positive and good or he could possibly become a good candidate for the title, the 'Dork of York' at the Fishbein reform school. His present life style was leading to a life of delinquency and deeper troubles.

It indeed was a blessing and answered prayer – at least in the beginning – that God had steered him, in his wandering search for something, to grab him early on in his troubles and send him into the hands and arms and direction of his new mentoring and tough friends.

Most kids with his lack of homeward direction, a kid wandering the streets looking for fulfillment in all the wrong places – with so many who laughed at him, taunted him or steered him into troubled waters. Billy's future needed realigning. It indeed was a miracle that new life entered in through 3 tough unlikely strangers and had befriended him and gave him new direction and hope. Maybe God does have a destiny for people.

Max's Gym became Billy's new home. It suited well his present needs. He found a new world, a fascinating world, that appealed to him. Especially intriguing to him was a section of the gym dedicated to the teaching of the Martial Arts – such as Karate and Tae Kwan Do, and Judo. It appealed to him for several practical reasons. First, it was good exercise, second, it taught personal defense for yourself. This he thought was a real need he had. So, he studied it and watched the classes for a few days and with the help of his new good buddies – finally enrolled in the class. He was excited and ready to start.

The class would start at 4 PM and that would fit in great after school. Because of his new friends, he referred to them as the 3 Amigos, he now tried to go to school every day, but he still didn't let go of his truancy times at school. These times were narrowing in amount – he hadn't yet caught on the reason for the importance of schooling – what was the gain?

From his neighborhood only, a few went on to college. It was a low to mid income area of town and most people found manual labor of some variety. The garbage truck driver, the city street workers, electricians and air condition repair serviceman. It was trying to become a middle-class small city in Illinois – and slowly achieving some success. Anyone who was ambitious headed out of York – or was lucky enough to find a way out through college and academics or a few small few, who made their way out through athletics. Small town/cities often provided a great source for talented baseball, football or basketball professional stars and great talents. The City of York had spawned a few. Especially famous: were two baseball players, a big-league NBA Pro and a huge lineman for the Chicago Bears. Not bad for a small non-descript, middle class small city in America. The famous were few indeed.

Billy's folks had noticed a certain change in their son, since something happened. They had never heard that he'd been beaten up by a street gang in their neighborhood. Nor, had they heard about Billy's new-found friends. They only knew that the principal called a lot to say that their son was in detention or not there at school – and to come and pick him up. Too often this was the case and they didn't know what to do with him. He didn't seem to be a violent or troublesome boy, yet he seemed to find violence and find mischief wherever he went.

But recently they had noticed a certain change, for the good, and the teachers at school also noticed the change for the better. Billy himself felt a certain change. In fact, he was maturing, and the hormones were running wild. Billy found his mind and outlook was changing. He suddenly decided to take school seriously as he perceived it as a way out for a better life than remaining forever in York. He forecast his life learning would be enhanced through association with Big John, Little Dave and Heavy Lou – they were older and more 'mature and wise' and they had visions of where they wanted to go.

Yet, as locked in as his friends seemed stuck in the small city of York, they had been and seen other places, towns and cities.

They had had a glimpse of the outside world – and it would be advantageous to Billy to befriend his new acquaintances and learn as much as possible from them. School was school and it had advantages, but personally it didn't do for him what his new friends could offer through mentoring. He would stick with his new friends – Big John, Little Dave and heavy Lou – They liked him and treated him with respect; and Billy thought, "I want respect."

Billy was maturing as his teenage hormones kicked in. His mind, spirit, and body changes were evident; and with the help of the 3-Amigos leading him to Max's gym, he was going to change his physical body. He saw what exercise, weight training and defense instruction could do – for most anyone – that would stick with it, for years. His new buddies had drilled those thoughts into his head. With their encouragement he could do it – and make himself new and totally improved. Billy liked those thoughts and decided to stick with them. He also came to realize that while his buddies had all transfigured their bodies into weapons for destruction, they were at least now destined to remain in York for the rest of their life. They didn't seem to have a plan to extricate themselves from York. But, thought young Billy, maybe someday and someway, his friends could rise up through their labors and goodness and lift and use their talents to elevate their status – and maybe their city into a classy middleclass enterprising and thriving unique and successful small city in America. "All things were possible," so said God who caveated a "to those that believe." Belief had a lot to do with change and success. His friends had a lot of energy, certainly determination and much creativity as well as a collective desire to do well. Miracles have been spawned from much lesser circumstances.

CHAPTER THREE

Billy began to feel new life and he was finding new reasons to do things. His interest turned from wandering the streets and seeing what trouble and intrigue he could find while mellowing out into a space of nothingness. His soul seemed to need some boosting and purpose.

He now was doing something seemingly worthwhile and satisfying to him. That rested well with him and he did a lot of thinking about who he was and where his life was headed. He knew deep down he had to change and his new friends were the opportunity and springboard for it. He was going to give himself the fuel to someday flee his present confines.

Monday came and Billy decided to show up early for school. This was unusual for when he did show up; it was usually late, even mid-first class. Most of the teachers at Bowman Middle School knew of him and his truancy and had tried to befriend him and help him with some direction and a sense of responsibility about the importance of school – plus the fact that the State of Illinois required his attendance at some school – preferably through 12th grade high school. He had barely survived 6th grade with a promotion into 7th.

But he came to school this day with a spirit of determination that not only was he going to change his physical body – but he knew he had the stuff to do well at academics – he only needed to try and do it! As his friends had said to him, it would take him 3 to 4 years of hard work before his body responded with very noticeable improvement change. He figured it would be the same effort required with school academics.

The teacher was shocked to see him sitting in math class when he walked into his classroom. Mr. Steel quickly noted in his logbook the fact that he was there. He even noted that Billy was seated in the front row. This day he was beginning algebra basics.

So, Billy got to begin right at the front of this discipline of Math. The other kids all looked surprised to see the reputable

"Dork of York" sitting in their classroom. His reputation wherever was preceding him most anywhere he went.

Some kids avoided him, and adults didn't see him, some kids taunted him, the girls ignored him. He was like a stick figure – without any social value or social skills of any kind.

Billy sat in class – his mind drifting a bit, thinking and feeling a certain aloneness in his new mindset. He was startled back into reality when Mr. Steel said to him, "Mr. Brewer," I must digress for a minute before I get into the subject for today and say it is good to have you back in class. The subject today is different than most math because it hinges on everyday progression of solving problems, which means it's necessary to do each day's lessons and complete it and it will definitely help you in doing each new lesson daily. It just so happens that algebra builds on each lesson. It's just how it is. Today we start afresh so open up your new book on your desk to page six. There we will start.

Billy had not forgotten his name was Brewer, in fact "Billy Joe Brewer." It was good to hear someone call his name – and not "The Dork of York." Billy listened attentively and took notes. He was a little timid to ask questions as he soon learned that was another hurdle he had to jump over. He also decided that in the classroom, he would not be put down for asking pertinent questions to the subject matter. That concluded in his mind – yes, he would speak up whenever he needed clarification on a matter. He was going to try to stick this out and do well – he thought asking questions a serious form of learning.

At the conclusion of his math class, Mr. Steel came over to him and thanked him for showing up and participating. "I for one think if you stick to this, as I've described, you can do well as I said, algebra is a progressional type of math. I hope to see you tomorrow, with your homework done and ready to learn the next progression. I think you might find it all actually enjoyable and challenging – I sense you enjoy challenges. See you in tomorrow's class, Billy, OK?"

"OK, Mr. Steel I'll be here. I'll try my best at getting this stuff, even though I haven't a clue what it's good for." Tomorrow would be another day.

CHAPTER FOUR

After his school day, Billy headed for Max's gym to meet with his friends the 3 Amigos. This would be the start of a new routine and he felt a change within himself. One for the better. A certain good feeling and proudness crept into his soul and expelled a new excitement of determination and purpose.

Yet he was still in an old wineskin; he felt a new wineskin growing inside of himself. It was a direction to better himself. His countenance had changed – as well as his confidence. For some reason he no longer felt the feelings of being a "wimp" – the scrawny – skinny kid – even though he physically still was. He felt the feelings of who he was to become – though he knew not what that was, but it was somewhere in the likeness of his new friends. He wanted them to be proud of him. He would pay them back for their friendship and caring investment they were making in him. Their teachings, kindnesses. He swore to God that with this His help he would succeed.

Dave spotted Billy coming through the entrance door at Max's gym. He had just finished a workout routine and sparring with another fellow boxer. He was preparing for the upcoming "Golden Gloves" tournament for the State of Illinois. He was hopeful in winning his weight class championship this year.

Dave ran over to greet Billy saying, "Hey, how's your day been? This was your first day back to school, right? How'd it go?"

Billy was glad to see Dave and told him of his time in the classroom and of his new feelings about himself. "I told Mr. Steel, my math teacher, I'd be there tomorrow prepared for a new lesson."

"Great Billy, you stick with it. You'll see that between school and working out here, you will become a new person, strong in body and mind. You will enjoy those things."

The two of them wandered over to watch Lou and big John work the weights. They both saw Billy and Dave and stopped to rest a few minutes, and grabbed a towel. They came over to Billy and Billy again told them of his day. They were pleased. Then Big John said, "Go get changed and get your butt out here for a workout. Karate is at 5PM – meanwhile you can do stretches and weights 'til then. We'll help you there!"

Billy felt life come into him as he headed off to the locker room to change. This he thought as a worthwhile life.

Billy found his locker the guys had secured for him, which contained some sweatpants, sweatshirt along with a Max's gym 'T' shirt. He had on a pair of gym type shoes. As he changed into his workout outfit, he actually felt a newness overcome him and a knowing that he was doing the right thing. Funny he thought, "I actually already feel stronger and bigger." He knew that was yet to be, as he looked at himself in the locker room mirror while in his skivvies – thinking, "I've got a long way to go!"

Billy left the locker room and headed out into his new world of muscle and skill-building – a land weaving mind, muscle, and co-ordination motor skills. He was eager to start. Funny, it felt he was on to something the same feeling he had at school. A directional change and for the better. He didn't like his rambling loose life – with no direction or purpose. He felt fulfilment here rising up at Max's gym. Dave saw him coming out of the locker room and approached him saying, "Come with me, we're going to start Karate Class – Mr. DeButts is the instructor. This man has a black belt in the sport and he is tough as nails – he knows his business. However, he is a really nice guy and a very good instructor – so pay attention to him. He was my instructor a few years back – so I know. I'll introduce him to you."

They both approached the section of the gym where Karate was taught and Dave went up to Mr. DeButts and said a few words to him. Billy couldn't hear the conversation – then they stepped toward Billy and introduction commenced. The instructor introduced himself as Bill DeButts – and added "My nickname is "Nickel" – you can call me whatever you like and comfortable with. Glad you can be with us, we meet every Monday, Wednesday and Friday at 4PM. I also teach "Judo" after the conclusion of Karate Class. Hope you'll come to those too!"

Turning to his new class he said, "O.K., everybody listen up. Today we will start with balance and motion of Karate. I assume you all have a basic understanding of what Karate is or you wouldn't be here. Right now, what you have on is fine, but soon you will have to get appropriately dressed for Karate. If you don't have the proper gear, we can loan you them for the course. Just let me know after this first session.

Dave saw that I was O.K. with the days plan and headed back to his boxing ring and area workout equipment. He stopped by where Heavy Lou and Big John were working out and spoke with them. It took but a few moments and he then went over to start jump-roping followed by some bag punching routines. Later, he would get in the ring, with his instructor and punch his hands covered with stuffed mitts. Twice a week he actually boxed for real against other in-house boxers in training. He was working diligently to prepare for the golden glove tournament for The State, then the regional, then for the Yearly Nationals – a year from then.

Likewise, Big John was aggressively pumping iron to get himself muscle honed to the 'T', for a regional body building contest to be held in Chicago in early spring.

Heavy Lou was preparing for a regional weight lifters competition to be held in Indianapolis – also early spring and his eyes were big on the national's due late summer. 'WOW' – thought Billy when he heard Lou talk about it – he thought another way to get out of "York." He dreamed big for the moment aspiring Lou a gold medalist and that he knew him - a new friend.

The afternoon went by quickly for all of them; Billy thanked the guys for all they had done and were doing and bid them goodbye and headed home.

His folks were at home as he came through the front door. They greeted him with mom saying they would have dinner in about a half hour. Billy went into the kitchen and asked if he could help her do anything – she about dropped her frying pan from shock and said – "Well, you could pour the water at the table."

"Sure," said Billy and filled the pitcher up to carry it to the table. Mom looked at 'Pop' sitting nearby saying, "Looks like we have a new son."

Pop replied, "Yeah, let's see how long it lasts – give it a week at most." Billy returned, placed the pitcher down and said, "What else can I do?"

"Well," said mom – wanting to feed this new frenzy, "You can take the serving platters to dads place and put 3 plates at his placemat." Off Billy went when mom had served the platters up. He was into a new dimension and things rested well with him.

Billy, his mom and dad gathered around the dining room table to have dinner. He opened up to his folks bringing them up to date on his new activities and school renewal. Billy's parents were not the most demonstrative type, but if you had been there you would have noticed their up-lifted demeanor having heard their son telling them so enthusiastically of his new friends, his activities and school work going on.

It indeed was something to be excited about from an outside perspective looking in. Like sunlight breaking through the clouds, positive vibes were dancing all around. After dinner, Billy helped his dad do dishes before he headed upstairs to attack his homework.

He felt different and a little 'stiff' from all his gym workouts – but his outlook demeanor was very different. Seemed like he had a purpose that charged his batteries. He kept telling himself to be patient, hold the course and work hard. The guys had all told him to get aboard and stay focused.

At the end of his school year, June 6th he would turn 13 and the Lord willin' he would be headed for 8th grade. Where he was at school, 8th grade was still in middle school and 9th grade would put him into a high school situation. At the moment he was about 5 foot 9 inches tall and around 145 pounds. He was proportionally still pretty skinny looking, but he knew and thought things would become different over the next few high school growth years – he certainly hoped so for he was going to do everything in his power to change his physical body that he could. He vowed to hold himself to the challenge. He determined not to fail.

CHAPTER FIVE

Billy opened up his algebra book and assignment. He remembered that Mr. Steel had said to read and study all the examples shown in the book, follow them through, and then tackle the homework samples. He read the chapter and worked through the problems and seemed to understand the process shown. And so, he started in on his homework assignment. It was slow, but he knew it would be and that some problems were more difficult than others. But as he worked his way along, he realized there was a certain pattern that occurred and he saw those connections. This was all new to him, but if others had to do this stuff, he'd give it his best shot.

He finished his five problems and turned then to his history lesson. This would mean his reading about 15 pages on U.S. History – no more forever colonies repeated he had in the lower grades. He was looking forward to advancing his knowledge of the founding of his country he lived in. He enjoyed reading and devouring information – all kinds of books, T.V., and movies. He also had become quite skilled in computer knowledge and all of its nuances. He really was not the nerd and hardnosed addict on computer games but did know a few and he was deadly at those. He desired to know much more in this area of electronics.

Billy looked at his watch; it showed 11:15 P.M. He was through with all his homework and he headed for the bathroom to get ready for bed and a good night's sleep. He suddenly felt tired and got into his P. J's and slipped under the covers. He was soon asleep.

CHAPTER SIX

New life was emerging for Billy as he doubled down on his efforts to toe the line and stay in school. After his first week back at school every day and followed by attending his new routine of gym classes at Max's, the early on transition from his truancy life to new normal school life lifted his ego up and he started to enjoy fitting into a normal lifestyle.

New friends at school were slow in coming, but that was alright for he had his '3' Amigos new friends at the gym. His reputation as a different and loner type lost soul still kept him separated from his class peers – at least for a while.

His new gym friends, older and wiser, helped him prepare, not only physically but mentally as they constantly said to him, "It's the mental toughness to do what is necessary to become the person you want or think you want to become. Results," they said, "equals hard work and patience." He had a lot of both to learn about but with each new day gathering behind him the depth, breadth and newness, he felt within himself, seemed to propel his determination to rise up and face the day.

Billy was finding himself and he found it to his liking. Fitting in was more pleasurable than thinking everybody is the enemy. He also realized that being his own person distinguished himself from everybody else. He determined in his mind that he could travel the road in life and gather what he needed and determine for himself his pathway in life. Others were smarter, bigger, faster, more talented than he, indeed individuals, but they were not he, and he was not them.

Change was a major word for Billy. He embraced it thoroughly, for he realized his truancy ways were going nowhere and something had to be done. In most of life things don't change but for an outside force interjecting itself. For Billy, it was the 3 Amigos. The more he hung around with them, the stronger he felt, both physically and mentally. He felt good about himself and indeed with time, he was changing and that was good.　　School took on a new meaning in Billy's life as he progressively took responsibility for his daily attendance. He also fortified himself with a 'Can do' attitude and ground out homework production.

The teachers he had, found Billy's new presence quite surprising and all of them took note of his new ways. Indeed, they were talking among themselves about his attitude and good efforts.

His middle school last year seemed to fly by rapidly, especially as he kept his nose clean and remained focused on executing his plan for his new life. School and self-development were his new priorities. And, he daily reminded himself that he would not revert back to his old ways of drifting his life away and press on with the daily vigor of pledging himself to work at conquering all the tasks that entered into his future daily life.

Billy thought in terms of it all as being a game to be played, incrementally, beholding the challenges of everyday life, and so he set his mind that this was his chosen way of life in which success or failures would show on his scorecard with personal growth. It was a new life he now felt comfortable with and embraced. He no longer felt the pain and agony of a drifter with no future or goals – No satisfaction or success and a mindset stuck at zero on the scorecard of life.

Billy reminisced as he walked to Max's gym that afternoon. He was walking tall with good posture and a zip in his step – a desire to get where he was going. His mind fashioned on his immediate past and a smile came on his face as he posted new thoughts and recent accomplishments on the chart of his mind. He was pleased with himself and pumped those thoughts into his well-house storage tank. His foundation was looming larger and stronger. He just needed to keep on, keeping on, every day. This would take some doing.

He remembered the words of that civil rights activist, Martin Luther King, who said, "We shall overcome" and attached his own personal life to it as, "I shall overcome." He took up his own personal cross – and lifted his own banner to on high.

Billy entered into Max's gym spotted his 3 Amigo buddies, waved and headed for his locker to change out. He felt warm, comfortable, and confident and knew he was in the right spot. His joy erupted inside of him and he knew and felt that he was right, exactly, where God wanted him. He was moved greatly at that thought and had peace about it.

Billy exchanged his street clothes for his workout duds and turned and went back out into the gym area. He headed for the area where he was now training for Karate and Judo with Mr. 'Nickel' DuButts, his teacher instructor. He was finding these disciplines much to his liking, - enjoying the mindset and the exercise of self-defense training he was getting. He was eager to participate with the class. Indeed, he was learning balance, self-sufficiency, resistance and assertiveness in his new martial arts formats.

He had a goal to one day possess in both the martial arts forms – a black belt status – the highest attainable honor bestowed on and to the students in training. At this point he would assess himself as a potential personal weapon of destruction, self-protection, as well as control of his body in a fighting occurrence. These things encircled his mind and his inner self filled with confidence and power.

Billy's new buddies beamed with pride in their new-found friend and they surrounded him with their friendship and encouragement. Billy was ever thankful to them and told them so. It indeed was a circle of closeness, and the beginning of a long-time friendship. He had the mentoring and they had a friendship and teachable student that listened and took seriously their advice and it bode well for everybody.

CHAPTER SEVEN

Freshman year high school was a new adventure for Billy and he found his successes rewarding. He found that doing his daily school work, homework and going to the gym after school gave him a good healthy feeling. It strengthened and encouraged him to participate every day.

Somehow his thought process led him toward the carrying out of completing his every day existence. He slept well and ate well at home. His life was becoming progressively rewarding and meaningful to him. He actually felt that he could see his personal persona maturing well as his physical body was improving in strength, agility and power. Slow as all this developed, his thoughts held steady to the course.

His math teacher, Mr. Steel was ecstatic that he was doing so well, math seemed to flow naturally out of him and the computer teacher saw that he had a talent for computer workings – a natural flow out of a math-oriented mind.

Billy enjoyed history, American history that was currently being taught to him. Other courses like English, he bulled his way through, Spanish he seemed to take on with a challenge to learn as he had many new friends with Spanish speaking backgrounds – he knew a little from just hanging out with some of them. Basic biology he tried to muddle through and wasn't particularly interested or talented at.

Team sports at York High didn't seem to grab his interest presently as his physical activities were being satisfied at Max's gym with his new friends, Little Dave, Heavy Lou, and Big John. He was developing a close tight friendship with his new mentors and he was not about to split off from his new and fun routines he daily performed at Max's gym. These guys were really special to him and he liked them like big brothers and they likewise regarded him as their 'little gold coin' in their midst. He was special to them and the mutual admiration society between them grew every day and every way.

When you are having fun and enjoying life, time seems to go by quickly. The days flew by. Months at a time. Fall then winter, spring and summer. Billy's time frame moved much the direction the planned functions took it. His wholeness improved in all the Realms of his efforts. The teachers were quite taken by his all-out efforts in schooling shown by his grades he was getting, and the attitude he was exerting. Billy was changing, he had put in the past any truancy departures from school and was pursuing a pathway of concentrated progressive attendance inclusive with good report, that called for living one day at a time. It was a plan that pursued positive results. It was working.

Teachers all, saw the change, his parents did so also, including the principal who no longer entertained Billy in holding detention in his office. The 3 Amigos dogged him and watched closely his progress for this was the beginning of new life for William Joseph Brewer- AKA Billy or Billy Joe.

While Billy was yet a freshman in high school, he was in the early peak of physically maturing. Yet still somewhat tall and lanky, by his June 6th birthday at freshman year's school end, he was now 6-foot-tall and weighed in at 160 pounds – not exactly an oak tree, more like a wispy willow. However, his mind was consolidating into some real soundness and fundamental firmness of intellectual acuteness. He was in awareness of his progression, as the 3 Amigos continued their ongoing appraisal and heaping of encouragement on him every day. The school faculty, in their own way, added their positive blessings on him as the school year went along. He finished up freshman year high school with A's and B's – reading his final freshman grades from York high school, Billy beamed – proud of himself that truly in his efforts, difference and satisfaction had shone brightly. He was pleased as was his parents, and the 3 Amigos.

CHAPTER EIGHT

Summer drifted in on York, and the demeanor of the tiny community wilted a bit as the summer heat took its toll. People in York were workers, but its employment was sporadic. It was indeed a middle-class community but it had a self-reliant penchant about themselves. People pitched in to help each other. What wealth they had was spread around and no one went starving. They were of the mind set of 'Can do' Citizens' – practical, common sense and true flag flying Americans for America. Solid mid-west stock.

Wimps and pussycats, free loaders and the politically correct government folks didn't survive long in the York environment. They were workers, not freeloaders.

Billy found a job that summer as a janitor at his high school in the athletic department. He was to pick up and clean everything – as his high school provided summer camp programs all summer long. He cut grass, raked, lined fields, maintained cleanliness all around and within the fieldhouse – and picked up and disposed of trash occasionally washed windows. When he was through, he went to Max's gym to work out. He was on the way to becoming a work addict and a sleep expert. He was enjoying his life.

Billy really did not have much time to play or have fun free time. He even worked most Saturdays to add income to his benefit. However, on Sundays were his days to rest – sleep in if he chose. On warm days he would take himself to the community pool his side of town – there he would tan, swim and look at the bevy of girls actively indulging in sunshine and pool dipping – forever chatting.

Should those days turn out to be dreary, dank or rainy, he would appear at the local "Y" for basketball pick-up games in the gym. He enjoyed this time and got to be friends with many levels of young teens. Here in the now, being taller and somewhat heavier with signs of physically muscular shapeliness, he self-proclaimed himself a peer and competitor among others and did away with any thought of the 'dork of York' label. Indeed, things were changing – for the better, and his getting into trouble and fights diminished as his stature grew. He now had not only his own earned reputation as a friend of the 3 Amigos. He was not to be messed with.

They without a doubt, had earned a solid good reputation, as Billy grew to know and the community regarded them with fondness and good repute. Several times Billy came across some of the 'Thugs' that had called him bad names and had beaten him up –but they gave him wide berth, though they were still somewhat bigger, if not taller than he was. He let the past all go – put behind him – let bygones be bygones, there was no point or need to settle scores. Billy's feelings just didn't hold angst against any past detractors – it just wasn't worth the energy – the sapping of strength to carry those burdens along in his mind or on his shoulders. IN effect he forgave them their past idiot transgressions and just moved on with his life.

Billy's freshman year was a transitional year in his life. He had grown another couple inches taller, put on ten pounds or so and was definitely sprouting some new muscle. He so much as attempted to go out for the fresh-soph basketball team and his height was a helpful advantage. He was in full enjoyment at learning the teaching he got from the enthusiastic coaches that year. He found that more than just a game, there was much to be learned about the intricacies and finesse of it. He was an eager learner – when he desired to give himself fully to something. Being 6 foot and a freshman – they had him play a forward and alter at center. He was thrilled and sought to improve himself daily. His work ethic learning at the gym was aiding his results in basketball. He was learning and saw the connection to improvement in whatever it was he was doing. Hard work spawned mental toughness and combined produced good results. Good results which produced good feelings and accomplishment also produced a certain perfection which qualities led to leadership and competitive excellence.

All his personal growth led to social growth of which both his teachers at school and at Max's gym as well as his peers fully noticed. His past reputation was suddenly changing and from a negative existence, a slow change was suddenly noticed. "The

Dork of York" was becoming a new human life form. Billy had a certain realization of all of this, as did his mom and dad, who took a new look at their son – and their relationship to him. It was an exciting time, a fun time, and hearts and minds were being mended.

CHAPTER NINE

Summer went by swiftly that year as Billy's life was full and active. There was no rest – though he was not weary. He was excited, daily. He actually looked forward for school to start up again. He was beginning to fit in. There was no more truancy and schlepping the streets of York looking for trouble. No more just sittin' and watching the trains go through town and hopping them in short ways through the slow section of town taking him to the edge of town where he'd get off with his fishing rod to fish at a pond nearby. He enjoyed that – a place where he could daydream about all sorts of things. Except for the absence from school here he was out of trouble.

Now things were different; and his business of involvement and re-aligned enthusiasm was taking him into new life – a life seemingly more outward and rewarding. Billy found his new life had purpose to presently create a positive environment.

He was for that and as a sophomore teenager with rarely no interest in life except just living it; He felt positive the newness about his decisions, its direction, and his choices. He hadn't a clue as to where or what lay ahead, but he knew that his new life's directions were taking him somewhere positive and his feelings positively said, 'Keep on, keepin' on.'

So it was that Billy addressed his future with enthusiasm. He noticed he was being noticed more as his schoolwork improved measurably. He was getting 'A's in math and history, and B's in Social Studies and Science. Because he was on the Frosh-Soph basketball team, he didn't have to take phys-ed per se, but instead was allowed to individually play basketball in the gym – pretty much just practicing his shooting skills. He wasn't allowed to participate off season in a team situation – until regular basketball season started. This was a league rule. But there were others on the team participating like he was and lots of pick-up – one on one games were available off campus.

This was all he needed for now and provided him opportunity to practice his quickness and perfect his shooting from different spots on the court. This he did with fervor, knowing the training ethic his 3 Amigos had taught him. His time and payday would come along the way. He knew this in his craw, even at his raw young age. Thank god, for his new friendships, he indeed felt his future before him positive. He would be careful of what he did and how he did it.

Through his training at the gym after school time, Billy had not only learned sports disciplines, but that those translated into personal discipline of mind and body. The gym offered a short course in nutrition – another area he had not much knowledge of.

Once he grabbed hold of the advantages of following good nutrition offered, he tried to amend his ways and develop new and improved eating habits. There weren't many foods he didn't like with the exceptions of rutabagas and lima beans. He couldn't stand those and avoided them like the plague.

As fall kicked in Billy began finding himself full time busy – early breakfast at home –with mom and dad, homework done, and school bag packed ready to go and heading for the bus down at the corner.

School got going at 8:00 AM – earlier than normal of the year before. It meant a longer school day now, newly implemented to give the students more education time on a yearly basis. This was a good thing, provided the curriculum was good and the teachers good. The two, were high credentials for a modern world necessity education. There was plenty of room for improvement as the bureaucracy levels between the Department of Education as well as the teacher's union impeding greatly the forward quality of the students' education in America and it was serious time to get it on as America was reverting to backward educational results on a world basis. The international ratings have propelled us downward from 26 to 37-a terrible stat.

There was no humor in these dismal facts emerging. The government was bereft of its duties once again and once again another division of some bureaucracy was failing to keep up and modernize and like a house of cards imploding upon themselves. The past levels of inefficiency, traditional hierarchy and because of its huge size and cronyism mentality the tower of educational pizza tilted too far to sustain its rotten to the core self.

People deserve change – governments do not like it one bit, and all politicians follow the wrong people, tenure and throw money and more money at the problem. Well America doesn't have money and certainly not to waste it throwing it at old ways of doing business only to find nothing improves. It doesn't take a rocket scientist to figure some of this out –only a willingness of voters to get up off their rear-ends and make a change. The status quo has to 'go.'

Starting earlier in the morning and lengthening the school day some is but a mosquito like advancement to advance the possibility of greater quality education. As someone so apply put it. "Baby, you have a long way to go!" Yes, the bear is over the mountain, the problem is in the pursuit of a path over it.

Real life is different than the modern era perception, where people get free stuff, don't or can't work, and get themselves attached by an umbilical cord to those things and people who control the money, jobs or opportunities. Our future is today at a crossroads of greatness or submission to greatly inferior lifestyles. It is not funny but critical to a normal democratic way of life. Life as one perceives it today, cannot determine its reality because our leadership is so poor and delivers so few honorable men and women of leadership, to take back our great land to a front and center world status we once had. Indeed, there are forces, obvious and subverted, which are actively pursuing the demise of our great and wonderful lifestyle and country.

Digressing some from the story, but essential to it, is its progress flow and revelation and revolution of men and boys (women too) in their maturing life or host, our belly is exposed to all the world and we are taking serious blows to it, from others at will. We are at the crossroads and in the crosshairs of history. Will we do what it takes to rise again?

We are sons of our fathers and our fathers are not doing their job. It is not entirely the fault of those adults; our government, its restrictions, laws, and timidity have bottled up the true functioning of our society. This does not and has not boded well for the wellness and the future of America.

Too few have responded along the lines of our young men, Billy in this life story of a youth growing up into manhood. Fathers are critical and central to the core family and prosperity within it. As in many cases, fathers are so busy attending their jobs, finding one, or being derelict of their duties of one, that virtually no time and positive energy is given or spent in quality time with their spawned children. Mama gets the notorious and heavy bequeathal of the children raising job. It is not fair nor is it a healthy position to be in. Generally, it is too much to lay hold of –as noble and as hard as they try to make it work.

Families are the creation that when it properly performs, the central cornerstone of society, and in its created functions a nation is healthy.

CHAPTER TEN

Billy's home life took on a new meaning and cohesiveness as he now found his relationship to his mom and dad more enjoyable and less irritating on a daily basis. A turn in his outlook as he transferred rebellion into cohesive positive vibes through accomplishment in other areas of his life that were proving to be most rewarding.

Essential in Billy's new lifestyle was the mentoring by the three Amigos and core grouping teachers at his high school. School, when one is enjoying it – was providing Billy with additional confidence levels and maturing.

His physical body and mind were responding well as he persevered every day learning and exercising various skills. It was an astute development of the mind as well, and Billy absorbed all these things like a sponge.

Heavy Lou, Big John and little Dave – kept after him daily watching over him and directing and advising him as to the programs he was taking as well as teaching him appropriate skill information. At the gym, Billy seemed to respond with pride and confidence as his mentors issued complimentary and positive input weekly to him.

The 3 Amigos were tuning up for some fall competition in each of their skill areas. Indeed, they were heightening and tightening their bodies and minds for upcoming prime competition and placement nationally for the extent of their talents.

Fall was always a great season weather wise, as well as for the personal enjoyment it served to mankind. It was kind of a reinvigoration of the soul, to crank up the spirit, body and outlook on life. It was a new time a breath of fresh air as fall eventuated into a crisper air temperature; beautiful leaf color, and football extinguishing itself inch by inch. It seemed like the Super Bowl game came just before summer started.

Billy liked the fall, the weather invigorated him. His outlook and energy level were high and though he didn't play football, he kept after perfecting his shooting and developing quick moves on the basketball court – ever practicing. His appetite was increasing and he noticed that as he neared basketball season he had grown to six foot two and his weight had increased to 175 pounds. He was still pretty skinny, but his body carried some new muscle along with it. Big John told him just last week he was proud of his progress and not to worry or care about how tall he was or his size. "All that will come as you mature out – You're on the way!" The Lord knows you don't argue with Big John.

One Saturday evening after gym time at Max's, he (John) invited him to join the 3 Amigos for a party at his house. Little Dave would have his combo there to play – a drummer, saxophone, keyboard and a banjo player. He was inviting a small group of his friends – and some girls to celebrate their 10th year together as the 3 Amigos. Would Billy come?

Billy was thrilled at the invitation as he had really no social life, now or in the days past, at least none of a joyful kind. Little Dave said to him – "Billy, there will be some girls there – friends and sisters, maybe you'll meet one you like and certainly you might like to dance with one. Some of them have boyfriends but you dance with them – they know you are our friend and safe. You may find one single and fun. Do you think you'd be interested in coming?

Billy responded right away with an edge of excitement. He was in new territory here, a new episode in his life and it was a safe environment. He said, "Yes, I would love to come to the party to honor the 3 Amigos many years of close friendship. Saturday week at 6 o'clock for a cook out sounded great! "Thanks Big John for the invitation – is there anything I can bring for the party?" said Billy.

"No, you just come and enjoy yourself – have fun, meet some

people, have some food. By the way, do you know how to cook?"
Big John asked aside.

"No, other than hot dogs and hamburgers on a grill. I'm vacant
of cooking talent I'm afraid." Responded Billy. "Well, that'll work
for me – come a little early and I'll put you to work. O.K?"

"O.K!"

"Well glad you can come. See you tomorrow at the gym." Said
Big John.

"Yeah, see you there on Monday." Billy said his goodbye.

The two parted ways and Billy headed home to catch dinner
with his family. Saturday night at home would be spent with his
mom and dad who would be watching T.V. together – each
sitting in their favorite comfy chair. They were having spaghetti
and meatballs this night. He would be doing the dishes to help
out and then join them watching T.V. at least for a while. They
liked to watch "Charlie Schrader" and his lively band. They were
a vintage band group – lots of brass– sax's, trombones and
'Charlie' played his clarinet 'licorice' stick.

They weren't the current hot electric guitars, big drums and
loud sounds trend of the day, but they were good musicians
doing good sounds of an era past. Kind of straight away music
minus the loud electric guitar volume.

Billy enjoyed sitting and listening with his parents. It felt good
to him to draw near being in their presence for at least some
time together. He didn't have to talk much, just be there. They
like-wise, enjoyed his time with them and indeed felt a closeness
of family. These were happy times at the Brewer house.

After two hours of adult T.V., he cutout to his room upstairs to
do some reading. He enjoyed reading, especially about people,
history and adventures of real stories about them. He had a
library card and actively used it and their services and take out
books and DVD's. He had his room setup with a TV with a DVD
player attached and a pair of good speakers that could 'crank' up
some pretty good quality decibels at his pleasure. Not of course
while his folks were home, unless he used his earphones.

Billy had a wide variety of taste when it came to music and as
he was learning guitar from Little Dave. He was learning country
western and a few Eric Clapton pieces who was exotically

talented on the electric guitar. He also had found some interest in some old CD's his dad had who enjoyed the bygone era of Dixieland jazz and people like Louis Armstrong 'Satchmo' as he was known, also a wild coronet player by the name of 'Wild Bill Davison.' Billy loved the up-tempo staccato beat and cross mixing of the instruments and strong drumbeat. Even some Dixieland had an occasional guitar player –one well known musician was a guy named Eddie Condon; apparently, he was quite famous and well known a musician and accompanist with many band groups.

Billy turned on some music to read by on a local FM station and selected a book for his flavor of the evening. Ah, yes, a story of a marine and his heroism in wartime, his courage as a Navy Seal at least a censored version of it. He admired folks like that, that put themselves in harm's way for the benefit and protection of others and serving preserving of freedom it allotted a lot of folks. To him, these were the epitome of a man's man doing duty in life -- actually laying down one's life for another. He thought it extraordinary a human being would take it upon himself to individually perform and serve in such a capacity, putting one's life in the gap, in jeopardy to preserve another. He was fascinated by their courage and the training it required.

At midnight his body and eyelids said it was close up shop time and he reached and turned off the radio and placed marked his book, then getting in bed and turning off the light. It had been a good day.

CHAPTER ELEVEN

Sunday, he arose early as he usually did. The sun was easing in from the east through his partly opened window. There was a small breeze which filtered into his room. It actually smelled good and fresh. He sat there on his bed, with his feet on the floor, and stretched his arms and twisted his body until it all felt aligned.

He got up and went over to the window to see out and look over the little city of York. His view was pretty expansive as they lived just outside on the edge of town on the hill. To the one side through the window he sighted the big Presbyterian Church and steeple downtown York and the fort like Bank building. He turned and went to his other window facing another direction and looked out. It was a totally different view. He viewed a valley of flatland, cornrows and a farm house some distance away.

He stared at the bucolic scene and his mind took hold of a very different set of thoughts; and he froze there in a Time Warp drift letting his mind spin around. That, out there seemed to draw his attention but he wasn't seeming to be focusing in on any specifics. He noted the vacancy of any particular mind picture coming to him his only feeling was a pull towards "out there" Somewhere, was where he belonged. He made a mental note of that feeling and stored it away.

He jarred himself back to reality that he was a sophomore in high school in York, Illinois. That he was living with his folks and a nice middle-class home. That both his folks had good jobs and he didn't, but that his job was to go to school and learn what they taught. It dawned on him at the moment, that that thought was the key to his future.

He returned to the other window that looked downtown York and opened his window fully up. The warm fresh morning air filtered in with tentacles of thought-provoking information and feelings. He felt the air waft over him in his pajama bottoms and a t-shirt, and felt stimulatingly good. He breathed in and then he did a couple of arm and body exercises looking much like some of the movements in karate and Judo he'd done. He moved then towards his full mirrored closet door and looked at himself. Yes, he was still some skinny, but getting taller and indeed, he was adding a little bulk to his body, even some muscle. He smiled a little at the thought of what 'Big John' had said, "have patience, keep working out, I think you have potential to becoming bigger than I am. Work, patience, determination that you want to change, go for it." Obviously good advice.

'Yes, indeed' thought Billy again looking in the mirror. He was now 6'2"and 175 pounds. His body was firm and muscled to that present time frame. He smiled a little smile as he added up just where he was in his present life. He was pleased, not discouraged, no in fact encouraged by his assessment of the moment.

He was doing well at school, he was in attendance every day; he was doing his homework and work satisfactorily, his grades were good to great and improving as time went by. His physical conditioning and skill dexterity were progressing, and basketball season was coming up, which he really was looking forward to and he was developing and absorbing any teaching he could avail himself to.

His home life was really making headway and he and his folks were enjoying themselves to the fullest. "WOW" he thought, things were good.

Billy came to after his many thoughts and feelings overwhelming him, and he changed out of his night stuff into a pair of jeans and a t-shirt that had a Chicago Bulls 3 Peat inscribed on it. It was one of his favorite t-shirts. He was an admirer of Michael Jordan and Scottie Pippen. Such talent, super basketball players.

He went downstairs to fix breakfast. He taught himself to short-order cook a few things as mom and dad usually had gone to work early and he had gone toward school; but used to play hooky all day long and double back to the house and cooked himself up some grub.

Today he would have some eggs and whip up some pancakes. As he looked into the fridge, he saw that Mom had gotten some bacon. So, he hauled all the good stuff out, and began assembling a breakfast for all his family. They would surely smell the bacon cooking and the coffee brewing and wind their way down to see what was going on. He got the orange juice out and poured three glasses, setting them at the table while the bacon was slow cooking on the stove. He whipped together the pancake batter until it looked ready to pour on the large frying pan griddle. He set aside the egg carton readying it for delivery to the skillet, in which first he sprayed some Pam on. He was ready when his folks appeared in their wonderment.

Indeed, it didn't take long before he heard the footsteps, shuffling and the patter of feet coming down the back staircase. Yep, that was right on time as he started his breakfast gig procedure. It was to be a good Sunday morning - with family.

His mom was first on the scene and she saw all that Billy was doing. She smiled big time as Dad appeared behind her. Mom said, "What in the world are you doing?" Dad said, "I don't care what it is, but it sure smells good."

And Billy responded with, "I thought a few good smells might lift you out of bed! Breakfast is almost ready. Have a seat. Bacon, eggs and pancakes and orange juice this morning."

"Where in the world did you learn all this?" Mom said.

"Oh, I picked it up during my wayward days of hooky, hope you like it!"

"Well at least you learned something then." Dad blurted out.

Mom and Dad sat down and Billy hustled up his cooking progress and soon it all came together, as mom got the butter and syrup out of the fridge for the pancakes.

Billy put the eggs over hard like on a plate, and then removed the pancakes from the griddle, pouring some more batter back on it for more pancakes. The bacon was ready and it all came together - just like he hoped. He thought that a bit of a miracle. They all set there together and Billy said Grace over it all and for the day. All things are becoming new in the Brewer household. There was much joy to be found.

Well mom did the dishes as Billy cleaned off. Dad wiped them as they were cleaned along with Billy's help. They were a family on the mend and all in the family looked bright for new life.

When all the breakfast things were finished, Billy said, he was going down to the city rec area for some pick-up basketball and that he'd see them later.

Mom and dad said, "Take care, have fun," and they went upstairs to clean up, shower, and dress for the day, Sunday. Sunday was looking good, a day of rest and play. They respected the Lord's Day to their enjoyment and to his honor. And this particular day, it seemed, would be remembered well by the Brewer family.

Billy hopped on his bike and headed downtown to the recreation park to try to find a pickup basketball game. There always seemed to be a few guys shooting hoops hanging around. So, it was today, and he recognized a few from his school team that were doing the same thing he was, practicing. It always was about competition, skill development and dexterity and execution of the body and mind. It always was about having fun, while learning.

To Billy this was more than just having fun. He thoughtfully attempted to practice skills the coach taught. He tried to execute taught skills before improvising his own. His ambition in his mind was to again make the fresh-soph team as the last year was so exhilarating and fun. Billy wanted to be as good as he could get and be, so he played that way and not just hacking around at the basketball court, like most.

Every Sunday, prior to the season, this time event took place, hopefully the team would come together when the season started officially for me and would pave the way to a winning one.

The rest of Sunday would be spent listening to music, reading, and reviewing and doing any homework necessary, not in any particular order.

As Billy sat in his room, he picked up his guitar, put up some sheet music on a stand and began to play and teach himself. He listened to himself play for quality and tone and assessment of his forward progress in reading and hand implementation of chords. It was imbedded within him the desire to do well no matter what it was he was doing; at least to his best abilities which he determined came through work; just plain work. He early learned his villain side was procrastination and he strove to fight it whenever it revealed its nasty head, which for a teenager was often.

As he played, he thought of 'Little Dave' who had started him playing on an old guitar of his he didn't use anymore and his early teaching him how to play and learn its intricacies of expression. Yeah, the instrument talks its own pretty language, Billy heard that sound as Dave played his guitar and songs he liked. Indeed, it was a 'pretty sound' to Billy's ears and he wanted to own those notes. Practice and doing were the new mantra espoused by the 3 Amigos and Billy was catching on under their mentoring. At his stage of life, he thought himself fully blessed. He thanked God often in his prayers for all he was doing in his life. Billy wanted to do his Part. His life was almost entirely before him, he was only now just beginning.

CHAPTER TWELVE

The weeks flew by as Billy's new routine took its course. Breakfast, early to school, classes, basketball practices, an hour plus at Max's gym, home dinner, homework, then finally bed. It was a very full day every day. Billy was relishing his new life. It was much better than his old days and ways of truancy from school and bumming out.

Billy felt increasingly confident and a part of society in general, not the me against it feeling. It was more like me included in all the midst of everything and being true to his definitely wanting to be an individual among many. Then he determined that being his best was tantamount to becoming exceptional. Exceptional people got ahead, the Michael Jordan's, The Dick Butkiss's of Chicago Bear fame, even the Steve Jobs and Warren Buffets in the worlds. They had singled themselves out among the vast society of people and self-determined their future; and just as 'Big John' had said, "Through hard work, diligence and perseverance they were never satisfied with the status quo, where they were presently in life. No, they worked their way through it all and on to greater heights and fortune. There were always emerging leaders in all the fields of endeavors, as well as levels of excellence and character.

Billy admired good character and honesty and fortitude and especially caring enough to do good for others and not be boisterous and self-aggrandizing. He enjoyed being below the self- centeredness that society was propelling on to the entire world; the look at 'me' I'm wonderful so follow me and you should be like me. It was a fallacious attitude, self-deceiving. He was still a fledgling in all of it.

Billy was maturing in mind and body and he kept busy doing the best he could be at all he did. He wasn't the most talented in all that he did but he wanted to be the very best that he could be. He would be the best at working at it; that was what the 3 Amigos had taught him. No one would attempt to work harder than he at whatever he was doing. That's how the 3 Amigos got to where they were. Big John's goal was to become Mr. America.

Heavy Lou desired to win his division of weight lifting at the Olympics upcoming and take home a gold medal. 'Little Dave's' desire was to win the Golden Gloves in his weight class at the nationals then try for the gold in the Olympics. They had set their goals and spent hours and days perfecting the possibility of reaching them. Their attitude was positive and good every living day. Goals like these just do not happen overnight.

Because of Billy's surroundings day to day, he was confined pretty much to doing, sophomore things -- things 15-year-olds did. Well this Saturday was Big John's party he'd been invited to. This would take him out of his sophomore comfort zone some and present him opportunity to stretch a little. Indeed, he would be confronting the opposite sex in a social environment, and he was a little uneasy about all of it.

One afternoon during the week at the gym, he pulled Little Dave aside and confided his anxieties about his being uncomfortable, as it was all new to him. He found Little Dave the same friend he was about everything else he'd talked with him about. Not alarmed or over concerned, but steady and helpful. There was no condescension of his naivete or laughing at his timidity. He'd been there and remembered the feelings.

His words for the most part were "Just be yourself, always the best policy; then you won't have to remember for all the lies and sayings that weren't who you really are. No having to back track to cover your butt for words that weren't you; or you trying to be someone else, like 'Joe Cool.' Definitely not a 'Joe Cool.'"

Well Billy thanked 'Little Dave' for his advice and friendship and they parted ways that day. He still really hadn't a clue how he should or would act at the party, but his being himself certainly would be the most comfortable, it seemed. He would try to do that however it went down.

Billy arrived early at the party because it was his understanding that he was going to be the 'Main Cook' of hot dogs and hamburgers. That would be his job one, that evening. He could do that and would as Big John had invited him to do so.

Big John greeted him with a big smile and a slap on the back. He almost fell over from Big John's little back-slap. He was a very powerful fellow, and sometimes miscalculated his power a bit.

Billy was glad that he was "Big John's" Friend and not someone he was angry with. God help whoever that might be.

Glad you got here a little early, good buddy, I put on the briquettes and fired them up to heat. They should be ready soon when everybody arrives. Then you can start loading the grill with dogs and patties. There will be around 15 or so people coming so you might judge how many to put on of each. The buns are over there on that table, along with the 'stuff' to put on them, including lettuce and tomatoes.

As you can see the soft drinks, ice tea, lemonade and water are over at that other table in ice buckets. And over on the table there, are the plates, finger food like cheese and Ritz crackers, and deviled eggs and potato salad.

Billy noticed that there were lanterns lit all around the patio which added much enjoyment and atmosphere- he also had a big stereo system playing softly the 3 Amigos various favorite music.

It was a most pleasant evening weather wise, the sun had not yet set, a slight breeze wafted in the air and a predicted full moon was due around 9 to 10 o'clock in the East.

Billy got on his chef's apron, with Max's gym embedded on it. Big John had it made for him - then Billy asked Big John if there was anything more that he could do to help with.

Big John looked around and said, "No, I think we're pretty much ready - all the chairs, tables, and a space to dance, records, tapes, CDs, and space for Little Dave's band. Thanks for bringing your own guitar - you and Dave might find the time to use them. I hear you're gettin' good on it."

Billy smiled at Big John's appreciation - respecting his compliment. These guys were the closest and best of friends. He loved these three 'Amigos' with a manly passion of much respect. He was totally thankful for all of them. They had changed his world.

The party area was on a patio. Around the backside of Big John's small home. It was surrounded by small trees and a 6-foot white fence surrounding 3 sides giving privacy. It wasn't lavish but indeed quaint and nice, and after all it wasn't the where, but the who you were with that made a party good. This was a potential good one in its happening.

Heavy Lou and his date and girlfriend, Cindy, arrived along with Little Dave and his girlfriend, Mary Jo. They were most attractive girls thought Billy as he greeted them all. He quickly asks them which 'entre' they preferred for dinner: dogs or hamburgers. Keeping a tab on how many of what to cook.

They all greeted Big John warmly as he backslapped Heavy Lou with a jolt — which he didn't give an inch. Billy noticed that and chuckled a little under his breath — that slap was sterner than the light one he received so be it!

Dave said to Big John "Where's Charlotte, I don't see her here?"

Big John responded, "Oh, she'll be here momentarily, she was picking up some special ice cream on the way here. You know some of that 'Tasty Teds' frozen custard stuff we all like."

"Oh, do I, great — already looking forward to dessert," spoke Dave. Turning to Heavy Lou, Big John said, "You might help Charlotte in with the ice cream and special cake for our 10th anniversary friendship celebration. She'd appreciate that. I told her we'd help her get back here. Keep an eye out for her. I told her to come back here and let us know — we'd get it all out of her car.

As the early group gathered some things to drink and get some snack food — other friends began to arrive. These were all friends of the 3 Amigos — another 8 people or so. It looks about 3 guys and four girls. Several of them younger around Billy's age. These were younger sisters of the guy guests that came. Obviously, they all knew one another as they were quite comfortable among themselves.

Someone yelled "Charlotte's here!", and two guys headed around to the front door area to her car to retrieve the desserts. Charlotte put in her appearance carrying a couple of gallons of ice cream and handed them to some guy to put in the freezer until it was needed. She then came over to Big John and threw her arms around him and kissed him lovingly. Billy witnessed this as he attended his duties cooking and said to himself as he first saw her, 'She's beautiful.' It was a simple statement to a simple truth. She was stunning!

Billy managed to successfully cook the dogs and burgers the right amount and get them into warm buns, telling Little Dave to call everybody to come get their food. Everyone hurried to collect their paper plates and food and move to the condiment table along it for other meal items. Things went smoothly and everyone said it tasted great. Many of the boys came back for some more — which Billy had anticipated and was ready for. All was well so far at the party, as everyone sat and ate their meal and drinks, and chatting among themselves.

Heavy Lou spoke up loudly, "I want to propose a toast and introduce to all here, our new and good friend — and chef for the night, Billy Brewer." Billy, with his apron on, stood up and bowed to all. Lou continued, "This is a special time for us, it being the 10th anniversary of the 3 Amigos friendship (Everybody clapped and cheered). Billy is our new-found friend we are mentoring and all of you will be proud to say, 'we knew him when.' Right now, he is in training and learning as many mind and body curriculum as we can get him to take. We think we have not only a new good friend, but a high potential prime candidate for something very special should he stay with our program and his general direction to his fullness of life. He is a very willing student with us and is now doing very well at school also. We are pleased to call him our brother — please introduce yourselves and make him feel welcome here.

Big John entered in adding, "I want to predict here and now before my friends, that Billy will be taller, bigger and stronger than I someday. — He is just now growing and his schooling is progressing well also. I have no idea where he will be in the future, but I will say this, based on his past since we found him — goofing off and bumming around York — looking at his track record of his work ethic and overall progress made, I predict great things ahead for him — if he keeps going like he has been — York will have a great citizen we will all be proud of." Big John put out his hand and arm towards Billy — who again stood acknowledging Big John's accolade of himself. He was thoroughly embarrassed — even among his new friends. "And now everybody just have fun — turn up the music," said Big John.

The kitchen closed down and everyone dumped their paper plates and plasticware into a large container things were now ready for dessert and dancing.

Little Dave took Billy in hand to introduce him around to everybody. They all were especially happy to meet this newly adopted Amigo member, and realized he indeed was young and under construction of Big John's group. They were excited for him.

As Billy followed Dave around glad handing all he was introduced to, Dave introduced him to a young gal seemingly his age, the younger sister of one of Dave's good friends. She said her name was Anita. She had long auburn hair, a wonderful smile, and a very pretty face — and when she spoke to him, he felt himself melting under her spell. "What was that?" thought Billy, as his body electrified and came to life at her meeting. She put out her hand and said something he assumed nice, but all he heard was a warm outflow of sound that put his mind into dysfunction. He felt as if he was double-clutching his words as he attempted to speak courteously and sensibly to her warming kind words to him. His mind was ajar for the moment as well as his mouth seemed to be. He wondered if he looked as dumb as he felt at the moment.

Apparently, she thought him to be attractive enough and said to him, "Would you like to dance?"

Well that floored him, and he would have to come up from under the table to answer her on that one. He shook his mind to consciousness and saw that he was still standing and feebly said, "Yes!" and took her hand and stepped back onto the dance floor area, to tread the know not what to do next dance.

Anita was amused at Billy and saw that he was uncomfortable and attempted to direct him into a slow-motion dance step, kind of on the spot dance lesson — basic 101, foxtrot. She held her distance as they silently tried their best to keep step with the music. It was awkward — but doable. After a few minutes, Billy loosened up a little and she did too.

The music switched to a fast, live beat, where holding each other was pretty much abandoned, and you just wiggled and shook to the beat. This was a little bit better to Billy's liking, maybe safer — 'Yes,' thought Billy, "This is more doable." They stayed on the dance floor through several tunes, talking intermittently and to Billy's thoughts none of which made sense.

Anita seemed to tune into Billy and found him rather charming and nice, so she turned up her charm a notch or two and Billy responded with a smile and twinkle in his eyes. They agreed to take a break, get something to drink and sit down, and talk. They did so with a sigh of relief.

Billy and Anita didn't go unnoticed out on the dance floor by the Amigos, especially Little Dave whose friend's younger sister he was dancing with. They drew together and commiserated thoughts with Big John saying, "You know that's quite a pair!" Heavy Lou said, "Yeah, looks like two dumb kids in love." Dave replied, "Not bad for a first time special social time for Billy — looks like he's getting the knack of it pretty well — she's a charmer and looker. He seems to be loosening up and having fun."

The ice cream custard was delicious and all the men folks licked it up a lot. Everybody got some dancing in, some with several partners and even Billy instigated another dance or two with Anita, before some started to leave just before midnight. Billy was cool and wise enough to get Anita's number and address on a napkin before she left.

He found out she was a student at York high school and in the same sophomore class as he. He only knew but a few people at school and virtually no girls. The few students were in his classes or on the basketball team. Indeed, his wandering years had led him to a vacancy of friends — and no close friends of any kind.

He helped the 3 Amigos clean up and put things away. Willing hands make short work and soon all was ready to go home — as Billy thanked the 3 Amigos profusely for inviting him. He said he had a really good time — from the cooking to his coming out time on the dance floor. It all was new and exciting to him and he was ready to head homeward and retire for the night. His clock was sprung!

CHAPTER THIRTEEN

Fall and winter times were good times for Billy. He continued along his pathways and routines. Schoolwork was progressing nicely and he continued to excel in his math courses and history, where he was pulling A's. The other subjects he was taking for his efforts resulted in 'B' level grades. He was pleased and continued to make maximum effort in all his academics. It of course, was basketball season; that time of the year when he participated in a school sports program. Of course, he could be found down at Max's gym on any free hours he had. His days were full, and it was good that he kept himself in such good physical condition as he did — which was considerable. Time was demanding.

They had him at guard on the basketball squad as he had become quite proficient in shooting 3 pointers outside of the line. His hands were getting big as he was ever growing and he was able to palm the ball. He wasn't the only one growing taller. Several guys were taller than him on the sophomore team — one was six foot five — and he played center.

The season was a long 20 games with an added-on tournament for the league at the end of the season on into February. So, Billy found himself fully booked for fall-winter time of schooling. Except for Sundays, there wasn't an edge of time available as personal time. He belonged to a routine and gave it his all. He was glad to be having a real life instead of his past bumming around York all day trying to avoid life, schooling, thinking, he was in control of it, by doing his own thing. He was much more satisfied with his present lifestyle of busyness. There was fulfillment in what he was doing. The 3 Amigos kept him on keel and focused on the long haul, otherwise he would be self-inflicted with dwelling on the moment.

It was good to have the friends he had, that were wiser and older, that had purpose generating their lives. Billy was able to see all this as the 3 Amigos often pointed things like this out to him — the long haul. What you do now affects the long term of your life — even the longer short haul of it — like a year from now. How it can make a difference.

Billy thought about this and concluded that what and how he did things performed now had effect on what happened even a year hence. Billy was maturing in the midst of all that went on in his life. He found there was a certain stability— realized, at home, school and his life by doing the things he presently was doing.

Well to make a long season short, Billy had a good basketball season, and was elected MVP of the team by his peers. It turned out he was 3rd high scorer in the league at the frosh- soph level. Quite the accomplishment. His life became somewhat transitioned into a temporary star/limelight — as his notoriety and talent emerged. Indeed, who did appear in his life again but, Anita — you remember Anita — the girl he danced and made acquaintance with at Big John's party. You see, she was on the 'cheerleader squad' — (You knew she would be) didn't you?! Of course!

Well it seems Billy was totally too busy in his daily life to be even thinking about girls — they were different and didn't work out and muscle up and rough it out in boy land basketball and male roughness stuff.

He hadn't seen her much as they didn't take any classes together. He hadn't paid any attention to the cheerleaders — that was their thing and didn't have anything to do with the boys or team, or so he thought.

It happened at the season end in the school gym, where the varsity and frosh-soph teams were being honored for their outstanding seasons. It seems that all the teams were in chairs facing the school students in the stands as the program and MC was passionately waxing poetic about both teams records for that year and mentioning a few outstanding performers. It was then when the cheerleaders arranged themselves into a pyramid like assembly — when one girl couldn't handle her part — lost her secureness, and the whole thing came tumbling down and the top girl hit the floor, rolled over, got up and lost her balance and fell bewildered backwards landing in Billy's lap.

To Billy's total surprise of that happening, there sitting on his lap was Anita. She wrapped her arms around his to steady herself and to her surprise there was Billy — to nobody's surprise reading this.

Well he and she were a little shell shocked, but pleasantly so. "Anita!" said Billy and likewise she said, "Billy!" Their eyes met in the big surprise fall out moment and she lingered in his lap a moment longer. She smiled her pretty smile and said, "Well hello again, we've got to stop meeting like this, people will talk." She sighed, smiled again, and got up off Billy's lap and stood before him in her cute cheerleaders' outfit.

Billy took the view all in and got up to talk with her but she said to him, "great seeing you again, I gotta go" — and off she flew along with the rest of the cheerleader squad.

Again, Billy's mind and emotions tossed and turned and he experienced another over-all feeling of refreshing exuberance. It was the same feeling he'd had before, when dancing with her in his arms — slow at Big John's party. She sure was cute and such a charming smile — pretty teeth. He hadn't noticed the lipstick she wore before. Those lips weren't for sampling — yet. It didn't even occur that they were.

It had been a good day and he had been singled out for an honor. That was a new experience for him — he kind of liked that. It made him feel proud of himself, his team and his school. Anita was icing on the cake.

Billy came home that night and told his parents about all that had gone on — everything except about Anita. He didn't want to get her involved with his parents. They didn't need to be involved. Personally, he didn't understand much at all about it either. It was all too new a subject matter to talk about. He'd have to chew on it more when he had time or inclination to do so and inclining such subject matter of the female nature was not on his familiar list for conversations. Still, through it all, Anita seemed to linger in his memory bank — somewhere near the top. He remembered he'd saved a napkin with her phone number and address on it somewhere. 'Think I put it in my top dresser drawer,' thought Billy.

Christmas had come and gone as the team had played in a vacation tournament. They had taken runner-up spot having gotten beaten by a single point as the bell sounded. No more school sports until next year. He would spend more time down at Max's gym working on weight training and different exercises and defense training programs. Indeed, he felt his growth was far from over, he finally began to feel what Big John had by faith seen in him. Beside all the work, he felt great, full of energy and his mind seemed sharp. He was 15 years young and maturing normally. It all felt good and healthy from his vantage point.

CHAPTER FOURTEEN

Down at the gym things were humming, especially for Little Dave. He was at the end of his preparations and training for the regional upcoming golden gloves tournament. Billy could see his excitement and serious side of determination at perfecting his boxing skills.

Little Dave indeed was very actively honing himself in body training and boxing skills. Yes, there was an art to boxing — as opposed to fighting. It required first of all, toughness, followed up by punching skill prowess, combinations and power of delivery. These things could all be taught to many, but there were few that possessed natural or talent in the skills of boxing. There were the sluggers. Skills of the 'old line boxers' and the single power punch guys — who let you have it suddenly with an uppercut, and there were the quick boxers who danced and kept their feet moving and moved in and out on an opponent with flurries of punches and combinations of them eventually getting past an opponent's defenses for a strike or combo of strikes to the head to put him down for the count. Little Dave, was exceptionally good and talented at the art of boxing in the middle weight division — the 180 to 200 pound weight class.

Little Dave's goal was to win the U.S. Amateur middle weight championship which if he did, so would qualify him for a spot on the Olympic boxing team — and that he had his totality of all he was geared for — why he was and all the training he did. His purpose of life was for the grand prize he desired and had been striving for, a gold Olympic medal.

Heavy Lou was also in training and preparing for weightlifting trials, a pre-cursor for Olympic competition and selection of its U.S.A. weightlifting team. As Billy was to come to realize these 3 Amigos were every bit worthy of going all the way in their chosen sport. He indeed, was dwelling in the realm of greatness, and notoriety. The guys weren't there yet, but their chances were very promising, and if they didn't make it, it wasn't for lack of trying. It was after all in the trying, and grunt work ethic plus ability that truly made the difference.

Thinking about these guys, Billy dwelled on the totality of all of it of who he was, who he associated with, and the type of friendships he was so blessed with having. The thought of all this, kind of took his breath away, a stunned silence of greatness, a renewal within him to become all he could be and follow the mentoring of the 3 Amigos.

So it was that Billy cranked up his enthusiasm for physical training under the watchful eye of his 3 new friends. They obviously knew their stuff and did what was necessary to reach their goals. He was building a work ethic so it became almost natural for him to be gaining ground in his pathway of life. He was definitely "Throwing the bum out" of his life and re-establishing positive purpose and direction to it. This pleased him and he found much pleasure in working hard at everything. There was nothing more pleasurable than accomplishing something, having worked hard to attain it.

By the end of the day, Billy was ready to sleep — get horizontal and renew his strength — giving thanks to God for all that he was, had and was to become. God was good and Billy not only knew it for sure, but he knew Him and found His Joy.

Billy owed a debt of much gratitude to Big John who was so willing to adopt him into his Amigo family. John was a gentle giant of a young man, who happened to be very smart about most everything. Right now, he was in high training mode for a preliminary Mr. America competition next month leading forward to the Big Mr. America title commencing in Las Vegas sometime during the summer. It was to him the equivalent to a gold medal at the Olympics.

It was even more prestigious than the Mr. World title. It had more value added to the title and offered a whole lot more opportunities for financial gain as well as advertising endorsements associated as spokesperson for all kinds and sorts of products. There was big money opportunity in that, plus the national exposure of his name and fame Big John, Billy thought, would make an ideal, "Mr. America." He was exceptionally muscled and slim in all the right places, and he was one handsome dude also. He had a great personality and he was a smart person of high integrity.

Billy couldn't think of a single reason why he shouldn't become Mr. America. He would make a good representative of the title, and be all it would ask of him as a Mr. America winner. Billy kept Big John in his prayers daily, for he loved John and his new friends very much and desired that God would bless them in their life and future.

CHAPTER FIFTEEN

Billy was in the throes of mid-teen development and so engrossed in a variety of things he was doing that he really just flowed from Max's gym to school sports. Now that basketball season was finished, he no longer had a school sport he was involved in. He was glad for a respite and accepted some 2nd level instruction Karate and Judo. He continued lifting and working with weights trying to bulk himself up with weight and muscle.

Basketball had kept his legs in very good shape — and that running kept him in good physical condition overall. He felt good about himself and looked forward to a more-less strenuous daily routine, or at least less organized and time demanding.

During this time, he got the opportunity to begin basic boxing. Occasionally his friend, Little Dave, stepped in to teach him some basic rudiments of the sport. Dave didn't have to do this as he was in high effort training for the upcoming golden gloves finals tournament.

One or the other of the 3 Amigos always kept an eye on him and his progress at Max's. It was a secure feeling which only developed a closer walk with the 3 of them. They were such a positive and enthusiastic group. It was enjoyable to work hard at all he had to do — and it was not a drudgery. The guys would notice his progress and improvement long before he himself ever realized it. They encouraged him along the way. Life was worth living. All these things of course, bred good mental health and that showed up in the school classroom. His record there was exemplary.

Billy's life now was now totally different. He was in attendance every day at school. His teachers were actually thrilled about having him in their classes. His grades reflected his effort and attitude. His grading periods said much about his accomplishments.

He had to show the 3 Amigos his report cards from school — that was part of the overall deal he had with them. That was called accountability. He didn't mind at all this detail along the way. He even shared them with his parents — they were thrilled and their spirits were lifted by their son's new lifestyle.

'Little Dave's' Coach was priming him much to perfection as was possible. Watching Dave go through his routines, workouts and boxing routine exercises, was tantamount to amazing viewing. If whoever gets in the ring with Little Dave, they will have a formidable opponent to deal with. It will be fun to watch Dave at the tournament. Dave had already won his weight class for state and regional matches and he was now slated for the golden gloves' finals, held in another city in another state. Dave had invited him to be part of his team during this exciting time. Billy was thrilled to be helping out any way he could.

Billy planned his calendar ahead of time for all the places the 3 Amigos were to go for their amateur finals, before any of them were selected to an Olympic team representing the U.S.A. It wasn't far off, but seemed that way, as the next four months played out. It would be fast and furious time for the 3 Amigos — hard work, training and travel away from their home and comfortable base of York, Illinois. They would have the reputation as the "Farm boys from the farm belt. They were the 'boys' from where America was fed 'corn and beef.' The country boy image was in fact a slight advantage psychologically and took off the edge of toughness and determination and training quality that was as good as anywhere in the U.S.A. What it didn't project was the character and work ethic the 3 Amigos pursued. They were a tucked away stealth entity.

Billy was amazed at his 3 friends as he daily watched them workout and train. They pursued at being the best they could be and to reach the sports perfection levels. On the flip side, Billy witnessed their play-party side of their leisure time allotted — they weren't here on earth to play, but pursue a goal, as part of their destiny they had set which encompassed the spirit of excellence and hard work. They personified those attributes, and maintained a semblance of balance in their lives. It was not easy — but the fact was they were not doing it alone. They were indeed the three Amigos, best and closest friends who supported each other through encouragement and being true in their relationship.

Billy had a chill go through him as he thought through all of this, — it all was being embedded in his 'craw' or soul daily. He felt a certain assurance and positive juices flowing through him —a confidence to promote his efforts within himself for a moment, a picture, of his future — vaguely flashed across his screen of life. It was a good portrayal.

Billy finished his school day with a good feeling of confidence. He was even beginning to enjoy the subjects he was taking. He looked upon them as 'challenges' rather than just getting through them mentally. It was beginning to show dividends to his character and well-being. He felt more at home with his peers as he began to befriend some and deepen some relationships. His world was expanding and his place in it was stabilizing to his likeness and positive personal comfort.

School days flew by and spring testing was upon students at York high school, even the PSAT and the SAT college entrance tests. He was not into those yet, as they started at the Junior class level, but he was getting some preliminary pre-testing training the school provided. They were now promoting this curriculum as they saw it as a benefit to the general student body in promoting a general higher level of individual academic attainment which hopefully would accentuate the people of York to an eventual higher level of prosperity and personal attainment. Hopefully York would become a more self-sufficient and prosperous community in the days ahead.

CHAPTER SIXTEEN

The community was indeed changing for the better. The quality of life was definitely improving. From the mayor on down, the people ages were getting younger and more versatile and efficient — they were having new and different ideas to the old line of thinking. The desire was there for change — real practical change. Words were no longer a sufficient basis for voting people in. Cronyism was losing its hold and the people deplored it — it was old thought steeped in crooked ways and means. It only padded the pockets of a few who propagated the process to continue the same process and way — lining the same pockets. It wasn't working, only corrupting.

York had been traveling the same road as the 'Big City' north of them did — it was a bad cold made worse by corrupt winds of the north freezing and windy. The headline in the 'York Patter' read "Windy City Style Rejected." The stories of corruption and cronyism gone awry brought change at the voting booth. Things were changing — time ran slow to change — but finally the people got mad, then wise and when the voting opportunity arose — all York jumped aboard to cast their lot with the 'New blood,' new thought, and attitude, and cast their vote in rebellion of the old irreverent ways of doing things and business.

It sparked new energy, and faces in the administration halls of local government business. Confidence of the people grew enthusiastic and in prosperity. Newness was received with glee and relief — for their future and the shedding of the past. It seemed that York was but a small city-town in America, that its citizens finally grabbed hold of the reigns and steered their future towards a new direction — a direction with character in leadership and a people desiring to follow brazen and stalwart stewardship representation which emerged out of the new city management movement.

Billy's parents were talking about all this 'newness' going on in the public arena. In the light of his 'history' fondness, Billy took it all in, talking to anyone who would breach the subject of Politics and Policy. He found it all fascinating and realized his sophomore understanding and comprehension was much lacking. He took in what he could, and stored away his input and conveyed to himself future pursuit of the matters, as he got older. Such interests would follow him throughout his life.

Indeed, America was in need of change — as government was always notorious to react to the needs of the people. It too, was leading in the way in corruption and do-nothing efforts. Not the by-partisanship that once kept America powerful and admired. It no longer was the 'light' on the proverbial hill — as it once was. But things were changing ever so slowly. It would take a generation or so to get to that point and time.

Billy only caught the message sent out by the present societal conditions, being only 15 years old and hearing the news as interpreted by his parents and other adults. It was not in his bailiwick of influence at his age and place to do much of anything to create change. The only thing he had power over was himself — and what he did. So, he worked hard at the 'present' of his life, it being sufficient for his realm of purpose in his own life.

CHAPTER SEVENTEEN

The 3 Amigos helped him keep his balance and focus in life. It was a good thing as he would drift off course if not mentored by them. They kept him on track to do his tasks even as they were so focused to perfecting their own. There was hard work ahead for all of them as they ramped up their due process to peak out at finals time. They needed to be at their best when the final tournaments were pending.

As springtime was elapsing and summer was drawing near, the 3 Amigos would be in finals competition — except for Big John, for the placement on the U.S.A. Olympic team. That was Little Dave and Heavy Lou's primary goal. It was their 'All.'

As for Big John, all he had to do was show up and look good — the best — of all the contestants. Based on what Billy saw of him — he thought him far the most superior specimen of a "hunk" he'd ever seen. How could he not win? Well it wouldn't be long now, another 15 days before the competition started for the Mr. America pageant.

Billy looked forward to being with Big John while he was in Las Vegas. He could only miss one day of school — a Monday, but was able to be there Friday evening thru Monday afternoon. Monday was a school teacher day and he got the day off. That would be enough to see the final selection for Mr. America.

He was really joyful that he would be able to witness Big John's coronation as Mr. America. He certainly hoped so.

Sophomore school year was wrapping up for Billy at York high school and his late spring-summer was already full with helping the 3 Amigos prepare for their competitions leading to the summer Olympics that summer. It would be most eventful and fun.

Billy pulled out some shorts and a pair of jeans a collared t-shirt or two and several regular t-shirts with a Max's gym logo on them. He would wear those to the actual competition Big John would be in. Because he was Big John's assistant for whatever he needed, he got in free to all the body building events.

Big John and Max saw to that, and previously had prepared for Big John's living quarters and entre fee — as well as for the information as to the procedures and times for appearing and posing for his event categories and judging.

The excitement was building including all of Max's gym as they cheered for their York ambassadors to high honors and accolades, — two going to the Olympic Games and one striving to win the Mr. America Crown. This was paramount to winning an Oscar in prestige and fame for Max's gym.

Big John and Heavy Lou and Little Dave knew it was hard work, plus a tad of luck, determination and perseverance, — it was a total package of high effort to accomplish a goal. Nothing was easy when reaching a goal in life, and they were determined and focused to do everything in their power to succeed.

Billy satisfied himself about all he was going to take with him for the trip to Las Vegas. They were driving — taking a van. It was around 1600-1700 miles and several days — and he would be doing some of the driving. Indeed, he had passed his driver's test, but didn't have a car.

He decided to do some research into just what made up a Mr. America contest, and found that was far more involved than one thought or could imagine. There are three general category rounds. The second round is a Muscularity Round — a comparison of muscle groups — are they developed evenly?

The first round is called the standing-relaxed-symmetry Round. There is no direct flexing in this round. Every muscle must be tight. Competitors are viewed from front, both sides and rear. And round 3 is finally called 'free-posing.' One is allowed to pose as he wishes. He found that in some pageant contests as many as 8 general mandatory poses are required in which points are given by the Judges. As Billy read the list, he realized he was into a new vocabulary list of words — in anatomy 101. Each set of muscles had to be developed to the max yet had to be symmetrically appearing as coordinated with other muscles. 'Hmm' — he thought — there's more than meets the average eye here. He found that over the many years of the Mr. America contests there were as many varieties of competition requirements — poses — as each pageant held important to its own criteria for winning. They all slightly differed.

After reading up on all this background material he was on overload. Words like biceps, double biceps, lat spread, side lifted rib cage, triceps, flexing calves, flex hamstrings and many more poses to determine quality and symmetry of muscle groups — all in comparison with other contestants being a judge would totally be difficult. Billy thought that job might be harder than being a contestant — maybe not.

Ones accumulation of my points determined placement to winning first place honors. In the old days if two winners were tied — then the most handsome would win. Well, thought Billy, in our case 'Big John' would win hands down. He also believed that Big John would win the title; he was just the right guy to do it. He'd be very good. At 270 pounds, Big John was imposingly imposing — and was such a nice guy in person to start with.

CHAPTER EIGHTEEN

The day came, when the traveling support team all met at Max's gym. There they assembled their bags and everything Big John would need prior to the meet. Everybody was in good spirits as they packed everything into the Maxi-van with the big logo on side reading Max's Gym, YORK ILLINOIS. You could feel the excitement among those going: Big John, Max, Max's gym body builder, "Rocky" the trainer and Billy. You could see the joy in their eyes, the expectation in their demeanor. This was business; it was the field goal for the winning point at the bell, at the super bowl.

After about a half hour they were ready for the long drive to Las Vegas and the Mr. America contest. The doors all closed, the engines revved up and off they went.

The trip was uneventful, long and yet everybody seemed still in a good mood. No one seemed tired, but contrary, pumped up in anticipation of coming away and returning back home with the coveted Mr. America trophy and he himself, 'Big John Michaels, Mr. America. It would be the first time that anybody had heard Big John's last name, but besides hearing it at every event and contestant judging, should he win, it would become a household name the world around, instant recognition.

The Mr. America pageant had finally reached the equivalency to the Miss America pageant. It was no way as popular — for one the numbers of participants included were from all the states in the union. This was not how the Mr. America's pageant worked. There were no questions, speeches, or talent shows. Basically, just a robe, slippers, and a 'v' type swimsuit showing off the physical entirety of the male body and the special muscle treatment each participant displayed. It was a male thing.

There were however, the female groupies that flocked after all that male testosterone in swooning and oohing over male muscle. There were of course, females who participated in body building but didn't have a venue to show off their female muscled bodies. These groupies were part of tag-a-longers —

that followed the male muscle contests — much like musicians and rock star groupies.

The hotel Max's team stayed at in Las Vegas was a low priced — off the main drag type of hotel. They had a two-bedroom suite — nothing extravagant. They weren't there for a vacation party time. They were there on business and a destiny trip. It was serious stuff in the making — and it all involved around one person and how he presented himself — not to people or the public, but to the eye seeking judges. It was all about anatomy arrangement of the male body. It was a two-day event and a finalist selected and declared at a banquet the second night for all, contestants, support people and the 'press.' It would be televised over the national ESPN Network from 8 to 9 P.M. — Sunday night. Big time exposure. The winning would be crowned as he presented himself fully unclothed, except for his V'd briefs swimsuit, appropriate for T.V. viewing. Even Miss America would be watching this show — it's a skin and testosterone event that would have limited viewing. Much like the roller derby thing. It would gather the boxing, and kick-boxing, wrestling, and adventure in the wilderness type viewers. There are lots of those. Lady Duchess and Lady Dafney probably wouldn't catch its viewing, or graduates of the 'Lady' petunia debutante circle social club — but the T.V. channel surfers might hang on.

As a national event in America, it was yet a minor pageant, but slowly gaining interest.

The days were organized into sections by muscle categories and not judged all at once. Muscle categories presentations required certain poses in order to accentuate them for judging. The judges' eye was the final pass and as Billy watched each contestant — he couldn't feel that one guys 'lat' sets were any better than another. It wasn't his eye that could differentiate or know what to look for. But after the first couple of rounds Billy said to himself — 'Big John' looked overall the best big body he'd seen — certainly the handsomest.

Big John, his trainer and Max were together excited with the results of the preliminary rounds of judging. He had big scores.

By the end of the day, Big John was in second place. A contestant named 'Herman' was leading. Herman was a big German young man of extraction, who definitely wouldn't win any beauty contests. But right now in the competition, that feature didn't matter.

There were still yet ahead many varieties of muscle areas yet to be evaluated and then the overall viewing of the whole body and its full appeal of perfection. Billy knew that Big John would win in this final event hands down — and as handsome as he was, it should be no contest.

The second day found Big John along with the others, repeating poses selected by the judges to show off particular muscle coordinates.

There had been eight finalists selected from 8 regional sections of the United States, who participated in the Mr. America contest. They were each selected by A.A.U. certified judge members from their region of the country. Eliminations were done at the regional levels and represented (the contestant) that group of states. The whole process worked pretty well and unlike the Miss America contest in the extracting process for the winner.

Obviously because of the gender, Mr. America hype and its extensiveness couldn't possibly match all the falderal of all the feminine pulchritude involved in the Miss America pageant, but it did have a loyal following of core people.

The third day was a last chance for each contestant to show their best. Each contestant could choose five of his favorite poses and the judges would add these points to the others and add them all up to declare the winner which would be established at the luncheon Sunday. These on National T.V. would be the declaration of the winner of The Mr. America contest for that year. A presentation award, and interviews would follow of course, then a segment of special poses to finalize his talents would be shown. He would receive the special white cape and while the T.V. was rolling, two very shapely well-muscled female beauties would adorn him with his kingly honors, and crown. In their brief bikinis of white long shapely legs, effervescing smiles, long blonde locks, the winner of Mr. America would be announced.

It was a good time spent on TV for an hour. For all involved it was business, fun and rewarding. For Mr. America it was the beginning of an active year of traveling around the country to special events presenting himself as the Mr. America for 2014. His financial rewards would come later after his first year of reign, and then he could capitalize on his accomplishment wherever and whenever he went somewhere. Endorsement would follow him especially if he was good looking and had any sort of gregarious personality. He might become 'popular' for years as representing Mr. America. In that case endorsements for all kinds of things were possible — and his personal wealth could exceed any expectations.

It was indeed Herman the German and Big John in the finals with only the behind the closed doors tally and decision making going on by the judges. The time slot for ESPN to cover the presentation of the winner and crowning, along with a plethora of news people there, plus photo shoots was heart beating exciting to Billy, Max and B.J's trainer. The crowd was silent in expectation all were as they listened to someone count down 4-3-2-1, you're on! The camera turned to a colorful curtain on stage and just adjacent standing was the A.A.U. official judge ready to declare the winner — Mr. America.

"And now, ladies and gentlemen, we bring to you the winner of the 2014 Mr. America title and he is — — — (a loud drum roll) none other than — — John Michaels!"

The horns blazed away — the drums chattered — everyone cheered, especially loud were the cadre of York Illinois people. All those back home at the gym and throughout all of York watching heaved a huge "hooray!" silently as the banquet people audibly shouted affirmatively and with approval which all the TV audience heard.

Big John came out on to the stage. He was all in his winner's regalia and under many lights. They allowed him to give a few poses — most impressively to the audience there and on TV. He was then crowned and he looked awesome in his entire splendor.

Thought Billy as he watched his friend 'Shine' in the moment of greatness! John was displaying his big friendly smile — his natural smile, and turned several directions, bowing to the audience slightly in thanks — giving for the honor just bestowed upon him.

After some time the reporters were allowed to surround him, photoshoot him — and pelt him with their questions. He graciously answered all of them as he could discern them. Anybody who personally knew him was deeply touched by his winning. They knew just how long and hard he had worked at assembling himself these many years and months. What an accomplishment. Indeed it was, what excitement. At long last — it was over. And it was, and a proud moment.

The TV's shut down, the crowd faded away and all those invited for the winners' feast celebration sat down and ate a hearty Sunday dinner, and fellowshipped together in the harmony of excitement and joy.

York city fathers gathered together quickly to put together a 'Grande occasion' parade for Big John, — all the gentry would be there and all of York. Proud of their own making good and joyously celebrating — the birth of a new era in York. They awaited the Mr. America entourage to return to York from Las Vegas. It would be an all-out turnout of York — the young, the old and the rest of its citizens in a boisterous parade of fun, celebration and the high school band blazing away.

The little city of York was now a recognized spot on the map. WGN television — out of Chicago, was there to cover the return arrival of the New Mr. America and his trainers in their van as well as other affiliates and print media. This was a big fish from a small pond news event. The Mayor of York would speak, the Governor made an appearance, and his two amigos friends made comments. 'Big John' said a few words of thanks for prayers for success — with the hopes of his success would bring people

together in friendship to help make the city of York a better
place to live.

CHAPTER NINETEEN

Billy came down from his mountain high upon returning from all the activity in Las Vegas. He felt like he'd learned a lot besides being so enamored with the show biz and the pageantry surrounding the Mr. America selection. The fact that there was so much more to something than the surface glitz associated with some event or project.

The business side, logistics, the economics and costs of production, the organization of people, places and things — all surfaced to his mind. He felt a certain maturity level he'd never felt before. There was so much more in life that made up the universe he lived in. It was a micro and macro world.

York was just a small city and seemingly didn't have the sophistication of the bigger cities. Billy thought that was probably a good thing, more manageable perhaps. Most people helped their neighbors if needed. There was a certain comradery that the community often generated. Billy felt proud of York and proud to be a citizen — teenager of it. He hoped someday— someway to be able to help this community he found so pleasant. He swore under his breath that he would.

Things began to settle down some and Billy turned to his new efforts of that summer toward preparation for the Olympics later that summer. Little Dave was training vigorously toward his participation as the U.S.A representative for the middleweight boxing gold medalist as part of the USA Olympic boxing team.

Also, Heavy Lou was still training for his participation as a heavy weight lifter to the USA Olympic weight lifting team. There was much to do for his other two Amigo friends in such a short time. Billy knew they were well prepared, as Max, of Max's gym, would see to that. He was a perfectionist and a true physical trainer health specialist. He also was very well liked by all who came to know him — and was greatly loved and venerated — admired as a leader. The young men and women followed and believed in him — the 3 Amigos were his ultimate students in life transformation through health and conditioning training. He added and promoted a strong psychological and spiritual dimension to building the best personal character within each individual that came through his gym. Max's reputation was impeccable, and he was respected, for all of York knew him as a loved promoter of their Youth. He held their trust.

Little Dave, as all who know him and whose proper name was David Murmine — was trying to peek his boxing performance to the Olympic Games time frame. He had to be at his very best at that time. Billy noticed the demeanor Little Dave projected in attitude and effort as he approached the upcoming Olympic Games. If anybody was ready, thought Billy, it was Dave.

Max was diligently attuned to Little Dave's case and he definitely knew the intricacies of boxing, having been a US national middleweight boxing champion himself. Max loved Little Dave; all could see that if they ever watched the two of them work together Max was there directing every move with encouragement.

Little Dave obviously was a good student. He greatly loved and admired his teacher, Max. They were a good team. Billy kind of pitied anyone who had to get in the ring with Dave. He envisioned him being pelted by a woodpecker and not a downy woodpecker either, but a pileated form of that breed. He envisioned Dave's opponent in terms of a large Excedrin headache. He admired Little Dave greatly for tutoring him and for teaching him to learn the guitar.

One day about a week prior to the Olympics, Billy came to Max's gym to work out and Little Dave was punching the bag. That thing was flying back and forth at high speed. Billy was mesmerized by it and stood and watched him pound the bag with amazement — what rhythm and power.

Billy's program at the gym found him finishing up the second degree in Judo and Tae-kwon-do; He was taking boxing lessons with Little Dave mentoring him - when he could. Heavy Lou was overseeing his weight training program and Big John was directing weight management for specific sets of muscles — enlarging his bulk.

Indeed, Billy was finally bulking up as he continued to grow taller. At the moment he was 6'2 and around 180 pounds. He was still kind of wiry, yet looking quite muscled and very fit. His basketball kept his legs in excellent shape for running and that would bode him well come fall.

CHAPTER TWENTY

Time flew by that summer. Always does when things are really busy. Billy was and he had no complaints. He thrived on useful busyness it only promoted his gaining more mental and physical growth. He was into 'growth.'

In August that year the summer Olympics were to take place in Montreal, Canada. A marvelous place to hold it. It was drivable and a pleasant eastern U.S. American trip of some 23 hours or 1300 miles. This time though, the town of York picked up the 'tab' for a cruise liner bus. One night on the road stay and a week's stay and expenses at the Olympic village.

After Big John had brought home the 'bacon' it was easy to gather the 'chips' to fund the two Amigos Olympic trip to participate that year. All of York was their backer and enthusiastic supporters. The air was charged full of hope.

The cruise-line bus was loaded with everybody's gear and all the necessary equipment plus some food and medical supplies. They had to be there early to prepare to participate in the opening ceremony flag walk — and pageantry. All those going on the trip had their cell phone cameras ready to go. There was a large send-off crowd surrounding Max's gym — shouting and cheering — wishing their Olympians a fond farewell and wonderful success. It was indeed splendiferous with a big York, Illinois sign plastered across the side of the bus. Underneath that signage was another that read, "Olympic bound."

Expectations were high, attitudes positive and they were on their way to Montreal. Once they were all quietly on the bus, Max gathered them around him and said they were going to say a prayer for this special occasioned trip — for safety, confidence, good health, and favor in their preparations of efforts in representing their country at the World Summer Olympics, 2014.

As Max lead the prayers, it was quiet, yet everyone there felt empowered by Max's prayer and time together. It indeed was special.

After the prayer time — everyone found their seats and tried to relax — it was hard to do with all of the excitement and they had a long two days of travel. They had made arrangements for two bus drivers to be in attendance because of the long hours of travel. It also involved safety — the driver could switch off whenever they started to get tired — it was worth the expense for all the reasons aforementioned.

Billy thought how lucky and blessed he was to be included. Yes, he had a job to do, mainly that of taking video of the two amigos — along the way and at the games themselves — while they were performing and preparing for their participation times including all the pageantry before and after the games.

Max provided all the cameras and tapes for his ownership record and how they would be distributed as well as to whom. He was in charge of the "troupedores Olympic" and spokesperson, whenever his two contestants needed one. Max took charge as well as good care of his team he brought with him to oversee. It was a processed coordination necessary for everyone participating.

His students did what he said — and if he said to 'win' — they would. They didn't want to disappoint Max. Expectations were high — "high hopes" as the old song went.

The bus ride, night stop and next day trip all went smoothly. They were rested and revved-up when they pulled into the Olympic village, where they would be living the next five days.

They had one day to settle in their new sleep facilities and to schmooze with their fellow Olympians from all over the world. They had lots of fun walking around together, observing everybody and everything in the village. The public was not admitted to those areas. It was an exclusive club — and race was not an issue for admittance. Only talent let you in or should it be said that talent and long — hard work were the entrance requirements. Yes, that would do.

Billy was in seventh heaven in the midst of all the world class talent and excitement of everyone who was there. It seems the world was at peace, in fact nationalities, races, sexes, sizes mingled with anticipation of wanting to know each other and celebrate a mutual ceremonial happening. There was no animosity for another while in the village, though certain countries tended to keep to themselves while being there.

The atmosphere was electrical all over the Olympics. The participants, the fans, coaches, vendors and police — whose presence was everywhere. It was a place and venue where it was meant to be safe — for all. The host country bet on it.

Swimming and soccer were the big popular events. The swimming would be fierce and the soccer loud and boisterous by nationalities involved. Weightlifting is a more subdued sport, individually important to participants and not a crowd thriller. Boxing on the other hand provided a point and time to be vocal for your men in the ring. It could be long or very short — good or great a pugilistic match-up. Talent did rain true in this sport — usually. Quite often out of the winner's circle of Olympic boxers, there became world famous professional boxers. The Olympics was a place for world class athletes that turn professional in their talents and secure themselves usually with the world class incomes. Thus the saying "To the winner goes the spoils." Olympians usually spawn future wellness of financial success.

CHAPTER TWENTY-ONE

Well, 'Little Dave' made it to the finals where in the second round he got suckered into a surprise left hook which floored him. Fortunately, the bell saved him, he revived enough to come back in the next round and pelted his opponent with his patented staccato of flurries to the gut then face and as his opponent was bent over, he plastered him with a right cross which put the guys lights out for the count of 10. That cinched his win and made him the middle weight Olympic boxing champion for his prize of the Gold Medal for his weight division.

Max was out of his mind joyous — ecstatic over Little Dave's BIG win. All that training, teaching, determination and long hard hours of pure sweat work paid off. Wow! As he hugged 'Dave' and kissed him on the cheek raising Dave's hand 'The Winner'! As the referee had done in the ring.

Max's crew maxed out in celebration that night — with chocolate milkshakes for everyone supporting Dave housed at the village, A visit to the Village Ice Cream Bistro — on Max.

It would be in two days before the finals of the heavy weightlifting competition. So, while one was finished Heavy Lou was yet to perform. But he was thrilled and ecstatic that his buddy Amigo had won the World Championship Gold Medal — Middleweight Boxing title. He just knew that he would win it, and gave Dave a big bear hug in response. They laughed with much joy, shouting "Hallelujah" — what a wonderful day. It indeed was exciting and when the news got back to York and when the TV interviewed Little Dave the horns and drums started blazing away in all of York.

All the excitement and work that paid off dwelt deeply with Heavy Lou. He was moved inside by the joy he saw in his buddy Little Dave. He was touched by his success — knowing the length and depth his little buddy had gone through. He was empowered to give his event his all. More than just winning his upcoming event, he would be in humbleness and thankfulness to God and to all that helped him attain his dream. He wanted to have that feeling also. He wanted to win for them.

The day came for Heavy Lou's final lift sequence against very stiff competition. They were inching by small pounds and ounces into new weight territory. Every one of the competitors wanted the BIG PRIZE! The prize Heavy Lou at 240 pounds wanted more than becoming a winner, was the personal satisfaction that he'd came full circle to his destination and dream. He had been true to himself. Sure, others would be proud of him, even look up to him, but he had to live with himself and so far he liked who he was. His "all" would be forthcoming.

It indeed was his challenge. He knew that all of York and Dave and Big John were undergirding his every lift — his expectation was high and he challenged himself to a zenith lift.

He took a deep breath, looked and concentrated on the steel bar in front of him. The weights had inched up one full pound from the last lift in which his opponent had matched.

He said a simple prayer — "to your Glory, Lord," then put his hands comfortably on the bar, and comfortably distant apart, set his feet for the final power lift of his life — then gave a resounding, "Harrumph" as he hoisted with all his strength he could muster. The bar and weights rose up above his head and as he stood erect — holding the bar for the required seconds over his head with arms straight. The bell sounded — signaling he can lower and release the barbells — which he did with a resounding 'thud.' Everyone in the room thought it would go through the floor. It didn't and he stepped aside and off stage to let his opponent opportune himself at lifting.

The big Austrian hulk set up paused, grunted and lifted — he got half way up and everyone could see him grimacing with difficulty — and finally he had to let it drop — he just couldn't make it — one more pound was too much.

"The winner for the heavyweight lifting division and The Gold Medal goes to Mr. Lou Bronski — USA."

Max and the whole York contingency maxed out with a loud joyous hoorays and hugging one another as Heavy Lou stepped to the center platform to accept the Gold Medal as the Star Spangled Banner played full sound. As Heavy Lou stood there tears came to his eyes, and with hand over his heart — and a bouquet of roses held ever so carefully in his other hand, he faced the trilogy of flags with the Stars and Stripes high in the middle. It was a sight to behold — and Billy got every second of all of it — the lift, the placing of the medal around his big neck and the tears. It indeed was a highlight moment.

The final night extravaganza was just that. It was big and final for all in attendance and on media coverage. The town-city of York contingency everywhere, was on 'cloud nine' and all the Gold Medal winners homeward bound didn't remember taking the bus trip home. It was all unreal.

CHAPTER TWENTY-TWO

All of York was in chaotic disarray — every home pot and pan sounded like a symphony of kettledrums. It was a joyous little community come alive with life, friendship and pride. They couldn't wait for the returning heroes to arrive — and when they did; it would be hard to constrain them — for all of York wanted a piece of them to hug. Maybe the headlines in the York Patter would read — "Heroes, Welcome Home — Olympic Gold Medalists." Indeed it would be a Gold Medal hug-a-thon or — "Town-City of York goes Berserk." Other headlines — "City Fathers Host Parade"; "Kids Let Out of School for Day." "Police, Firemen Join Parade. - No Looting, Violence, Protests or Name Calling Involved."

"Pride and Love Filled the Air," "Heroes Honored by All," and "York Wins Big Time" These were headlines in the York Patter — there right on top of its Local Rag.

According to the State Highway Patrol the returning Olympic bus was just a half hour away from downtown York. The streets were lined with people in anticipation of the bus funneling through them and down to York square — the public park area of downtown.

The high school band was awaiting the director's whistle to blaze away with their big sound — the whole place was giddy with joy —- as the town poised together to unleash its welcome home heroes' cheers, signs, and trombones. And that is exactly how it came off as the bus came to a stop in the square and Billy and the coaches stepped off — followed by Little Dave and Heavy Lou wearing their gold medals around their necks.

The time and sight were extraordinary and loud as the celebration madness had set in upon their hometown boys making good the name of York, Illinois. There were 3 Amigos - no knowns, from a small Illinois City that together suddenly made good on their destiny of dreams and installed adrenaline in York, Illinois an unknown, middle class, unappreciated city that just came alive — before the world and showed that they all were world-class citizens. It was a triumph, in hard work, perseverance and guts by the three Amigos and their coaches. It was teamwork at its best. York, indeed, was so proud and showed it joyously.

It was a good story, one that deserved to be told throughout America, the print media swarmed in, as well as the TV news — especially the sports programing, WGN TV and Fox out of St. Louis, sent crews to interview the 3 Amigos. USA Today had their people writing up its coverage and storyline. The three Amigos of York had never seen such business and intent interest, all these media folk demanding interview time.

Indeed, the scramble was on and they were the core recipients of wide spread interest. It would be at least a week before all the 'hoopla' died down and the newsworthiness began to die out.

York enjoyed the notoriety for a while, but grew tired of all the media folk nosing around — they hoped they'd leave and let York return to its own level of living.

It was about a week before everything started to calm down and return to normal. Max's Gym, Max and his staff, the three Amigos and Billy needed some relief and quiet time to recoup. The last month had been extraordinary upon all; intense, active and physically exhausting, not to mention how mentally fatiguing it was to all. Everyone needed some downtime.

Billy took all the videos home to show mom and dad before he turned them in into Max's hand for keepsake. They really enjoyed those and were so excited for Billy — that he was a part of all the central goings on.

Billy took some days off. It would soon become time for another school year to start. It would be his junior year — but he wouldn't be 16 until next June. At the moment he was measuring 6'4" and around 200 pounds. He was still growing and had another two years of growth in him. He knew he hadn't fulfilled all his growing — God definitely was not finished with him yet.

CHAPTER TWENTY-THREE

Billy tried to take time to rest, as he was 15 and too restless to sit still. On Sundays, he occasionally went down to the square to do some pick-up basketball. He loved sports.

This particular Sunday, he found only a few guys playing basketball. One of them was a kid named Eddy Brandon. It so happened that he was the rising senior quarterback on the varsity football team. He was keeping active 'till football practice pre-season started in a week.

Billy took note of that as it rang a bell in his brain. The two of them hit off really well and they hung out all day long together. It was good bonding between them. Later that day, after some rousing one on one ball, Eddy said to Billy, "You coming out for football?" Billy replied, "I haven't thought about it at all — no, I hadn't planned to."

"Well," said Eddy, "we could use and need an 'end' this year, our best end graduated last spring, I need a good end to throw to. I've noticed how quick you are on your feet, and you have very large hands — and obviously you have soft hands — I can tell by the way you handle the basketball and shoot it — you're good — I've seen you play on the Fresh-Soph team last year and know you're an honored player by the league. Why don't you think on it — between the two of us? I think we could make a good team — I love to pass and I get to call most plays. Football season shouldn't interfere with the basketball season program. Let me know?"

They exchanged names, addresses and phone numbers. Eddy continued, "Look, if you think you'd like to play, call me, I'll introduce you to the coach and you can talk with him. His name is "MAC" McCarthy. He's terrific — I know you'd like him a lot — he's got a really good record and has been at York for 15 years. All the kids love him."

"Yeah, I'll think it over and let you know. It intrigues me very much just thinking about it. Yeah, I'll give it some close thought. Sounds like Coach McCarthy is someone you can enjoy playing for. I think I would enjoy playing on your team with you. I have a feeling we'd match up pretty well if I tried out for end. Thanks for thinking of me. Well, I gotta go, see you later — great pick-up game. Really glad to meet you — it's been fun."

They parted company and headed home. Billy always came home after Sunday pick-up basketball games jacked up. It was always fun and kept him honed for competition.

He made himself a Dagwood sandwich, grabbed a glass of chocolate milk and headed for his room. There he would relax and put on some of his favorite music and maybe pick some guitar. The weather was beautiful and he threw open a couple of windows.

He sat down on his Chicago Bear bean bag chair, stretched his legs and took a big bite out of his sandwich. What a great day, he thought. As he sat there looking out the window, his thought turned to remembering what Eddy had said about the current football program and coach. It sounded mighty interesting and alluring. He weighed in on his academics — he was doing pretty well there, and he wanted to play varsity basketball — mmm — He was pretty sure others had played two major sports programs at other schools — may be even here at York. He remembered that Eddy did.

York's varsity football team had done well last season taking second place in the league — it would be fun if they perchance could win the league this coming fall — mmm! He'd have to learn the ropes of football and specifically the position of end. He'd never played it, but had watched a ton of it on TV. There were some great ends throughout professional football. Especially over the years.

He recalled several pro-tight ends that went both ways, and a defensive end way back that he greatly admired, who was a hall of famer from the Green Bay Packers, Willie Davis, a 5-time pro-bowler. And he recalled several others like 13-time pro-bowler and 6 foot 5 inches Tony Gonzales having scored 103 touchdowns in his career as a slot receiver. He was a former basketball player from CAL, last playing for Atlanta.

Then there was the more modern giant of a tight end, who caught 90 passes in one season, and weighing in at 265 pounds and standing 6 foot 6. In two seasons he caught 17 touchdown passes. Most of the tight ends play in at 245-265 pounds — they were formidable hunks.

Billy thought to himself, "I'm a junior high schooler, presently 15 years old and 6 foot 2 inches tall and about 200 pounds. I'm pretty fast and wiry, solid of body, I'm smart and aggressive. Do I think I can play at end on our football team?"— Mmm — He held those thoughts a long time — weighing them all — plus his desire to play football. It would need a commitment to the sport — all out.

He assessed his prospects, feeling like he had more growth potential left in him. Even Big John said he thought he'd be larger than him. Well, if John thought he'd be larger than him — so be it — it will happen!

He was really inclined to 'rough it some' in his life and football seemed a sure-fire way to go to satisfy that! "Yes, I will play!!"

He found the paper he'd scratched Eddy's phone number on, grabbed his cell phone and called him. Eddy happened to answer right away, and Billy said, "This is Billy — I've given my decision to play football serious thought, and I'm going to do it! So set me up with the coach and I'll be there. Hopefully, we two can make a good team together — that I would like to see. I think we connect well — but I'll need lots of help to catch on playing the sport — and learning that end position."

"Great!" — responded Eddy, "That's terrific — you'll do well absorbing everything you need to become an outstanding player. I feel it in my bones. You are a natural athlete. I think my passing hand is tingling with excitement!" He laughed — they both laughed. "OK Billy I'll be back to you as soon as I make arrangements with the coach. Thanks for calling, I wasn't sure you'd say yes, but I'm glad you did."

Billy picked up his guitar and started pickin' and singin'. He felt good and happy about his decision. He felt anxious to get going at it — right away. He wanted to know if he could do it — it was a challenge. He loved challenges.

The season was up coming and looming soon and the pre-season conditioning and play learning time was ever presenting itself. Eddy called the coach.

"Hi, Coach, this is Eddy Brandon, how are you? — Good. — The reason I'm calling is I have a new recruit for you — I think he would be the perfect replacement for end Darrel — who graduated. This kid is talented, quick, fast and tough as nails. He was on the first team fresh-soph basketball squad — has soft and big hands and is already in superb shape — I just got through playing 2 hours of pick-up — one on one basketball with him — we spent all afternoon together. He's a first-class kid. I'd like him to interview with you and sign him up for varsity football. I seriously see him as a big asset for our team. By the way he's still growing — he tells me he has more inches to grow and he'll be much bigger in a year or two. That's his opinion and he tells me it's the opinion of Big John Michaels — his mentor and personal fitness coach."

"Holy Cow! He's Big John's Student?! Yes, I know Billy's reputation and achievements here at York High. They are significant — and you say he wants to come out for varsity football?"

"Yes," stated Eddy, "He's anxious to get started, and says he's a willing student to learn all about the game — says he's an avid watcher of college and pro games — and a big fan of the Chicago Bears."

"Well Eddy, we really need a good receiver at end this coming year — and if you have a hot hand to deliver the ball, with him we could possibly take the helm of our league this fall. It would be nice. We'll have over 90% veterans coming back — so we should be really strong. Have him in my office tomorrow around 8am and I'll interview him and find out what you already told me about him — based on what you say — I'd bring him onboard — we need him!"

"OK coach, if I don't call back, plan on him being in your office at 8 o'clock. Thanks for hearing me out — see you tomorrow — bye," said Eddy.

They hung up, both looking forward to the meeting with Billy.

Eddy called Billy and told him he'd talked with Coach McCarthy and that he wanted to talk with him at 8AM tomorrow morning —- "Is that OK?"

Billy said to Eddy, "I'll be there in his school office. Thanks for putting a good word in for me. Will you be there?"

"Yes," replied Eddy, "I wouldn't miss it." "See you there," said Billy — and hung up.

Billy arose early as the sun was appearing over the eastern horizon. He put on a new pair of jeans and a collared York athletic department t-shirt he'd gotten during basketball season.

What muscles he had, his outfit showed them off. He scrambled downstairs to the kitchen to fix a decent breakfast. He fixed his own food when mom was not able to. He thought nothing to do this.

The day was sunny, 65 degrees and a beautiful morning. He hopped on his Schwinn cross bike and headed off to York High School a couple of miles away from his house. Billy arrived about 7:50 AM and stored and locked his bike into a bike rack — then headed to Coach Mac's office.

The door was open, the lights on — so he walked right into the coach's office. He saw that coach 'Mac' was on the phone — so he stood and waited for him to get off. It was just a minute before he was.

Just before coach 'Mac' got off the phone, Eddy came in and he stood alongside. Mac arose, extended a handshake to Billy saying, "You're the young man Eddy wanted me to interview. Nice of you to be here so early in the morning." 'Coach 'Mac' motioned them to sit down — as he surveyed Billy from top to bottom. He was impressed with his posture and his body proportions. For a 16-year-old — he was quite well put together. He wasn't a short and stocky type or heavyweight slightly out of shape lineman type. He was what the coach thought as a sleek fairly husky — well muscled boy of 6 foot 2, 200 pounds — long well-muscled arms and a tight muscled torso elongated for his height.

Mac thought to himself what Eddy had said, that Big John had said about Billy's physique — He's still growing, picture him really big someday. Mac could vision that also, and saw the raw potential in Billy, so he took Billy in by saying, "So you're interested in football — but never played it. Eddy said you follow college and pro football often, is that right?"

"Yes sir," said Billy fortunately — looking the coach right in the eye. "OK," followed coach Mac, "Several preliminary things. We need you to get a physical and we need to have your parents sign off on your playing for us. Think that's possible?"

"Yes sir" Billy stated again.

"If you don't have a family physician, I'll be happy to give you the school's 'DOC'!" Mac said.

"That would be good" said Billy. Continuing, "Mom and Dad will sign the release form so I can play."

"Good, I'll get right on it, because we start practice in ten days and I like my players to be in top shape for the long season of 9 games plus any play offs. I'll call your cellphone and let you know what time and where to see Doctor Stevens. Also, here are some pre-season papers covering schedules of practice, a season game schedule, rules and regulations and conduct issues, and costs involved for each player — student for the season — and dress code requirements when needed."

"OK, now let's just chat for a while, so we get to know each other a little better." Said coach Mac. They proceeded to ask questions as Billy related his story as it had unfolded the last 16 years and Billy learned about the coach's background credentials and history also. Eddy was just there for the ride and kept quiet — unless the coach spoke to him.

When the interview session was through, they all stood up, shook hands again, and bid farewell until they next would meet. The coach asked Eddy to stay a few minutes and Eddy said, "Yes." And told Billy he'd be with him in a couple of minutes — see him outside.

So Billy went outside into the hallway, and looked at all the trophy cases lining the hallway — admiring the amazing display of all the various school trophies won. Not bad for a small city like York, thought Billy.

Eddy emerged from within the hallowed office of York's beloved coach. He'd been there a long time and looked like he'd been there much longer than that. Eddy stated, "I thought that went well, coach is happy that you want to come on board, and is looking forward to working with you. He is a taskmaster, but a fair one and you'll learn much from him because he loves to teach us kids.

The season should be a real gas, and you may be the 'key' to unlocking a winning season. So now my friend, I say good hunting — and play hard — our goal is to win it all this year. Give me a call anytime — meanwhile study those play sheets in that binder he gave you — especially right end. I'll see you later, Billy."

"Thanks for everything — see ya!" said Billy.

CHAPTER TWENTY-FOUR

Billy took the permission letter home to get signed by his folks. And after a short discussion with his dad — they signed it. He would call and let the coach know it was signed — now he must pass the physical standard testing by Dr. Stevens. He'd ask Coach Mac if any appointment had been set.

Billy called the coach and luckily found him in and was able to speak to him. The coach said, "Great!" to his folks signing the release form, and continued with, "got you a physical testing time at 4 o'clock today — can you make it?"

Billy responded affirmatively that he'd be there — repeating the doctor's address of Suite 210, Crenshaw building, 1540 Yorktown Avenue, and his phone number.

Billy thanked him and said he was looking forward to making the team and playing for him. He affirmed that he'd do all he could to help the York Raiders win a championship.

The coach said to Billy — "I like your attitude. Glad you're coming out. See you next week at practice. Take care. Thanks for calling me. — Good-bye." and they hung up.

Well Billy had a little over a week to do those things he had free time for. No school yet, but his daily workouts at Max's gym — taking martial arts courses, boxing and weight and fitness training under the watchful eyes of the 3 Amigos — who in spite of their new high status and notoriety, were still going to Max's gym to keep fit.

Their goals had been reached but life went on and they still wanted to keep fit and be in top shape. They, however, being new celebrities on the scene had to go to many places for one reason or another because of their new-found Olympic status. They all were booked pretty solid for months to come, on TV shows, commercials of one sort or another and endorsements for products of multi-sorts for which they received financial benefits under various contract arrangements. These things only added to their new-found stardom and celebrate, also to their bank account.

All the demand that came with their new now famous status was not without some irritation and troubling times. Being famous and in the spotlight is not an easy position to be in. It gets complicated sometimes. Depending on the type of athletic star you are. Sometimes, determines your length of 'dollar' production you're good for; like a one-time ad for a cause, product or event, or a multi-time contract for a certain length of time. At the moment all three of them were on the front of the Wheaties cereal box — just pick your hero — sports star — for whatever reason. These commercial ventures usually have a timeline of being alive — of course with some commercials they often reappear.

When popularity is pulsating, many noted athletes turn to business managers for managing their business needs and some come with high fees — some are good, others not so good. Some had good reputations and success and those were to be found. The three Amigos pooled their thought and put a search on for a one personal business manager that would handle them all. An all-for -one, one-for-all guy. It became imperative they select one soon.

Max was again a help here. He had a lawyer customer-friend, who had a brother who lived in Chicago and was a partner of a firm that catered to the sports world as business and career managers.

A check on them by this local lawyer found the firm very reputable, good and costly. Celebrities held much favor in the public eye if they had and were keeping their nose clean- especially if they esteemed themselves as people with a good story and were honest folk — like a good neighbor type person. Good managers could feed the bank accounts of those they represented if the personal reputations, and conduct, were above reproach and intact.

The three Amigos indeed, fit the image and form of these criteria and a meeting of all of them with Tom O'Brien of the Chicago firm, O'Brien, Norton and Goldberg.' — sports managers. All were lawyers that chose the business field of managing sports personality stars — representing them in all kinds of endorsement and appearance deals, short and long-term contracts. They also provided tax and income C.P.A people to manage those problems. They were a full-service legal sports business career management and C.P.A services firm.

Max's customer/friend lawyer, suggested to the 3 Amigos to form themselves as a small corporation, for tax reasons and benefits, with limited liability. This was explained to the three of them — in the presence of Max and Billy. Billy was indeed included - on the insistence of Big John — who wanted Billy involved in every aspect of life that was possibly made available to him. His object was to enlarge his parameters, and possibility thinking — providing a liberal education wherever it could be found. In school, out of school life learning takes place everywhere one goes — 'grab it', absorb it, it will expand your thinking and improve your choices you make along life's journey.

These were the things Big John wanted for Billy — He loved this kid and desired for his best. Indeed, it was important to him, for he had strong premonition of greatness for Billy's life.

CHAPTER TWENTY-FIVE

Indeed, Billy's greatness was just getting started — the moment he attached himself to the three Amigos. For they all had good heads on their very fit shoulders and had good core values to sustain their conduct which made possible the good choices and reputations they had. These things were very hard to come by in their world and time of living. It was not easy to alone make it without falter and back-sliding momentum.

In fact, they kept each other honest and through agreement ran their lives through each other as filters for any darkness coming into any of their lives. They were open and discussed everything — they refused to hide stuff that potentially could wound them somehow. It was a good and unusual friendship. A strong one with good binding.

Billy was in their midst now, along with his now appreciation of his folks, and they of him. It was for Billy, a godsend vested his way, indeed an intervention in his life that afforded a grand potential opening for a lifetime ahead.

So far Billy was meeting all expectations, in school and out of school. He was young, but maturing fast and taking responsibility for his life and conduct. His mentors, because of their conduct and criteria they set for themselves, provided ample good 'examples' of rightness and righteousness for the core living of the life and soul in Billy's future life. He was learning right ways in the pathway of a God he knew. He felt God's touch on his life.

Billy's problem, as in most of us, was dealing with where the rubber meets the road, where choices have to be made and determination to follow those pathways, one way or another as he processed forward. Old slew foot is always there to throw you curves, lies, and huge divots to separate you from God and your good choices that you are making for yourself. He hates, "good success" for goodness sake! It's beneath his corrupted dignity, to do good anytime or any place.

It was that time of the year when football rang its starting bell — the U.S.A. over. It was time for that nip in the air, yet relinquishing slowly the summer heat still lingering in spurts.

Players were out in shorts, and 'T's, running sprints, laps around the field, push-ups, bar chin ups, then up and down the stadium stairs, and any hills nearby and of course — jumping jacks with everybody yelling "hep" while swinging their arms from their sides to over their heads — clapping hands at the top-again sounding off — "hep."

Indeed, it was running plays throwing passes, kicking field goals, kick-offs, blocking and tackling routines. It was teaching time for the coaches. To dig hard with the kids to install football knowledge, skills, and to hone talent to perfection limits.

Enthusiasm and inclusiveness were categorical imperative for the 'spirit,' component necessary for 'oil slick' coordination and team functionality. Semper-fi type thing.

The problem was time constraints for preliminary pre-season practice. Indeed, you were at the beginning of the season — not at the end — when you got closer to perfection and coordination among the teammates in pursuit of winning — and the desire to win — the 'dig-deep' stuff that boys and men are made of. With young men, it takes a special breed of coach, an esteemed leader towing the line - edging them onward and upward to do their best. It had to be a total team effort to win.

Winning was the name of the league game of football. Football was a team sport, a rough sport and a win was calculated by an individual's best one-on-one effort on behalf of the whole team's success. Breakdowns occurred when someone gave way to the fullness of his assignment and a play didn't work.

Second chances usually presented themselves throughout a game, such as when an offensive guard let up on the defensive guard coming through him. Someone is outfoxed, overwhelmed or quicker in movement than the other. Adjustments need to be made, especially if repeated times ensue. Maybe a trap play — or a double team on that defenseman will stop him. The coach's' job is to spot that, and heal the wound.

Billy was pretty worn out after the first day of practice. However, he thought himself in much better shape than most that day. Most the boys his age didn't do physical fitness the way and as often as he did — daily.

Billy could see the handwriting on the wall. He was going to have to learn a lot to be good at this game. He thought momentarily of the videos Coach 'Mac' had given him. He would get those out and play them. He needed instruction, like a Marine recruit at boot-camp. Actually, school would begin in a week — so he'd have time now — this week to watch all the videos and absorb as much of them as possible.

Coach 'Mac' didn't do all the coaching alone. He had a few assistants and some volunteer folks, former players of college, and one rather large soul, a veteran of the esteemed Chicago Bears offensive line. He was assigned to the tackle to tackle coaching and both sides of the line.

Sure, he was the big guy protecting the quarterback — but he had to know all the tricks and shenanigans of the defensive guys trying to get through him. He had been a godsend to coach 'Mac.' York, had a good crop of 'heavy-lifters' as lineman candidates and 'Big Bo' Mineke — number 76 of the Bears, and volunteer line coach — challenged the Yorkmen 'heavy-lifters'- to their fullest.

Most games were lost or won in the trenches. The line play — both sides were critical to winning ways. They made possible the good things that the backfield could do to move the football up the field. It wasn't all talent that was the necessary ingredient for winning, but the hard work of grinding each play out — just getting the job done, that ensured the greatest possibility of making progress — and eventually winning. It was the 'grunt' stuff that did it.

Billy sat for hours viewing his football videos coach Mac had given him. Things like the fundamentals of football, tackle to tackle line play, ends — both ways — and individual tapes on the backfield positions. He would view those last — maybe view the half backs and all their pass patterns. But mainly it was the study of the 'ends' — both ways, that interested him and needed viewing.

He viewed the 'ends' video first and after its finish — he rewound it and played it again for a third time. The third time the why's and wherefores sunk in why and how the 'end' functioned correctly. It established the patterns they ran. The blocking they did. The art of catching — emphasizing the art of soft-hands being a 'key' to receiving and holding on to football passes at any speed thrown. It was amazing the intricate things needed to perform positively in game situations.

He took note in the video of a section in them denoting the so called 'art' of folding after catching the ball — as the defender collided with him in a tackle attempt. How to spin — and when, or step aside right after the catch, or relax for a moment as you are hit — then determining your move or to fold. He never had experienced the likes of those type hard backside tackles the defensive linebackers doled out — some were fierce. Not all were executed cleanly — and you could easily get hurt.

Billy was thoroughly enlightened after viewing the "end" video and was glad he did — glad the coach had those. When he finished the 'end' video, he put in one of the others, first on the linemen — then the backfield positions. He was getting a good study on the inside of football. Obviously from his recollection of watching and listening to college and pro games, these tapes re-lived many of the player's actions and position movements in action. It all seemed to come together in his mind and now he only needed to remember the stuff as he played out his 'end' position on the team.

Always was the transition from theory to live reality. Billy finished viewing the tapes and got up and went to his computer console table. He booted it up and began to look up the top ten all-time great 'ends' in the pro-game. To read and gleam if there was any information he might use to add to his further knowledge of his position at end. Those top ten were quite impressive, a few were hall of famers, others multi-pro bowlers chosen each year. The best of the best.

Between the videos and computer, Billy took and prepared some notes of special interest to himself he wished to particularly remember. He placed these in his playbook where he could find and use them. He'd spent the day studying film and computer stuff and it was time to head for another practice session when the sun wasn't so hot. He was hungry and hit the fridge before he headed out the door. He piled some cold meats between two slices of Rye bread and adds a little 1,000 island dressing. Then poured a glass of chocolate milk — sat down and chowed out. — Mmm — that was good! He went and lied down for a short time — before he had to "bike" his way to York high. He was old enough but hadn't learned to drive yet and didn't have a car. It wasn't yet important to him — the bike did just fine and was good exercise besides.

The coach gave a lecture before getting into actual practice. The team needed to learn and hear how they were going to win and play their games. It was in the fundamentals that they were practicing right now. Learn and play hard now and that's what you'll do in the real game. "Alright, out for warm-up exercises!" One of the assistant coaches led them through the exercise routines and then sent them all running five laps around the football field — "No cutting corners he yelled — "That'll add laps for whoever did so!"

Billy did all the exercises and unlike some — was not winded. He felt anxious about getting to the point of actually playing in games. He pictured himself on the team in actual play at his position of end. The picture was sitting well in his mind and he dwelled on that a few minutes. It wasn't to be that day — too many fundamentals to learn and do, and fundamental play was the glue that made wins possible. Many a running back would break loose from a poorly executed tackle that was fundamentally unsound. Fundamentals were essential for good execution in most every endeavor in life. Fundamentals, Billy understood could mean the difference between success or failure and maybe really getting hurt or even winning or losing a game, so he practiced what the coaches taught and took the exercises to heart. His gameplay maybe dependent of how well he executes the fundamentals necessary.

At 5:30 PM the coaches all blew their whistles to signify the end of that day's practice session. Always to follow was a short homily by Coach Mac summarizing the day and where they had accumulated progress to and any other side note he had for them. Today's little ditty was the summary of the upcoming season. There was a regular season. There were a regular season

games, plus five possible play-off games. Most games would be on Friday night starting at 7 PM. This year's offensive formation would consist of the 'winged-t' and the shotgun. We've found success running these formations. This year we are without Ozzie Syzmanski — our right end, but we feel our new recruit, Billy Brewer, a junior, will fill in well at that position. With everybody doing their job well, he may more than do well and deliver the goods for us. He's 6'4" and 200+ pounds full of readiness to get started, which I'm sure you are — Hoo. ———
Dismissed ——

"See you tomorrow ready to go." Everyone fled to the locker room to shower and get out of there and back home.

CHAPTER TWENTY-SIX

The upcoming days duplicated drills, running, blocking and tackling. However, more time each day was devoted to the practice of plays — their refinement and timing. The practicing of blocking the correct way and correct defensive man were small things important to the success of the whole play in order to maximize potential yardage gained. Each player learned that he held the key to winning — play-by-play, to do his job well.

Coach Mac kept a close eye on the training of his new recruit Billy Brewer. Billy worked with the quarterback coach who was also the ends coach. This proved very interesting to Billy as he learned the quarterback position while executing his end position and receiver routes, the slants, outs, deep routes, the stutter steps and spinning just after hauling in the ball.

It was an adventure that he liked. The video tape viewing was paying off in his mind and he learned that seeing the ball clearly and letting it kind of fall into his hands using them as shock absorbers promoted good reception of the ball — whether it had been thrown at high speed or softly. Hard hands only acted as reflectors — like two walls — and the ball would bounce off — often.

He was enjoying his improved ability to catch the ball whether on an in-route where he stood still or if on a slant route full speed and catching a hard-thrown pass.

He needed to work on all the different catch receiving technology of bringing in the bacon on his downfield long-haul routes. He found these most challenging to him. So, the end coach Sidney Hill, worked with he and Eddy to develop cohesion and timing of the pass plays — there had to be a weddedness between the two of them — the quarterback and the ends. He also worked with the running backs and fullbacks to shoot the gap, and turn receiving the passed ball, then turn and head up field or plow — driving his legs into the tacklers.

The coach was good, informative and knew his stuff. Billy thought himself lucky and blessed that all his so- called mentors, teachers, and coaches were first class people that took their jobs seriously and obviously loved what they did. That was certainly the epitome of quality teaching. The unknowns were personalities and attitudes. The best had both, that made learning more palatable and enjoyable, which in turn turned out the best 'fruit' as in results for their students.

School days once again began as Billy arrived early on the first day. He was really enjoying York High School. It was now his "hay-day" of high school. He was flourishing as though he was right smack dab in the middle of his element. He was developing into an energetic and exciting young man who had begun to seriously take his schooling seriously and enjoy his athletic endeavors to the fullest. It all seemed to be coming together.

Billy was filling out nicely as he had continued to grow taller at 6 foot four inches and presently weighing in at a little over 200 pounds. His long lean muscles were beginning to accentuate into very noticeable size. His mentors were making much headway with his body development, attitude, and mental acuity by holding him accountable for his grades at school. They hovered over him while he did whatever 'thing' it was he was doing at the gym, and he hung out with them a lot in free times. They were cool together and enjoyed "joshing' with one another and singing to tunes Little Dave would pick on his guitar.

The three Amigos and Billy were getting to be fixtures around town and the townspeople would all say 'hi' to them — recognizing them as they were now celebrity status. While Big John was on the road making appearances as Mr. America, so too were Little Dave and Heavy Lou as Gold Medal Olympians, thus Billy didn't see them all as often as usual anymore.

Billy was to be plenty busy for the fall season now, besides schooling, he was entrenched in football with the York varsity team. It would be a season he would never forget. It was new territory for him — a new sport and one he had never played. He was certainly learning and learning it fast, and very much enjoying it. However, as yet, the reality of it, he had yet to experience. He had yet to make contact with an opponent. That would be new and different. It would be where the rubber meets the road.

One thing Billy thought about was making practical use of all he was learning from videos and coach's practice was one thing, but a real game was another. Teams were arch enemies on the field — no 'pussy footin' around. Smash, bam thank you Sam stuff. As he let his mind wander over the thought of his playing in reality — he got a feeling of enjoyment, and good expectation. He was looking forward to his putting himself against others, after all that's what athletes do. He wanted to be good — not just participate in whatever he did. Perfectionist maybe, maybe not, but definitely a fierce competitor.

After all, if you're playing against someone — some team, the idea is to win. Not everybody gets a ribbon or trophy for participating. If it's a team sport there has to be a winner, play-offs — a winner — finals — a winner. In war, there are winners — both sides don't get trophies for their participation. 'Yeah, like a nice game, let's do it again another day thing.' Don't think so, thought Billy, sports in particular, are a winners and losers type thing. Getting better is a way to winning, it's a gradual persevering effort, called practice, repetitions, striving, extra effort, reaching, setting goals and doing it. Insistence on best efforts, against resistance from opposing players. The best effort and better team play for the day, is declared the winner. Billy thought it's certainly more fun to win than lose. Go for it!

CHAPTER TWENTY-SEVEN

The first week went by in school and the weekend fired up with the York high school Raiders playing their first football game come Friday night at 7PM — under the lights. Billy could see himself in action, he was getting excited. He had that day received his full uniform, pads, shoes, helmet, and maroon and white home jersey with a big lettered number 89 on it — front and back. "Boy, that looked good." He was anxious to see himself in it all, and even more excited to picture himself filing out of the locker room with all the team — out onto the field into the lights, cheers, cheerleading antics and thunderous noise — with all the great York high school band. "Wow! Can't wait!"

The three Amigos would be there if they're all in town and his Mom and Dad. He backed up his thinking a second over the cheerleading part — and wondered if Anita was on the cheerleading squad. He really didn't know — he'd been too busy to even think of her. He did like her, and felt attracted to her. He had no idea whether she had a boyfriend — or not! Well, anyway — he hoped she'd be there.

Friday night came none too soon for Billy. He was ready to rough it up in reality time. He wanted his team to play the *victory* march after the game. He was ready.

After a late afternoon meal, he showed up at the school locker room around 5:30 PM for the coach's pre-game meeting, rally talk and review of game plans. After that, it was dress out time with the game pads et al. Billy seemed elated with each item he attached to his body, the rib pads, shoulder pads, jock, t-shirt and finally the socks and shoes. Then the maroon and white jersey, with the big number 89 on it. "Wow!", he thought. He dressed out, put his helmet on, and went over to the full-sized mirror to see himself. 'Ahh!' terrific, hope I play even better than I look. I look formidable — at least I think so, he thought. It was time to find out as the time came to exit the locker room with the team. The team was rather quiet before the game, as all were busy putting on their war gear. His teammates looked often at one another — he could see the look in their eyes that said with great anticipation — "I wanna get out there and murder those bums." The energy level was definitely building — and fast. All were ready — full armored. Coach Mac came into the locker room from his office. All got quiet and attentive. They were to hear his last words of inspirations and encouragements before the starting kick off.

Coach Mac, along with his staff, assembled all in front of them. He looked each player in the eye as he said, "Men, today is the first game of a winning season. We play one game at a time — reassemble to learn from our mistakes, and return next week to the gridiron to battle again. This is a war — us against them. Today we win, they lose, that means we have to play our very best. We are a can-do team, 'cause we play together and together we will win. Alright everyone put a hand in — that's right — 1, 2, 3 — play-hard!"

Everyone gave it their verbal best, pumped up all — they stormed out of the locker room with determination and pent up energy. If you'd been there, you'd have been impressed!

CHAPTER TWENTY-EIGHT

THE FIRST FOOTBALL GAME FOR BILLY BREWER
at
YORK HIGH SCHOOL

by STAN ZALINSKI

The recounting of the York high Raiders football teams' first season game versus the Midlothian "Bruins" high school found the raiders edging out the Bruins by one point, 21 to 20. It was a hard-fought contest. Neither team could get it going the first quarter and the biggest offense by either was the punting game.

In the second quarter, Midlothian scored first early on, with the raiders grinding out a lot of running plays by fullback, Bobby Brummel. His play was determined and aggressive. The line looked real tough and blocked well. Finally, at the 2nd quarters end, they advanced into the red-zone and scored. Half time score 7 to 7.

Coach McCarthy must have given the team a good rally talk as they came back in the 3rd quarter to score twice. The first scoring occurred when the 'heavy lifters' in the line allowed Bobby Brumell to have his way down into the red zone. The first score came on a slant pass from Eddy Brandon into the hands of the new junior 'raider' recruit, Billy Brewer, who faked a long route and cut across behind the linebackers to haul in the ball and use his size and speed to reach the end zone.

The second Raider score developed when the raiders pounded the ball to the Bruins 40 yard line. Then proceeded to run a split end play where Brewer blocked the end, then headed downfield about 10-12 yards whereby he broke off into a drag route across the field as Eddy Brandon hit him perfectly and Billy then put on the speed actually running over one potential tackler and on into the end zone. Score 21-7 Raiders.

The Bruins again scored when a punt was poorly executed and went out of bounds only 20 yards up field. The Bruins capitalized on the error and scored a touchdown but the Raiders blocked the extra point. Third quarter score — 21-13 Raiders.

The fourth quarter found the Raiders struggling and losing a fumble in their Red Zone in which the Bruins capitalized on the error and were able to punch it in on a trick end-a-round that actually worked. Raiders 21, Bruins 20.

No further scoring took place as both teams tightened up their defenses. All in all, it was a hard-fought good game. Bobby Brumell looked particularly good and the new recruit, Billy Brewer, looked very promising as a replacement for last years end Ozzie Syzmanski. Coach Mac should be proud of his first win.

END OF ARTICLE IN 'PATTER'

Well the locker room was joyous and loud — they had their first season win, if by a too narrow a margin.

Coach Mac came in — all got quiet as he gave his little homily. "Guys —- you played pretty good for this opener. We were a bit sloppy here and there, but we'll be tightening it up this week."

"We were lucky tonight — getting that win — next week we play Canton high school at their place — our first away game. We've always done well at away games and I expect no less next Friday night. Enjoy your win — see you at practice Monday.

Everyone cheered and shouted knowing that they were going to be worked hard. They had been sloppy in their play. Truth is truth.

The stands had been packed full opening game. Yes, the cheerleaders were in top form and mom and dad Brewer were very proud of their son. He was a very different boy than a few years ago. They hugged each other and headed home to await Billy's return home that evening.

Eddy came by Billy as they were finishing dressing after their showers. He spoke to Billy and asked if he could give him and his bike a ride home and stop at the local DQ for a shake. Billy looked up, smiled and said, "Great, thanks — sure — sounds good!" The two headed out the gym locker room jabbering away about the game. It looked like the two of them would make a good tandem team — and great friends.

Billy arrived home and unloaded his bike out of Eddy's car and thanked Eddy, each saying, "Goodnight. See ya!" The fellowship and shake endeared Billy to Eddy. He respected Eddy as a senior quarterback — who was a good leader as well as a top quarterback. He felt very positive about the season's prospects and the connectedness he and Eddy seemed to have both on the field and off.

Billy's folks were awaiting him home with joy in their hearts. He gave them a hug and sat down to talk with them before hitting the sack. It was nice to talk and share with them. It indeed felt like family and that raised his love for them. He thought of the three Amigos having been there tonight to watch him in particular and was anxious to see them tomorrow.

After half an hour with his folks, he excused himself and headed upstairs to bed. It had been a good day. He was proud of himself, but not satisfied. They had eight games to go. He was anxious to get to practice and back in next week's game.

Billy sat on his bed with his guitar in his hand and started pickin' out a slow country melody. It didn't last very long and he put it down, threw his legs under the covers, turned the light out and drifted off to slumber land. He was tired.

That Saturday he slept in arising around 9AM. He put his jeans on and t-shirt that advertised 'Pepsi' — a winner. He liked Pepsi. Billy headed downstairs to the kitchen for breakfast. A couple of fried eggs and English muffin — slathered in butter and a glass of chocolate milk. That should hold him for a while. Teenagers loved to eat — often. He found fixing his own stuff to eat fun and challenging.

As he ate, he thought of his buddies. They'd be down at the gym if they were in town. He didn't know their schedules as they were too busy in their celebrity status. He felt so privileged to know such now famous Olympians and Mr. America — all from right here in York, Illinois. He felt and dreamed that someday he would hold a similar status as they — in some regard for which he had absolutely no idea of what. Billy tucked that thought away in his retro-file mind. He'd tap into that again somewhere along the line of his life.

He arrived by bike at Max's gym, deciding to work out whether any of the Amigos were there or not. No one, including

Max — was there. Max's assistant, Kenny Heiberger was there running the place.

Billy went into Max's gym and headed for the locker room to change into his usual workout clothes. It was fairly busy — especially with working week employed folk. Many there spoke to him, and said "you played a good game Friday — good luck on next week's game — "go get um!" He thanked them for coming out and said his team would do better. "

Billy changed out, and worked out for two hours before stopping. He felt stronger and he checked his weight — 210 pounds. He felt like he had yet more growth ahead in store for him. That would portend greater opportunity for upcoming basketball season and give him advantage at end on the football team — a bigger target for Eddy to hit.

As he walked to his bike, another thought hit him — how nice it would be to have a car to get around instead of this bike. At 6'4", he kind of looked 'gorky' riding it around. Even an old used one would be good. "Mmm!" If he ever had a date — he'd need transportation — yes, he needed to pursue that thought. He'd approach his buddies and seek their input — maybe talk with his dad.

He got on his bike and headed down to the park and the basketball court where he hoped he could find a pick-up game of hoops. There were a few guys there and they recognized him and included him in their game. It felt good and natural expressing himself playing 'hoops' again. He enjoyed all of his new-found height he'd grown and hoped it would help him come basketball season again. Right now, it was football season — a new sport he was enjoying and his legs were in top shape for that. He was pleased with his progress overall.

Once again, looking forward to Monday — and practice. He was getting bored. So he headed home, to relax and listen to some music and play his guitar — maybe get his karaoke honkin' and sing a few tunes.

Sunday came and for some reason he felt a pull to go to church. He hadn't one and thought where one might be — oh, yes — the big Presbyterian Church he passed on his way to his Sunday basketball pick-up games — maybe he'd try that? He didn't know what to do — or how, heck he'd just go and ask — he was sure they'd help him — and they did.

It was the First Presbyterian Church of York and he entered through the large sanctuary door. They were gathering their flock for 10 AM service. There were many people, and everyone was taking their place seating. It was mostly full, so he entered in and slipped into a pew in the back row. He was dressed as he was so he felt comfortable. An usher gave him a program and he sat and read through it. He discovered the music was to be done by the Youth Choir that day — 'mmm' he mused. He'd see what they had.

The pastor came to the front and spoke, greetings in the name of the Lord. May his blessings be upon you all-the-day. The head elder came forward and read the church news, events of that week and stated those that were sick — then offered a prayer for them. So far, he was comfortable. Nobody had asked him to give his life to Christ yet. He thought about that and said to himself — I know my maker already — he's my maker and Lord of my life.

Next after the announcements, came the Youth Choir up on stage behind the pulpit. They formed a semi-circle. The organ went big time and the Youth Choir sang out. "Pretty good," thought Billy. Then 3 of the youth stepped forward to 3 mics. One had a guitar. They sang a contemporary tune praising Jesus. They too sounded pretty good. Then they all sang a contemporary piece in unison harmony. He counted 52 kids in the choir. Pretty good — and they looked like they were having fun.

Well the Youth Choir was followed by the main sermon by Pastor David Burr — which was titled, "The Spirit empowerment." Billy saw that the pastor was a good-looking man and had a strong clear voice. He listened to the sermon and thought it really good. The pastor wrapped it up by saying with his hands lifted upward, "Praise the Lord!" everyone said in response — "Amen!"

There were a few people in the church while leaving that recognized him and said "Hello." It seemed to be a friendly place — maybe he'd comeback. On his way out, he was greeted by the pastor at the door and shook hands saying to him — "enjoyed your sermon." the pastor did a double take on that — a high school kid — alone — who actually must have listened to his sermon. Pastor Burr — engaged Billy speaking to him with a question — "Are you here alone?" "Yes," said Billy. "What's your name?" Billy said, "Billy Brewer." "Don't you play end for The York Raiders?" Again, Billy answered, "Yes." He was impressed with Pastor Burr's questions. The pastor again asked the question, "Did you fill out a new guest slip and put it in the offering plate?" Again, Billy confirmed that he did. "Good" said pastor Burr, looking Billy in the eye said, "Look forward to your coming back — we have a terrific youth director. Have a blessed day young man — goodbye."   They parted their ways and Billy headed home on his bike. It had been much better than he had expected.

CHAPTER TWENTY-NINE

The following weeks were spent in routine activities. School and academic studies, sports, workouts, practice — building confidence. It was daily progress. Things were running smoothly and he went to bed each night tired — but fulfilled. His football practices proceeded to hone better connections between Eddy and himself on the timing of pass plays. The coaches were working the team on the fundamentals of blocking and tackling — they spent some time teaching the defensive linebackers how to read offensive formations and what to look for — and to 'key' certain offensive backs to tipping off play direction and decoy movements. Coach Mac was plugging the loopholes he'd seen in the last game. Coach Mac knew how to do these things and get the most out of his players. He was a most respected coach and faculty member.

Also, that week a few new 'trick' plays were introduced into the playbook — like the end-a-round reverse that we got shellacked on by Midlothian High School last week. He also set up defenses to read the tell-tale offensive backfield movements and how to position his defensive ends and linebackers. The coach was hitting all of his potential defects we had last game. So, the likelihood of being fooled again would be lessened.

The upcoming Friday night away game with Canton High School went surprisingly well. The Raiders scored in every quarter and came off with a substantial win — 28 to 7. Billy scored two touchdowns on pass plays — one a crossover, and the other a long haul-in. Billy was pleased with his deep route straight away catch over his left shoulder on the dead run.

Everyone was thrilled at that and he received and a great ovation. The Raider team of Eddy and Billy were 'hot' and well connected. It would be a productive season.

Two touchdowns were scored by Bobby Brumell the fullback from 6-10 yards out. He was a real force to be reckoned with, and he was improving weekly.

The atmosphere at York high school was joyous with each win during the season. They came one after another as the season progressed. The trio of Eddy, Billy, and Bobby became known as the triumphant trio. Mac continued to be the attitude leveler pointing out without good blocking nothing would get done. Talent is one thing, but necessary support is the key. The heavy 'lifters' were — doing their jobs well. Both ways.

By the completion of the 3rd game with Northwest Military academy at home things were hummin' pretty well. The team was hittin' stride in most every area. Practice was paying off. Eddy and Billy were spot on — working all their passing formations. The 0 line was doing its heavy lifting on defenses to open holes for Bobby Brumell.

Coach McCarthy had been a quarterback at the University of Illinois in his prime. He also was an honors student while there. Thus, it was no surprise to his players, no matter what the sport, that he gave emphasis and importance to any future proper attention to his students' education in the classroom. He was a spearhead, educator addition to the York faculty.

The faculty was a dedicated group of teachers, whose job one was the education of their students. SAT and ACT scores had been rising for several of the last years and that was good news to all of the York community and bore good future citizenship tidings.

Only three games had taken place. It was a season of 9 — which would take them into the last week of October — with 3 weeks into November — should they get into the play offs. That would conclude the season around November 28th — a Friday.

The official basketball season started December 1, a Tuesday. Unofficial practice would start two weeks prior to that. Billy had been doing Sunday basketball, one on one, and team like pickups year around — and was pretty well tuned for the sport already, but right now he was having the time of his life playing end on the football team. A championship was in the making and he wanted to be a part of that. His teammates were all revved to bring it on this season. The focus was there as well as the effort to make it happen.

Silverton, Jasper City and Dumont high schools all folded under the Raiders determination to win. With each win the team seemed to double up on their practice time esteeming perfection as it could be ingested. Sure there were momentary set-backs and mishaps like when the Raider's punter got off one that went straight up in the air and came back down just behind their own line of scrimmage and bounced backward some 10 yards. You could hear the crowd groan to their toes on that one. The defense tightened up and the opposition team never gained a first down. Mistakes were to them just glitches on their way to progress.

The 3 Amigos attended every Friday night game to watch Billy — and really got excited when they saw the Raiders determinedly exert their will against whoever they played. It wasn't as though other teams were bad, but that the Raiders were so good. With each game Billy increased his confidence — in his routes and how to deftly finesse catching Eddy's passes.

Big John commented to heavy Lou and Dave, "Our boy is growing into manhood. Look how he plays — and practices full tilt."

"Yeah," said Lou, "He's using his height and weight to his advantage — no question about it. This has got to be their year as several of their better players graduate this year — especially Eddy Brandon. That'll be a big loss."

Dave jumped in, "He'll be hard to replace — he's certainly a big college prospect!"

"No, question about that!" said Big John. I wonder who would ever replace him here. The coach has his work cut out for him to find a good follow up. Nobody's ever seen the back-up quarterback play — maybe if we get way ahead he might come in."

Dave responded, "Yeah, knowing Coach Mac for developing talent, he might have him primed for his opportunity time next year. It's in the realm of possibilities under Coach Mac."

"We shall see." came back heavy Lou.

This Friday the Raiders played West Haven, an away game. The team was running on all eight pistons with precision. Eddy was threading the needle to both ends and to his fullback on traps. The 'O' line kept the varmints out of Eddy's way and the defense looked like the proverbial Chinese fire drill penetrating the opponents 'O' line. The problem all opponents had was that the Raiders were such a balanced team. There weren't weak spots. If any, the punter position was lacking distance but Jason Mason, the field goal kicker was greatly improving as the season moved along, and was nailing them at 40 yards or less He was in his junior year.

Scores by the opponents came few and far between especially after the half season elapsed. However fittingly, the other powerhouse in the league, Jamestown high school was the last game and it was played at home on the Raiders field.

The problem with a winning team can be complacency and over confidence — those lead to costly mistakes. It was indeed a problem that Coach Mac was aware of and fought hard to keep his team attitude such that 'swagger' didn't enter in and affect his team in a derogatory manner. He kept after them to do their job each individually — everyday. Action and accomplishment would take care of themselves when all worked together. It was a good thing — as the next two games came on stream.

Belmont gave the Raiders a very tight game the first half holding the score at 14 to 14. However, the safeties just couldn't keep Billy and his height from pulling down the ball in deep routes. Billy was getting the hang of tweaking the ball from the sky as Eddy, with good protection sailed the pig skin downfield in radar like fashion.

Also, the pounding of the '0' and 'D' lines weakened the Belmont will, and the final score mirrored the problem. At the bells end, the Raiders won it 33-17. That left the last game of the year to prepare for. It portended to be the toughest and hottest contested game that season, and it would propel the winner into first place for the conference championship trophy. They then would have to prepare for the regional play offs and if winning, the then state play offs. It was a big thing to be there — an honor, and to win the state title — a huge accomplishment — and a long, long season. It would take him into the basketball season and that was OK for Billy and the basketball coach.

CHAPTER THIRTY

York High School was ginning up their enthusiasm for the Jamestown game being played in their backyard. It was a large high school out of Kankakee and they had the reputation as tough and usually good with winning records. And it was for the league conference championship — 1st place. That excitement factored into the overall attitude of the teams and students of both schools.

The week went by fast. School work was of primary concern at York — but literally everyone was waiting for Friday night under the lights. The principal of York, Perry Dunlop, tried hard to keep a lid on all the excitement. Of course, there had to be a big rally — couldn't get away from that. The gym was full Thursday night — the mighty school band was there to blow off steam. The cheerleaders were in top form and Billy glimpsed Anita again. Jumping, twirling and cartwheeling across the floor. Climbing the human pyramid was what landed Anita in Billy's lap some time ago — he secretly hoped that might occur again. Meanwhile, this time with the football team he would keep an eye on her. She was special. However, she need not interfere with his job at hand — the reason for the rally.

Billy was looming large at the rally — he definitely was the tallest dude on the team. He was by far not the heaviest. Their interior lineman ranged from 250 to 275 pounds — and due to Coach "Bo" Mineke, they were not the rotund type linemen. Every one of them were college prospects and not to small colleges, but to Division I type schools.

The rally night was blazing loud, active and fun — all had a marvelous time trying to spur the team onto victory on the 'morrow night. Hopefully thought Billy, a regular school day would calm him down some. But the 'buzz' would be going on around the academic day. It was inevitable.

The team, as it was, Billy's junior year, was the best it had been over the last decade. It had all the ingredients of a Winner — a Champion. Next year it would be different, as key players were graduating. Right now, they were a balanced team of determination and hard work. No matter what the outcome tomorrow night, it won't be for lack of hard work or trying. That was a given. It would be talent and perfection pitted against each other. It would be the mistakes, turnovers and surprise happenings that would cause loss. That's why Coach 'Mac' continually drilled into them to continue doing exactly what they had been taught and drilled. Their jobs done well. Billy thought "If we execute well, we'll win this thing."

Billy returned home that evening around 8 o'clock from the rally end hanging with his teammates. They were jacked up as he was and anxious to get it on and done. Things were as positive as they could be. He visited with his folks for an hour and they expressed how proud they were of him in all he was doing in school and athletics.

His dad surprised him with the announcement that he had gotten a raise and promotion at his company. Billy could see his mother beaming at that news as he told Billy. Indeed, it was good news — as Billy knew how dedicated an employee his dad was over the long years he was with the company.

Billy got up and went over and gave his dad a hug and congratulated him — saying he well deserved it. Billy excused himself and headed up to his room. He needed to calm down and think things through. He put some music on — played his guitar and then got into his 'Jammies.' That was his immediate need and desire tomorrow was another and busy day — he needed his rest.

Friday the big day arrived with the sun arising with scattered white clouds abounding here and there. He must have been tired, as he felt very rested from what he thought as a good night's sleep. He arose and did his bathroom routine and went and put on his jeans, collared t-shirt and light V-necked sweatshirt with the Chicago Bears on it. He checked himself out in the full-sized mirror on the back of his door, approved and headed downstairs for breakfast. Surprised was he to find his mom in the kitchen fixing breakfast. She said as he approached, "Good Morning — today is a huge day in your life and I wanted you to start off with a big 'mom' breakfast." He gave his mom a hug — thanked her — and looked over the table. A large orange juice was awaiting him.

Mom was busy dropping several eggs into one pan as she dipped several pieces of bread into some batter and put them on to the flat griddle — French toast.

The smell of sausage filled the kitchen air as she cooked them on the skillet. 'Wow' whatta breakfast he thought! He sat down and within minutes it all came together, on the plate before him. Indeed, he was hungry and dug in heartily.

"Boy, was that ever good." said Billy to his mom. He assembled all the dirty dishes and took them to the sink He gave his mom another hug — thanked her and picked up his packed lunch and books and said, "Have a great day mom — thanks again —" and headed out the door to the school bus pickup.

Billy thought to himself — based on that great breakfast, this should be a super day — good!

The school day seemed to progress slowly. Obviously, he was anxious to get through it all and get his battle garments on for the game. Everyone was anxious to get through with the schoolwork and move onto all the excitement surrounding the big game. The teachers were having a hard time holding the students' attention in the classroom. It wasn't a normal Friday. Even the nerd group was fidgety and seemingly distracted. The air was explosive with teen energy.

The campus was full of banners — ribbons, signs and anything wearable with "York" — on it. The campus was alive. The principal felt like he was sitting in an electric chair that day and even he was caught up in all the falderal and excitement.

CHAPTER THIRTY-ONE

At 3:30 PM the school day ended. The dismissal bell sounded and everybody scattered. The varsity football team was to meet in the gym's conference room for some words the coach had for them. All the team showed up on time and they got right to listening to the coach.

In essence Coach Mac covered his pep talk — that this game was just another game on the schedule. Yes, it was now the most important one, but the results would surface best if we played every play just like that had been the best effort you could give on that play. Just do your job and the rest will take care of itself. Only mistakes and turnovers might beat them. Tackle, block, hold onto the ball were keys, and work together for the good of all. He wished them good luck which he said happens to those who work hard and smart.

His little 'homily' to the guys took only 15 minutes. He dismissed them — telling them to eat something before 5:30 PM and rest and show up ready to work hard. The winning will take care of itself. "Dismissed!"

Everyone shouted "Go" and they all scattered to do whatever they had to before returning to campus to dress out for the game. One could feel the electricity in the air. It was alive!

Everyone had to eat sometime before the game and had specific things that needed preparation work. The cheerleaders had new cheers that needed tweaking and the grounds people needed to check out the stands, field, line work on the field, communication system and locker rooms for supplies and things needed for the York team and guest.

This game in particular needed to be spot on good. All the vendors were ready with inventory plenty enough for the large crowd expected. There was rumor that even pro- scouts were expected to assess players. All players knew that was so.

It was approaching 6:00 PM Billy was through eating a well-balanced meal fixed by his mom. He was thankful for his mom. She was always concerned for and about him and she was an excellent cook. This night she fixed him a couple of large Bison burgers — with lettuce, tomatoes — just add ketchup for perfection. He had some cut green beans and a baked potato. This was one of Billy's very favorite meals. Billy had time and devoured his food with the delicacy of a hungry lion. It was the best, a taste treat!

His dad had come home early, that Friday night and told Billy he'd take him back to school around 6:00 PM. When Coach Mac said to be there to start dressing out. That meal should supply my every energy need, he thought.

Billy arrived promptly at 6:00 PM. The campus of York high school was buzzing. The gates were open starting at 6:00 PM and already people — fans were filing into the 15,000-seat stadium. There was limited seating. As Billy entered the locker room, about half the guys were presently there. Another 15 minutes all were there and diligently shedding their street clothes and putting on the pads and 'armored suit' as Billy termed them. Indeed, when all the garb was on, including the helmet, each looked rather ominous and fierce.

The locker room was rather quiet that evening. It wasn't really just another ordinary day. This one was special and had consequences for everyone — the opponents involved, the York football team and the communities involved of the participants in the contest.

It was called 'prestige' — of winning the Conference Championship. One step at a time thought Billy — and one more step toward the state title and championship trophy. That of course, was still a long way off. First things first — and this would be a really tough one.

Billy looked around, after tying his cleats. He was finished out. Most of the team was also finishing up — another 5 to 10 minutes should find everyone suited up and ready. The coach said he'd meet with them 20 minutes before kickoff and lead the way out to the field for brief work outs, exercising — and loosening up. Actually, the game didn't start until 7:15 PM — until the National Anthem and starting line-ups were announced.

Then the coin toss for kick-off or choice of end of field to start from.

Promptly on time Coach Mac appeared and led the team outside to the field. After they all gave a 'fist' to the air, then shouted together, "Let's go!" Each player was instantly engendered with a united power jolt and they all stormed the field like lions after prey.

The crowd roared, screamed and yelled, as the teams all started exercising, loosening up, sprinting and Eddy and his ends practiced passing, and receiving. The captains of each team went to the sideline where the 'refs' were standing for the coin toss. Jamestown won and elected to receive. York took the side with the wind to their back. All the stadium arose, and sang the National Anthem — the teams were ready for kick-off — and combat.

CHAPTER THIRTY-TWO

York kicked off; It was a long high one deep to the one-yard line. Their kick-off return specialist fielded the ball without dropping it and got to the 15 yard line before a Yorkman sliced in and took him down. It was a beautiful tackle. First and ten for Jamestown. It was Jamestown's plan to early jump on York and score in the first set of downs. Being on their 15 yard line was not the place to be to make that happen.

The Yorkmen not only relented ground to them, but wanted to get the ball back, and score themselves. So the battle of the frontlines early emerged. The Yorkmen yielded about nine yards and firmed up to stop Jamestown from getting a first down. Jamestown had to reluctantly punt the ball away.

York received the ball on their 20 and moved it to the forty yard line. They had 60 yards to go. York opened with a fullback trap up the middle — with a wide receiver decoy flanked out right. Jamestown knew of Eddy's talents and set their defense up for the pass. The trap fooled them and York gained about 20 yards to the Jamestown 40.

Eddy called on end slant pass to his other end figuring they scouted Billy being the main receiver. Billy headed straight downfield as if to catch a long ball, drawing the middle defense with him. Eddy hit his mark and they had another 15 yards into Jamestown territory.

Eddy set up his next play splitting his wide receivers outside of the ends. They would take short routes and flare to the sidelines pulling the defenses with them. However, the heavy front would be pick blocking to open a hole for Bobby Brumell to power through. The line did and Bobby did — they were now 1st and ten on the 10.

Eddy would now dump a hook to Billy in the end zone which he did for a T.D. perfectly executed. York kept up the pressure and offensive devastation so at halftime the score was 28 to 7 —

hardly the game plan Jamestown was looking for; indeed they were somewhat taken back by their predicament.

The halftime show was really good as high schools go. The 100-member marching band of York was excellent and the cheerleaders and their formations were showy and precisely done.

In the second half, York received the ball on the kick off, their back to the wind, which was in fact pretty much a negative factor that evening. That's one element Eddy didn't have to give much worry about. The Jamestown Wildcats must have gotten a good talking to at halftime, because they certainly were toughened up and were enlightened when they caused a recovered fumble on a pass play to Eddy's left end it ricocheted off his chest pad into the lap of a Jamestown defensive back, who took it back in for the score and extra point.

To the York team — that was a cheap score — one they did not earn — the hard way. They swore the Wildcats would pay dearly for that infringement.

Jamestown kicked off; it wasn't a particularly long one, being taken on the York 49 yard line and finally being hauled down on the Wildcats 48 yard line. A 13 yard return. Eddy circled the wagons and called for a quarterback shuffle-pass right to the halfback with Billy in fairly tight and Bobby behind the '0' tackle. If there was blocking to be done — it would get done.

Eddy took the ball, turned to his left, faked a hand-off to the left halfback who crashed the line and then headed the other direction and shuttle passed it to the right half who took it around the outside — for 25 yards to the 23 yard line. Mac's and Eddy's play calling were keeping the Jamestown Wildcats off balance and unsure.

It was now 1st and 10 on the 23 yard line. He called for a 'Y'-out down pass to Billy. Billy lined up about 5 yards wide of the tackle looking like he was to receive the ball on a down route pass. However, after he ran some 12 yards, he Y'd right then straight downfield as fast as he could hoof it. The line held fast and Eddy unleashed one to crosshair about the goal line and everybody held their breath as it sailed to the spot — Billy was glad he had really hustled as the ball softly landed in his hands

— over his shoulder and he scored to the crowd's wild enjoyment and astonishment.

It was a marvelous catch — a great play well executed. The after point was done and the score was 35-14 Raiders.

The rest of the 3rd quarter and most of the 4th found each side going back and forth mid-field between the 40's. Both teams seemed a little tired and Jamestown put on a push late in the quarter, but were stymied at the 9 yard line and the York defense held firm and the Wildcats tried a field goal for 3 points. Score York 35- Jamestown 17.

With 12 minutes to go in the game, York received kick off and their best kickoff returner running back took off like he was doing the 100 yard dash at a track meet. He got the ball to the 35 yard line of the Wildcats. Everyone — the whole of York in the stands cheered. It was one of the best returns that year. They all knew Jerry Witherell was good, but this was a treat to see. He almost made it all the way except for the deep defensive back, an all-state candidate, forced him out of bounds.

The York Raiders now had the ball on the 35 with 2 minutes left to play in the game. They could run out the clock with running plays or keep on maybe trying some new plays. They showed a new alignment for the backfield as they set up for the next play. It was called a crossbuck right out of the 't' formation. The quarterback under the center, two halfbacks behind with fullback slightly deeper in the middle.

The coach and the entire Jamestown team gave each other a look of wonderment and puzzlement. Nobody ever used the 't' formation anymore — it was antiquated — or was it?

Coach 'Mac' didn't think so, and with the lead he had, he thought he'd try and spring it and see what happened. There was a hike, hut-hut-hut. Eddy got the ball, spun left and faked a hand-off to the right halfback crossing full speed into hopefully the space made between the right guard and right tackle. The team had practiced it, but to what perfection they didn't know. The play was designed to fool the defensive linebackers to cover the running back coming through on the left side vacating space on the right side for the actual ball carried to wedge through the line and break open for whatever yards he could get.

The decoys were the split ends out far for deep routes — keeping the deep defense backs to guard those areas. Thus, leaving the middle defensive area primarily open and unguarded. If the play worked, really good yardage could be gained — if not — well, back to the drawing board.

Well, it sure worked, and totally took Jamestown by surprise. They wound up on the Wildcats 20 yard line inside the red zone. Now with 43 seconds left on the clock, Eddy called his favorite slant pass play 89- slant to Billy — who did the down and across the field. They'd practiced that hundreds of times. The line held long enough to see Billy flashing across the field behind the linebackers and between the deep defenders. He was a big target and Eddy didn't miss it. Billy caught it, and turned to the goal line 5 yards ahead, with all he had — he would not be denied and wasn't. With the point after, the time ran out. The final score was 42 to 17. It was a great victory.

The Jamestown Wildcats were essentially humiliated, defeated by a better and stronger team that day. The fans went bonkers in delight over their league championship team. York was a proud community of most ordinary people with big hearts. This night was to be a celebration night — the dairy queen would be busy.

Mac McCarthy would have a week for workouts before York had to play the state quarter final game for their division of the state tournament. Winning that, would be a coup — a feather in their crown. After the League Championship game — a game against the two top winning state powerhouse teams, the team felt they were qualified to take on any high school team — anywhere, that they faced.

The stats and quality personnel they possessed showed well that possibility. Reputations, exaggerations or rumors of other teams — didn't have much if any effect on the York players, they wouldn't be intimidated. Working hard and executing well was the team 'motto', in the locker room and in the point of public opinion. Distraction epitaphs about them had little or no significance. They knew who they were and what they were capable of. They weren't playing college ball, but hard-nosed high school ball — yes. They could handle that.

CHAPTER THIRTY-THREE

The fall air was chilling up and a few trees were turning early. Billy was determined to enjoy himself for a few days and it was good the weekend was ahead of him. In a way he wished the season was over, it had been fun and educational, but tiring and a little stressful. He had stretched himself, which was good and he thoroughly enjoyed all his teammates and had become close — uptight with them.

He loved Coach 'Mac' and the Coach Hill. In spite of all the attention the football team and its games received, he tried hard not to neglect his studies. After all, starting junior year, colleges were peering into his life evermore, taking seriously his effort toward academic work. Billy wanted to do well so in his senior year he could take several AP courses — where if he got a B or better, he would receive academic college credits — wherever he went.

That was another concern he had on his mind. Where he wanted to go. College seemed far away, but in reality it was just around the corner. He needed to give it some thought.

Right now, Billy needed to stay in good shape at the gym under the 3 Amigos watchful eye. He was now into the black belt segment of Judo and finishing up his taekwondo course. Dave was still teaching him the refinements of boxing and Big John was taking him through weight training for different sections of his body-enhancing the muscles and strengthening his total framework, sculpting muscle units, mainly the torso and upper body muscles. To augment his legs and all the running he did, he had Big John work a leg-weight program to strengthen the connecting leg muscles for added protection, for all the leg use he was putting out daily. He would need that as he finished out football season and basketball when he started that. His mentors were serious in their mentoring efforts and investment. They were proud of Billy and his work ethic, attitude and progress development. They also were especially proud of his grades attained at school. As were all his teachers.

All the team received a congratulatory letter from the principal Perry Dunlop for their stellar efforts and winning the league championship — bringing home the trophy. It was always a big thing to have accomplished that.

Friday night came and again the Raiders played their game, winning the quarter final state game 34 to 21. Billy caught 5 of 6 passes thrown to him, two for touchdowns. The scouts from colleges were flocking to the Illinois state playoff games. If they'd been watching Billy, they'd be writing lots of notes. For the novice player he was, he had refinements of a seasoned senior dedicated player. He was just beginning his outstanding player days ahead as he finished out the playoffs. The Raiders were indeed getting better with each game. They continued to gain confidence and with confidence — assuredness in what they were doing. That bode well for the overall attitude of the entire team.

The next game, the following Friday night would be the state finals as the state was cordoned out into four territorial sections. Two sections played each other, the winner playing then in the finals — against the winner of the other state sections it was the traditional public Illinois school association playoff schedule. The best 4 records in the state participated in the state playoffs.

It would be the York high school Raiders versus a large high school from the suburb north of Chicago called 'New Trier' high school. It was from a wealthy community with always high caliber sports programs. This one was especially talented.

The state public high school playoff games were traditionally played in Soldier Field — downtown Chicago. It could hold close to 100,000 fans. The Chicago Bears professional football team played their home games there. It would be a really big time thing to be a part of that scene. The team was really excited to be playing in a big time pro-league stadium and knowing it was for the Illinois State high school football championship.

The trouble with sports programs like this one, it was quite a distraction to the students, school and community — especially like York where the community was so into their one public high school. With such a grand event for the folks of York as this state championship, you'd thought every family there had a son on the team. The community was small enough, that everyone knew someone who knew or was related to a member of the team.

As soon as York had staked out its claim to the championship game — everyone clamored as to how they were going to get tickets and transportation to the game. The team would take a school bus and the townsfolk would board one of a fleet of tour busses that would be procured.

How it was that the school functioned as well as it did through the playoffs was due to the principal and city leaders adjusting attitudes, priorities and behavior. The excitement was somewhat diminished. The whole scenario played out with high expectations for the Raiders and confidence that they would come home, triumphant.

The Chicago Tribune paper and area rag sheets, were promoting their own Chicagoland 'Monsters of the Midway' vs the Davids of the mini-city of York, Illinois. York was not the favored pick by the Vegas/Chicago bookies — by a lot. Well, they had it wrong with the tiny City when the 3 Amigos brought home the 'bacon' this past year. The Raiders had their slingshots ready for Goliath. The team would follow coach 'Mac' and his staff into the valley of the giants. They would take their chances there, boldly — and all together. There was no fear of Goliath. They were as ready, as York could be. It seemed like the City of York would be without its citizens that Friday night. The police department would be all out on the prowl covering the protection of its city inhabitants that evening.

Well the big night was drawing near and everyone going to the game in Chicago was checking the weather twice, and taking everything necessary — like *'bumpershoots'* in case it would rain. The York city spirits were indeed high, lots of laughing, joy, and confidence in their team.

The fleet of busses departed all together like a bomber run on Chicago. There was supposed to be a full moon that evening and the weather in the 40's. Yes, it was to be nippy, but the excitement level and voluminous yelling and screaming would certainly raise the temperature some of Soldier Field.

But being hearty mid-westerners they were, they knew how to dress appropriately. The busses were full of chatter and laughter, cheerfulness was everywhere. The York team took their usual school traveling bus for away games. The less cushioned seats were not noticed by the young energized Raider football team. The team bus was jovial and full of laughter trying to keep their cool and be loose before the biggest game of the year. They'd gotten this far but didn't want to lose any marbles. The coach and staff were aboard and let the boys be boys — within reason. The concentration and serious stuff would be upcoming all too quickly. Most all the team had water bottles, the coach didn't want any soft drink consumed before the game, but wanted them well hydrated. All the excitement made the trip shorter than it was, and it was assured the stadium seats were to be as uncomfortable as usual.

The 'big shoulders' city was coming into view and in a little time it would be havoc in the parking lots prior to the kickoff. The media trucks were nearby the stadium with their large satellite antennas pointed starward. It would be a good 20-30 minutes to find their seats. The York Team Raiders found their locker room entrance and proceeded to it under the watchful eyes of Chicago's finest (blue and white) with their famous leather black winter coats and black and white checker ribbed visor caps. They looked good, and tough. The boys all spoke to them as they paraded by filing into the locker room following the coaches.

The coach huddled the players together for a few words of instruction in effort to settle and preserve the energy level that was poised to explode. They needed that for the game. The team automatically sensed a regrouping time to get dressed into their gear and get things football into their heads. There was high excitement and anticipation welling up in each of them. It took all of them 30 to 45 minutes to don their battle armor. There was another 30 minutes before they all would be running out onto the field for pre-game practice routines.

The time arrived and the coaches led the Raiders out the tunnel onto the field. It sounded like a 100,000 people erupted yelling, screaming. The paper in reporting the event expected some 60,000 to show up. Pretty amazing for a high school playoff game, albeit a championship one. Of course, both teams had their large school bands there and they revved up for all they were worth. Both side's cheerleaders and mascots were ready and willing. It, indeed, was a spectacle. Probably the biggest Billy thought, he'd ever — see being from York. Little would he know of his future. After about 25 minutes both teams retreated to their locker rooms for short instruction time from their respective coaches. Meanwhile the bands struck up the National Anthem as the local lyric opera star baritone blew his pipes loudly and proudly. It was over in ten minutes and the field was ready for both teams' entry back on the field. Of course, they had to run through smoke and mirrors to the screams of their respective fans. The cheerleaders ran ahead of them — doing cartwheels and flips. Anita was among them — but Billy wasn't looking for her, he was busy.

The team captains huddled with the referees in the center of the field for the coin flip, and goal choices. That finished, the captains returned to their sidelines to huddle up with all the team for their arm and fist "Go Raiders" yell. Then out onto the field for the kick-off.

The stadium announcer announced the 'York Raiders' versus The New Trier 'Trevians' and their playing records. New Trier would kickoff.

The whistle blew and the ball was in the air. Coach Mac had sent his receiving team to the field. His main return runner Trevor Armstrong received the ball and headed up the right side of the field. He was swift and quick — with long strides when he was on a breakaway. His teammates made checkmate with the first six tacklers and he finally got trapped along the sidelines and stepped out of bounds at the 49. Not a bad return everyone at York thought.

The first sets of downs were all running plays to test the defense line of scrimmage. They made 10 yards for a first down, barely. New Trier had a formidable line. Mac wondered just how long that could last. He was betting on the Raiders superb conditioning to outlast the 'Trevian's in the 'trenches'.

Mac kept up the line plays — over center, off center, off guard, tackle slices and then he threw in a tight end tuck pass that found its mark behind the linebackers; and Mike Chandler reeled one in and gained another 10 yards after the reception. New Trier took a hit on the short pass. The Raiders were now on the 18 yard line — inside the red zone.

The defense of the 'Trevians' was expected to tighten up. It did, and they pulled their deep defensemen up to better cover gains of the short passes. Of course, this left their deep zone coverage somewhat vacant. When Eddy saw this, he called a verbal for a deep side line pass to Billy. Billy was hungry for one of these and was ready to strike out on his route.

Billy lined up at tight end and placed himself a little further wider than normal but not way wide right. The defensive linebackers were on to him as the ball was snapped and he slanted in 3 strides and turned back right and then downfield as fast as he could go. The linebackers were outfoxed and left in a lurch crowding up the middle, and thought their deep guys would pick him up. Billy zoomed by those guys who picked him up late — too late, and he was 3-4 strides ahead of them.

Eddy knew it was a hit time and delivered a strike to Billy over his left shoulder close to the sideline. It was so perfectly thrown, Billy's reception looked easy. There was no one to stop him and Billy eased into the end zone. Mac's series of plays were a terrific set-up for the deep strike team of Eddy and Billy. Indeed, they had a certain pro- quality to their playing. The player scouts in attendance all noted the quality play of the two of them.

The Raider crowd went nuts over the touchdown. The New Trier fans couldn't believe they had been scored upon and they vowed it wouldn't happen again — so far in the game they hadn't touched the football. Half the first quarter was gone. The line play by the Raiders had eaten up many minutes on the clock.

The Raiders kicked off it was deep on the one yard line. The receiver momentarily fumbled the ball but quickly recovered and headed straight up the field. The fumble delay kept his blockers looking at him while the Raider penetrators plotted angles for their tackles. He got to the 8 yard line. One of the Raiders angled a superb tackle on him and leveled him good.

New Trier pulled it together to forge an advance up to their forty-five yard line. They fought like hell to get there. The Raiders were firm, coordinated and tough. Coach Mac had drilled them good and well at spotting tell-tale tips on offensive lineups and position poses and stances. The Raiders defense wasn't always right but precautions invariably worked to their good.

New Trier took a time out towards the end of the 1st quarter. They needed it and the Raiders used it well, planning how to better defend against the tough Trevians on the March. They needed to disrupt or strip the ball; they needed a turnover.

The Raiders were excited and determined in their play after the timeout. They began to stunt and crossover their charging patterns and it began to pay off as New Trier was not picking them up and didn't seem to know what to do. Coach Mac saw this and kept the pressure on. He was a proponent of the Chicago Bears defensive style as was 'Bo Mineke' line coach, a former Bear lineman. The linemen of both sides were large and many times it was who was the quickest to get the strong block on the other first, that made the difference. Coaches like "Bo" Mineke helped make the difference.

The raiders finally stopped the Trevian Star running back on a sweep when he stuck his helmet in the "Stars' midsection where the ball was as he tackled him. That dislodged the ball out of the running backs hands and it went ground-ward where another Raider linebacker pounced on it for a turnover. That loss took a marked toll on the Trevians as they were on a roll and optimistic and confident to advance the ball down-field.

The quarter horn and whistle sounded and they switched ends on the field after a short break. The ball was presently on the 42 yard line of the Raiders when the ball came out.

The quarter recorded each team scoring again, so at the half time the score was 14-7 Raiders.

Each locker room espoused that it was a hard-fought game and that the score was close. They spent time with both the defenses and offenses separately, advancing ideas on how to improve their play. Each team's records and general make up were similar — the difference would be determination, skills, conditioning, luck and turnovers, even individual effort.

The rest of the game reflected these attributes. The third quarter found the duo of Eddy to his ends resulted in two more scores, 21-7.

New Trier game back in the late 3rd quarter with a hard-earned score 21-14. Bobby Brumel! Got going in the 4th quarter as the guards and tackles began to move their opposites around a bit. He piled up record yardage for play offs, and finally scored on a fullback trap pass play that caught the defense off guard, making it 28-14.

New Trier came back with another score on a reverse making it 28-21. They were playing a hot hand. They continued to press York as the closing minutes drew down, and seemed to be overwhelming York's defense. With two minutes left in the game New Trier pressed and found itself on the 12 yard line and scored on a wide out double spread — the score being 28-27. New trier decided to go for the tie — as they were on a roll offensively speaking.

The stage was set for the point after on the touchdown. New Trier would tie the game, score — if completed — and it would go into overtime, with them receiving the kick-off. The teams were lined up — when York called for a time out. In the huddle Coach Mac told Billy to play right guard in place of Murray and he and 'Bo' told the center and right tackle on how to block the offensive linemen to the side in order to let Billy charge through the 'hole' and leap block the field goal attempt, the point after kick. Coach Mac said to 6 foot 4" 220-pound Billy — "when you break through leap as high as you can — arms extended out and try to block or tip it. He then said to the team, "They will be expecting a playoff overtime, let's end the game right here. Everybody-fists- GO!!"

The referee blew his whistle and both teams filed back onto the field and assumed their positions for the point after kick. The lines both exploded at the hike of the ball. York's internal heavyweights leaned hard on their assignments and Billy rocketed through the hole, then leapt high his tall body into the air — his hands and arms extended. He felt the ball hit his hands hard as he then crashed to the ground. He had done it! "Oh, my God" Half the stands said, he blocked it! The end of the game whistles blew the scoreboard clock read zero, and they the York Raiders had just won the Illinois football State Championship game 28-27. What a game!

All of York descended onto the field and swamped Billy in particular and the team in general and all the coaching staff. It was finished, it was done — all but the 'trophy' giving and the governor saying, "Congratulations, York Raiders!"

Billy felt elated, tired, spent, satisfied, and jumped up and down with his screaming teammates in jubilation. The team circled for a thanksgiving Prayer — then separated to joyfully hug their families and friends — and girlfriends. Billy was looking around and spotted the cheerleaders and Anita — he ran over to Anita — picked her up like a feather, put her down and gave her a big, big, hug. She was surprised — and delighted at the same time. It was a good time to be alive.

Eddy Brandon, York's quarterback was voted most valuable player of the game. The team itself, including Eddy voted special accolades for Billy Brewer, for his extra effort given in blocking the point after tip — in actuality — winning the game for York. It had been an extraordinary effort and it wouldn't not have happened but for the "heavy lifters at center and tackle doing their job so well. Again, it was one for all and all for one mentality — that paid off. Individual and extraordinary efforts pay day paid off for coach Mac and his staff. They were very proud of their team and told them so in the locker room after the game.

The celebration held off until the next day as all returned to York — a parade, — time for banners, bands, and gross expression of Victory and Celebration. It indeed was a 'Coup' for the City of York. Score two for York this year. Suddenly York was maturing itself into a new and vibrant community. Especially within the State of Illinois — which didn't have much favorable things going for it.

Mayor Arthur Swartzman pontificated his heart out at the York Square Celebration. The next day, the band outplayed itself; balloons galore rose skyward and waved in the breeze. Everyone seemed to be leaping and jumping with praise for the York Raiders. They had brought pride and joy to the community. Everyone was arm in arm, brother and sister, standing unified as one family.

Two signs were erected, entering the City of York proclaimed, "YORK 2015 — STATE FOOTBALL CHAMPIONS." Transformation was in motion with the City of York. It was becoming a small city of notoriety and increased economic activity. By years end the mayor announced York had balanced its budget and was head long to establishing a surplus. The old politicians were being turned out and the new breed were stretching their wings for solidarity and fiscal soundness — a better life for the city and the citizens of York, Illinois. Truly they were a proud nation-er-city.

CHAPTER THIRTY-FOUR

The celebration carried on pretty actively through the weekend. The city was proud of their young men, and coach Mac and his staff were lifted up in adoration for producing such fine young men and a state championship team. These type teams do not come around very often and Mac had been crafting this one and fitting the last piece of the puzzle with Billy Brewer. For a first-time player of football, he was a compelling athlete — his work ethic, raw talent and attitude for learning propelled him to the forefront of high school special talent. He had yet another year to go and another year to grow. He wasn't done in that department. The 3 Amigos were not through with him yet either. Their influence and time limit was nearing the end as Billy would be headed off to some college after next year. They had only one plan for Billy — to assure him of the full measure of his confidence and physicality and of his academic potential for excellence that Indeed he would be secure in himself for pressing into all of life and his future. Big John stood in awe of his mentoring student. What a genuine young human being in the making. The 3 Amigos saw their challenge for the next year as one of triumph and joy. They were pleased with their investment of time and money. The 'wimpy' kid of old ways now was transformed into a man mountain dean figure. Presently at 6' 4" and 220 pounds, they literally drooled over the prospects of one last year of mentoring and training for Billy. That 'boy' was becoming a 'hunk' as some would say.

Billy showed up the next Monday for Varsity Basketball. Practice had finished and they had already played one game. So, he had some catching up to do. It wouldn't be too bad, as he had kept his shooting up — and one on one play every Sunday at the park recreation center.

He and Eddy mainly were squaring off on each other weekly. Eddy had the same catch-up problem, but he had already spent a year on the varsity team and knew his teammates and plays and signals. But thought Billy, how nice to already know a varsity player. It would afford him faster learning and a certain camaraderie. Indeed it would and did. He already was in superb shape but needed to learn the signals, plays, defenses, and become aggressive in new ways — unlike football, bigness was good, but quickness was key. Of course, good shooting paved the way to excellence. Billy was a good shooter — both inside the paint and on the rim. He'd been practicing long shots after scrimmages with Eddy. They were falling pretty well and often. He only needed to retrieve the feel in his shooting and motion. Being bigger, taller, and larger would keep him very competitive with opponents. He wouldn't be shoved around as much anymore — he'd out grown the old "wimpy" Billy of his younger years.

Billy turned his energy into his academics. Grades were evermore becoming important to his future. He actually was enjoying most of the subjects this Junior Year, and realized the importance his grades would be in assessing his overall qualifications for College — especially if he perchance wanted to go to West Point. The more he thought about attending that institution the more he thought it the right choice for him. He needed good solid academic credentials — he knew he physically could make it — so he set his mind to doing his best in the school room.

He would need the recommendation of a U.S. Senator or Congressman plus his total school record. West Point only took the best all-rounded students in. He needed to have his application in by early spring his senior year, along with the congressman's personal recommendation; Congressman Jonas Sterling would be the one he'd have to go through.

Other important persons for recommendations would be the school principal and homeroom teacher, and of course a primary coach or coaches of the areas of sports he participated in. From an outside perspective there seems little problem as indeed Billy had a superb accumulated record ever since he returned to school full time and under the tutelage of the 3 Amigos. Billy's parents were probably the most impressed with their son's progress in fact they were even shocked as to the degree he had attained in school. They were very proud. As a family, they had drawn nearer and dearer to each other. The home front atmosphere was most stable.

Billy showed up at varsity basketball practice the first day he could after the championship football game. His height was recorded at 6'4" and weight at 220 pounds. He was pretty rock-solid between his football workouts and his contingency work out under the tutelage of the 3 Amigos. He felt he was not through growing in height and weight, as he continued his weight training, boxing and Black belt Judo final year.

He felt more comfortable back in the classroom without the strain of all the play-off games in front of him. He pressed with his studies and classroom performance.

His classmates were now getting to know him better every day and tried to befriend him whenever they could. Of course, since the play offs and his famous leap of faith, blocking the tying point after field goal in the championship game — all of York knew and were fans of his — blooming friendships.

All the girls were now seemingly interested and in attendance to him. Billy was the hero on campus. Now with basketball the girls and guys would now be able to view his beautiful new and powerful physique in his team basketball uniform. There was no question about the attractiveness of Billy's physique and his ever better looks as he was maturing. The young teenage looks were transforming into pre-manhood and development.

Basketball coach Stilman as well as head football coach Mac McCarthy were fully aware of Billy's presence on the scene stature and his acute mind.

Billy was poised for new things ahead in his life. He was ready and willing-ever wanting to absorb all that came his way.

Only a few things were absent in his life. A girlfriend and a car. They would come, as for Billy, his girlfriend in his estimation was Anita — a classmate, but she was unaware of her status. As for a car, well he had the money or some miracle transformed, he would use his tried and true mode of transportation — his trusted bike — and walking. That kept his legs in constant good shape.

Between all the successes in athletics and in the classroom up to the present, his life was good — really good. He was very much enjoying life on every facet of it and pressing on to his high calling which he knew not.

In God's perspective, his life destiny was spot-on line, and would continue. Billy took times, in his room to dwell and focus on his life so far. He engendered a spark of pride in his overall progress thus far.

That night, a school night, as he sat in his bean-bag lounge chair in his room he pulled over his guitar and started playing tunes that popped into his head — singing sporadically — words of refrain. Finishing with "Thank you Lord for your kind and caring presence — every day." His night time sleep was deep and abiding.

CHAPTER THIRTY-FIVE

York settled back into a semblance of normality and peacefulness. However, York was not the same little city it once was. Everyone seemed to notice the atmospheric change of attitude of its citizens. Things seemed different — a new energy attitude adjustments and striving to rise up the level of York to a strong community of brotherly love and care. It was good — all of it.

Mayor Swartzman was ecstatic over his new administration team — and the progress the City of York was making. The York paper, The York Patter, announced in its Saturday edition the honors the City of York was receiving from the State of Illinois, its House and Senate resolution declaring "The City of York shall receive the small city of the Year award." A best small city of all small cities in the State of Illinois.

It wasn't 24 hours after the announcement that the mayor had city entering and exiting signs erected on the main highway going through York announcing the fact. Also, a huge billboard advertising sign plastered downtown saying, "The State of Illinois announced York best small city award 2015 — City of Faith, Hope and Charity. It was signed by Arthur J. Swartzman, Mayor.

Well besides the mayor, every citizen became a self-promoting advocate of York. It was catching and they were letting folks know that their city was the "New" York — that it was re-inventing itself — and enjoying it.

The environment that Billy was maturing in was so positive, fun and adventurous — it was hard to think of living anywhere else. The bad, corrupt years were now behind it and York's roses were growing with gusto.

Winter was blowing in; the temperatures were dropping and the wind picking up — out of the north. Basketball was the sport of the season and die-hard fans flocked to see it happen. The York Raiders again were blessed with a group of seniors matured from the previous year and it looked like the possibility of getting to the play-offs and was very real. Again — Billy's height and weight would greatly help the team — especially under the boards.

He enjoyed basketball a lot and his record with the Frosh-Soph team was positive and rewarding. He had received several honors. This year he would be playing a power forward. He was and had been, quite deadly at 3 pointer shooting and the coach was hoping for him to become a force to reckon with under the boards in rebounding. The team lacked size and weight rebounding the previous year and Billy could very well fit that missing link to the Raider '5.'

Indeed, it was late November and Christmas was soon to be looming its cheerful tones. Thanksgiving week was coming up and the Raiders had a tournament to participate in. It was a small one with the top four teams in the league playing "single elimination" tournament over the Thanksgiving 4-day break. Billy and his team would play in that.

Billy's new friend Eddy (the star quarterback) was and had been the high scorer on the last year's varsity team. Surely his talent would rise again this year. Eddy was not only a good student but a very talented athlete. He was smart and aggressive in all that he did. That may have been why the two of them became such good friends — like personalities, intellect, and joy of sports. Both were aggressive and assertive in all that they did. When they were together, they fed off of each other --kind of kindred brothers.

It became clearly so, during the basketball season, as the two of them teamed up — much like their football positions of passer and receiver. They found how often the two of them would feed each other with passes — much like on set plays — when driving the ball to the net. Eddy would drive to the net and Billy would follow up to take rebounds and dunk it. Their combination plays rarely were stopped. They were fast and accurate. Scoring was their game.

The season would be like that. The team was full of scrappers — fighters and what talents they lacked, they made up in effort and determination. They had a very good coach in varsity, Coach Hank Stillman, who befriended his team with his honesty and knowledge of the game — plus he had been a star player in his day at Division III Illinois Central. He knew his stuff and got the max out of the boys.

The winter months were especially cold that year — ever windy and harsh. Everybody bundled up in their warmest wraps as each day passed. That winter it seemed like on every weekend it snowed — at least some.

Billy was on the bus to school every day and hooked a ride home from after school sports with Eddy, who had a car. It was there that they learned about each other — about Billy's relationship and story with the 3 Amigos.

Eddy was genuinely touched by Billy's story and Billy certainly enjoyed learning more about Eddy and his family. Eddy's dad was the president of the biggest bank in York — the Illinois central bank of York. Eddy's folks were prominent citizens of York yielding much influence within the York community. Though they were prominent folks, they were down to earth real people. His dad had played quarterback at Iowa State — where he graduated, and went on to get his MBA — in finance from the University of Iowa.

"Stone Brandon" was a pillar of York's society and chairman of the city's chamber of commerce — which was very active. His mom had been a nurse at the York community hospital having gotten her RN degree from Northwestern University School of Nursing at Northwestern medical School Chicago campus.

They had met, according to Eddy said to Billy, at a York chamber blood drive, she was 21 and he 22. They fell in love and married, and had Eddy and older sister, Marla.

Indeed, Eddy was and had an upper-class background who inherited his father's athletic abilities, good looks, and both his parents' ambitious and determined personalities.

The two of them were becoming good close friends — even though Eddy was a year ahead of Billy. They would always stay in touch. Unbeknownst to them now they would be attending the same college institution.

At this time frame, late basketball season. February, Eddy was making application to several college level schools. The University of Michigan, Iowa State, and the Military School of

West Point. For that he needed to procure the blessings of Congressman Jonas Sterling from the 12th district of Illinois.

That choice caught Billy's attention and intrigued him — he'd keep that thought in the back of his mind. He had never even thought of a military career as a future life choice. "Hmmmmm."

CHAPTER THIRTY-SIX

The Raiders Varsity basketball schedule was surging along quickly. They finished 2nd in the 'Turkey days tournament,' and finished first in the Christmas holiday tourney. They were headed for a conference winning championship record. There were 19 games on the varsity schedule and then the 'March Madness' play offs — the end of March should there be a tied winning record at the end of the regular season basketball schedule.

Christmas vacation time was spent mostly with Billy playing in the Christmas holiday tourney held in West Haven — some 100 miles away. Before Christmas vacation occurred, the school provided a large Christmas party and dance on campus. A big loud band that played all the music the generation preferred. Billy was there with Anita, after getting his nerve up to ask her out to the dance, requiring coordination with Eddy since he would be driving. That saved Billy's day - good friends with transportation.

Eddy had a high school sweetheart named 'Penny'. She was a really cute blonde bomber — a star on the women's soccer team. Well, in hindsight it seemed the dates went really well that evening and Billy got loaded up with several kisses that evening long — and lots of dances. Yes, Billy had loosened up a lot and learned how to wiggle his large body to the rhythm of the music. He actually began to find it fun — especially looking upon Anita's very pretty face with its wide smile showing her beautiful white teeth and ruby red lips. "Golly, she was pretty," — he said to himself.

The four of them laughed themselves silly that evening — all got along well as closer friendship engulfed them. They would maintain that a bond and kindred spirit of friendship for a lifetime ahead. What fun he had with Anita. She was somethin' special and he delighted in her. He seemed to flow in conversation that evening — it may have been because he was with Eddy and felt so comfortable. All he knew was that when he got home — he felt joyously happy. He thought, "Isn't that how it's supposed to be?" He thought so, and chalked it off as a most positive experience along his lifeline so far. He slept well that night. Sugarplums were flowing.

Once again in the basketball arena Eddy looked to be the high scorer on the team. Billy followed up with the most 3 pointers scored and the most rebounds. He was a terror under the boards under the basket and fought for every rebound off the boards. He had the most points — rebound tips and stuffs under the net on offense. His size and ability were paramount to his aggressive play in getting the ball. He used his new-found heft to power his way around and under the net. Some of the opponent's forwards or centers would literally bounce off of him in collisions around the net.

Once again, the school students flocked out to see the York Raiders play. The girls came up with a nickname for Billy, 'The Hunk.' Well he wasn't yet the likes of heavy Lou and Big John, but there was yet time for the possibility. He had time yet being still 16 years of age. At the end of his junior year — on June 6th he'd be 17 — 3 months before his senior academic year. Plenty of time to grow mentally and physically — meanwhile Billy worked out daily appropriately as he pursued his academic and sports endeavors. He desired his body to be much like Big John's as possible minus a lot of the refinements and ripples — and have the strength of heavy Lou, a mountain of a man, without rippling muscles, just raw strength. God forbid should he grasp you in a bear hug and apply pressure ooh-wee doggie — no breath! Crushed ribs! No thanks!

Indeed, the girls of York High were high on the 'beef' handsomely ensconced in those maroon and white uniforms. Eddy was pretty well put together guy too at six foot one — a hundred and ninety-five pounds — solid. Billy and Eddy were two of the most muscled of the starting five.

Most of the team was leaner and thinner — a few taller, but without the heft factor. Both Eddy and Billy were pretty good looking young 'studs' — so there was no give away imperfection there. Eddy was more effusive and outgoing than Billy who was a little more reserved and quiet type. Both young men were very respectful to others, especially their elders. They were respecters of authority, the flag, and service men and women of the armed forces. As for politicians, much like the American people, they were on the bottom of the respectful and respected list by both Eddy and Billy. Respect is earned.

One of Billy's favorite subjects was history — pretty much any history, but particularly U.S. History. History involves always leadership and leadership policies that cause governments to run and rule. Policies cause people prosperity or loss of something at the expense of someone or something else, group or in general. Generally, one leader's personal policy, social outlook, personal preferences and general level of money, power or sex, (are they not related?) determines the agenda for the country. A Czar like a Czar, a King like a King, and a brave heart like a gem on display. Experience is the best communication for leadership and good personal character is by far and away key to matching what the people want. Skullduggery, deceit and thuggery corrupts everybody from top on down — it gives them permission to pass the graft on or along. It's catching and choking. Usually its cause is in the name of votes. Bribery is the highest form of graft in getting votes. Bribery by deceit, blame and declared innocence of any wrongdoing perpetuate the continuation of corruption. The "I" confess, he did it mentality is the pass-through mind set.

York had been through all of this, but the people finally had enough and rose up on the next election and voted in 'new' people — turning the 'old out! Good riddance. The new, York City administration — from the mayor on down were now doing a very impressive job from finances to project management. There was a new connectedness and discussion and actual using of common sense in decision making goings on in the chambers of City Hall. Things were changing and getting done under a new City Motto — "If it's good for our citizens, it's a done deal." Mayor Arthur Swartzman originated that one. He was spearheading a lot of good policy and accomplishment. That gets attention — and votes. It also boosted the coffers of York and its progress.

Bond referendums were passed to boost infrastructure improvements, streets, sidewalks, water, sewer and their 1st rate police department and fire departments. York was on the move. The little quaint City of York was blossoming in the fullness of maturing itself into a new metropolis — small city with a bright, energetic, prosperous future.

Billy and his family and families of York together at the dining tables talked about York and its present and future hope. The people were ready for change and abhorred the old status quo. Now was the time and opportunity to change York, from a mediocre dull community to a vibrant, joyful place to live and raise a family. The Brandon's' and Brewer's families were actively discussing York's hopes and future.

The middle-class community would chance to improve their lot in life. Hopes were raised in all its citizens for a brighter tomorrow. The level of attitude changed and the people of York responded with hope and faith. Things were new attitudes positive.

The basketball season was drawing to a close. The Raiders taking the league championship trophy home. Eddy was the MVP of the league and Billy was the most prolific 3-point shooter and rebounder.

They certainly were a team — and they inspired their teammates to shoot, shoot, shoot — which they did. This year, much like football season, was York's finest show time production. Next year they would be minus Eddy — their top scorer and playmaker.

Spring, April through May 30th would be academic time and studies effort to clean up his junior year credentials. He turned his sports time back towards Max's gym and with his 3 mentors, the 3 Amigos.

Renewing his strength and bodybuilding regimens he took up a new martial art called, 'chimpoo,' a Chinese street fighting course. These moves pitted the opponent's moves back towards themselves with serious repercussions and devastation. Smaller people could defend themselves against hoodlum attacks on the street. It was an unusual discipline. In the hands of a large strong man it was truly offensive in nature. Bones broken, hands crippled and breath taken from you. It was scary stuff. Not for the light hearted.

Billy had had a terrific school year. At 16 he was the epitome of a high school star. His academics were soaring and his athletic involvement was as good as it possibly could get. The 3 Amigos were ecstatically pleased with their investment friendship as they mentored him. They would have one more year before he flew the coup from York and Max's gym influence and teachings. They were determined to make the most of it. So they called a meeting between themselves — Billy excluded, to review and plan the next 9 months they would have Billy under their mentorship.

None of the Amigos had gone to college. Dave and Lou had attended the local Community College for two years — but neither finished up. In spite of the educational lack they like big John were men of determination and knew what they wanted — and set their sights and ambitious desires squarely on their goals — and blindsided everything else out of their vision. Obviously, they had succeeded in spades and were experiencing the rewards of their serious long-haul efforts. They knew what the word 'focus' meant. They watched Billy to come to know that word too. Their exemplary conduct, presence and character certainly were being embedded within Billy. He was a fine boy — young man, by the best of measure.

He was developing leadership in all his doings. On the field, floor or in the classroom. He stood well before his peers and public. He was indeed maturing with humbleness and positive vibes. They saw leadership painted all over their mentee and at that meeting pronounced Billy on solid ground for becoming a full member of society and respectability. He knew right from wrong, understood thinking ways to problems and used his underrated strength for problems related to physical force employment when needed. His judgement was good and sound, his logic and thought expressed well. He was realizing his ability to control his environments and think through problems with much clarity. He was young 16 plus, but his maturity level exceeded his age.

CHAPTER THIRTY-SEVEN

Everyone was glad to see Billy back at Max's gym again, between football and basketball his daily workouts were resigned to some weekend drop in stuff. Billy had been just too busy with school and after school athletics. The 3 Amigos didn't mind as he was in a discipline of physical workouts almost daily. He got in some weight work during football season and not much during basketball season. But he was extremely active and in a learning mode under fine coaches.

He felt good being back with all his friends in the gym and being under the watchful eye of MAX – or big John. The 3 Amigos and MAX were family to him away from home. He enjoyed their fellowship especially as he was Maturing. He felt closeness and even likeness to his Amigo friends.

His routines were set forth by big John to build muscle in all the right places – not necessarily to those areas of the body a body builder and sculptor would have. Billy was developing great abs, pectoral and arm-by-cep muscles. He was yet not fully grown and by his body size a lot more meat would be required to fill out his expanding muscles and frame. Big John was exceptionally pleased and thrilled that Billy was indeed fulfilling his assessment he had predicted when Billy was first discovered around age 12 – skinny and wimpish!

Every now and then big John would fold him into his big arms and give him a big bear hug – and praise him. Billy loved that time – right now Billy was 6 feet 6 inches and heading for around 240 pounds. Big John was 6 feet 2 inches and about 260-270 pounds. A Sculpted body beautiful – a Typical Mr. America – and he was so good looking – a man's man handsome dude. He also was about the nicest guy around. Big John had a wide variety of friends and lots of them.

Billy Continued taking 'Kempo' The Chinese Street Fighting discipline as he worked on his overall body building. It would be another 3 months until Senior Year Football would begin training. He wanted to be in top Shape to round out his Senior Year of Athletics. Right now, he had a 3rd degree black belt in

Judo, a brown belt in taekwondo and was the leading weight lifter in several categories at Max's gym – outside of heavy Lou and big John.

All Max could ever say about Billy was that he was "awesome." Max was an all-around good guy – an ex-Marine drill Sargent who was respected by all – at the gym and in the greater public Arena. People in the body health training business far and wide knew of Max Snellinger. Much like the famously known name of 'Vic Tanney' – the physical fitness guru, who had a String of physical fitness gyms across America. Max's notoriety propelled with the 3 Amigos Success.

On June 6th, that early Summer day, Billy became 17 years old. Big John threw the Party at his new home – A larger one that he and Charlotte had purchased with funds from his previous house and others by his Mr. America status endorsements, and product associations. These were many and considerable. It was a small farm of Some 50 plus Acres. It was really Pretty. It was fenced in at the property line and surrounded his 4500 sq. foot home. His home had a workout gym and a gourmet Kitchen for his wife – who absolutely loved to Cook.

He had brought in a 4-piece band – drums, electric guitar, saxophone and Keyboard Vocalist to play that evening. All of the Amigos and girlfriend/wives were there including Anita. Others there were his folks, Close School mates, Coaches and Max's gym instructors and wives. It was held on a Friday evening starting at 5PM – with finger food and BBQ Ribs – American Style potato salad, soft drinks and Kraftig-light beer-cold in ice buckets. Hopefully it would be a nice Summer evening of Sundown enjoyment. All-in-all, about 50-75 people were invited. That would make a nice size and enjoyable party – not too crowded or loud.

Now when the invites went out to all, Eddy and his Girlfriend 'Penny' were to pick up Anita and bring her. She was familiar and Comfortable with them and was excited to be with Billy on his 17th birthday bash in his honor. It would be fun.

The night brought about much activity. Everyone enjoyed dancing and schmoozing with each other. Billy took advantage of her attendance having come with Eddy and Penny to the Party.

The highlight of the evening was a big beautiful 3 story cake with 17 candles on it. It was Scrumptious Chocolate. Then Ice Cream and Cake after Ribs and Chicken wings that about did everyone in – it was a hit!

Billy's highlight however, was dancing and talking with Anita – getting to know her more. Anita definitely seemed to be attracted to him. They seemed to get along together well, and the wave lengths seemed to be in sync. There indeed was much joy when they were together – as he held her in his arms dancing. He was totally transfixed with affection for her. Billy had some trouble talking with girls in general, but no trouble now doing So with Anita. Anita was to be 17 also in August – and soon to be a rising Senior.

The only thing Billy felt he was missing now in his life was a car. Though he had done without one for some time since he had turned 16. It really hadn't been a need – except when he felt at a loss when desiring to ask Anita out – or just swing by her house to see her, whenever.

Billy and all the partiers had a great fellowship time at his 17th birthday bash. The band had been good, and it seemed like everyone enjoyed themselves and dancing to the music. It had been a pretty and delightful evening weather wise, even as the party broke up around 11 o'clock at night. Billy's parents went home early and Max and some of the instructors did likewise.

The evening finished out with Eddy, Penney, the 2 Amigos and their dates, and Anita. They all pitched in cleaning up before they left. These were good folks, responsible young people – and lots of fun.

Billy again thanked everyone and collected Anita and headed to Eddy's car along with Penney. It was so much fun, and his enjoyment level was high. Eddy drove to Anita's home, where Billy walked her to the door. They chatted for a few moments and Billy held and kissed her for a short time before she entered her home. "That was really good" thought Billy as his mones shook with good feelings. There had been no withdrawal – or body abeyance on Anita's part – and if you asked her, she would have said; her heart was elevated with special feelings.

Billy's Saturday found him cooking breakfast for he and his folks. Cleaning up and returning to his room where he picked up his guitar and proceeded to pick and sing songs he knew. He was relaxed and in a good mood. When he was through, he headed downstairs and out the door, mounted his bike and headed off to Max's gym to work out. Life was good.

Billy entered the gym and instantly felt comfortable. Now that he was a mostly full-grown young man, and having proven so diligent in all that he was doing at Max's and in school. His acceptance level was full measure. Billy, indeed, was a learning machine, who literally soaked up instruction of any kind and transferred it into personal reality. He was gaining on heavy Lou and Big John – it would only take some time, which he had plenty of.

At his present height he was now four inches taller than both heavy Lou and Big John at 6 feet two inches. He was close to heavy Lou's weight around 240 pounds and short by 30 pounds to Big John. His muscle characteristics were now vastly accentuated and muscled and toned like Big John, but nowhere near his refined sculpture, he didn't intend to follow Big John's path as a body builder – but he did wish to achieve a combination of pure strength and muscle dimensions – combining both of their talents. He also wished to be limber and flexible for basketball and football, thus keeping his body and legs fluent for speed.

Billy said, "Hello" to everyone and went and got into his workout duds. He did his weight routine for forty minutes, punched the bags for 15, did a bunch of floor exercises and push-ups, Jump rope, pull-ups, gut crunches and practiced Tae-Kwan-do movements. Soon an hour and a half had passed – he'd had a good workout. Big Lou had come in, waved at him and went to change. He was no longer training for anything but was maintaining his overall tone. When he came back out, he came over to where Billy was to speak with him. They talked about Billy's birthday party – Billy thanked him for throwing the bash.

Big John asked Billy how he looked to the future as he approached his summer and senior year. Billy responded with that he was going to proceed with normal daily workouts – doing basketball on Sundays down at the park with his friends – then teaming up with Eddy in the open areas throwing passes, and pass catching.

Eddy was keeping in shape for fall football at West Point. He'd been accepted there – recruited by freshman Coach 'Danny' Murdoch. Congressman Jonas Sterling had taken one look at Eddy's resume, and record and immediately wrote his recommendation to the academy.

Thus, Eddy was unofficially a Pre-cadet at West Point. His arrival for early football Season workouts after September 1st, would be just around the corner. The two of them really had hit it off – that sparred well with themselves to keep fit and sharp. They would be separating soon, and they swore they would keep in touch. Eddy had turned down other very enticing full loads to other colleges and occasionally he 'tweaked' Billy to think about going to West Point too. He'd say to Billy "We Could be the new team of Blanchard and Davis." Billy gave it some thought as he had yet to make choices up to mid-February of 2016. That would find him beyond Senior football and most of basketball Season. He would be in the midst of his advance academics' regimen carrying 3 A. P. Courses, history, math and Computer Science. His other Courses included Spanish and English 4.

Billy and Eddy hung out with each other, double dating as Eddy drove and Billy supplied the gas. It was a good summer of fun as the four of them always seemed to enjoy each other's company immensely.

York had several public swimming pools opened for the summer which were a favorite place for the four of them to go. They developed a deep summer tan by mid-August and found a few swimming skills long ago practiced. Summer was a time to relax for a short time and assess the next future ahead of them.

On the very hot days they would just sit in the pool and talk. These days just more deeply drew the four of them into closer relationship and strengthened it.

Soon Eddy would be off to West Point Academy. He'd go early as he had to be there for pre-football season practice. He already had been assigned a room and roommate – another football recruit living in the Athletic dorm. He had to be there Sept 2nd.

Billy had to, on the same date, be showing up for Varsity football practice at York High School. It would be his Senior and final year at York. Right now, they all were enjoying Just being teenagers, having fun, relaxing from school work. It was all as it should be.

Billy was cooking breakfast for he and his mom and dad that Sunday – and as he prepared it, his thoughts turned to the fact that they all would be separating. He and Anita would be returning to York. Eddy would be off to West Point and Penny would be attending the University of Illinois. It sunk into him the loss he felt he would feel of Penny and Eddy – maybe forever. He certainly hoped not. He swore to himself that he would always keep in touch with both of them.

Mom and dad had wakened and were heard coming down the stairs. The aroma of eggs, bacon and Flap-Jacks was too much to miss. It was ready to serve as his folks walked into the kitchen to sit down. They all loved this time together. It indeed produced family togetherness, and bonding. Billy would remember these times as he too was but a year away from attending some college himself. He would be among the many departed from their parents – away from home. It all would be too soon. They all sensed the future and rejoiced in the present. The family was the important thing they all realized that truth and realized it in the moment.

Today, thought Billy, I'm going to church – Just up the street to the big Presbyterian one. He'd get there early enough to see Anita sing in the youth choir. She had a pretty good voice and sometimes did a solo with the group back-ups. He was very fond of Anita and looked forward to their relationship senior year.

The sermon that day was on "The sins of the father." (not God) How they can be visited upon the sons on down through the generations. Billy thought to himself, "My father doesn't sin." What's that all about? The pastor greeted Billy as he left with Anita on his arm. Billy mumbled something to him as they shook hands like, "Still not sure about the sermon!" And the pastor said, "You will retain what the Holy Spirit thinks you need, no more, no less." He and Anita bid him good day – and walked down to Anita's car. She said, "Get in and I'll take you home."

Later, after a small lunch, he headed off on his bike to the city athletic fields and the basketball courts where he would play pick-up games. Hopefully Eddy would appear, and they'd battle one-on-one. Eddy didn't show that day, but he found some others to play with. He then headed home on his bike and on up to his room.

He decided to take a nap and lapsed into an hour and a half sleep-a-thon. He felt really good after – with all his windows open and his ceiling fan on. He put on some music CD's he liked. About half way through he reached for his guitar and played along with the next song.

He played and relaxed – singing along whenever, enjoying his freedom that day. The days of junior year Summer were closing in and fall start up for school was only weeks away. He felt joy in his present life, and gave way to what was yet before him – with assuredness of a senior – with a purpose. More work, struggles, busy-ness, conquering each day, one at a time. It would be a tough year academically and a challenging one in his athletic endeavors. He felt ready for his senior war at York. He would give it his all and best. He would give all his supporters, family, teachers, coaches and friends reason to be proud of him – and continue their support. That night, when he put his head down on the pillow, he had no trouble dozing off into dreamland. None at all.

CHAPTER THIRTY-EIGHT

Billy gave Eddy a call and asked him if there was anything he could do to help him with getting prepared to go off to West Point. Eddy thanked him for thinking of him – but, said, "No," he pretty much had it all under control, and that his parents were doing a lot to help him get ready. They chatted about going to miss each other, but decreed loyalty in keeping in touch with each other during the year.

Once again Eddy dropped a thought line on Billy to look into joining him at West Point – that we'd make a good combo on the football team. It would be great! Billy told Eddy that he'd do that – look into West Point – and maybe a career Army person. He didn't know anything about it at all, but the thought of hooking up with Eddy – as a team – intrigued him. He would definitely look into it.

Eddy and Billy finished up their chat saying they'd see each other before he left -play some 'hoops' down at the park. They agreed said "good-bye" and hung up.

Billy sat there a few moments, sadly thinking of Eddy's departure and how he'd miss him. They had become such good friends. They had to keep in touch. Billy had a vision like picture of them. Combining their talents on the Army gridiron, as cadets on the Army football team. There was a certain pull he had while thinking about it. Proud to be a member of the notorious grand establishment of West Point Academy. It wasn't just another college, but an institution with a certifiably proud history of professional protectors of America. He liked the feeling and thoughts he had about the academy. He was used to certain regimens in his life between school, workouts at the gym, sports, and his academics. He took all of these seriously and accepting his life and lifestyle as normal for him.

Billy continued to sit there, after talking with Eddy – contemplating his future. Not many kids had any idea about their possible future short or long-term tomorrows. Billy had always ... since the 3 amigos drafted him into their orbit ... had a sense of purpose, a sense of some direction in his life that was establishing itself.

He felt a certain destiny was generating energy in his life. He felt it so strongly that he gave it credence in his thought life, and much consideration towards trying to follow the choices and directions the Spirit seemed to show him.

Billy had always thought that he had a special relationship with God, he just seemed to feel it within himself. And, he gave into those urges in his thinking, believing he was being directed by and in God's pathway for his life. He didn't know where all these feelings came from, but he strongly felt it was God nudging him on, almost directing his ways. Where else would the 3 amigos have come from like they did, and what they'd done – befriend him and teach him and lead him in directions for which he became the person he was today. No, it wasn't happenstance, luck or pre-conceived human inter-diction. Overlooking his life there was a plan for his life attached by an outside force directing his pathways.

Billy felt a certain obligation to this force. Indeed, he was most appreciative. Everything had turned around for him since the turbulent truant days of ditching school and bumming around town all day doing not much more than fishing, killing time, and getting into minor delinquent trouble.

Since his skinny, talk, wondering, antisocial behavior at 12 years of age, he, at the moment, felt great joy in being exactly who and where he was.

He had no jealousy of anybody, envious of none. He liked who he was and what he was doing. He felt purpose in his life and was attacking it with gusto and determination – which gave him strength to head into the wind – no matter what!

He thought just how much better his life now was, not only in regards as to how it might have gone, back in his younger days, but that it was exciting, accomplishing and fun in all that 'in the now' was visiting upon him.

Billy came to form his dreamland of thoughts and regrouped his thinking and direction. He found some paper and wrote down about his thoughts – and getting info on West Point as Eddy suggested. It would be fun playing ball with Eddy at West

Point – might just be a good team together. He would dwell on these thoughts as his school year went on. It was about to change his life. Reality was about to set in as school was starting. He was now a senior and 17 years old. He felt a certain change in his life, a tinge more of responsibility, and he welcomed whatever it was that would be set before him. He felt prepared for the struggles that would be coming forth. There would be many.

Senior year would be his last year in high school before he left home and its comfortable surroundings. York High and the town would then be in his past when he took on the higher learning levels of college. But, first things first.

The football season was officially starting – with a week of hard practice with Mac McCarthy as head coach. Again, he'd be working with end Coach 'Sidney' Hill and Line Coach Big 'Bo' Mineke. Both he and another end – Mike Chandler, a senior – would be coordinating power players on the offensive line. The Raiders would be missing mainly their quarterback – Eddy and fullback of notoriety Bobby Brumell. Those would be big losses except for one point, the head coach and his ability to bring in new players and raise them up to become players greater than they were. His reputation and respect preceded his presence on the field, where he was the field marshal.

The morning practice was full of warm ups, body conditioning, repetitions and some pass formations run at two-thirds speed. The idea was to again get familiar with the ball – the feel, the sight of it, the techniques of pass receiving in different spots and conditions. Oh, yes, laps for all -- leg conditioning was very important to have come game times. The first day workout lasted 2 hours from 8 to 10am. There would be a second one late afternoon when the heat was less. It was shorts and T shirt times.

Increase in temps and drill routines increased during the week. The first game was Friday week, 11 days away from right then. Coach Mac had a schedule printed up for all to see and do. He had pages of comments attached to the handout – and you'd better read the small print too!

The week went fast, and school was to officially start the next Monday. Summer would officially be over for the students and faculty at York High School. It again would b e a time of busyness for all. Billy was looking forward to getting it on. It all would be challenging. He felt up to it!

The first week of school for Billy was football practice and he was excited to return to the full activities of the academic year ahead. That Monday the classroom was running a normal daily academic schedule. 8am to noon, lunch, class resumption at 1pm until 3:30pm. Interspersed during the day was a homeroom time and time for personal expression of extracurricular activities, like art, music, speech, debate, or theatre. After academic time was Phys ed for all and then varsity sports. It was a full day.

The City of York worked hard to give their kids as much quality and varied opportunity times as time allowed, and their budget would support. The kids of York were blessed as the community was now fully committed to the excellence in education for the children, who were priority one!

The new city administration was on top of it all. Things in York were changing across the board noticeably. The whole community was again re-united with Mayor Arthur Swartzman, recently elected. He was an outspoken leader type who really represented all the people of York. He was well liked and won his election by a landslide.

York was becoming a very vibrant and nice place to raise a family and to live. The general economics and wellbeing of its citizens was improving. The mayor emphasized "family" values and a prosperity mindset for York's citizens. Everybody was now on the bandwagon.

Billy once again dug in to his classroom activities. The first week of school found him realizing that the academic levels had been raised. They were escalating to pre-college levels as he dwelt among those qualifiers into advanced placement courses. It would be challenging and the competition sharp. Billy had an attitude he'd been developing over the last five years of his taking his academics seriously and trying hard to apply himself with vigor and excellence. He enjoyed the rewards of seeking excellence in his studies and sports. He realized he had the "STUFF" to contend with whatever was thrown at him and rise to the point of securing himself a place at the top of his class. He enjoyed all types of competition; he enjoyed knowing things and being able to do things. He realized that he was blessed with many God-given talents and never in his prayers ever forgot to thank God for his blessings and grace. He knew from where his strengths came from – it was not just because he worked hard – which he did, but that he was able to conquer his subjects with understanding.

He thought of Anita one day in study hall. He wondered just how she was doing academically, he'd never delved into her school success or background since he'd known her. He guessed that was because he felt like he was 'snooping.' Well, that was just the type of thing 'Anita' liked to talk about – about her and him. He would ask her about those things sometime. Yes, they were getting to know each other more. That was good – and so far comfortable. He missed her.

CHAPTER THIRTY-NINE

Eddy was off to college at West Point Academy. It was his choice of direction. His grandfather had attended the famous military academy in the WWII era. His grandpa rose to a full-bird colonel with many distinguishing honors following him. Most of his service related to active duty details.

"The long Gray Line" as the academy refers to itself, has around 65,000 alumni, including two presidents, Ulysses S. Grant and Dwight D. Eisenhower. A long line of known generals have shown their starts from Robert E. Lee to General Norman Schwarzkopf to General David Petraeus, recent director of the CIA. Even George A. Custer, who graduated last in his class in 1861. Six current public servants, congressman, governors, and senators are graduates serving our American constituency.

Eddy felt a certain honor in his selection of West Point, and he was recruited hard by Coach Murdock, fresh-soph coach. It wasn't a hard recruit choice by the coach, and though Eddy had half a dozen prime division one coaches recruiting him, he focused on West Point football. The academy was building a really good solid team and Eddy felt positive in going there and contributing his talents. Now if he could only get Billy there.

West Point is a highly selective college. Each applicant needs a nomination from a member of Congress. Founded in 1802, it is the oldest service academy in the country and is located on the Hudson River in upstate New York. As a cadet, you are a member of the U.S. Army. You receive a full scholarship and an annual salary from which you pay for your uniforms, textbooks, a personal computer and incidentals. There is no tuition charge. There is a requirement for an initial deposit. Room, board, medical, and dental care is provided by the U.S. government. Upon graduation you will be awarded a Bachelor of Science degree and a commission in the U.S. Army. In turn, you are obligated to serve five years on active duty in the U.S. Army and 3 years in the inactive reserve status.

Your study choices include civil engineering, economics, foreign languages, history, legal professions, management information systems, management science, mechanical engineering, and political science.

Eddy was favorably inclined towards the legal profession. He was ready to grow up and get on with life – he was ready for new horizons and training. He was a leader, as his high school time had given him early opportunity for stepping up.

Billy was a cut from the same character values as Eddy. However, their backgrounds were different as to household economic status. Eddy was now having to march to the tune of values called "duty, honor, country" geared for a career of professional excellence and service to a nation – as an officer in the United States Army. It was a monumental task for young men fresh out of high school to adjust to in four short years.

Coming from a small city in the shadow of Chicago, Eddy's new life would be very different. He wouldn't have the freedoms that he would have had at a college anywhere else in America. This was the military and the military way of life, totally different. It was a proud tradition he was in, highly respected and daring at many levels.

For the most part, it was a regimented lifestyle. You did and performed as others instructed you. You were judged on how well you did these things, your character, and 'your esprit de corps' while serving, if well, gets you advancement in ranks over time. There were visible rewards. One worked hard for those rewards, and family life was also hard but taken care of.

Eddy's class was in the neighborhood of some 1300 cadets. West Point was administered by a superintendent – a Lt. General, a Dean – a brigadier general, and a commandant also a brigadier general, all former graduates of the academy. The academic staff topped out a 580 and the students numbered around 4600. The academy colors were black, gray, and gold. They were known as the 'Black Knights' and as everybody knows, their mascot – a mule, which if he could – roam the 16,080 acres of all of West Point acres of landscape.

As Billy began looking over many different colleges, West Point was on his list. He already had some division I schools looking at him and sending him promo – information about their college and its programs – highlighting athletic achievements in all their sports offerings. Athletic wise, it was to his advantage to have picked up accolades list 1st team all-state in football, and 1st team all-state in basketball his junior year. It was no wonder of his high recruitment level after looking at his academic achievements as well. They were outstanding – tops in his class – his progression of grades continued to excel from freshman year on and his character and personality were highly esteemed by his peers and teachers. He indeed was 'prime ribs' for college material – to any he might wish to go to.

Several other universities Billy was intrigued with were the University of Michigan, Northwestern in the Midwest, and Stanford out West, also Auburn University down South. Any of these schools were excellent academic schools and most with high powered football programs.

He was looking for excellence and exceptionalism in colleges. Athletic scholarships would be important to him – and if he did well this fall in football and basketball senior year the likelihood of getting a part or full scholarship was most probable.

The first week of actual school was drawing to a close. Though it was physically tough because of football workouts and practices, academics bided for his time also. Indeed, a new regimen was being again established.

The Brewer household once again resumed the familiar school schedule routine. Billy's dad was doing well in his new position at the company. His dad and mom were in good health at ages of 42 or so. The Brewer family was doing well over-all. It was a closing out year for the both of them, as Billy would be going off to school someplace after that present year. They weren't looking forward to losing their son. It had been 17 years of raising him – the last 4 or 5 years were the best as Billy came under the mentoring of the 3 amigos. Their influence had been neither short of amazing, wonderous, highly significant.

It had brought their son and them much closer together – in love. How could it get any better than those years seeing Billy's growth in his personal life and in his astounding physical growth – really beyond measure of their wildest dreams. His person and personality were exciting, and exemplary to others. "Such a fine young man" so many said of him, more than they deserved or thought, but they were so proud to be his parents.

Billy indeed was a delight to be with, to know, and he was such a level-headed kid – er – big kid. He became very popular at York High School and even in the community he lived in. Many knew him, a ton of folk wanted to. His notoriety only increased as he strove to be his best in an appreciative community that would recognize excellence in athletics, in character, and in the public arena. He was a pleasure to be around, joyful and outgoing – he laughed a lot and was pretty easy on the eyes – especially to all the girls.

Billy felt the admiration and downright love of so many – none more than his buddies – the 3 amigos. He felt like a son to them even though he was only six or seven years their younger. He had a destiny to fulfill, the one God had engendered within him. He absolutely felt it – more every living day – and swore to God and himself to rise to the gratitude level of attitude in all that he did or was or would be. He determined he could become those things, by God's grace, and his belief, while working to accomplish his best in his every-day efforts.

The 2016 football schedule looked much the same as last year. The team seemed to be tightening up pretty well – coordinating better every day, and their enthusiasm was percolating pretty well.

Billy was coordinating very well with the new quarterback, Jackson Andrews. Jackson seemed to be honing his skills at that position quite quickly. His spirals were true, and his speed pretty strong. They weren't, Billy thought, up to speed and force Eddy had on the ball – though they were pretty accurate. He had a good eye and had perception when he was going at top speed. That was good.

Mike Chandler, the other end, was not quite as big as Billy, but he was fast and quick and had good hands. If the line could hold this year, the passing game they had could tear up the league. Coach Mac counted on them this year as he didn't have fullback par excellence Bobby Brumell to be the assured power threat up the middle. The new fullback was lighter and nowhere near the quickness, but was a determined ball carrier.

The team never counted themselves out of any game knowing Coach Mac could or would find a way to win. They had real-time confidence in him – and most all the players loved him like a "Dad." They all played extra hard for him.

When the York paper, 'The York Patter' interviewed Coach McCarthy, he said, "We will have a good team this year and while we lost our very-talented quarterback Eddy Brandon, our new quarterback is developing very well, and our strengths will be in our two talented ends Billy Brewer and Mike Chandlier. This year we will be counting on our senior halfbacks to be our ball carriers. They are seasoned and have gained speed and quickness – you'll be seeing a lot of them. Our lines will be strong and aggressive this year and a few pounds have been added as well as increased strength. Our kicking department will be the same good quality as last year. So, all in all, I expect great things happening for the 'Raiders' this season. Thank you."

The article finished up with the schedule and some publicity comments about new cute routines by the Raiders' cheer leaders led by head cheer leader 'Anita Cantina.' A news bulletin that the hot dog brands were changed to a bigger and better tasting dog. That was big and good news to all of York's vociferous fans.

The rest of the articles on the sports page gave statistics on last year's seasonal games, and yardages attained type things. The 'Patter' was a good small-city paper. What with all that was going on this last year – the Patter was abuzz in much news reporting. It had lots of pictures supporting the articles. People love pictures. This year they posted 'good photo-op-collector-type sharpness quality of the new potential stars and individual photos of the York 'O' line and 'D' line. In the final paper before the first game all York had a collage with the names and numbers of the whole team – sans helmets – with uniforms. This was a gigantic hit with the entire community. The York citizens really got into their sports stuff with gusto – most enthusiastically.

York had transitioned and between all the 'hoopla' surrounding the winner of the Mr. America contest, and two

Olympic gold medals, a state high school football championship, the people of the fair city of York, Illinois, were primed for the upcoming football season and anything else the high school could field on grass or hardwood. They were totally enthusiastic followers and fans of any York team. 'York forever more," -- might have been the overall city-wide cheer. York was a quiet small-town city community, but now it had become a "somebody city." Certainly, it now was an important and worthy city in the eyes of its citizens. It had gone from a looser, depressing place to live into an inspiring, joyful, and desirable, even enviable place to call home. What a difference a year made – well, maybe two.

CHAPTER FORTY

Eddy now wore the gray uniform of the United States military officer-in-training. He was known as a cadet. He was now ensconced within the neogothic buildings of gray and black granite. He was a part of 1300 incoming freshmen cadets collectively known as the United States Corps of Cadets. He was on full scholarship, compliments of the U.S. citizenry via the United States government. He and his fellow soldiers had hard work ahead of them. It indeed would not be easy – and certainly not as free as having gone to a regular university or college.

They had honor codes where he was, the cadet honor code stating, "I will not lie, cheat, steal, or tolerate those who do." It was a different environment entirely – not a civilian lifestyle. They were being prepared for life and war, in that order.

When he graduated, he would have three pillars of performance; academics, physical, and military. He would then be commissioned as a second lieutenant in the U.S. Army.

Eddy's time would be filled with academics, physical training, and personal habits of cleanliness. He would have successfully surmounted the broad academic programs, military leadership performance, and mandatory participation in competitive athletics.

All in all, his life was about to be transformed into a learned, gentleman presenting, lean leader, officer, and killing machine. It was to be his duty to become the protection element for the American people, a leader of men and women in the acts of war and peace.

In order and discipline were code words for cadets. Approximately 81% of the freshman class would graduate from West Point with their bachelor of science degree. Until 1975, the venerable establishment for Army Military housed only males. Women now compose approximately 15%. The first female captain, the highest-ranking senior cadet, was appointed so, in 1989, West Point was an early adapter of the internet in the mid-

1990's and in 2006 was recognized as one of the nation's 'most wired' campuses.

Eddy would now be among the forerunners of notoriety of generals having graduated and serving their country. The likes of General Schwarzkopf, generals Petraeus, Odierno, Stanley, McCrystal, and David Rodriguez, to mention a few. Eddy's life would be full should he stay in the service of his country.

In preparation for that journey, Eddy had to select the curriculum he wished to pursue in his undergraduate state at the academy. His selections focused on the legal profession – wending his way through the military version of law school. The whole thing – these next 4 years would be the challenge of his life – was he prepared, as much as anybody could for his age.

After arriving on the West Point campus, he settled into his quarters with meeting his new fellow cadet roommate – he too was a football jock. He was a very large fellow with lots of muscles. When Eddy asked him what position he played, he said 'center.' Eddy thought 'perfect' – and a good person he needed to know. It was, of course, very important, the relationship between the center and the quarterback – especially on audible plays – there needed to be precise coordination between them. He would press to get to know his new roommate this season. He too was an incoming cadet – or freshman, in civilian terms.

Billy suited up for York's first football game of the season vs. Jamestown. It would be traditionally one of the toughest schedule challenges. They were the last game of the previous season, and it had been a really rough one to win. He was chatting with his teammates helping each other don their armaments for the game.

Everybody had all their equipment on and headed for the coach's office before going out the tunnel of the locker room area and on to the field. It was here that they all prepared by pumping themselves and each other up to rush out on to the field together.

Coach Mac would lead the way. The cheerleaders would be running ahead, doing flip-flops and cartwheels, trying to excite the crowd into a frenzy. This, of course, would instill the York 'Raiders' onto victory. The coach came into the room and spoke a few words of encouragement to the eager young men. His words were, "Play together, as a team, together teams win." That's all he had to say – they got the picture – it was not one for the 'gipper,' but one more for Coach McCarthy. And they all flew out the coach's room door, through the tunnel on out onto the field. It was always exciting to do that routine – never boring. The test was here!

Super bowls are big deals, but weekly York football games were big splashes for the citizens of York – they backed their teams with full enthusiasm and numbers. The home stadium was always full. Oscar Meyer was king of the eats and Pepsi the sauce of choice.

The team warmed up along the sidelines of their bench as announcement over the P.A. system blurted out information. The national anthem was played, and the opposing captains joined the referees at the center of the field for the coin toss. York lost the toss and took the wind at their back side. There wasn't a whole lot. The key would be passing accuracy, not wind speed.

York kicked off to Jamestown – the game was on. Each side ran the first series of plays running the ball – testing each other's line strengths. Each side punted with York's punter out-distancing the Jamestown 'Wildcats' by twenty yards, an excellent punt.

Most the 'Wildcats' returnees were rising seniors. Their powerhouse players last year, about half a squad, were lost to graduation. York had lost a critical two to college direction, the rest were intact for senior year with war time experience under their belt. Hopefully, thought 'Mac' this would provide good tidings for his 2015-16 team. For the most part, the season would be very successful and, in many cases, they dominated games.

In the second half, Mac moved his point of attack to his passing game. Jackson to Chandler and Brewer. Right off the bat, Jackson made connection with Billy. They kept sending fake halfback draws in the center area of the line, with York ends began having a hay-day running their passing routes downs across the field. York's 'O' line was terrific and rarely did infringement get to the quarterback before he could spot and hit his target 8-15 yards downfield.

Jackson was good – he was determined to be the best he could be. That was plenty good enough that evening Friday night under the lights at Quigley Stadium. You could see it in their eyes when each of the team huddled up for the next play. It was called the 'semper fi' attitude adjustment. They had it.

The defense hadn't lost any of their first-string players and they knew their way around in the forest. They knew the feeling of winning, shutting down the other team. Big 'Bo' Mineke had taught them well – having been an all-pro lineman with the Chicago Bears.

He got down and dirty with the lineman during practice – showing them the "how to's" and nuances of offensive and defensive playing. It was most useful when it came to game-time reality.

Information input and execution output. It worked good for York linemen. Coach Mac taught the backfields – both offensive and defensive – their job and strategies needed to be aware and play effectively and smart. But, 'Mac' was best at the overall establishment of a game plan for the team against their opponents each week. He and his team of staffers were young men leaders who were followed and listened to that which they taught. It is what was transferred to the team that promoted extra effort – that extra that made the difference for winning ways.

Jackson Andrews, York's senior quarterback, was developing a good relationship with the center on the team, George Huff. George was a big guy for a kid, weighing in at 249 and 5'11' tall. He was college gridiron material. The two of them developed a staggered-count cadence, which was instituted to draw their opponents offside. It worked at practice but hadn't been game tested. It was a new feature 'Mac' thought of – to have yet another play in his strategy basket. Such a staggered cadence's timing use would be needed when they needed a yard or two to reach a first down – catch the defense anxious to 'stuff' an offense from getting it. Off-sides would cost the defense 5-yard penalty, thus a first down for the offense, to resume their attack, resulting in a first down and 10 to go. The defense giving a play away – free.

The York Patter covered the game well in synopsis form. Stan Zielinski was their prime sports reporter and he indeed was a total York Raiders fanatic. He picked the game apart and covered the play action and overall game plan well. Enthusiastic he was. It was good that he had such great material to work with. Here is a synopsis from Stan's article.

HEADLINE: Raiders Route Wildcats 28-0

The Raiders showed their strength last night under the lights of Quigley Field, with fullback Bobby Brumell graduated, Coach Mac took to the air. The game was over from the beginning, with the eleven, try as they might.

Their efforts were much in vain. Rookie varsity quarterback Jackson Andrews showed the crowd his talents, as he hit Billy Brewer 3 times for touchdowns. Twice on long hauls and once on a fake touchdown shot as he crossed across the field to take a bullet to the gut and a 20-yard run – dragging tacklers with him.

Left end Mike Chandler faked a cross over and cut loose downfield as Andrews laid one in the palm of his hands – over the shoulder. It was quite spectacular.

The solid 'O' line and 'D' line held fast and the 'O' line was almost impenetrable. The 'D' line, like a Panzer division, punched holes in the Wildcats' line at will all evening long.

It was a change of plan strategy as Mac McCarthy plugged in his computer innovation of plays – right out of his fertile mind. It was not much of a doubt that he would get the Coach of the Year award – again. And if Mike Chandler and Billy Brewer continue on – they will most certainly be candidates for first-team all-state.

Though it's far too early for assuredness, let me speculate. I'll be putting my chips down on the York Raiders to pick up the league trophy – come December again. Their strengths and losses have only been replaced by high-quality players. The quarterback position looks solid and the halfbacks have stepped up to replace the power fullback Bobby Bromell, with quickness.

See you next week at Quigley Field. CHEERS! He signed off as 'Stan Zielinski.' Everyone in York subscribed to the "York Patter"

– with pride. They eagerly read every word of it. It was a good small-city paper, but it had improved immeasurably the last few years. If there was news in York – they reported it. People flocked to the Patter.

Eddy's girlfriend Penny had gone off to the University of Illinois. It was a huge school, but she found lots of new friends from small towns and cities from Illinois with like-minded and down-to-earth character types. She felt more at home with these type kids as opposed to the big city or even some suburban high school incomers.

Eddy had written her about his routines he had to perform at West Point on a daily basis. The best part of the day was football practice, where everybody was big, good, and talented. He told her Freshmen Coach Murdoch was a personable, good coach and demanding and well respected.

He was known as Coach Murdoch, SIR! And he was Cadet Brandon Jump! It didn't take Coach Murdoch long to get us drilled to his specifications. When he spoke, we listened. Then to action. So far, Eddy said, he was doing well and catching on to the various directions and orders he was told to do.

If you go with the flow, instead of procrastinating, it makes the irritation of being ordered around by faculty officers, and senior cadet wannabees, a lot less painful. Oh, the fun part is the football. Got to go – miss you a bunch. Will be home for Christmas – Love, Eddy.

Penny wrote him back that she indeed liked the U of I quite well. Though it was huge – everybody found small clicks of students to hang out with and enjoy. I will enjoy very much seeing you come Christmas – in your cadet uniform – I like men in uniforms.

I know you like girls in tight sweaters – Ha, Ha! I'll keep in touch with your folks when I get back home. Thanks for the picture you gave me – and the one of us at senior prom. You're a doll – see ya – Love, Penny

They both decided to put their nose to the grindstone. It would make the time go faster – less time dawdling and feeling antisocial or lonely. They were smart doing so. Christmas would come soon enough.

Once again Billy was hailed the 'star' of the game and he received a lot of attention from his peers. He would defer from himself that he was just part of the team and Jackson Andrews and Mike Chandler were and played outstanding. He also mentioned the great play by the linemen – all. He pointed out it's the guys in the trenches that let us do what we do – best. Our linemen are really good.

Billy tried hard to defer any glory from himself and on to others. He knew his strength and opportunity to shine depended on all his teammates' efforts. One didn't make yardage unless a proper block had been made somewhere, by someone. It was that simple.

Billy switched his stripes as soon as Mondays showed up. With his life so active, there was no time to waste reminiscing over yesterday. There just was just too much going on. The days of yester-year were as they were – etched or stamped in the history books. The present time was where it was at. Billy threw himself whole-heartedly into the here and now. That was his history; that was his plan.

York High School, since Billy returned to school from his truancy younger days, was good to Billy as well as good for him. He was happy to be alive, in this place with the people he was with. He was expanding his friendships and enjoying greatly his close buddies all, the 3 amigos, Eddy, Penny, and Anita. There were others, his math teacher, history teacher – all faculty members he had, his coaches of course, and his closest friends these days – his parents.

Things were good, but they would get better and different. Life changes daily, weekly, and yearly. It evolves and either you incorporate it, or it washes you aside. Life is not stagnant – though it sometimes feels that way. Billy was a high-energy guy and he only seemed to wind down when his head hit the pillow at night.

After several weeks into the semester, he was being challenged mentally in his new "A.P." courses – history, math, and computer science. His brain was on high charge and all his synapses were snapping well, like pistons fired by high-octane gas. He knew he had to do well in his courses in order to get into good schools. It was important.

His assigned teacher counselor was his Varsity Football Coach "Mac" McCarthy. It was a blessing that Billy deemed 'God' directed. Coach Mac had been an academic all-American at his college and took his duties as a student counselor very seriously. It would prove out to be a blessing. So, again when it came time to accumulate personal references for college admissions. Billy had yet to make a college selection choice. He had picked the schools that appealed to him from around the country. He needed to make early decision on several of his choices. Billy was now considering West Point – with a military career attached as a possible choice. He kept in touch with his buddy, Eddy, and his encouragement to come to West Point – and let's be a teammate together – a one-two punch of Blanchard and Davis of Army football past notoriety. It definitely intrigued him – a lot.

Such a choice would give him focus – keep him busy – and cut the free dawdling time to a minimum. He was used to being busy – have schedules – doing things. His days were full – he liked it that way. It also had the advantage of "keeping his nose clean" – no time to get into trouble stuff. That had been yester-year. The 3 amigos had salvaged him from those troubled times. Thank God, for his human angels appearing and sharing love. He felt certain grace upon his life and his assigned angels watching over him. Billy was unaware just how many there were – but he felt their results and presence often.

The temperature of life was now beginning to ramp up. His senior year was his entry into early manhood, a time of more responsibilities and requirements. He had had lots of help so far along his life, and only 8 more months of support systems graciously available to him. He was preparing himself to stand alone against the world, drawing on what possible support he had access to if needed. For years yet ahead, these times in high school would draw dearly to a close. His certain freedoms found to age 17 would be changing to more adult thought and deeds, Billy was growing up!

Though he was not consciously thinking of these things, they were impressively happening at what seemed a rapid pace. Right now, his mind snapped back to the next football game with Belmont High School.

Belmont High School had lost its opener by a touchdown and 3 points. Coach Mac said, 'They will be charged up to redeem themselves and possibly be a surprise package this Friday night. While they would be hard-pressed to win over York this season, all things were possible if York had a bad day's night. Mac was on top of it and all were confident in his plans and the team's outlook.

The York Raiders were ready as they could be. The kids and cheerleaders were all jacked up to do their part. The vendors again were "beefed up" with a new brand of "dog" and the citizens of York were ready to flee their homes for Quigly Field Friday night.

The noise level of York fans centered at the football stadium, and the rest of town drawn near to their radio and WMAK – the local called it "WANK" station 1430 FM on the dial. There was no television coverage as yet. WMAK had a radius of about 100-plus miles, and the Announcers were a hearty expressive duo. They could make a high school game sound like it was the Super Bowl.

Between the superb York band and 25 strong charged up cheerleaders who were excellent gymnasts and show girl combination, the halftime show was pretty exciting as a high school halftime entertainment went. It was equal or better than most college halftime shows.

CHAPTER FORTY-ONE

Belmont High School was game number two on the schedule of nine games. It was the second home game. The next three games would be away games. The time for kickoff was drawing near. In an hour and a half at 7:00 pm. The team would be eating dinner around 4:30 to 5:00 pm, and be at the campus around 6:00 pm sharp, to suit up and receive instructions from Coach Mac before the game. It was a routine procedure and protocol for home games.

Stan Zielinski was already on the campus wandering around talking with people, players, refs, assistant coaches and the gold posts (for inside information). NO wonder when he posted his story of the game, it was an exciting adventure of all Friday night at Quigley Field under the lights. The York residents ate it up, enthusiastically. He was good and infected humor.

The end of the first quarter found the two teams sharing touchdowns at 7 to 7. It was a hard-fought quarter. Quarterback Jackson Andrews wasn't on his game or as sharp as his potential, but he kept trying. He was not a quitter by any means.

In the second quarter, Andrews called for a reverse, with a double spread on the right since. Everybody thought it would be a hit to Billy or fullback wide out Nick McKiever. The play started with the quarterback under center, taking it back as to pass, but handing it to the left half Jerry Summers, who took off right where all the blockers were, only to hand the ball off to the right half, Don Tartak coming his way going in the opposite direction, a naked reverse. It was daring, and many yards would be lost if it didn't work.

Well, it was in the timing of the play, and Mac's impeccable sense of it, that caught the entire defense unprepared. All the defense was looking and running to the pass receiving zone and had their backs towards where the ball was going around left end.

Right halfback Don Tartak was a very fast runner and he had it on high gear, high-tailing it around left end. Nobody was near him for at least 15-20 yards as the deep defense saw what was developing and came up to meet him. This run would probably get him to around the ten-yard line of Belmont. He got close at the 12-yard line before getting hammered.

A down and in pass to Billy produced a perfect pass and catch and Billy marched on into the end zone. Jason Mason nailed the extra point and York was up by 7 at 14 to 7. The game stalemate had been broken. Belmont felt the embarrassment and it had a negative effect on the team spirit who were thinking a win over York. They were, it seemed, a bit over-confident with their good playtime.

Mac's hammering words of "You play every play hard to your best and do it to the full games last play." No slouching. As Yogi Berra, the famous Yankees catcher once said, "It ain't over 'til it's over." Of course, he's the same guy who said, "When you come to a fork in the road, take it!" Yoggi-isms, hmm.

The second half saw York's Quarterback, Jackson Andrews performing surgery on the field. He was threading the needle with York's ends right and left. It must have been disheartening to Belmont as York picked up three touchdowns in the third quarter. It was now 35-7, York was overpowering them across the board. It seemed like ends Chandler and Brewer had double bodies on the field. They were everywhere going on their prescribed routes crisscrossing and downfield. While Mike Chandler was quick to escape tacklers after contact, he came down fairly easily if the tackler hit solid, whereas Billy was terribly hard to stop and bring down. He was too strong and big for high school defensemen backs. If you didn't get him around the ankles, you weren't going to slow him down.

The game lightened up a bit through the fourth quarter, but no improvements on the scoring resulted. The final score, unchanged, was 35 to 7. York Raiders. Once again Mac's strategies worked out. So far, his season was the extension of last year's record. The team itself looked even better than the state champion team of last year. Certainly, the pass game flourished at no detriment at the quarterback position. Andrews looked positively really good. Billy was reeling in everything delivered his way in the neighborhood, and Chandler was slick as a greased monkey on the loose.

The next 5 games were away games. With Westhaven, Dumont, Jasper City, Silverton and Northwest Military Academy. York followers went to all the away games on bus caravans. They were enthusiastic supporters. All the games were won by York, again some by small margins and two by large scores.

It was hard to temper down the enthusiasm and whoopla of the York fans. They were nuts over the team. Soon the attitude changed to the prospect of the possibility that once again they might be headed into State Championship play. Most certainly the league championship. A cheer from the cheerleaders blasted out "Ramp-Up-Champ, Ramp-Up-Champ! Go, Go!" Banners appeared, bumper stickers sold like crazy, and the local paper and radio blurbs even caught the fever.

Fortunately for the raiders and Mac McCarthy, no one had been seriously hurt or injured during the season. While Mac was a compassionate guy, he basically said, "If you're somewhat hurt, bring it out, I'll tape it up and get you back into the action." All his past and present players quoted this about playing for Mac, but while they were hurt Mac took care to doctor his players up with good medicine and lots of TLC. Parents of hurt players recognized Mac's concerning attention to their sons. Many things were so that held the "Coach" in high regard- they knew he "loved" his boys and drew respect.

The transformation was exciting to all of York, amazing what winning seasons do to all its citizens as excitement and positive thinking grew rampant. Pride of the school, the city and its people were evident in all its forms. They would take it and run with it until all that "Sha-boom" runs its path and recedes into another form.

It was "go with the flow' time, stay in the middle of the stream, while the "gettin' was good." Billy sent the York patter to Eddy and Penny's mom; made sure she got the "ragsheet" too. Billy would get emails from Eddy with encouraging words to "keep, keepin' on" with all he was doing, and "Thanks" for all the info on he, the school and Anita. Eddy said he really enjoyed it all.

Eddy emailed pictures of himself in his cadet uniform, his football uniform and updated him on all his freshman year football and academic year. He always at the end stuck in an "advertisement" to come join me here at the academy. "I need your help. We can make a good team!"

Billy always enjoyed hearing from Eddy. He would shortly have to make up his mind if he too would apply at West Point. He presently thought so and needed to get started in the process and paperwork.

That week Billy sat down with his college counselor, his parents, to talk seriously about his choices and applications procedures. Those procedures were all a little different. Some required a short story essay, others didn't. He needed to ask his high school counselor how to secure a nomination from his Congressman Jonas Sterling from the 12th district of Illinois. Billy was fortunate mainly because of both his athletic status as well as his academic status that the teachers and coaches, two being his main coaches, could help him how to proceed in filling out and sending in his West Point application. He would make applications to Northwestern University in Evanston, Illinois, University of Michigan at Ann Arbor and UCLA in Los Angeles and Auburn University down south, and West Point, New York state. Actually, he had all the formal applications in hand and needed to coordinate it all with Coach "Mac" McCarthy, his college counselor and school counselor. He needed to collect recommendations from his academic teachers as well as anyone else he could think of.

As Billy thought processed all of this, he would probably have a dozen recommendations at hand. He had no idea just what they would say, but he thought they'd all be positive and favorable. He'd been trying so hard to do good for himself and make the 3 amigos and his parents proud. His good academic record, showing improvement every year since he returned to school back in middle school was proof of his abilities being tested each year!

Since his junior year, his grades were all A's, some plus, some minus. He didn't have free time to dawdle around and kept to things important to his success at school. It would show his good work after the first semester of senior year. Hopefully, those grades would be good also.

"Mac" called in Billy for an appointment one afternoon after lunchtime to talk with him about his college choices and applications. He was glad to see Billy as he had been busy with fall football. They got along really well, and Mac especially liked Billy for the personal character he possessed. He was essentially a trouble-free young man maturing rapidly. Billy was well respected by his peers and adults and was treated that way. It was the way he treated others. He was a very presentable young man. Self-possessed, good-looking and large. His 6'6" frame at 240 pounds presented a formidable human being on display, and if you knew him intimately, you knew he was packed with substance. He was to be respected.

The session went well, and they had a lot of laughs and bonded closer. Billy thought "Mac" a really good man, kind, sharp and related well with high schoolers. He was a professional teacher and coach. He had a class in biology at freshman level. Everybody that had him loved his class despite the subject matter. Cutting up dead frogs doesn't grab everybody! But somehow Mac got them through it. For that, a lot of students were thankful. It was an act of mercy.

Billy seemed to feel that his college application time had been used wisely and by the end of the week he had them ready to go. He only lacked an interview with Congressman Sterling and that was scheduled on the coming Saturday at 10:00 am in his office in Springfield, Illinois. The Congressman was working in his office that Saturday finishing up a bill to be introduced on the floor and made time for Billy's appointment. Billy's dad drove him down there as it would take them an hour-and-half. There was plenty of time to awaken, eat and leave. Plus, he'd get to talk with his dad alone. He was looking forward to a personal time spent with his father.

The trip to Springfield went well, and fast, and the time with Congressman Sterling proved to be outstanding. He was a good man, dedicated to representing his constituency of the 12th district. He actually had seen Billy play ball twice and said he was thoroughly impressed. The two of them hit it off graciously. He said he'd played high school ball as a lineman for St. Francis Catholic School in South Suburban Chicago. It was in a rock-em, sock-em Catholic League.

The Congressman said he'd get right on writing the recommendation as soon as he received his high school grades, and faculty recommendations. Billy said he had those things and would leave them with him now.

"Good," said Congressman Sterling, "I will have some time this week and have something ready for West Point. I know Mac McCarthy pretty well and will lean heavily on what he has to say. Oh, he's your counselor, even better for you, he's a marvelous man. He has a great reputation, a man of character."

They stood, shook hands and Billy departed feeling really good about his interview. His dad was well pleased, as he put his arm around his son's broad shoulders, and they left the Congressman's office to head home to York. It was a worthwhile time.

The balance of the week found Billy finishing out the other application papers for his college choices. He needed to get them all out in the next two weeks. It was pretty much standard procedure for all seniors that hadn't yet applied for early admission. It wasn't fun duty doing these things, but it definitely had to be done.

Billy kept his nose to the grindstone, doing the everyday work necessary for daily classes and homework. When afternoon Phys Ed came, football practice for him, he felt relieved and more relaxed when he was doing physical exertion. He concentrated on ball retrieval, soft hand reception. There weren't many dropped balls thrown with any near accuracy in his direction. Mac always said, "What you do in practice always show up in games." In his case, concentration was a big plus.

One day at practice, Billy caught sight of the cheerleaders performing their routines. It was unusual for them to do this outside. Usually they did their thing in the gym. Of course, he looked to catch a glimpse of Anita. This year she was the head cheerleader directing others in all their routines.

He spotted her barking out calls of direction to her squad of high school beauties. Most of the girls sported "blonde" long hair while Anita had long dark hair. He thought a long thought of how pretty she was, how her hair literally glistened in the sun, how soft it felt and was and...then...

"Mr. Brewer, are you with us today? We need your help here," came Coach Hills loud voice and whistle. Billy looked sheepishly at the coach who in turn looked and smiled at Billy knowing he was lost in thought watching Anita. He knew they were an item on campus and was glad he was having a normal high school female relationship. It was healthy and potentially encouraging and good for athletic performance – "my hero" type thing. It was good for the ego, healthy for the mind, and calming to the body, but distracting to the present need of performing the duties required at football practice.

Billy retracted back into his shell and returned to his workouts at practice. Conditioning was high on Coach Mac's staff list. Better, stronger, longer lasting bodies for the grueling games on York's schedule. It made a difference as a game got into the depth of time last quarter. It showed and proved out many times as other teams seemed to wind down prior to games end. York would take advantage and push other teams around with ease when they started to clog up.

"Mac" could see this happening and was glad his boys worked as hard as they did in practice. It made a difference, it made for wins. Winning wasn't everything, but it sure made a difference in the standing.

The last two games were at home, Canton High School and Midlothian. Both teams were loaded this year with seniors. They too, had their battle ribbons, and experience counted a lot at the high school level of sports. The games would be maybe closer and better than last year. Coach Mac looked forward to their contests with them.

Fall was in the air; the Elm trees and Maples were fiercely showing their bright colors with orange and red. Tree lines of either were stunning to look at but were a mess to clean up when they shed their leaves.

Fall was an invigorating time of the seasons, the beginning of a nip in the air after the summer heat wave. It felt good to the body and psyche. It was school time, busy time, football season. Soccer was the back-up sport for both boys and girls. It was a popular sport drawing lesser crowds, but the players were highly charged to play the sport. Fans of soccer were small but very loyal and enthusiastic supporters.

The York boys' soccer team was pretty good, and the girls' team was currently in first place in their league. Fall indeed, was an active time for students of York High School. Perry Dunlop, principal, was a very busy man, a proud leader of his students, faculty, and all the coaches of its various teams. He was a hands-on leader and wasn't a sit-in the-office kind of guy. He intermingled a lot with his students and knew a lot of them by name. The kids loved him, not feared him. The school's code of "respect your fellow students, faculty as you respect yourself." The students came up with that themselves and strived to live up to it. What happened overall was an attitude that begot the spirit of excellence in effort and in personal results. It reflected well with all of York.

It, of course, spilled over onto the citizens of York and caught on to a wellspring of neighbors touching neighbors. It had been a long time coming with York's past receding and its lively new vibrant attitude affecting its citizenry. What it resulted in was the transformation of bad business doings in City Hall to good will accomplishments by its newly elected government with the people's backing and support. Respect made the difference – it was now being earned. Respect is hard to come by, it must be earned, and York itself now had it and it was flowing rivers of living waters. Good things were happening in abundance. Prosperity in one fashion or another was the new life in York,

Illinois. It was a great place to live and call home and raise children.

Billy, Eddy, Anita, Penny and all their friends and families were greatly joyful in their beings and how they went about their everyday living. Some people now called the city "New York," knowing it was nothing like the namesake of that nine million coagulation city of people in the state of New York.

York's reputation glowed with new era light. There even were people moving into their city, because they heard such and such good about the tiny city. Small city life was still personal in its orientation and operation. It still personified the notion of people and families knowing others and wanting to participate in the community and somehow to contribute to the general over-all good of their city. People helping people type of thing. It indeed was a forerunner of what societies were in need of – brotherly love and concern for one another's welfare. They were the personification of an all-American small city. Their sign said so right under the city's name at the edge of town.

CHAPTER FORTY-TWO

Once again Quigley Stadium was full Friday night. It was the Canton game. Last year York had won rather easily, but this year Canton would be an improved team, having had a year's experience under their belt. Most were now seniors. This would hold true also for York's last game with Midlothian.

As for Mac's concern, he was concentrating on preparing his team to do better the things they did every day. The same old, same old with new niches and more perfection. Coach Mac would call it all "work hard everyday stuff."

One of these new offensive venues was what he called the quarterback roll-out-hidden ball play, where the quarterback takes the ball back after receiving it from under the center, then rolling to his right, fake handing the ball to the halfback going his opposite direction and keeping the ball all the time next to his hip and leg opposite to the defensive players. Mac referred to it as a bootleg right. They practiced and fine-tuned Jackson Andrews repetitively until he felt comfortable and executed it with deceitful precision.

One of Mac's favorite quarterbacks of all time was named Johnny Lujak who played quarterback at Notre Dame in the 1950's. He was an excellent passer and ran the "bootleg" with deceitful vengeance. He produced many long yardage passing plays and enjoyed some good running yards himself.

Mac instigated another new play, which basically was a fake field goal attempt. He worked with Jason Mason, the field goal kicker, and the place kick holder, Benny Hampton.

The first thing Mac did was to check the size of Benny's hands. He found them more than adequate to be able to hold and pass a ball. So, Mac had him throwing tons of practice passes until he actually got good at it.

So, it was that Coach Mac was as well prepared as he could get for the Canton game this coming Friday night. He felt the team very well prepared for the Canton High "Rough Riders." The teamwork of Andrews, Chandler and Brewer was humming along with much precision. It seemed that the two halfbacks were executing their plays faster and picking their way running with better determination.

York high was on a high once again as Friday afternoon school let out. The banners were flying, the food and drink stuff was ready for consumption, only the fans themselves needed to show. Kids were all over the place in anticipation of kickoff. The football players had gone home to get some home cooked early dinner and back to suit up for game time. The referees were due at six o'clock and the gate and security forces were meeting beforehand to prepare for the crowds. Other than fan exuberance, they were pretty well behaved, it was the York way.

Expectations were high as the band played the "Star Spangled Banner" while all those in the stadium sang it out. There were no flag burners, protesters, anti-anti-American folk attending the game in York. These folks were the heartland of the country, all Red, White and Blue patriotic Americans. Our government wasn't running this show at Quigley Stadium. These people of York were moderates, practical, honest and verbal and didn't vote to the far right or left at the voting booth.

The kickoff, a booming high one above the crowd, and deep to the goal line. Canton had the ball. The runback was returned to their 20-yard line as they drove it back straight up the middle. The ball returner was totally flattened by Charlie Brown, York's middle tackle of the kickoff squad. Charlie was a really BIG ol' boy, the son of a farmer who lived outside the town of York.

Charlie not only played right tackle on the offense, but also on defense. He was big and fast and exceptionally quick. He was a protégé of and student of "Bo" Mineke. He was much like him as a high school student. "Bo" spent a lot of extra time with Charlie, mentoring him with his knowledge of line play and strategy. As a senior, Charlie's line play was of All-State caliber quality. He was known for his aggressive and fierce playing. At 6' 1"and 260 pounds and in excellent shape, he indeed was a prime candidate for any division I college material. He would prove to be most effective in this Canton game. As a backfield running back, you wanted to run behind Charlie's blocking, you would expect to make yardage. Charlie could move anybody aside and did. He was a mountain of an already 18-year-old young man. He also was a smart student in school. His college prospects would be many and his choices excellent.

The quality of York's lines, both the O-line and the D-line, were such that their opponents usually couldn't compete with them for any length of time. They were that good a high school football line, not only locally and statewide but probably nationally too! AS the Canton game progressed the trio of Andrews, Chandler and Brewer were hummin' true to form and the score was 21 to 0 at halftime. And scores were by the ends catching Jackson Andrew's passes. Two of them by Billy doing his short crossover then turning downfield and hauling the ball in deep and on into the end zone.

Mike Chandler outran the short defensive back and caught one over his shoulder, sprinting around a deep defender who attempted to flatten him, but couldn't detect Mike's fake cut in time and he trotted into the end zone. The Raiders were good. They blocked, tackled and outran, over powered and literally out smarted their opponents. It was another year of formidable strength and talent that propelled them in their winning ways.

It was indeed, one of those truly talented teams with all the right ingredients needed to attain a championship status. Teams like this were few and far between. There would be many players getting scholarships at college and an unusual number for York. Seniors would be honored with many honors. Coach Mac McCarthy would see his love of football and coaching kids come to fruition again in his illustrious career as a high school coach. He would probably be elected as Coach of the Year in the league, and if he again won the State Championship, to State Coach of the Year. He definitely was headed for the state Hall of Fame for coaches in the near future.

The second half let in the Canton Rough Raiders to the scoreboard. It was now 21-7. It was a jumble by the quarterback as the ball was snapped and Canton got the ball very near the goal line and converted the turnover into a touchdown. It was a costly mistake, one that can easily happen to any quarter back.

Canton kicked off deep into the Raiders territory and specialist kickoff return back, Jerry Witherell, took the ball back to the 50-yard line. Were it not for the good blocking of York's kickoff receiving team, he never would have gotten as far as he did.

Andrews would now be in great position to start a drive on the Rough Riders. Although they had a lead on them, they would not let up on their march to finish the game. There was still too much time left for bad things to happen. They were not a perfect team and they were most vulnerable if they should ever let down.

It was under Coach Mac that they listened attentively and, again, he reiterated the by-line "to play the full game to the most, 'cause it ain't over 'til it's over." In letdown times, you can get burned, which funnels negativity into a team.

The running game came alive with the duo of half-backs performing their feats of talent. Fake passes, with hand-offs to them and occasionally to a fullback power up the middle between center and the right tackle area. They found the D-line of the Rough Riders vulnerable at that position with George Huff and Charlie Brown literally removing the lineman in their opposite positions.

Two sets of downs later, the raiders again scored on a fake fullback up the middle with Nick McKiever and delivered a bullet pass to Billy on one of his famous crossover pass pattern receptions. He got to the five-yard line. Then Andrews reversed the final play, a fake pass to Billy and a draw power run with McKiever doing the honors to score and Tony Diago adding the extra point, score; 27 to 7 – Raiders.

The last quarter found the Raiders adding two more touchdowns, one, hitting Billy on a long ball thrown on a straight-away pattern bringing in the ball five yards short of the goal line and on in.

The other score to Chandler on a down and in and down pattern where Billy comes across to wipe out a would-be tackler of Chandler after the catch, freeing Mike up to possibly score. He did.

The game ended 41-14 – Raiders. Eight league game wins so far with only Midlothian High School left to play before possibly going on to the state play offs, and state championship. They were playing again, and better than last year and the enthusiasm and confidence levels were soaring. They were primed to go the whole way. The excitement levels at York High and the city of York were elevating with vigor, with each day passing.

The Patter City paper and radio station were gallantly expressing the accolades of York's football Raiders. Stan Zielinski was at his pontificating best once again. The paper was flying off the shelves.

Nobody had the record of the York Raiders this season. All wins, with one more game to go. As Stan Zielinski pointed out in his summary of the Midlothian Bruins, their quarter back was a really good one and they too directed their attack through the air with much success. It would be the toughest and overall efficiency of the O-lines that would make the difference.

On a total assessment of line play, Stan gave the nod to York based on experience and quality of the players and Coach Mac's ability to assess and provide a way to win. Stan Zielinski's sports column was always read and not many in York ever missed it. The larger paper like The Chicago Tribune would sometimes publish columns from the Patter, often Zielinski's column was quoted. "Stan Zielinski, of The York Patter, said such and such." Ed Martin, owner of the York Patter, was really proud of what his little paper had become over these last few years. Its notoriety had taken it to a lot of nearby towns and the circulation was gaining ground dramatically.

It was the end of football season, only the tail-end wrap-up games and any play-offs were left, and it looked like York might certainly play into the playoffs again this year. There was excitement still ahead for the City of York, and they had been through the mill of it all last year and were waiting to again participate in the winners' circle once again with enthusiasm.

CHAPTER FORTY-THREE

The headlines of the York Patter read; "Raiders Route Bruins' for league title.

By beating the Midlothian Bruins, the York Raiders cinched the League Championship title trophy. The last game of the season secured all the hard work put in prior and during the season. A reward well deserved. We as a community should indeed be proud of our high school's football team, not only for their excellent play, but for the quality of the young men playing. Dedication to excellence, exerted with smart coaching by Mac McCarthy and his talented staff helped the Raiders to another successful year.

Fortunately, success breeds opportunity for further success as the Raiders will once again be in the state high school, Division II Championship play offs. A winner of four play-off games will become the state of Illinois champion. "Cheers" for the York Raiders.

On the back page of the Patter was an account of the last seasonal football game, with Midlothian High School.

The Raiders entered the game usually taking charge early on. However, Midlothian asserted its muscle right from the start and pelted York with its talented quarter back's passing game. They scored in the middle of the first quarter, to lead 7 – 0, a lead they maintained the first quarter. In the huddle for a time out, the word was just keep playing our brand of ball, do what we do best, and the game will shape up in our direction. Never give up! Go Raiders! So said Coach Mac.

The second quarter was hard fought good running, and Mike Chandler and Billy Brewer performing with exciting catches gaining many yards, provided a tying touchdown going into halftime.

The third quarter efforts by the Raiders opened up the game with a couple of breakout runs as the O-line opened holes for substantial yardage by Sommers, Tartak and McKiever. The entire "O" and "D" lines were putting the pressure on as York positioned themselves and scored, making it 14-7.

The fourth quarter posted several hidden bootlegs by Andrews which totally spaced out the defense, one on a deep wide out pass to Billy, the other was a straight away quarter back run. These plays happened back-to-back effectively confusing the defense. A drilling of several more passes provided another score for the Raiders, score now, 21-7. The Raiders were growing momentum.

On a timeout, several of the D-lineman told the Coach the D-line of the Bruins were slowing down some as they were tightening up. Things were changing, and Mac saw the light.

"OK, keep the pressure on, work together, team up. We are steering for a breakout. Concentrate, focus on your job, do what we do at your best. Now let's do it!" Those were an electric socket coming to life with juice. Those were fightin' words.

After the pep talk by Coach Mac the team came to life, out blocking, tackling and passes threading the proverbial needle with abundance. It was a veritable machine turned on to high gear.

Midlothian fell into a series of several dropped passes or blocked ones, as well as a critical fourth down blown offsides caused by Andrews' stutter counts. A Bruin's receiver was stuffed by a Raider tackler only to have the ball fly out of his hands and into one of York's finest, thus thwarting a key Bruin drive. The attitude and altitude were changing, and the Raiders took seriously their offense.

Each and every Raider player felt the electric juice energize them. It was a spirit of Coordination between team members in both the offensive and defensive lines. They would not be denied victory in the game.

As the clock wound down and with the score as it was, Andrews play calls got bolder. Instead of lessening up, they pressed harder to try to get another score in before the bell. Thus, quarter back Jackson once again took to the air with Chandler and Brewer as main targets. Several times, showing the big ends as receivers, he threw short to the fullback, McKiever, just over the line of scrimmage and threaded his way up field for some good, short gaining yardage. He wasn't big like Bobby Brumell of last year, but he was tough and fast.

With less than two minutes on the clock, the Raiders found themselves on the 36-yard line, first and ten. After several fakes to the ends, and handing off to McKiever, the fullback, they gained another first down. Now at the 25-yard line, the devastating duo of targets, end Chandler and Brewer, rose up to become the receivers they were. Andrews faked to the fullback going through the line, backed up a few paces, looked left, pump-faked a pass and gave Billy Brewer time to haul tail down field into the end zone, where upon he stepped back and let go a zinger off his front foot to Billy who was approaching the end zone.

It was one of those picture-perfect film passes you show prospects on how to deliver and receive long passes. Billy let the ball drift into his hands with softness of assuredness in its reception. There was no doubt in any of the Quigley Field attendance that he would miss or drop the ball. They were right, and the score was now 28-7.

Midlothian was humiliated at their performance, one would have a twinge of feeling sorry for them, but football was football. There was no bad luck or good luck in this game. One team was just better than the other, today.

The clock ran out soon after the Raider touchdown. The fans screamed, hollered and ran down on the field to surround the Raider's team with warm hugs, back slaps, jumping up and down-waving banners. The cheerleader squad was doing flips and running around shouting "Go Raiders! Go." Together shouting and counting off 28-Yo-times- doing flips and cartwheels. Quigley Stadium came alive with what it was built for and once again York responded with love and admiration for their team. They propelled their emotions while the air caught the winning tide.

League Championship again visited the Raider campus. State play-off championship was next with, again, the planning of buses, motels, overnights to wherever the winning prospects would take them.

Again, the Illinois State title was theirs for the taking. The season was new now, with a total of four more games to win the whole shootin' match. This would test to the max the Raiders' varsity football team. Mac had his work cut out for him over the next few weeks, times of stress. Back-to-back championships would really be a nice coup for the folks at York. How nice the two State Championship trophies would look in the school's display case, next to each other under the York banner.

On the inside of the back page of the York Patter, was the diagram of all the brackets and high school names for marching to the finish line for the Illinois State Football Championship games.

The Illinois State final playoffs are composed of two districts. Each district is composed of four sections. Each two sections have a winner who in turn plays each other and those winners are state runner's up. They play each other for the Championship trophy. Stay posted for all playoff game reviews and pull for the home team – Go York Raiders!

Well, the City of York was once again ramping up for a joint effort of support, organization of buses for those wishing to travel to the games. The Championship game would again be in Chicago's Soldier's Field, on a Saturday afternoon 1:00 pm game time.

Stay tuned! Stan Zielinski. Sports editor York Patter.

The York Patter was always sold out these last few years. Lots of things were and had been going on in York. The notoriety of the Three Amigos, Big John winning the Mr. America title. Heavy Lou winning the Olympic Gold Medal for heavyweight lifting and "Little" Dave winning the USA Golden Glove title and a gold medal title for Middle Weight Division Olympiad.

That was followed by the York Raiders winning their league title in football and going on to win the State High School Football Championship trophy and title that fall. All-in-all it was an immense time for the City of York.

And now, again, the York Raiders were in contention for another state football championship. If won, would be the first back-to-back championship by a high school Illinois team ever. No wonder expectations were high. Hopes effervescing, and hard work ahead to achieve those goals. It was possible because all of York, including the players, thought that they could do it. The possible was possible, the impossibility of it was dismissed. York had four weeks to devour the supposed impossible and establish the possible.

It all had come together – everything! But most of all, hard work. Mac McCarthy was experienced in that regard. His accomplishments as a high school coach over the years exemplified greatness, fairness, toughness, leadership, assertiveness and love for his players through the years. He was unique as a man, a leader and as a mentor of young men. His name was "respect." He would be on the high school football Hall of Fame, he epitomized the word "Coach," He was an assured prospect in waiting.

CHAPTER FORTY-FOUR

Fast forward four weeks to the fall of 2016. The leaves were beginning to turn and the chill in the air was increasing. Some days were downright cold. The York Patter, with Stan Zielinski reporting, took its York citizenry through the York wins of the section one first round district and then the section one playoff game placing the Raiders into the runners-up section one versus like team of Section two playoff. The winner of which became the State Champion for the Illinois State Championship Title.

The post season playoffs were completed with York facing off with a powerhouse team from Edwardsville, Illinois of District Two. It was the first time Edwardsville Killian High School had advanced into any playoffs. They were high on themselves with confidence and loaded for bear for the playoff title game. They had come through a lot and their cannons were indeed loaded full strength for the Chicago Soldiers Field contest.

It was being billed as the inexperienced Rookies versus the experienced "been there before" hard core team.

"The Championship Game"

The game of fame teetered back and forth in the first half. Each team testing the other for weaknesses. At halftime it was the proverbial Mexican standoff at 28 to 28. Both teams threw their best talent and efforts in trying to outdo each other. It was a total crowd pleaser of a game and hard fought; There was an abundance of college scouts in attendance. They were licking their "chops" over the talent involved in both teams. Zielinski continued...

Then of course there was a second half, where if no slip ups occur, experience counts. It would be those turnovers, missed timing, missed blocking, and execution, that made the difference.

The York Raiders, just out worked, out played, out smarted, and out communicated the Edwardsville Killian "Tigers." Mac McCarthy's Raiders were skilled, experienced, tough and their conditioning kept them going full throttle the whole game. The Raiders' stars were at their best all game long. Scouts and college recruiters had to be drooling over the prospects on both sides of the ball that day in Soldiers Field.

While the Raiders offensive unit was able to take full charge, the last ten minutes of the game to win 35-28, was because of their experienced defensive team that literally shut down the "Tigers" from about anything they threw at the Raiders. Line Coach Big "Bo" Mineke was beaming ear to ear with the D-line and the linebacker defensive performance. They were a wall of confidence and aggressiveness.

Well, champions they were, most deservedly. They were a well-coached team, a team that had a terrific work ethic, a group of young men who had much fun, taking responsibility for themselves and the job of the position they played. The team all raised up Coach Mac on their shoulders, parading him around field like a trophy. They did that too, with Billy Brewer holding high the state championship trophy and jumping up and down. Anita was leading all the cheerleaders in front of the victory celebrants, around the field – a celebration lap with band members blazing away in no particular formation. It was a grand and glorious high school victory spectacular. York had accomplished the impossible and replaced it with the possible. They had known, with this team that all things were possible. They just proved it!

The article was signed by Stan Zielinski. The Patter was full of commentaries and comments by people having watched the game from the stands. The celebration would take hold most on the following Saturday and Sunday in York. The talking about it would last weeks – maybe months. The city would honor the team with a special rally, with band playing and city dignitaries espousing many accolades of praise.

It was the first time York had ever won back-to-back championships in any of the sports they played. So the Mayor was most effusive in his speech denoting such an achievement level, which fired up the audience into a "Go – Go – Go – Raiders" chant.

Billy took all these festivities in alongside his teammates. It was a good feeling of accomplishment and satisfaction in doing a good job. He hadn't won the MVP award, but quarterback

Jackson Andrew did, and he was glad for him. He had really done well all through the season and especially so through the playoffs. Andrews wasn't quite the natural athlete that Eddie Brandon had been or was, but he definitely was a "can do kind of guy." He always made the effort to get the job done.

The football scouts would marvel at this year's team, pretty much across the board, they were a mature bunch. They really did look, in many respects, like a college caliber team. Many would receive "full boat" scholarships to colleges – many Division I schools.

During the week, Stan Zielinski prepared several articles on the outstanding play and the Raiders various team players, emphasizing their talents on and off the field. It was close friendly townsfolk who were anxious to know about their favorite teams they supported at York High School. He did a profile of each starting player for both the offense and defensive teams. This was very popular with the avid readers of the Patter, and the players themselves. It was kind of a collectors' kind of thing made for scrapbooks. Many happy remembrances held sway in 25 years or so.

The scouts, of course, would actually have attained full stats of the players they were interested in from the athletic office of the coach. The coach was quite knowledgeable about these things as he kept files on each student/player himself – a Dossier on each. He also expected his assistant coaches to maintain active files on their players they coached.

The football season was now over and with the seasonal change brought on basketball season. Of all the football players, only two played on the varsity basketball team. Both ends, Mike Chandler and Billy Brewer. They'd been playing since 9th grade on the Frosh-Soph team and now the varsity team as seniors.

For Billy it was his usual thing to be busy all the time. Athletics were not over for him when football season stopped. He easily transferred his alliance and attachment to basketball. This would be his last and final varsity sport he would ever play in at York High School. He looked forward to getting going.

Of course, Billy would have to catch up to speed with the team as they had been practicing for several weeks. Both he and

Mike had drawn together over the last two years and would hit stride quickly.

Right now, schoolwork was a priority, always was. Billy kept his nose to the grindstone as he needed to keep his grades up for going to West Point.

Billy had all his applications in to the schools of his choice and was now waiting for their replies, which would probably come sometime in January or February. He hoped that he'd be accepted at West Point Military Academy. He looked forward to that happening.

His grades seemed to be holding up well, despite his busyness. Apparently, he was able to prioritize his time and concentrate on doing things as needed. He really, this year, had no spare time. So it was indeed a challenge to fulfill all his agenda. It was called discipline and will power. It would become a blessing over the years to him, His future would depend on these attributes.

Coach Mac McCarthy, his folks and friends were all mega proud of his football achievements, as well as his personal persona and integrity as a young man growing up. He loved his parents, Coach Mac and all his coaches for that matter. He loved the 3 Amigos and had a heavy crush on Anita – that was kind of last on his priority list. He'd have to up-kindle his interest and effort with her.

Anita came into Billy's head with feelings of need to see her. So, he called her to see if she going to be at church that Sunday. She was. He told her he was going and had wondered if she would be there. She was glad to hear he was going too. He said he'd be there at 9:00 am for Sunday School and she said that she'd meet him there at 9:00. Ah, thought Billy, so far so good. Somehow after having talked with her for a while, he felt energized. It felt good to feel that way. He always felt that way when she was around or talking to him. He liked her a lot and had no other interest or feelings about any other girl. She seemed to be right for him.

Other friends had said to him that they were a good couple – made for each other. At the moment Billy thought so too. He didn't really know any other girls except to say "hi" to. Girls were kind of scary anyway. He didn't know much about them.

Sunday morning arrived, and Billy had gotten up around 7:00 am. He dressed for church and headed downstairs to fix breakfast for his family. They weren't going to church, but usually got up early. Billy headed downstairs took his sports jacket off put his Barbeque Chicago Bears apron on covering all his front. He got some eggs, bread, OJ out and some sausage links. Then sprayed a skillet with some PAM, turned on the stove and fired it up.

Mom and Pop came down the back stairs into the kitchen smelling the good breakfast and coffee smells. They sat down as Billy did a short order breakfast treat for them. Eggs over easy, sausage links, toast with butter, coffee. It all was enough along with orange juice and vitamins to fill the morning satisfaction quotient just right. Two cups of coffee for Mom and Dad – there, done.

Billy removed the dishes while still talking to his parents. They expressed to him their love and how proud they were of him, and asked how he and Anita were doing – they hadn't seen her in a while.

Billy brought them up to date and told them he was meeting her at church that morning for Sunday School, then regular Church Service. Billy's dad reached in his pocket and peeled off some cash and handed it to Billy saying, "Get Anita to take you for lunch and you pay for it if she wants to go or can." Mom looked surprised but happy as he did so. She really liked Anita.

Billy said, "Why thank you Dad. I'll ask her if she can go but will return the money if she can't. That was really thoughtful and nice of you. You guys are the greatest. That was music to his parents' ears.

Billy had walked to church, it being about a half mile towards town. He found the Sunday School classroom for senior high kids and there was Anita, and did she ever look pretty. She lit up with a big smile and came toward Billy. They moved over to a quiet corner to talk as they were a little early for class time. Before it got started. While he had the chance, he asked Anita if he could take her for lunch after church, but that she'd have to drive. She feigned thinking a few seconds and said, "Yes, that would be nice." She knew Billy didn't have a car, much less a driver's license, so she said, "I'll get you home after lunchtime." Billy said, "Thanks, that'll give us time to talk and catch up some. It's been a hectic fall so far."

She agreed and they both laughed because they needed to. Senior year was a stressful time in a young person's life. So much going on – always new and more grown-up responsibilities.

Both fell into their seats for the Sunday School lesson and discussion feedback to the extent they could participate. The Sunday School bell went off and some went home, and others went directly to the church service, wending their way through the church building.

The Sermon was on I Corinthians 13:4 on what the attributes of love are and what love is not. Both Anita and Billy sat down in the pew seat with their program and Billy said, "This should be an interesting sermon topic."

The pastor welcomed everyone and had a general prayer followed by announcements of the church, followed by a choir song of praise. Then the Pastor Reverend David Burr entered the pulpit to speak. He shuffled some notes, looked over the flock and proceeded in his sermon.

"Today's sermon is one all of us can improve on, 'What is Love?' Good question you ask, but I can't nail it down. Love is not nailed down. It is experienced by time, work and constant effort.

"It is said that knowledge puffs up, but love edifies, i.e. builds up, esteems and provides a platform for security, trust and deeper positive personal relationship. Love by Webster's definition uses these terms: strong affection, warm attachment, attraction based on sexual desire; beloved person, unselfish, loyal, benevolent concern for others. While these characterizations are good, they are not what love is.

First Corinthians 13:4 says what love is: Love is patient, love is kind; It does not boast, it is not proud. It is not rude nor is it self-seeking; It is not easily angered; it keeps no record of wrongs. Love does not delight in evil but rejoices in truth. It always protects, always trusts, always hopes always perseveres. Love never fails – (people do.)

"Now this is sound and fruitful stuff, and it should be, it is from God's Word. I have come up with 15 topics that are hopefully helpful in marriage and personal growth which ignites love if practiced.

First on my list is Communication: "you talk, or you die." Second, is Sexuality: this is a "touchy" subject with positive issues and negative producing issues. Third, Friendship: a good relationship for any length of time is looking for depth. Fourth, Forgiveness: is essential and central in a relationship. Fifth, Worship: someway, somehow is the need for a spiritual dimension and outreach. Six, Attitude. Seven, Priorities: assemble your daily life. Eight, Finances: This is tough duty, but critical for love to work. Nine, Honesty and Trust: transparency: enlightens a relationship. Ten, Passion: don't miss it, it rarely just happens. It is kindled by hard work. Eleven, Planning: here two heads are better than one in a marriage relationship. Twelve, Intentionality: to fulfill this generates longevity in a relationship. Thirteen, Patience: living daily strains it. Exercise your will. Fourteen, Fun: kick off the serious, relax together or with others. Fifteen, Choices: You choose, you own them. Choices are God's gift for sifting life.

"These subject matters and thoughts I've put together to prompt you to take a look at love, it's needs, for a healthy and productive life. We are only "cracked pots" on the wheel of life forging our life to fulfill God's destiny for us. Rules are to be broken and break them we do, but some things are much better for you than others and God has a plan for you, including some worthwhile suggestions for along the way. God bless you, you and your mate, and a life in abundance of His grace.

Amen."

There was a final hymn of grace and the service was over. Everyone stood and greeted others and slowly departed the sanctuary to finish their day. The pastor stepped to the doorway of the church and greeted his flock as they greeted him in love.

Billy and Anita greeted Rev. Burr on the way out and told him they had learned much from his sermon. They heard Rev. Burr compliment Billy for his outstanding playing on the football field and also to Anita for doing a great job as head cheerleader for the York Raiders.

Billy and Anita thanked him for the compliments and headed for her car. They were not going home, but were going to a nice restaurant for lunch on Dad Brewer's dime and generosity.

As they got into Anita's blue ford focus, Billy said to her "This is a really nice car, you like it?" Anita responded that she did, saying her dad was the manager of the local Ford Auto Agency here in town and they got a deal on it! "Well," said Billy, "you certainly look cute toolin' around in it. Your color is blue, bright blue, fits you perfectly."

"Why thank you," responded Anita.

Anita drove them to the restaurant; a nice one Billy had picked out. He wanted it to be a nice one because he thought Anita to be special and he wanted to do something special for her.

They entered the "Kings Inn" grill and bar known to have good food. It was a very nice restaurant and the York City folk named it one of the top five best in town. Billy felt much enjoyment escorting Anita to lunch and being able to sit with her privately and talk with her.

There was a certain aire of being proud to have the privilege of being seen with such an attractive young lady. So very pretty indeed. They were an attractive couple.

Billy spoke to Anita once they were seated at the table. He picked up the menus and handed one to her. "Let's order then talk," said Billy. They did so as they decided on a big breakfast instead of the Southern Fried Chicken special. The waitress took their order and left for the kitchen. Billy turned towards Anita and said, "You know that I think the world of you. I really like you and hope you will always be my girl. However, times are coming, and we will be separated by college choices until school is through for summer and vacations, like Christmas. I will be kept very busy by the regimen required where I'm going. My free time will be in short supply. I am going to miss you and your company so very much. I shall write you and email you hopefully often. I hope you will too!"

Continuing Billy went on, "I have been accepted at West Point Military Academy. My future for the next nine years. Four years at the Academy and a five-year service requirement upon graduation. Nine total years. I will at graduation hold a Bachelor of Science degree in my major, which I'm not sure of yet. My education will be paid for by the department of the Army, except for uniforms, textbooks and computer which will come out of my annual salary I will receive. I will be commissioned a 2nd Lieutenant in the Army. I will be playing, for my athletic requirement, football my four years there. I am excited to again being with Eddie Brandon. You know him from York last year as our quarterback. It will be a great reunion. He is one of my closest friends. We have been developing a plan, a strategy to play as a team unit. My goal is that one of us be nominated or win the Heisman trophy. We are planning a pattern after the famous tandem football stars of Army yester-year by the name of Blanchard and Davis, though they were running back stars. Anyway, that's my plan for the next four plus years and an Army life for a time after graduation. I think I could do well and advance rank through the years.

It isn't a safe civilian job, but a necessary one. Someone has to do it. I wanted you to know all this for your information. My life will be different from your traditional college style and homestyle work ethics. There may be lots of travel necessary to the job. Maybe tours of duty involved that I would be trained for. These would be possible dangerous times.

Somewhere during all this I hope you would be in the midst. You are very special to me. I just want you to know these things before our lives go crazy and we are apart. I feel like you're my girl and I'm your guy. I hope I have it right! I do love you. I have or love no other." Billy finished his daring soliloquy with Anita. Anita had been listening quietly and patiently and attentively with her eyes on him. She had not ever heard him wax poetic such as this. She was rather transfixed and unsure of how she should react or respond, but she tried.

"Billy," she said, "That was quite a spiel you shared with me. You know how much I like you, even love you, and I thank you for sharing all this with me. Indeed, it does give me 'meat' to chew on about our relationship – now and over the near future. I think I'm going to need time to do just that. I don't have any answers now about anything, but I know where you stand and with me. Again, I thank you for taking the time to share all this with me. Oh, here comes our breakfast. Let's eat while it's warm and give me time to think."

"Yeah," said Billy, "I'm famished. I'll say a short prayer." "Dear Lord, thank you for our lives. Thank you for putting us together that we can be with each other and share. Thank you for the love of life and for this food we are about to eat. In Jesus name. Amen"

They both looked up, took their forks and dug in. It tasted delicious, and they were certainly enjoying each other, sitting opposite at the table, thanks be to old Dad. It would all be related to him later, and much to his enjoyment. Billy was a good son.

The lunch eating was voraciously taken in and it was gone shortly. The energy levels that day and with Billy's talking, developed a hunger feast par excellence. They were surprised how little they talked and how much they ate. It all was very filling and good.

Finally, they were almost through and Anita said, "I've already stated I'm going to need to take some time to chew on all this you've told me. I really feel close to you, having you share with me as you do. I like and appreciate your communicating with me. I respond to that. So, have patience with me in getting back to you on this one. There is a lot there to think about."

"Well," said Billy, "Let me get our bill and then we can get out of here. I'm sure you have other things to do later. I thank you for listening to me so attentively. You are so easy on my eyes and I love to hear your voice and such a wonderful laugh."

As they got up after taking care of the bill. Billy lifted her chair back, as she got up, he gave her a big hug. Anita enjoyed that, always did when he hugged her. He was a big fuzzy bear – that image she liked. She liked big fuzzy bears named Billy.

As they ambled to the car, they both chit-chatted with themselves and did a lot of laughing. It was time to lighten up a little, as Billy's dissertation of his future was somewhat dismal to Anita. He would be gone from her, especially in everyday proximity. She needed to gather herself together in a quiet space and wrestle with her emotions over his news.

A career military man. She didn't know about that. Where did she fit in? Why, what were her future thoughts and desires and destiny? Certainly, Billy was her special guy friend. But how would it all weave its way forward? How serious was Billy about her? There were many questions. She needed some space and time to assess her life now, and its future. She was only 17, going on 18 soon. So was Billy.

Anita drove Billy home where Billy said to her, "Can you come in to say hello to Mom and Dad for a moment?" She replied, "Sure, I'd love to, but I need to get home myself. Just a few minutes, OK?" "Yes, that'd be great. They'd love to see you. They really like you a lot," replied Billy.

Billy and Anita headed for the door. As Billy opened it and let her enter. He hollered for his folks, who were in the kitchen at the time. They proceeded to where they were, and Anita hugged his mom and his dad. His dad had a great big grin, likewise his mom. They all sat down. Billy said to his folks, "Anita has to get home, but she wanted to say 'hello' for a minute or two."

Anita broke in saying, "I want to thank you for allowing us to have such a wonderful feast this lunch hour. Your son has given me a lot to dwell on about his future. You and I will soon be knowing him from a distance. It won't be easy. West Point and a career will be a long way from here. We will have to keep in touch often. It's going to take me much assessment of where this is all going versus my life and where it's going. There are a lot of 'If's' involved and 'I don't know's.' We have half a year left of high school Hopefully Billy and I can get it all worked out. Much can change in six months. I'm getting to not like change." Everybody laughed over that agreed statement.

Anita got up after her short visit. Again, thanked them and hugged them and started to the door with Billy. Billy thanked her for taking time to be with him and his folks and gave her a big fuzzy hug and a kiss and said he'd see her tomorrow at school. She departed to her car and to home. That surprise kiss would linger.

CHAPTER FORTY-FIVE

As Anita entered her home, she found that her brother, Nathan, was there sitting and talking with her parents. She came up to them greeting and saying "I'm calling a family council meeting here and now. It's very important to me. Are you all in for a while?"

They all looked at each other, and Dad said, "We were just sitting and talking. We are here for you now." Dad took charge.

Anita stated, "Thank you family, I need your dialogue and feedback on what I am going to tell you. First of all, I am not pregnant. Now that you are calm (getting laughter from her family) here's the spiel."

I'm glad you're all here to help me sort out a future scenario I see as perplexing and confusing. I think I need to be making a decision or pre-decision. As you all know, I have an ongoing relationship with Billy Brewer. We are more or less high school sweethearts. Neither of us has dated others and we are for the balance, a couple in love, we are fond of each other and I think sometime in the future might make a team together, might someday marry. I'm speculating here, based on my feelings and upon my sense of his unknown feelings or desires. I have not asked him about these future things or feelings he has. I don't think he knows those feelings at this time. It probably is premature speculating about these things, but I need to respond to Billy about his talking to me earlier about his near future life stuff.

Dad broke in asking, "what kind of 'stuff' did he talk about?"

Anita hesitated then spoke again, "Well, the gist of it all, he's going to West Point Military Academy for four years, then he's hooked into another five years payback duty and serving in the military. After that I and he have absolutely no idea. I have no idea where or what active duty he will perform, nor does he at this time."

"I think you can see my dilemma somewhat, and my concerns for me. He is committed to this pathway, his tuition is paid for by the government and he wants to play football for West Point along with Eddie Brandon, York last year's star quarterback, who is already attending there. They have some sort of plan to becoming the daring duo, Heisman trophy talk stuff. I have no idea what or who that is. Something about returning Army to football prominence. Billy, I think has high expectations and achievement in and for himself. I personally think he has greatness in him and will someday become that attribute." Anita stopped speaking and waited to hear her family's reaction.

Mom and Dad looked at each other as did her brother. They talked among themselves for a good ten minutes or so. Anita kept quiet while listening. It was an important moment for her, and she felt she needed their help. They were family, a tight-knit one at that. A good verbal Italian family.

The family quieted down, and Dad spoke up, "It's obvious to us that Billy has a lot going on in his life. We are concerned about and for you. It is also obvious you two are a fine couple of kids in the throes of maturing years. Indeed, the both of you are single with no specific attachments other than strong feelings for each other. There is assumption you two will continue a strong relationship at best. Other than that, there seems to be no agreements or contracts or promises. Therefore, it is our outlook that you two need to proceed with independent ways of direction, giving way to some space for time to develop both pathways for your own lives. If you two are meant for each other, God will cement the deal in His time. You both need to be making decisions as individuals for yourselves and not tying them to whims or decisions of the other. You may just have to pare down emotional heavy ties to each other in order to function in a balanced and healthful future way.

This I think is the crux of our talking among ourselves. I hope it somehow helps you in your thinking and decision making. Just know we love you very much – all of us, and don't want you hurt!"

Anita responded, "Thank you all, I think you've given me enough thought content to mull over and chew on for a while.

Any opinions from my family I know are sincere and with loving care. That's the way we are. It's wonderful."

Anita left the room and departed to her bedroom to think while lying down. It would be a time shared with the "Lord" of her life, Jesus. She needed him in on all of this. "Oh, Holy Spirit, come help and lead me in my thinking," she softly said as a prayer. She entered her private bedroom sanctuary and lied down. Her energy and emotions were thin at the moment. She might just fall asleep. As her head hit the pillow, indeed she became her thought and the lights went out. It would be the Holy Spirit's time to indwell. Monday arrived, the birds were chirping, the robins were searching for worms, and the big daddy crows were chiming out orders to whomever would listen. Anita awoke, got dressed and headed for the bus at the corner. She had two Krispy Kreme donuts with her and her lunch for the day. She'd take two bites and lick the frosting off her fingers. It was really good.

Billy was essentially doing the same thing without the Krispy Kreme's. He'd gotten up early enough to fix himself breakfast of eggs and toast, juice and vitamins.

They both arrived the same time at school and had a few minutes to chat, then went directly to their classrooms. She said to Billy, that she'd been chewing hard on all he had spoken to her about, and that she'd have a reply to that in the next few days. All Billy could say was "OK" to that, he'd have to wait. They heard the bell call everyone to class, so they departed different directions. They were both busy throughout the day, and he had basketball practice after hours and she had cheerleading activities. For each this would be the last athletic participation round up at the York High School for the both of them. It would be academics only the year out, another four months ahead then graduation.

The both of them had felt the loss that would be of the familiar high school repetition every day, the busyness, and fun of all the fellowships, teachers. They would be fading away and they would be starting at newness in life. It would be different. They would be growing up and away from home, at least some of them.

Some looked forward to it, others not so much, or even hated the change expected. Each senior was at this time still in "limbo" but actively busy with finishing studies and waiting and planning for the future to show up. Any slowing down for a 17-year-old senior, used to going all the time, was not normal. There was a certain suffering and painful aire that touched seniors parting way used to for 17 years at York schools. They would be on their own, taking care of themselves out from under the watchful eye and from under the roof and care of home. New life was drawing into reality and life of its own. It was a bit scary.

Billy's academics were perking along in high gear. His 3 AP courses, he thought, were not only tough, but fun. He was making "A's" in them as were his grade levels in his other courses.

Anita was doing really well grade-wise herself. He had heard she was going to get the Frances Hunter Art Award for artistic talent at graduation. She was an accomplished artist for her age. She had a real talent for drawing and painting. For her work of on canvas painting of "Cheerleaders in various forms of acrobatics." She was a "gold star" artist winner for talented high school art students. She said she wanted to donate her painting piece to the York Athletic Department upon graduation. This accolade and accomplishment came to past in her dossier given at her time of graduation.

She had a 3.8 grade point average, an A- total. She decided upon attending the University of Illinois Art and Graphic Design School in Champaign, Illinois, a four-year complete arts professional training school program. She was tickled that she had been accepted, as was her whole family.

She called Billy to tell him and he too, was thrilled to hear it and happy for her. It was a peg in her puzzle of what she was going to do while he was away at West Point and other places. A certain lessening of tension set in with her as she received notification of her acceptance.

She felt relieved that she now felt a certain breathing space in her life over the next four years. The program even had a special year to go to Paris for special painting tutorials and training. She looked forward to that. She was again happy and thankful to God for his "weaving His wonders" in her behalf. She was delighted Billy was so pleased for her. Their romance attachment would just have to wait in the wings – floating along, until God moved to unite them – well she hoped so – she still believed Billy was her future husband to be. If you asked Billy about that, he would have said "There is no one else. Anita will be my bride someday."

Included in the Art School package acceptance letter was a bunch of classes she would be taking over the years of studying. Options and programs like the overseas in Paris. She perused the part list of classes available like drawing, painting, sculpture, digital photography, design thinking, intro to Web technologies, methods of teaching and art teaching, even printmaking. She licked her "chops" at all the opportunities she saw before her. She was getting excited to be heading off to college after seeing her future in new light. She was pleased.

So, when it was, Anita got back on track with Billy to reply, the reply she had put off, she was now more comfortable and assured in herself. Billy faced her as they sat in her folk's garden room to talk. There she explained her delay and frustrations of hearing all Billy was going to do for the next four years and his onward filling out his government contract beyond that. She now knew and had a life before her of art learning for the next four years. Certainly, it would keep her busy pretty much full-time. She'd be able to pal around with Penny at the U of I on occasion and they could commiserate about their boyfriends off at war-er-football camp at West Point.

CHAPTER FORTY-SIX

Things now began to mold together for the both of them. Things that were potential roadblocks in their relationship faded away with the solving of sorts of Anita's frustration level about what was she going to do when Billy was so long gone to West Point, much less thereafter. The four-year time problem of much loneliness due to separation, suddenly lessened with her acceptance at the University of Illinois Arts and Design School. This would fill her time with something she loved and wanted to do. It also made her feel not guilty, having to make a choice to do the art thing had Billy been around more or gone elsewhere to school. It saved her from having to make a decision of hanging nearby and dating more or doing as she now was doing. Each would have their space and be guilty free to do their own thing. Under the circumstances it was the mature thinking that prevailed as certain uncertainties were cleared up.

Right now, high school was entering its last winter, a late snow storm moved across York, filling the streets, trees and rooftops with white fluffy glitter. It happened so fast, at such a rate, that the school system shut down for a day. Of course, the school kids made good use of the break sledding, snowboarding and pelting each other with snowballs. Everyone mostly hated winter, especially the long gray days. The cold and really windy days combinations were bad days for older folk, made it hard to breathe. A few lucky folk were already ensconced in Florida for escape time. But most everyone stood firm in York braving the storm and made the most of it.

No matter what the weather, Coach Hank Stillman had basketball practices with whomever could show up. The gymnasium was open. Billy would "hoof" it through the snow to York High and back. Heck, he was 17 and enjoyed the walk through the snow - many sidewalks having been plowed by "buster" the sidewalk-plower in his end of town. It was a neat little mini-dozer with rubber treads just the width of the sidewalk. It was a fascinating little machine.

When Billy arrived at the school gym, he went to his school locker for Varsity players and changed out into sweats and a varsity t-shirt, then headed upstairs to the gym. Mike had shown up also and was already practicing. They got together and played one-on-one just as they had so many times down in the park. They were both much alike in shooting abilities except for Billy's larger size they were pretty equal in talent. The coach gathered all those who were working out together and took them into his office to show them some film of last year's game with Jasper City. They had beaten them fairly well, but they had a supposedly good team coming against them again this year. Billy and Mike intensely watched those players who would be facing them in the game. They were returnees.

Coach Stillman pointed out some moves the Jasper players would give and had as typical play movements on their opponents. Billy and Mike noted what the coach was saying and stored them in their memory banks. Coach Stillman was good at doing and seeing those small nuances of the players and hopefully would be used against Jasper when they played them. Everything mattered, even the small stuff. This observation would define Billy's future and would stand him well many times in his lifetime. Little things add up to big mountains if not dealt with or recognized for what they were. Many times, it was the small things unrecognized that in review, would determine a future outcome. He would learn this more to the point during his experiences at West Point Academy. Such small things recognized in time, can save a life or lives. One can be trained to be observant but again one must retain and use such knowledge.

After viewing the films shown by the coach, they discussed the overall plan of execution for the Jasper City game that Friday night in the "Earl the Pearl" Montros gymnasium. Earl "The Pearl" Montros, was the famous NBA player, a guard, who made a name for himself for scoring a record number of points during his college career at the Winston-Salem State College, in Winston-Salem, NC. He was one of the few escaping the confines of York and making a name for himself, and York Illinois. If there was an athletic hall of fame of York, he would be prominently in it.

There was a statue of him in the lobby of the gymnasium along with the many trophies and awards in the school's trophy showcases. Everyone in the school knew of him, as each year a special video about his life and accomplishments would be shown in the school auditorium. Billy thought "good for him," he made it out of York, and left a legacy and many charitable doings in York. He eventually returned to live out his latter years in the Yorkshire Retirement Center and Community.

Billy and Mike were primed for the Jasper game and the Coach ran everybody hard that week in preparation. They were ready for the task when the opening whistle sounded Friday night at 7 o'clock.

It was a really hard-fought game. Both teams' defenses were very good, and the game wasn't in the big numbers. Billy and Mike upped the critical 3 pointers all night and Big Billy crashed the boards in rebounding plays. His size and weight were critical to making the difference as the final buzzer went off with York winning by 3 points.

Once again Anita was heard cheerleading her flashy crew of gals in their cute outfits. The crowd in York loved their antics and cheers and responded loudly to their bidding. York was most alive when its athletic events were going on. It was akin to having a professional sports team in town, only much cheaper, and actually probably more fun. Expenses were reasonable priced hot dogs, popcorn and Pepsi. No gum was allowed at athletic events – chew to your heart's desire – elsewhere. Everybody observed the request.

York fans were if anything, notoriously loud. They were well behaved overall but were a full power source of encouragement for their team and were sponsors of many York citizens spawned fan clubs. The York community was alive and well, Thank You! York was yet a big city – known as a small city-town, and now it was maturing and blossoming in good fertile soil. Good repercussions spiraled out from York and it was recently among the favored small cities in America, for families; a good school system, hospital, small symphony, good restaurants and a recent addition of a Krispy Kreme donut franchise, with seating. It became the early morning place to go. Mr. Vernon Rudolph, the founder, would be proud – also wealthier.

Winning the Jasper City game placed York in the first bracket of the playoffs. They went on to the finals but managed to fall short of winning the tournament. They took runner-up place. Mike and Billy carried the team in points scored and Billy led the conference in rebounds. They were able to outplay the Jasper City "Jays." It was close but for Jasper, no cigars, as they say. It indeed was a battle back and forth with the Jays taking advantage of planned play-making with two of their senior scorers sinking way too many. They were indeed good; the best York had played that year. If anybody deserved to win, they did.

Well the after-season playoff tournament was over, with York runner-up this year. It was now into early springtime and baseball season had already started its practice mode. Billy and Mike and Anita were finished with York athletics. It had been a great four years at York High School. It was time to give the finishing touches to academics.

After graduation it would be college time – a time for most. The academics had vastly improved at York over the last five years of planned programs under the progressive leadership of Perry Dunlop. The academic status quo was vastly raised as to quality across the board. Astute leadership was the key to it all, a highly regarded, talented, well-liked and appreciated man of integrity. The combination and attitude of his make-up and talent drove results favorably at York High School. Good things trended downward into the lower grades as quality tightened up and test scores rose. Colleges had taken notice and as a result more York kids were headed college bound. That in turn upgraded student motivation to greater heights and achievement levels which transpired into loftier jobs in the real marketplace.

Beyond that the community of York from its city government on down became more professional and the city more prosperous. From the city council to the state political representation and better qualified folks would run and then be voted in to serve the communities in their district. York in the

2015-16 was looking attractive as a place to live and settle in. Wage and job opportunities rose, and the community of York was feeling more prosperity than ever before.

Welfare as it had been, was almost non-existent – no more free-bees on the dole. Crime and laziness were greatly diminished as the police and fire department took on a new look of quality personnel, better pay. The standard of living numbers rose proportionately, and York no longer produces low rated bond issues. It was a small city on the move!

On May 28th, a Saturday, 2:00 pm rolled around. It was the senior year graduation time at York High School. Always a proud time for parents and faculty, at least most of them. It was a pleasant day to have an outdoor ceremony and the seniors were all gathered in their ceremonial robes and funny hats, which would become frisbees later.

The ceremony processed the senior class down to their seats in center front stage. The podium was off to the left of the class. Procession called for them to come up the right-hand side steps, cross the stage while to the Right was the faculty and to their right near the podium was Principal Perry Dunlop. Coach Mac McCarthy and Standley Steel, head of the Math and Computer Science field of studies. They would give out the diplomas for graduation at York High School.

The music department fell silent as the entire senior class sat down. All the seats were full that had been set out. Mom, Pops, relatives and friends all fell into witness of the senior graduates.

Mr. Dunlop, the principal, got up and approached the podium. He too, as was all the faculty, dressed in robes and special flat square hats with specific tassels hanging which denoted the education specialty of their chosen field of study.

"Welcome to graduation day. The Class of 2016 shall today matriculate on to greater achievements and experiences, many away from home. It shall be a new experience and exciting to all. Our school faculty, friends, families and community congratulate you all upon your hard-earned achievements here at York High School. You can be proud of yourselves. Good Job. So, without further wear and tear on your backside, we now present out the diplomas and special awards. Then immediately following the valedictorian of the class will say a few words on behalf of the senior class. And right after that will be the traditional "sailing of hats – a flat out fun experience – guests beware!"

A silent few minutes passed as all the presenters adjusted themselves and their notes and diplomas assisted by the honor students of the 11th grade. That was a nice touch.

Presenting honors was done by Principal Perry Dunlop, as Coach Mac read the senior class graduates' names. To the side of the graduates were the local media with Stan Zielinski again on the job. He had his program and pad ready to jot notes. All the graduates were listed alphabetically and after their listing were noted special awards and list of athletic and academic special awards.

Billy Brewer, aka William Joseph Brewer, was called to the stage. Coach Mac McCarthy started off by mentioning that Billy was top student in his class with a 4.0 grade point average. He said, "Most everybody knows your story and we are all most proud of your accomplishments. You are Valedictorian of your class. Also, for your outstanding athletic achievements and accomplishment in both football and basketball, two sports played four years here at York High School, you have earned the "Nathan Swift Athletic Excellence Award" for your four-year contribution to York High School's Athletic programs. It is an award for participation of excellence and for personal character quality.

The dispensers of the diplomas and awards presented Billy with these awards, to the applause of the entire audience, one felt the empathy of the awards as they were given. The community seemed to love Billy. He was kind of a local hero, well liked, admired and they were thankful for his athletic endeavors and efforts. He gave an appreciative slight bow as he left stage and went to sit down, slightly embarrassed.

When Mike Chandler received his diploma and comments, stating he was to attend Notre Dame University on a football scholarship, Billy raised and pumped his fist in the air shouting, "Woo, woo!!" Mike got a rousing hand from all.

Anita, the exciting and well-known head cheerleader, who AKA was Anita Anne Cantina, a good looking, pretty, peppy

Italian gal. She claimed also high academic achievement and the Frances Hunter Art Award for Outstanding Artistic Talent and Excellence. "The School accepts and thanks you for your donation to the Athletic Department of your beautiful painting you call, 'Cheerleaders in various forms of acrobatics.'" It is also a state sponsored "Gold Star Artist Award" painting. Again, our thanks and congratulations for your contribution to York High School."

After all graduates of the Class of 2016 were presented diplomas, it was time for the graduation commencement Valedictorian mini-speech.

It was announced and written in the commencement program that "Wm. 'Billy' Joseph Brewer" was the Valedictorian recipient that year. It was his honor to give the class final senior year speech.

As tall, handsome, big "Billy" Brewer stood before his classmates, the school, parents, teachers and guests, he looked over all that were assembled there. He had never done anything like this before. He was a little intimidated but that receded quickly as he got into his short speech.

"Fellow classmates, teachers all, parents, guests all, I humbly stand before you in awe of all you have done for me, my classmates, over my years at York High.

"From my shaky beginnings of truancy attendance to my miraculous finish here at graduation of York High School. Nobody is more surprised than I to be standing here – not in my wildest dreams. It has been hard work, great mentoring, tons of help, and determination of the will to complete all the requirements and courses, for this our graduation time. I am most proud of my classmates, they have worked very hard to be here today. They are great and fine young people on the move towards bettering their lives and the lives of those around them. The world and York will be a better place because of them.

"It has been an amazing and rewarding time here these last few years, especially back-to-back championship titles, winning basketball teams and teachers who did make a difference, who cared for our benefit. These people make York High School what it is today – quality one."

"Personally, for me, I specifically want to thank Mr. William Steel, Coach "Mac," and my 3 Amigo friends, my parents for their continued support, and specific interest in investing their talents and time my way. I have benefitted a literal "ton" from their helping me become what I am today. I just would not be who or where I am without these very fine folks. I thank you with all my heart."

To my fellow classmates a hearty "Ya-hoo, we did it! (Applause and great noise) SALUTE!!"

The house came down with caps flying every which way as the school band struck up the fight song. Perry Dunlop came forward to the mic and said into it, "Graduation's over. Class dismissed. Good Luck." Everyone stood up and commenced chatting with anyone around them. The air and mood were extremely lively and happy. The whole world at the moment seemed peaceful.

Everyone filed out of the ceremonies area and dispersed. Many groups formed and prepared to go somewhere to eat or go home. It had been a most successful day. It couldn't get any better.

A gathering surround Billy and his family; His amigo friends and girlfriend all headed for a sumptuous lunch at "Harvey's Hash House." There they would sit and reminisce over the last year's lamenting the time when Billy and others would be off to college or wherever. Times familiar would become times unfamiliar. Young people would become young men and women. Parents many, would become empty nesters, alone with spouse and households would become empty canyons of silence. New times, new world, different lifestyles and adjustments. One last summer of attachment and closeness before children go off and become young adults, some far away. It was a long tradition in American life and preparation towards becoming ready to face the world on their own. They raised up and headed out!

Billy would have to be at West Point Academy mid-summer for football orientation, the Academy orientation. Thank God, his friend Eddie would be there and help him orient himself to the task of facing up in a new place, a strange land. It would not be easy. But as Billy came to realize all this past, training, education, lifestyle and hard work would be a blessing towards sustaining him and his new life choices at West Point Academy. The Academy life would be tough, but

So was he – in spades!

BOOK 2

CHAPTER ONE

June 6th came around, Billy was now 18. He was closing in on 250 pounds on a body big John was proud of. At 6' 6" tall his framework was rather impressive and intimidating. He no longer showed the signs of youth but of a young man blossoming into young, very strong adulthood. He didn't appear the young high school athlete and student. His features and body were maturing differently, and his demeanor was changing to a more mature and formidable nature.

Billy continued to maintain his work ethic of body building and training, still under the watchful beaming eyes of his mentors, Dave, Heavy Lou and Big John. They were thrilled with what they had invested in and turned out. He was as the expression goes, "Somethin' else!" Amazing. They loved him and he them, always will. A solid admiration society.

Billy and Anita hung together as much as they could that busy summer. At the pool, hiking, eating and just talking under a shade tree somewhere. They needed to talk, talk out their feelings of upcoming separation from each other and their future as individuals and career building future. It would be different difficult and in need of careful attending to each other's needs through the highways and by-ways of modern communications. It would be their lifeblood survival of connectedness, an umbilical cord, if you will. They put in the effort on the front side of their future life ahead. It would suffice to help cement the bonding necessary for the two of them to endure. Plenty of talk, and understanding, empathy and young love energy released to satisfy questions and an appetite for their future.

It was a time together they needed. It was a time well spent considering the moving picture before them. It would be a long commitment for Billy, maybe even longer for Anita in her role of the stay at home framework. Though each would be separately very busy, they would be literally hundreds of miles apart. Four years' worth of Illinois to New York distance and few time-offs from their workloads.

Both Anita and Billy were very excited with their personal prospects and near-term college level times for their lives. She was very excited about her scholarship to the University of Illinois Art School and for the opportunity to learn and grow in the world as an artist and craftsman. This upped her self-esteem level considerably with her college acceptance and curriculum ahead the next four years. She would be sacrificing, missing, dear friends and family for increasing her competency and experiences in the world of the arts. She would turn her activity of cheerleading into private times of fitness whenever and wherever she would go. Plus, she would consider maybe some singing parts in local theatre productions in need of such talent. She was a bundle of energy and talent molded into the likeness of being part of Billy's destiny. They both knew and felt God's touch on their lives for each other and were now making preliminary plans on a togetherness basis. Both expressed no desire for any other person, nor desired to be free to look further. Their heads were turned to each other and there was a determination to have a coordinated plan, as much as possible, which would stay the course, for them, forever. They were in love, at least it surely looked that way.

Both parents were brought into the loop as to the two of them and their plans, hopes and feelings. It happened one Sunday for lunch after church service. It took place at Anita's home out on a patio where the summer flowers were blooming, and the greenery showing brightly across the landscape.

Billy and Anita in agreement spelled out for them all the plans that they personally had made, individually and collectively. There was no talk of marriage at this time or place. There was an assumption of marriage for their future, but nothing definite in the plans for the immediate future.

Both families seemed to have enjoyed the company of the other and nary a disparaging word was cast. That was a "big" mountain to be conquered in their estimation. And, both sighed with a sigh of relief when they were together after the families parted company that day. Their general plans and future living them out were now pending. Any adjustments along the way were jointly thought out. These talks held contact like for the next four years and were subject to renegotiation after that.

Included in these plans would take in Army assignments for duty or active duty upon Billy's completion of training at West Point. He would only know then any assignments he would get. Anita had no ideas just what phase she could see her way in fulfilling and pursuing her future at that time. Decisions for both were pending other inputs at those times and places.

Billy and Anita themselves parted company for the day until further desire or development was necessary. Things were progressing as summer was ending. Billy had to be off early to West Point for football pre-season practice. It was necessary to him and his desire to be prepared for whatever was forthcoming in his life. He had seen the benefit it was to others and likewise in his short-lived years.

Anita was much like Billy in so many ways, just a cute, feminine counterpart, smart, determined and assertive. She adored Billy with great respect and admiration. He was a giant of a gentleman, smart-talented and had a (Christlike) spirit about him that greatly attracted her. He knew his physical strength and the strengths of his personal attributes. He was pretty well in charge of his overall personality and in control. His assessment of his total self was realistic and intact. Manhood was pursuing him with an ever-increasing passion, as his life seemed to swiftly move forward.

Billy felt confidence and preparedness in his present status and that life so far, was totally a rewarding experience gifted to him by his Creator. He knew it was, and he thanked the "Good Lord" often for all his blessings. He determined to stick with God and His Grace. Other ways were temptations gone askew with repercussions awaiting ignition if taken. Good choices were high on his list of achievements.

Achievements were always relegated to those things of the past. One was able to look back and determine if one's choices were a positive or a negative thing. An overview of Billy's life gave him a good score on having made good choices along his way. Good solid trustworthy friends were definitely assets in one's life. Sometimes a committee of several heads were better than one. The equation always eventually came down to one person having to make a choice and decision. He was the one accountable, so he tried to weigh his choices wisely.

Upbringing, training, responsibility, experience and discipline all helped him to make quality decisions in a hellbent world. Billy's life got turned around by angels in disguise in God's hands, this his feelings of being blessed so much, and thankfulness. All of these qualities plus an established work ethic stood him well thus far in a world so dysfunctional.

Men of principle and honesty, trustworthiness and discipline were hard to come by in this age of corruption in about every facet of life. The societal sanctimonious approval and tolerance for everything in the name of political correctness was torpedoing the world all over. It's influence generating subversion of the mind and reason in deeds and speech and was tolerated by all at the gunpoint and in the name of evil doers spreading their diseased laden propaganda. The backbone of the establishment was already weakened and collapsing under the influences of the wicked and cunning. The worlds underpinnings were definitely coming loose.

The 3 Amigos were strong proponents of positive thoughts and actions. Strong for America, for individual rights and good choices. These things took strong and courageous backbones to produce. Blackness was moving its shadow across earth.

In simplistic terms Satan's forces were seemingly winning. After all, he hated and was jealous of God and wanted to be him. So, he is hellbent to destroy anything God has produced or touched. Obviously, he still reigns, but is on a short leash in which he will become null and void, in God's timing.

Most people see the world in two dimensions "me and them," and it always will be that way. Unfortunately, corruption of all nations and society has evolved and increased and it has become hard to escape its jagged long tentacles with its stingers at the ends.

This was a world Billy and Anita had before them in real life. It was and would not be pleasant always to live in. Their bonding was a grace God had opportuned them to become a positive force in His hands. Only God was able to raise up people of His choosing to stand up and be counted for Him. If God be for you, who shall be against you? Only an Evil empire, that who or what! Satan the evil perpetrator world-wide in scope.

Most people didn't see earth in that way, they were too in the middle of it all. Their eyes and hearts were dulled and oblivious to the bloodshed going on around them and when they did recognize it, it was then too late, and overpowering to dig out! People tend to be ostriches rather than lion kings. Snakes need to meet pest control folks, exterminators, with strong backbone and fortitude.

Billy and Anita were coming into this world of chaos and there were at first sight too many weeds in God's garden. York seemed to be producing the aire of what change can do for people. It was comforting and essential that people take matters into their own hands and take back what the "Evil One" had tried to take away. It is never easy, but when the heart gets right, righteous things can begin to happen and once again "Good choices" can prevail into positive actions for the betterment of all. ON the flipside, if good men do nothing, nothing changes to "worselley." That's called "apathy" or "spaghetti spine."

Billy and Anita assessed their strengths and concluded that as a team they would survive together rather than so called "hang separately."

CHAPTER TWO

Anita and Billy were maturing in to the fulness of young adults. They were not blind to the world, though they could not understand it all. Who could? From the president through the pillars of wisdom, the Congress, they too hadn't much of a clue as to understanding and certainly had few solutions for most any business coming their way. There was so much partisan politics the decision log jams were enormously piled high. They tripped over each other on the way to cross a bridge to nowhere. They all waxed poetic, in saying the problem was the other party's fault. While many's the time the log jam was in their own party.

Nobody ever heard of common sense or negotiating out a mutual solution. The president and congress were dancing a different dance to different music and were entirely out of hand and most dysfunctional.

Where were the statesmen; where was some backbone; where were the real patriots proclaiming American goodness and greatness. Words were words and had no meaning. Lines in the sand were meaningless and invisible. The government was evading its responsibilities and oaths of allegiance. Money talks, and money flew out the coffers like feather s in a wind storm. We the people were operating our precious blood secured land with a shadow government full of wimps. A gutless class of politicians trampling on the constitution, breaking laws, their own, and Gods. Laws were stacked so high congressional bills so long, nobody would read them. "Just pass them, read them later. Everything is fine." Right!? Fine is not a good word, it is next to meaningless as to its definition, vague at best.

This was the world Anita and Billy were living in and the direction it would continue to go if not for some drastic patriotic and courageous measures being taken. It would take a younger, fed up, educated and common-sense courageous generation to reform, to instigate and install, what America needed, action and a big slice of common sense.

America was currently headed for its brand of socialism which evolves into communism which eventuates into dictatorship of some form, where one loudmouth along with his "yes" men, tell everybody else what to do, say or think. Who pays for what. They establish a blood sucking tax code even more stringent than it already is.

If we are already now far overloaded in laws, more will be better? Common sense says however enforce the ones already on the books and amend and update the ones too antiquated for today's society purposes.

These scenarios and problems would be the issues cogent to Billy's and Anita's life time before they would be challenged to the fullest between societal desires for the country and the status quo of the present ineptitudes in charge. Government needed to step aside, across the board, and let the will of the people pay homage to and for a new America. A land of opportunity and freedom. The present outlook was not the America "shining on a hill" image. That would return one day If, much action and reform by both sides of the aisle would dare to exercise the will of the people and return government to its true rightful place and purposes. Negotiate in the name of America. Government of the USA are not a self-serving group of elitists, but in fact are voted representatives of the people and for the people. These are not privileged lawmakers who live by separate laws from those they represent. Those selfishly sown laws for themselves need to be undone and make all representatives of Congress subject to all the same laws that you and I and Joe Public live by every day. Laws cover everyone equally.

"Words to live by" was an article and column being featured in the "patter chatter" feature column. The Editor-in-chief and owner Carl T. Anderson was writing it. In it was featured politics, the lack of good politics and extensive poor-quality of present-day likeness of it. Clips and passages were devoured by its York avid readers. It was a sold-out weekly produced rag, except in-play off times of York High School when abbreviated extra issues were printed. These days York seemed to be alive with news and views. The paper was expanding its personnel and circulation coverage. People were being hired. York was growing as well as prospering. It was, after all, an award small city enclave of happy citizens It was a showcase of active change for the better example of town-city. York was growing up, maturing into a new modern form and creation of an "enlightened" small city in America.

Billy and Anita were now in the forefront of a new generation that was sick and tired of the way things were done, and witnessing current changes being instituted one by one injecting new life into the dead and corrupted "Status quo" of their city. Everybody in York could feel the change. They were now headed off to college with this early establishment for change biting at their heels and pushing them with opportunity and new future life, giving reason to grow and learn and return good for evil by becoming more educated and able to help fully become new leaders in the world around them. They knew they would be challenged and that they had a good solid education from teachers that cared for them and were aware of the needs for the future generation. They were prepared as the best the high schools of public schools in America could be.

Money could add bells and whistles to a school's curriculum, but the real difference was the quality and personal interest of the teachers that taught. Caring not just in a job, edged the difference. Anita, Billy, Eddy and Penny and others of their two classes were the graduates that received the benefits of the "New" York school system academic and sports programs. They were outstanding because of people who cared to make a difference. They would now be on their own, she at the University of Illinois School of Art at Champaign, Illinois, and he would be at West Point Military Academy in New York state. They had their bags and things packed, ready to go. It would be different, it would be challenging. They hoped it would also be fun. New friends would be forthcoming and that would be a new experience in a new location.

They would be in a home away from home, seemingly a long way from Mom and Dad and all that was so familiar for so long. New life, new place, new people and friends and a new level of educational challenges. They were moving up, it was called growing up in to the adult world. It was a bit scary underneath it all.

They knew they were ready, but certain uncertainty existed. They would greatly miss their many friends at York, and mostly their boy- or girlfriend so special. Indeed, they would have to be vigilant in keeping in touch, the invention of the computer and instant email would a blessing as well as texting and tweeting all instant communications. It will afford a certain comfort zone that letter writing delayed.

However, to those that can remember such communication, how letter writing was treasured as keepsakes, especially if perfumed, for years after love letters were kept for years. Much was to be pondered about. Life was about to bloom.

CHAPTER THREE

Billy arrived at West Point Academy with minimum clothing and things. Anita arrived with maximum things of hers, as she was a new co-ed on campus, and had been assigned to a dorm room with another roommate, a typical two roommate setup. Two beds, two desks, two dressers and a central ceiling light and two desk lamps. It was a sparse but enough for two 18-year-old girls.

Billy was ushered into a military, dark, stone-facade hall and into his dorm room. He too, had similar amenities in the room as Anita. Both had another roommate of similar status, in this case, another "plebe" cadet.

Indeed, they were the lowest of cadets, something so low that if they floated down a river on a dime, their feet wouldn't get wet dragging off it. "Well, thought Billy, this will change, and I'll start with football. He knew not just how much his words would become truth. He and Eddie would put their plan together, after all that's why he was mostly there. His work ethic, dogged determination to do well, and his past training, discipline and accomplishment would kick in as positive ammunition for success. He would opportune his time and effort to make the most of his new lifestyle and it would be very different.

Penny Hunter, Eddy's girlfriend, had settled out her new quarters at the Chi Omega Sorority house and found her way across campus to look up her old friend Anita in her new place of residence called Baily Hall.

As she found the hall, she entered in and asked some lady where Anita's room was. She said, "Upstairs on the right." So, she made her way up there, only to find Anita busy putting her things away and in place. She was the only one in there at the time. Anita looked up as Penny entered her room and let out a big scream of joy and rushed to her and put a big hug on her. "Penny!" "Anita!" They hugged a long moment and let their long-time friendship sink in. Both relaxed and laughed with excitement in their renewing friendship. Things were going to be alright. They had found each other. New relationship would grow and blossom. The seed that had been planted at York, and now renewed, would begin a close friendship for life.

Billy quickly settled the few things he had brought and talked with his new roommate who also he found out, was part of the Freshman football program. They would become good friends and teammates. He was recruited as a center position on the freshman cadet team. They both found out they were in the "Jock" plebe cadet hall, all 22 of them.

New plebe cadets, ripe for the pick by the other more senior cadets. Billy introduced himself as Billy Brewer, from York, Illinois. His roommate shook his hand and said he was Frank Consolo from Beaver Falls, Pennsylvania.

They both took a break in settling their things into the room and went to the Pepsi machine in the hall, plunked in some change and headed back to their room. They sat down in their desk chairs to talk. They both thumb-sketched their past lives and talked about why they came to West Point and football. It was new to the both of them, but each felt a certain togetherness and friendship that would help sustain them through West Point. It was a togetherness and one for another support system so much taught at West Point. Besides the concept of "Follow Orders" having each other's back would closely follow protocol for cadets and Army regulars.

At 5:00 pm that evening, Billy's first day on campus, was a called meeting for all the new freshmen "plebe" cadets to hear what their typical day would be like, which would actually take place and start the third day on campus. Two days were for orientation and familiarity of campus, facilities and amenities.

At 5:00 pm a bell sounded, time to have already gotten to the assembly room in the form for instruction and orders. Promptly as "plebes," and new on campus, everyone assembled and took their place.

Once all were seated, an Army regular, staff sergeant, James Mallory introduced himself and said, "Good evening. Know you all have been busy settling in. You haven't seen anything yet like the busyness that the days ahead will be. In three days, all of you will be in complete uniform and every day thereafter. You are no longer a civilian, you are "Corp," and subject to its protocol here at West Point Army Military Academy.

"As you probably know, West Point is one of the most selective colleges in the country. Also, as you know, its applicants need to have a nomination from a member of Congress. We take our recruiting seriously. West Point was founded in 1802 and is the oldest service academy in the nation. We sit on a huge piece of property on the Hudson River in upstate New York State. Every student here, receives a free education plus a small salary, along with a requirement after graduation to serve your country for five years, and three years subsequent in an inactive reserve status capacity. It is your business of protecting the entire confines and people, of the United States of America. You will be trained by the finest and become a soldier in the finest Army in the world.

"To those here in Athletic capacities, we the "Black Knights" compete in the NCAA division of the Patriot league. Our main goal is to beat Navy, Airforce and Notre Dame, if we play them.

"When you leave and graduate from the Academy, you will possess a Bachelor of Science degree and a commission in the US Army. You will be a leader of character, committed to the values of honor, duty and country. Your education will be one of excellence, professional, ready for service as an officer of the United States Army.

"We early on want to inform you of our honor code, which is that a "cadet" will not lie, cheat, steal or tolerate those who do. We base Cadet's leadership experience on a development of all three pillars of performance, academics, physical, and military.

Most graduates will receive a commission as a Second Lieutenant.

"Today I will give you a run through of a day and life of daily life here.

West Point Academy typically gets going at 6:00 am.
At 6:40 am is formation on Thursday and Friday are block schedules of 70 minutes.

Each Plebe's schedule is different. They vary on class and extra-curricular/corps squad activities scheduled.
The weekly schedule looks something like this:
0500 – 0615 Wake up time
0650 – Breakfast formation
0700 – Breakfast
0730 – Classes begin, units of 55 minutes with 15-minute break between them.
1205 – Lunch formation/Lunch
1250 – Deans hour. It may be free time to study or get ready for other classes or mandatory meetings or briefings to attend.
1355 – 1600 Classes
1610 – 1800 Company athletics, drill, study, workout time/unit training. This varies with the time of the year or week's activities.
1800 – 1930 Duties and dinner. Dinners are mandatory for plebes on Mondays, Wednesdays and Thursdays. Duties consist of delivering laundry.
1930 – 2130 Evening study period, mandatory study for academic courses.
2130 – 2330 Perform duties, clean rooms and free time.
2330 Taps and bed.

"Weekends are more relaxed in what you get to do. Usually these would include doing small errands, doing duties, going on details, and of course, for you all, memorizing "plebe" knowledge."

"Let me see here, a few miscellaneous tidbits. Main sports programs such as football generally start around 5:00 pm for practice. You are not exempt from our prescribed sports and athletic participations, except those during the times expected on your participation. Athletes are spread among the campus not retained in special dorms, except for the football team this year. You will choose your majors in the fall of Sophomore year. All cadets take the same curriculum until Junior year.

"We encourage connections between classes when appropriate. Oh, yes, your first vacation is a week at Christmas time, so plan ahead. So, if there are any questions, I remind you starting the day after tomorrow we officially get the year started and uniforms are mandatory. Give it your best and you will receive the best training in the world.

"DISMISSED."

Well, Billy and all the "plebes" took a deep breath and exhaled all. He was a now officially ensconced in the US Army official officer training facility. He left the area hall and traipsed back to his room along with Frank, his roommate. Thank God he wasn't alone. They both retreated to their room in "Patton Hall."

They sat down, talked for a few minutes then moved to their beds to cool-out and catch a nap. Frank wrote up on a blank paper "DO NOT DISTURB" and taped it on the front of their hall door. They were an intimidating twosome should someone other than an Army Reg bust through the door. With Frank at 6'2", 265 lbs. and Billy at 6'6", 260 lbs. They at first glance would send anybody packing quickly. They agreed to take an hour rest. Their beds weren't made but they pulled up the Army issued blankets supplied them and fell asleep.

CHAPTER FOUR

Billy's family was finding the home front lonesome without their son there. All the busyness had gone out, his room quiet with no life. Billy was their only child and they didn't even have a dog around. Mr. Brewer suggested that maybe they should get one. Mrs. Brewer suggested they think about it. After all, they were gone all day working. They agreed. Mr. Brewer turned on his computer email to see if any incoming word from their son had yet been written. None yet. They would wait for Billy to write. He promised he would. He said, "often." They would keep in touch with Eddy's parents and together weather the next growing years out with both kids distanced from them.

Meanwhile both Billy and Frank awoke, arose and went to their computers, then into their email to find no incoming mail and both clicked on to write a text. There they started writing their parents an accounting of their time.

Frank had a girlfriend back home also and he and Billy wrote them next after their folks. Billy had a list assembled on his computer to jointly write all a group together, one flash-mail from time to time.

Billy had on his list the 3 Amigos, Max, Coach Mac and Mr. Steel of York High. A one size fits all summary letter.

One thing each room had as a part of the Modern Army training ground was an in-house small refrigerator for those two behemoths, standard meals would not be enough energy source and they would have to pack in some fridge snacks. A must get project. Both agreed. After all, they were college age and men of action.

Since now both Frank and Billy were to begin the regular year, they had moved from the strictly jock dorm for pre-season practice over to their present "Corp" cadet Patton Hall dorm, where they would be for the rest of the year.

The real West Point year would start the day after tomorrow. A lot will have to be done including grocery shopping for the fridge and preparing their military clothing.

After writing time they assembled their beds and straightened their room to look respectably clean. This would be a continual must, Army style. A clean house. There would be inspections regularly especially for the new "plebes" cadets.

Unfortunately, the new class of plebe cadets were expected to be put through a lot, what some might be termed "Mickey Mouse" doings. It all had purpose and reason for their doing at West Point. Many of the regimens even during "Beast Week," the necessity to keep a good sense of humor was essential to surviving the rigors of Army life and teachings.

The Army system will find your weakness, but that's the point. West Point toughens you up, and that's the necessity of officer training and experience gained at the value of a West Point military training college. It trains you to become and live the values established by the Academy and unique to it. Boys became young men of confidence and purpose with lives changed and strengthened for life ahead no matter what field or career was eventually chosen.

Most graduates referred to their experience at the Academy as "superb training academically, and physically, prepared for all the world and its problems." The best educated, and the best physical personal training a young person can have.

Billy's experiences at West Point indeed would provide him many military learning programs, from more basic to extensive specific training in military matters which would provide opportunity and preparedness for service as a commissioned officer and careers in the Army service.

His training and daily life as a cadet at West Point would take him through a military science education training in small unit tactics and principles of war, individual tactical skills in rifle marksmanship, land navigation and movement techniques.

His cadet professional development was in officer conduct and decorum and professional ethic education, as well as a cadet's day-to-day military environment of unit training, chain of command duties, drill and ceremonies, including extra-curricular activities, and classroom duties. All these duties and training would one day bring Billy to the forefront of becoming an officer in the United States Army as a 2nd lieutenant. He then would be assigned to a new command location somewhere in the world.

At this level he had certain choices available, and upon graduation must prepare himself for a branch selection, i.e. what area of the Army he would like to serve in. Because of certain talents recognized by his teachers, regulars, he may have a special area he'd best be qualified to fulfill. In any event, he would find his niche in the Army.

On some free time, Billy walked alone around "Michie" Stadium and the gridiron. He envisioned success in that place alongside his friend Eddie, quarterback of the "Black Knights" and currently a sophomore cadet. He, Billy, currently was on the freshman team, playing end and tight end positions both ways. His defensive tight end hero was Willie Davis, of the Green Bay Packers - back in their early days of 1966-69 glory. He was a black man of much character, liked by all, highly respected, and an inveterate five-time pro bowler and later a successful business man and Hall of Fame inductee.

Billy's offensive end and more recent hero was a large 6'6", 265 lb. tight end who had 90 catches and 327 yards and 17 touchdowns under his belt. Young power end named Rob Gronkowski, a totally aggressive end who played for the Patriots, who knew his advantages, or his size propelled him to prominence and success in his hustle play routine.

He was big like Billy who at his current 260 lbs. and the same height. He knew he had not yet gotten to his full weight, but expected soon to be there. Indeed, an attained weight of 280 plus pounds would be possible by sophomore year. He was desirous of making a name for himself in a sport he truly loved. He would not be denied and would pursue excellence in attaining and doing his best. It was indeed possible to attain that which he wanted and if Eddie and he got it all together, they might attain the goals they had dreamed of in the next three years.

He left the field area and wandered over to the "Paulson Barracks Hall" where he wanted to look up Eddy. Many of the varsity football "jocks" resided there. Billy entered Paulson Hall and walked up to the postal box area. He looked over the names for Eddy Brandon. He found it located on the first floor, Paulson #102. He found it immediately down the hall to his right, second apartment. The door was closed so he knocked on it and waited at attention. After all Eddy was now a second-year cadet, no longer a plebe freshman. It was called "respect."

The door opened and there stood his best friend from York lookin' good, fit and Army official like in his cadet uniform. His eyes brightened up and face lit up seeing his friend Billy at the door.

"Come on in big guy," spoke Eddie, "What's the pleasure of your company?"

Billy spoke up, "Well, I had some free time, ya right, I thought I'd look you up and see if we could chat for a while. It's been so busy since I've been here, I just needed to talk with my friend!"

"Yeah, glad you did. What's up?" Billy got to the point and main reason he was there. Saying, "You know the main reason I'm here at West Point is to play football, with you!" I'm working hard trying to do the very best I can at being good at playing tight end and receiver on the fresh-soph team. You, of course, have moved up to starter quarterback on the varsity team. I knew you'd be there. You're the best out of high school anywhere. They're lucky to have you here. I came, of course, to hook up with you and make a name for ourselves in a "tandem" like "Blanchard and Davis." I'm looking forward for us to be getting at it as soon as I can do well enough to get promoted to varsity level. I still got the fabulous feelin' of great fun and play the old York way we had."

"Me too," stated Eddy. "I keep promoting you with varsity coaches Jeff Monkin and Bob Bodenhammer, the tight-end coach. They are watching you, so keep making catches and mowing people down. And on defense keep up the terror in our opponent's backfield. It won't be long before you're up here with me and then we can fly with your favorite routes."

"Yeah!" said Billy, "I'm kinda gettin' itchy to try to get some haulin' jobs done for the Army Mules. I'll keep tryin' to keep myself honed to good play. So far, I'm doing pretty good. I think we're lucky to have played at York under Mac. His crew was the best. We learned a lot.

"Yeah, they were special times and it was great times at York. Speaking of York, how's Anita doing? I'm sure she's missing you. Penny and I are doin' good. It's hard here with me doing this thing here. How are you two managing? It isn't going to be easy. We have set ourselves apart from the crowd and have a job and career ahead. My philosophy is to take one day at a time and to take this choice we have made as prepared as we can." Eddy was wise in his assessment, thought Billy.

Eddy said to Billy, "Billy, you're just gettin' started here. It's a lot of work, you have to set goals and challenges to yourself and be in effort to meet them. Knowing you as I do, I find that you should have no trouble in exceeding the necessary requirements they set. Your lifestyle in York will fare you well here. Anyway, we'll be on the road for our old fun times during football season. I'm looking forward to it myself."

"That's for sure," said Billy. Then he said, "Well, I've got to move along. Things to do you know. Great talking with you. See you later at practice."

Billy left Eddy's dorm hall and headed back to his dorm at Patton Hall. He entered his room. Frank was not there. So, he lay down for a few minutes and took out the large card containing the Academy athletic schedules. He perused the football schedule for both the Fresh-Soph team and the varsity. Not all the schedule matched up. The Fresh-Soph only played six games while the varsity nine. He would really have to concentrate on doing well with the short schedule. The first game was with Fordham University. No one knew what either of their teams were about. Well, it really didn't make too much of a difference as the emphasis was playing their own game, executing their playmaking well. He fell asleep right after that.

CHAPTER FIVE

Fordham University was the first scheduled football game for both academy football teams. There was a little squib on the back of the schedule about Fordham.

It stated they go back to 1882 for their first game. They were from the Bronx. Playing in Loftey Stadium seating 8,000 fans. Known as the "Rams," which the St. Louis team was named in their honor of heritage. In 1928 and 1936 their offensive line held the name of the "Seven Blocks of Granite." It was coached by "Sleepy" Jim Crowle, who was one of the famous four horsemen of Notre Dame, which included the famous Vince Lombardi, coach and founder of the Green Bay Packers. In 2014, they won the Patriot League Championship.

Billy thought quite an impressive school it is. It should be a scrapper of a battle on the field. The school enrollment was around 15,000. He also noted a couple of alumni recognizable names in Donald Trump and Denzel Washington, actor.

Billy looked at the clock and saw that he needed to move out to football practice – the last day before the game day. It would be filled with playmaking and new plays injected into the playmaking schedule for opportune times of need. He was ready and up and out he went.

Head held high, another challenge ahead. Football practice was exceptionally good. The team seemed coordinated in offensive flow and its defense seemed to be tuned up as well. He was ready for some action, the Army way – Let'er Rip!

The opening season game was upon them. Eddy Brandon was at the helm for the cadet "Black Knights." They were ready as head coach Jeff Monkin could get them. There were 12 games on the schedule this fall, and Fordham was loaded and a balanced team of talents. Of course, the main rivals every year were Air Force, Navy and Notre Dame when they played them, which was on this season's schedule. So, there was a tough schedule ahead for the "Black Knights!"

The whole of the cadets was assembled in Michie Stadium overlooking the Earl Blaik field. There was mandatory attendance at all home games. The cadets were a boisterous lot glad to have some fun time together in solidarity for their team.

Both teams were warming up on the field. It was a mild fall day in this opening season day, a great day for football. Soon the beginning festivities began with the singing of the National Anthem. The baritone singer from the "Men's Army Chorus" pitched his pipes and with all hats off, hands on their heart they belted out with gusto. It was done very well, and a rousing cheer erupted at his finish.

The field cleared off and the opposing team took the field for the kick off. The cadets lost the coin toss, so they kicked the ball on the opening round. The ball rose high into the air and sailed into the front part of the end zone. Fordham received it without fumbling and ran it back to the 22-yard line before a cadet lineman downed him with suddenness.
The first set of plays were to test the middle defensive line for weakness.

The Rams broke through on third down to push it to within two yards of a first down. However, the cadets held, and the Rams had to punt on fourth down. The punt lofted to the 35-yards line of the cadets and hit and rolled out of bounds.

It was now the cadet turn to move the ball at their own 35 yard line. Eddy Brandon and his teammates ran out to take the offense. He was the Commander of the brigade. He was the in-charge guy to lead his team. He too, tried to penetrate the defensive line, with a series of between the tackles plays. An off-tackle trap play got him about 15 yards, not bad. A first down. ON the first and ten, now in the red zone, he called for a sweep right. The ends and wide out took their spread positions preparing to block on the next play.

Eddy took the ball from under the center, faked a handoff to the halfback coming through the line and headed wide right with the ball. The tight end held his man and the wide out came in and blocked a linebacker positioned to stop the play.

As the coach said, "Execution, execution, execution!" The teammates sank their teeth into their blocks and Eddy scampered 15 yards to the five-yard line. The Rams "D" line held for 2 downs and it was now third down and five to go to the goal line., Both lines tightened up for a fullback shoot up through the middle. Eddie called for the tight end to take two steps and flair out. The play was "brilliant" and Eddy flipped a quick short pass to the tight end as he flared out. The defensive back was two steps behind him and didn't have a chance to stop the catch. The extra point was confirmed. West Point 7, Fordham 0.

The West Point band sounded off, the cadets roared approval and a cannon erupted its satisfaction victory salute.

The kickoff by West Point was long and low, bounding profusely up and down toward the Fordham goal line. The offensive kick return specialist awaited the ball, collected it on a favorable bounce and headed up field. He got to the 47-yard line before a cadet even touched him. A lucky set of blocking along the way. They were in good field position to start their offensive drive.

Several tries through the line and a trap pass got them to the 40-yard line of the Cadets. It was first and ten. Again, they advanced another 8 yards upfield before the cadets tightened up their defense. A play through the line made headway about 8 yards to the 39, but as the ball carrier went down, the ball got stripped out as a free ball. Fortunately for Fordham, they recovered it just short of the first down, on the 40-yard line.

They were now in a dilemma as to go one yard for the first down or punt and try to short kick it just short of the goal line of the cadets and put them in a hole.

They decided to punt, but it went too far and into the end zone a few yards. So, it was taken out to the 20-yard line for the Black Knights to restart a drive on offense. Substitutions were made, and Eddy found himself in the huddle with his old high school tight end "Billy Joe." He raised an eyebrow and smiled at Bill and called Billy's favorite catch pattern – down ten yards and cross over slant. Old, old patterns long established were not forgotten between these two closely tied friends and teammates. The play was precisely crafted, and they gained a quick 15-yards up to the 35. It certainly excited the entire cadet cadre of West Point. Sparks of excitement had been noted with the precision of execution that the play produced. Excitement was in the air, everybody not having a clue as to the magic they were about to witness in their future football arena.

Coach Monkin who was the only one on the inside knowledge of these two players past, gave a wry grin to nobody in particular, and pumped his fist with vigor as Eddy and Billy connected. He knew the magic was still there just by the manner of their execution of the play. He felt the jolt of joy in his craw. This may be a very good year. Indeed, it would be.

The overall playing of this year's present cadre squad of varsity players infused by a few of the new freshman talent would evolve into a close team who precisely understood the true nature of working together for the United oneness of Force. It was the epitome of West Point purposes and teaching. The spirit to the commitment of excellence. The 2016 fall season would build itself for future greatness in a manner of the past "Blanchard-Davis" heyday years.

Coach Monkin knew of the reasons for Eddy and Billy's attending West Point, at least the athletic pursuits they desired. He had been building his team talents over the last several years preparing, hopefully, for a true winning full season. Known for years of poor past performance, he was charged with making change, and his light went on, and his spirit arose, watching Eddy and Billy knit and weave newness into his varsity program. He felt a certain destiny in his future.

CHAPTER SIX

It was a hard-fought game, back and forth, a pitched battle. Coach had taken Billy out for a long while as his regular end again returned to action. It was not until the middle of the fourth quarter, when they were tied, that Billy reentered the game. Once again Eddy gave him the eyebrow raise and smile. It said volumes to the both of them. In the huddle he called another pass slant play deeper into the downfield.

Just before they exited the huddle, Eddy said, "Everybody tighten up on this play. We're goin' for the gold." It was the words of a warrior chief in battle. Everyone took note and resolved to give it their best. Best is good, and Eddy shone his wares again with precision, as Billy hauled in the pigskin for a 30-yard run including over a few tacklers. He was now a different young man, fully grown with maximum power in his 6'6" frame at 280 pounds of steel. He was something to see in the locker room, a chiseled body of muscle, most formidable and even intimidating.

The fullback power runner ran a crossbuck up through the middle and punched it in behind a line doing its job to the max. The cadets won the game by a touchdown and point after. The cadets were stunned and in euphoric delight. The Rams were just stunned. This was a great feeling to win, especially beating such a rated team of excellence. It indeed was fun for all.

The Coach had some confidence words to say to his team. They soaked it in and he said, "It was good!" That week at and on the West Point campus everyone seemed to be in high spirits and right in step. The tone of the cadets rang true to West Point, excellence for mind, spirit and body. Eddy and Billy commiserated the joy of their renewal and revival.

Game one on the schedule was now in the Win Column. Now it was onward, game for game – one at a time – conquering their demons along each day awaiting their next battle on the gridiron!

Coach Monkin sat in his office looking over his 2016 schedule. He thought long upon it realizing the enormity of the task he had before him this season. He had lost almost every game to these teams the previous year. He set everything down aside and said a prayer for God to guide him with favor this season with effort and wisdom to conquer this year's scheduled opponents. "Lord I need your help and invite you to come alongside our efforts for victory. Thank you, Jesus!" His prayer was short and sweet and to the point, in true meaningful belief that favor would be released on his team.

He realized he could do the possible, but he needed God in and on it to do the impossible. His hopes ran high after concluding his prayer, though nothing had changed, or so it seemed. He knew he was a good coach who had prepared for the season well and was counting on his freshmen recruits, carefully chosen, to spur a right balance for all the positions. This would put them in a formidable position of total excellence and spirit of winning, a team about their business.

He had been building a solid foundation over the last several years and he sensed he and his 2016 team were poised to take it all only if. They needed to concentrate on only one game at a time. They faced quality teams this year in particular. Coach Monkin would have to be versatile enough in using the players he had. They were experienced and or good solid players. The difference would be in the preparation and training and developing the will to win. Winning begot confidence and confidence translates into can-do thinking and accomplishment.

It was his job to promote and convince his players that winning was something they could do this year. Much had gone right with the Fordham game plan and the balance of the team was really good. Conditioning would be a factor and the Army was good at that!

Eddie and Billy got together after the game and celebrated their win. It was like old times, the two of them in collaboration and they really were excited, and they saw they still had it as a teammate twosome connected by pass plays. They saw and felt their potential and again, they made a new pact to give it their all.

Once again, life settled into Army training routines with early rise and work. Work, work, work all the days long. His past dedication to a strong work ethic was paying dividends to success in both his studies and football.

As time went by his strength of mind and body soon endeared him to senior officers, he had classes under and coaches he worked with. He was a student par excellence of all he did or attempted.

Soon it was a weekend again and this week's opponent was Eastern Michigan. It was a team they should beat without much difficulty, but on any given day anything can happen. As usual the pre-game training and head time with the coach, had the Black Knights perked and ready to go.

And play well they did, beating the "Eagles" 31 to 6. The Black Knights had their passing game humming with Billy scoring on two touchdowns and many long yards all over the field. The ground game was vastly improving with quickness and power being exerted by the running backs and power fullback.

Both the O-line held for the quarterback and the D-line was wildly aggressive and, in the backfield, too often for the Eagles to handle. Obviously, the Black Knights looked strong and good.

After the game, Coach Monkin praised the team for the balance displayed across the board and told them, "This is only the beginning of an increasingly hard schedule. Savor the win but don't take it in. Work hard and your excellence will show. Next week we play Duke University, who has been riding high on several wins this season. We will be playing them away. They were playing with a previous 8-5 record for the last year. They can be deceivingly tough. We will need to score early and often. So, it's work hard this week, play our game and clobber them." He was a man of few words, but those words carried punch and meaning. His words were not to be denied.

School work and the everyday life at West Point was much in duplicate, ye, varied enough to not be boring. One had to be alert, quick of mind and physically fit to make it through each day. Classes were progressive in sequence and one thing built on another. That was Army style of life. It was important to quickly get the swing of compartmentalizing your time and work so everything gets done. Billy was very good at doing these things as he had been taught and disciplined to be that way, mainly because of this athletic extension and energy levels needed to actually get through all he had to do in a day. His sacrifice daily was play or non-work time. He forfeited those benefits attainable for other benefits.

His time with people were to the point and task at hand. Just hangin' out was not in his schedule of living. Because it was not, he didn't really miss such free time. He did however, miss one thing though, Anita! And home with the folks.

Billy kept in touch with Anita by letter, cell phone and email, texting also. Same with his folks. They liked to hear his voice and gain satisfaction he was OK and healthy. They were concerned about his tight regimen and stress levels.

He assured them any stress was worked out through football. It was there "mama." I let it all hang out and cast it into the sea of physical work.

Anita seemed to be busy in her art world at the University of Illinois. She had much positive to say about all she was involved in and delighted she had applied there. She said she missed him, but with her busyness she realized his heavy workload and that he was happy as can be. They both commiserated their distance apart, renewed their love for the other and kissed a silent kiss to each other at their conversation end. Until next time. Meanwhile, letters and notes, short emails, texts would have to do.

Christmas break was coming up in a few months and that would place them together once again. Both of them couldn't wait!

The game was a barn burner. Duke got off to a fine start scoring two touchdowns in the first quarter. They got lucky on a long and down pass and were short passing us to death. That would have to stop. And stop it did, as Coach Monkin and his defense coordinator reassembled their defense strategy. They had to plug the hole in the dam.

Monkin and defensive coordinator, Jay Bateman, sprung a new defense and duplicated the Chicago Bears style of stunting attacks. They brought in one of their deep cornerbacks to help break up the short passing game. It worked well at solving the problem. In fact, on a critical third and short, Duke called a short over the center pass play that floated a little, only to have a Black

Knight linebacker come across to catch it and get a few yards in the process.

It would be the turnover that turned the game in favor of the cadets. The D-line tightened up and the O-line got fiercer in enforcing their territory. This gave Eddy time to deliver his pass options with precision. He and Billy, alternating the other end on down and long patterns, cut a swath of yardage down to the goal line ramming it in and over for a touchdown and point after.

At the half it was 14 to 7, blue devils on top. The half time locker room was quiet as Coach Monkin and Bateman reviewed their new strategy for the second half.

The cadet's center had been hurt on the last play of the first half. Getting cut from behind in his lower legs. He was now out of the game. He was replaced by freshman heavyweight Frank Consolo, Billy's roommate.

Billy knew him a mover and a shaker on the Fresh-Soph squad. He would do his position well., He was an all-out type of guy, much stronger, than he looked. This was not normal the kind of substitution Monkin made, but he knew his personnel well. It was Frank's opportunity to prove himself and he did and stayed in the rest of the game.

By the third quarter end the score was Duke 14 and the Cadets 21. Another interception on a wide out sideline pass that the cadets picked off and ran back to the five-yard line of the Blue Devils. A short fake pump pass to Billy and hitting the other end coming across the middle wide open for the needed second to receive a bullet by Eddy right in his gut.

Both teams fought hard as the Cadets further mastered their defense and offensive line play. You could see the "blood" in their eyes, the desire to win flowing into their veins and the military like precision of execution by Eddie and his receivers, who clinched the advantage on the Blue Devils who seemed to be fading and tiring. The game continued for another five minutes with no scoring until late in the fourth quarter when the cadets found themselves on the 38-yard line of the Blue Devils. It was there they called in their most accurate field goal kicker who promptly split the goal posts for another 3 points, making the score at the game's end 24-14. It was a hard-fought game. The defense held all game long against what had been an aggressive offense in the beginning of the game by Duke. Duke seemed over confident playing Army because of their previous year's record so unfavorable. This year Army was different and busting with talent and determination to reverse their losing ways. The roses were smelling good to all of West Point, winning teams invigorate the "Corp" of the camp and everything seemed to flow well.

CHAPTER SEVEN

The University of Illinois was having another bad football season. Even though they always seemed to have one or two players that got drafted into the pros. Even Northwestern University beat them in the opener of their season.

Penny, Eddy's girlfriend, was doing well in her studies and Anita was flourishing in her curriculum for first year freshman. Many of her studies were assigned freshman requirements she didn't particularly enjoy. However, anything associated with her core curriculum of art, she was excited about and blew those courses away. She was indeed, learning much that was new, absorbing all that got in her way like a sponge.

She thought a lot about Billy, and how they met and danced at their initial meeting at Big John's home party. She giggled to herself thinking about winding up in Billy's lap during a breakdown of a pyramid she was on top of at an athletic celebration gathering. She was distracted for a few moments while leaning on her elbow semi-dreaming about high school days. She felt an energy surge come on her while reading and doing homework at the art department library. She had been dreaming and dozing. She shook it off for a moment and sat up and renewed her studies. It was but 2:35 in the afternoon, daylight primetime.

Every weekend for 11 weeks was filled with football games, sandwiched in with hard practices during the week and cadet training and studies all week long. It made for hard and quality sleeping along with dogged determination to maintain precise scheduling to get it all done and accomplished on time.

While he was good at plying his time well, it was hard on the body, soul and spirit. It was good that Anita wasn't around, she'd be a real distraction although a very pleasant and desirable one.

Developing a lifestyle of discipline, days flew by. They out maneuvered the Air Force Academy 37 to 6 as their land machine was well oiled with high octane and Abraham tanks.

Wake Forest went down 45-42 in a tough one won by a field goal margin, nevertheless a win.

Billy and Eddy's stats were flying off the wall edging on breaking school records for single season yardage and catches. The backfield 3 were hitting new heights on gaining yardage as the cadet-o-line hung tough together allowing few opponents D-line men and linebackers access through them.

Hard work, good planning, winning, good attitudes, more hard work, plus Coach Monkin pressing with enthusiasm and determination resounding loudly in their ear. This season would be different and meaningful. It certainly was different as attitude and confidence was soaring, everybody on the team now wanted "it" badly and they were in on the sacrifice for it.

Billy sat down in his room to take a break. He reached for the football schedule card pinned to his cork board and looked it over reading Penn St – Away, Bucknell – Home, Tulane – Home. Every game was a potential upset by the other team. It was important to reach a positive weekly mindset in time to come into the next game. Five actual days to practice and shape strategy for the cadets next opponents.

The coaches were busy commiserating together over strategy and things to practice that week. Trick plays were a part of each week's strategies and awaiting the opportune time to spring them on in the game.

The fall season was really busy on the West Point campus as the plebes were pressed with so many responsibilities at seemingly such a young age. It was indeed, adult striving time pressed forward in West Point style. Each plebe would have to "fish or cut bait" the first freshman plebe year. West Point wasn't for everyone and a small percentage of the freshman class would drop out. Most of those would reappear at another college or university to continue their formal education.

West Point was unlike a college experience even those with ROTC programs. The freedom of college and the university lifestyle was so different from that of a service academy, lifestyles in particular.

You were chosen and chose to enter a separate way of living this one preparing a select few of the population to learn and become defenders of our nation and its security.

The professional Armed forces of the United States of America. It was their job one. They made a commitment for duty to the extent of nine years. Four years at West Point and five years on active duty with 3 years inactive reserve status. A student at West Point generally would consider themselves career military personnel Most generally putting in a 10-20-30 year service time cut out of their life, before retiring out of the military.

Billy thought on these things assessing his life momentarily, giving some thought of where it was taking him in what directions. Right now, he was immersed in plebe-freshman year and West Point fulltime occupation training and education. While he thought tentatively about his life it was essentially to be taken one day at a time. He currently was enjoying his choice of being at West Point. It was fulfilling at the present time frame. He didn't think he would make a full career of being in the service, but he was just starting his educational and early career lifestyle in the military. And then there was Anita? He had his youth years still before him and maturing to do as he gained experience and knowledge.

Little did he know just where his life would take him. His second tier of living was currently humming in place. It occupied his present life and thought. His life was good at the present time. He was full of confidence for the next day. He thought he better be, as the next few days would take him through basic physical military conditioning and foot training over obstacles, under fire of blank bullets as he wormed his way under barbed wire and low obstacles, over logs, through bramble and hiding behind trees. It was boot camp week of military war training exercises at West Point.

Next weeks was scheduled military weapons training and deployment of accuracy in firing them. This was just a preliminary practice to get the plebe's interest in absorbing some knowledge of weapons and foot training power and strategies. There would be more concentrated time frames specifically planned to indwell themselves deeper into war games, ground power and strategies. Proper use and timing of those would require more basic training and comprehension time to sharpen their military skills prior to graduation.

Meanwhile the plebes took regular college courses the Army thought would hone their skills the Army needed, but also preparing for civilian return of life and job opportunities. The West Point program was thought out with care and in response to a greater breadth of knowledge which in turn gave the military man an overall depth in facing the new military lifestyle.

It was now Friday, and Billy had finished the "boot camp" training. He still had his daily workout with the football team during the late afternoons and early evenings his bed looked like heaven every time he laid down to actually sleep. It was like a time machine he plugged into only to awaken with a body renewed and re-charged. Thank God, he was only 18 years-old, prime time for healthy hormones and life breath.

Billy kept his eye on the present tasks at hand, yet he was mature enough to see and believe that some of his high hopes would come to fruition. To win the Heisman Trophy and a national championship title much less a season within the league the Army "Black Knights" played in They had too many times secured the leadership of last place. He would be a partnership with his team in changing the results and attitude of this year's football season outcome. He felt a change in the players as Coach Monkin sought to inspire them to winning ways. Winning was always inspiring to the soul and for priming the pump to exceed in doing one's best at whatever was the task at hand.

The task this weekend was to destroy Penn State then Bucknell the following week. ON the surface Penn State had talent and a winning schedule so far. Bucknell was in the dumps with a losing season. The coach reiterated his slogan "It's not who we play, but how we play. When we play our game, we will win." That was this season and the hope was alive.

The odds at this point in the schedule did not conclude a winning season with two very tough teams looming as the last two games. Notre Dame and Navy traditionally were powerhouses and so far had winning seasons. The five-game completed schedule was too early on for any predictions of outcomes for success.

There would be the honing of the iron time for all good teams. Certainly, this year held Army among them, with four games yet to play. Army had their wars cut out for them. Battle plans had to be prepared as opponents' schedules played out and records were determined. Coach Monkin and his Army were determined to be in the running for a winning season. The coach reminded his team that a one-point win was just that a one-point win.

Monkin had done his recruiting well across the board these last two years. His field goal kicker looked to definitely be a winner up to some over 50 yards in practice. He had a strong leg and was very accurate so far. That position would serve the team well over the years ahead and especially welcomed this season.

The Army "Black Knights" found their stride in the Penn State game hitting on all 8 cylinders with added full race hubcaps and a high compression dip stick. That dipstick was Eddy and the full race hubcaps were Billy and the other end plus two dragsters in the halfbacks. It made for a full-blown engine O- and D-lines. To watch this team in action was made for extraordinary viewing. The harder they worked the more luck they had, and the end results were eventfully successful. So far, the plan was succeeding.

The weekend was once again upon them. Another Saturday game, this time at Penn State, located in University Park, PA. They would be playing before a potentially full house, Beaver Stadium, with a capacity of 106,572 screaming fans. At the time the "Nittany Lions" were sporting a record of 2 and 3, a 40%-win record.

It was home of the late Joe Paterno, before the scandal. In spite of that, it featured a winning record of 409 – 136.3 A huge winning record history. It was obvious they had cracks in their armor, so Coach Monkin was on the alert to breech their weaknesses.

They were tough on the run, especially tackle to tackle. Big, good, tough linemen doing their jobs well. It was imperative to go around them, over the top of them, but not through them. Fake cross bucks, traps and lots of variety of pass plays and off tackle and end runs were possibilities.

So, went the planning and practices of the Black Knights for the week.

As Saturday afternoon appeared with large crowds gathering on a mildly cold semi-winter day. The Nittany Lions and the Army cadets were aligned for kickoff. It was 1:00 pm, at 35 degrees everyone was Pennsylvania attired for cold as the ball came down to the Penn State running return.

He got to the 25-yard line before everybody in the stands heard the tackle. It was ferocious. It seemed a miracle that either got up. The first quarter was hard fought to a 7 to 7 tie. Everybody was full of energy. By the half end the cadets had the lead 14 to 7. This time they received the ball, and speed demon back Ramos Ramirez ran it back to the 41-yard line, a good dodging and slicing effort. The cadets had good field position.

The second half was another battle and battle plan for the Black Knights. For the most part of the first half, Coach Monkin had his team beating away with running all the slots. But this half he would edge his gunnery talents in Eddy to Billy and Elmore Davis at the other end. He would do trap passes just over the line to a fake fullback draw with a flair out after he got through the line and hit him with a quick short pass. It was a good alternative play that usually got short yardage.

Well, Eddy, and his gunnery mates had a field day in the backyard of the Nittany Lions for the rest of the game. The final score was 37 to 21. The cadets seemed upbeat and full of themselves with energy. By the end of the game, the Penn State defensive line seemed tired and frustrated. The fired-up cadets were looking like the word "together" had meaning.

The term "cover my back" took on new meaning on the football field. Even the Penn State band sounded muted along with the fans. There were few Army fans in attendance, but they were loud and strong, definitely excited about their team's performance. The ride home was verbose and very excited, the fans and cadets feeling so proud of what their team had done and was doing to bring winning ways to the gridiron. They knew it had taken hard work to bring about the "change" in results from the past performance levels of the past seasons.

Coach Monkin was becoming a hero on campus. All the cadets encouraged the players to keep on "Keepin' on" like they were. West Point had a new attitude to deal with and everybody was on board.

The next two games were at home at 'Michie' Stadium. All the cadets on campus and staff would be there to cheer the Black Knights on. The electricity would be 220 amps on the field and across the stadium.

Tulane, located in New Orleans, was originally founded as a public medical college in 1834. Today its current enrollment is 13449. It is a private research university. The team was known as the "Green Wave." They were not a powerhouse having a 2015 season of 3 and 9. The 'Green Wave' got crushed by Army 49-7. The ground game broke loose for Army and their loose cannons were too many, too often. It was the beginning of the end for a successful season.

The following game was with Connecticut University with an enrollment of 31,119 located in Storrs, CT. The "Huskies" all 42,000 of them would be in the stands, from East Hartford. Their record of 6 and 7 was disappointing to them. They were unfortunate to run into the Army Cadets when they did this season. The Army Black Knights were on a destiny so far destroying all that were 'pitched' against them. The 'Huskies' met the 'Hulk,' losing to them 38 to 0. A really one-sided game. It took the Huskies by surprise almost as much as it did the cadets. They were quite stunned by their poor performance on the field. If it wasn't the running game hitting on all 8's, it was through the air with bombing runs spot on by the cadets. The headline in all the papers including USA Today were reading "Army Black Knights fired up 87 points in the last two games. Looking toward a winning season for first time in ten years."

The superintendent of West Point Lt. General Caslet declared the Black Knights the General Patton armored division returned again. That of course set well with all the cadets, the regular

Army brass and a third of the Pentagon. It was an Army on the move.

However, an ever-living problem was immediately before them. Two in fact. Those mountains were not Iwo Jima and Okinawa, but the fighting Irish of Notre Dame and the US Naval Academy Midshipmen. Yes, they presented the most formidable opposition just around the corner. It was the last two games of the schedule.

Both teams had lost only two games so far and were "hot" on the grid iron. This would be the recognition of the Army Cadets 2016 mettle and backbone of reaching deep and not fainting.

This year, Coach Monkin and his staff was not only prepared for war but relished the skirmish and was stockpiling all the ammunition he could gather for the battles. It was assured that these games would indeed be major campaigns for the Army football Black Knights. The Rangers, Special Forces and Green Berets would all have to be brought to bear arms in defending the United States Army honor. There was a battle cry on campus "Charge." Support gathered without much difficulty on campus during the weeks prior to the games. It was as though it was to be looked upon as two major campaign battles.

Everyone was in high pitch, they would break the curse of losing to these two teams. They were greatly hopeful, as well as confident, that things and the score would be different. It was in the air at West Point.

CHAPTER EIGHT

It was Armageddon time on the campus of the Notre Dame Fighting Irish. Today the game was to be played on national TV, so was the next week's game of the traditional battle against Navy. The stakes were raised, the battle lines drawn as they faced each other on the fighting Irish Gridiron in South Bend, Indiana. Tradition loomed large for both schools with the notoriety biggies going to Notre Dame and its football tradition over the many years. The famous "Four Horsemen" and plethora of Hall of Fame and Heisman Trophy winners, went on and on.

This year the Fighting Irish again had developed talent going for them. They had recent seasons with poor showings but were into winning programs the last two years, increasingly finding ways to win.

The 2015 season they bludgeoned through with exceptions of Clemson, Stanford and Ohio State games who were besting their best this season. Coach Brien Kelly's lucky Irish season ran down in those latter games. However, Notre Dame was always traditionally tough. No matter their opponent.

Notre Dame always had large linemen, talented halfbacks and usually a first notch quarterback that got drafted into the pros. They were always aggressive. This last year they came up short. Today Notre Dame was confident that they would pulverize Army. Most of the team and coaches were looking at previous season accumulative records of poor showing by the cadets Army team.

The Army coaches and team were counting on their poor reputation past to smoke screen the present team's turn around performance. In fact, the Army PR people practiced a little decoy PR work in the public arena pointing out the poor performances of the past seasons. A bit of subterfuge strategy. Why not? All's fair in war and athletic competition.

To no one's surprise Notre Dame struck first on a "surprise" long "bomb" to their speedy end. It wouldn't happen again as

Monkin took note. The big Irish line presented an early problem, but later
the cadets loosened up with some unorthodox formations in the form of "stunts" different front line lineups and fake rushes on third downs. Notre Dame multi times into the game threw interceptions to those receivers who found very close coverage on them troublesome and provoking. The Army defense and offense kept up the diversification of position players keyed to their study of Notre Dames' best play gainers and procedures. The Fighting Irish just couldn't get their proverbial footage right to produce good plays.

Interceptions were too often or at critical timing and turnovers were killing them. Little David was slaying Goliath, slowly. Army took a while sparring with the behemoths, and its larger than life reputation, its PR and gaggle of trophy winners.

It was not enough to out gun the Army howitzers as machine gun Eddy, and the fierce playing of Billy and Willie doing long down field and cross patterns. They were skilled at all game long. The battlefield of the lines was just that, as they pitched a fit at each other. The Notre Dame line held to their reputation but near the fourth quarter began to tire and make mistakes.

The recruits by Monkin began paying off with their superb conditioning and finally this year, they had some king size tough trench fighters. All the hat tricks cooked up by Coach Monkin were executed with precision. Eddie was hot again, and Billy had hands of glue and after catches, carried half the Notre Dame defenders another 5-8 yards downfield before succumbing. Notre Dame was obviously bewildered by what the Army action was doing to them. It was too late to recoup, try as they did, but Army kept pressing always pressing onward. This was not the Army team they had heard reputation about.

The Army strategies worked their way and wonders, through the whole game, both halves. Notre Dame was perplexed. The big jumbotron showed the final score as 31-21, Army. It was quiet in the Irish Garden of greats; no line ups of the big green band blaring, and Louie the Leprechaun lost all his air. What Army fans that had made their way to South Bend, were hysterically loud that they could be heard back on campus at West Point, which said campus was absolutely "looney" over such a win that day.

The Army strategy, PR screen, execution and timing of plays, the tank formations of the offensive line, protecting Eddy and the storm troopers of the D-line breaching Notre Dame powerhouse monsters of their offensive line, all operations were successfully carried out. The ride home on the Stratoliner comfy Army busses (yeah right!) was totally exciting and most all fell asleep an hour before arriving back at West Point.

On arrival the busses were invaded by the entire West Point cadet campus. Cheers and bugles and drums helped propel anything loud adding to the voices of all. It was an amazing sight. Only a win next week over the Navy Midshipmen might be louder.

The on-campus cannons might be brought into actions. Yes, they were still operational, lately used often. The Army cadet varsity team recouped and began to practice on Tuesday that week, giving them plenty of rest after the Irish game. Campus studies were reduced some to give everybody some air time. It was a good gesture and thing to do, because while Navy was Army's usual final game of the season, they indeed were a formidable force this year and Army "Forces" rival.

Navy had an overall 20-year record of 369-234-8 with an 8-8-1 record for its 2015 season. With a split season Navy was vulnerable. Of course, they were always especially up for the Army contest. They would be playing hard.

The review of their season showed vulnerability in the backfield defense to passes and their line had not faced the likes of the New Army tank division of its O- and D-lines Army would throw at them this year.

With Army beating Notre Dame, a proverbial powerhouse, that occurrence might give Navy food for thought and hesitance in thinking Army would fold under their navel bombardment.

Navy Coach Ken Nivmalalo said to the press, "We will beat those landgrabbers right back into their foxholes," While it was an off the wall "bravado" comment, it didn't endear Army but for a response of "Yeah, right! We're not an army floating on inner tubes, this battle is land-based, and we take land – that's what we do!"

Well, Army led off with two touchdowns in the first quarter, a 14 to 0 score. Just before the half, Navy launched a carrier strike to score, but missed the point after.

Army scored twice more in the third quarter, leading. The fourth quarter Navy launched an all-out aerial strike along with end runs of every description. They were successful and scored, but they had spent their war effort and ran out of fuel as the end of the game came to its finish.

The 28 to 13 score was enough to declare it a landslide victory for the cadets. Four thousand plebes and West Point Cadets sent their hats into the air as the scoreboard broadcast 0 minutes. It looked like a fusillade of Howitzers had gone off, even as the cannons of West Point roared into action, and approval along the sidelines – K – K – BOOM! It had been a double successful season finishing with wins over Notre Dame and Navy. It was like the Chicago Bears beating the Green Bay Packers twice in one season.

The Commandant of West Point declared Sunday and Monday days off. No classes.

The plebes and regulars were excited and grateful the victor team rested and recovered from a very tough and hard season of physical labor, and mental control and toughness the season required. Eddy was voted MVP of the team, and Billy received the "scoring" trophy a high of 15 over the season by a tight end or any end for that matter.

There was an after season, The Sugar Bowl with match up Oklahoma State in which Army extended their victory march winning 24-21. The season of excitement was over, and all of West Point had had their minds blown away right on up to the Chief of Staff, a four-star general. From him on down the line, it was victory talk of the return of the Blanchard-Davis days of old when the Army football team had flourished, and awards flooded in in 1944 through 1946. They even appeared on the cover together of Time Magazine. The public couldn't get enough of the new dynamic duo. As sports and football players go, they had the stuff that made headlines and halls of fame museums.

Once again, the cadet campus simmered down back to normal levels of activity and daily routine. Billy and Eddy were not the big heroes any longer. They were cadets apart of the men and women of the Corp and as freshman and sophomores they were not secured in rank or experience to yet shine as leaders as the upper classmen did. Rank took leadership, responsibility and dedication in the Corp.

It was true that both Eddy and Billy were aggressive, smart and very fine cadets who established themselves with assertiveness and leadership qualities. These types were in line for promotions and responsibilities in the Army ways of life. It was in their blood.

Eddy was a natural quarterback the quality and skill of those greats that went before him from any school or college.

Billy not only was a formidable giant of a man, in superb shape, at 6'6" and 280 pounds, he had been under the tutelage and was honed and trained by 3 of the most renown trainers ever around in that timeframe, who he knew affectionately as the 3 Amigos, all Olympians, and gold medalists. He himself was accomplished in basketball, football, weightlifting, boxing, and several of the martial arts with black belts. All he needed was Army training in weaponry, strategy and logistics. Given these things you might say, he would be a one-man army. His peers gave him respect, room and a certain fear level. He was a gregarious type personality, but on the serious side when tasks had to be performed. He accomplished and did things right, followed the rules, but he was his own man who processed problems in his own way.

He greatly admired people with truth in their speaking, knowledge in doing, and determination to succeed. He also was a caring and passionate man, a gentle giant with extraordinary physical strength, and control of the emotions.

The sum of his parts was gathered from his family, his genes and his growing young years in training with the 3 Amigos. He was taught much well and educated to its finest achievement levels available in York, Illinois. He was a young man on the go and for his time. Only he, would determine his future.

CHAPTER NINE

As things on the West Point campus settled back towards the normal flow, Billy continued to take what spare time he could muster to write and contact his family and girlfriend, Anita. Likewise, with Eddy. Billy had a good talk with his folks, who were so proud of his accomplishments at the Academy. His Freshman year there was nothing short of phenomenal. Their little skinny wimpish child was now such an amazing human hunk of a young man. They, indeed, were proud of him. They definitely missed him terribly but realized he had to get on with his life. He was after all, now a young man away from home, living his life essentially on his own.

Billy missed not being home. The fixing of breakfasts for his Mom and Dad, the walking to school or taking the bus, his bicycle riding everywhere in York. He really rarely hadn't missed a car. The pickup games of basketball with Eddy and others in the park. It was a good life. Lots of love generated and promoted in Billy's life through 18 years.

His times and the pull of the church Anita and he went to. He missed that, all of it, at West Point. He realized that he was about to serve a president who was eliminating anything religious in the service or for that matter, the market place and that he concluded was essentially and primarily wrong. He was wrong in promoting such directives and policies. God will remember. Billy wasn't sure what religious form his president was or believed in. Nor whether he was even born in America, there was much controversy over that. It was unclear, and he desired it that that way. His presidency was unclear to many just who's side he was on; his wife clarified her feeling about her beliefs about America but his were obtuse and opaque. Hers negative and anti.

Generals and regulars in the service were being demoted, let go, or transferred by the president. The Army and all the services were being trampled on and funding and projects cut back or removed from the pipeline and drawing board. Pretty soon he will have our military fighting with left over muskets, sling shots and our Navy mounting machine guns atop inner tubes awaiting favorable winds. It was not a good time to be in the magazine of the military. The only hope was in a change of administration through new change in leadership and party. New thinking for the future way of doing things was essential to the renewing of the old American leadership way of life and lifestyle and a prosperity the world never knew and was so envious of. Times were evolving, hopefully for the better. A reality had to return to those in government service, they had forgotten the people and went on blindfolded in their own behalf – along for the easy ride. They became the privileged few who policed everybody but themselves.

The laws they made were not for them, the salary increased were for them, but not others. "There will always be the poor," said Jesus, but despite government's false promises, there was now a poor middle class. Now where'd the money go? You guessed it, into the pockets of the politicians – yes, your elected representatives to Congress – who invited lobbyists – fellow pocket-pickers, to follow them to grandiose retirement homes on the Riviera-er, Palm Beach, wherever. Corruption corrupts – absolutely. It was Rome all over again. Tammany Hall revisited.

This was the political climate that hopefully would change in the fall of 2016. It was imperative if American society wanted any semblance of the grace of God for its future. The people will have a golden road to nowhere laid out before them if they listen to all the biased pundits and their neighbors and neglect to vote their conscious beliefs amid desires for a prosperous, healthy, vigorous and secure country.

The "new" had to be brazen and bold to resist the counterfeit culture being fed them by all the freeloaders and faux vote getters and far leaning strategies taking America down the primrose path of destruction. It was a simple scenario for all Americans to rise, fight back and to regain, modesty, reality, truth and their good consequences. We the people have been put on the "dung heap" hill of unhappiness by the dark side of life among us who are laughing their way to hell. America needs new backbone of steel, and minds versatile with passion for new ideas, new revisions of old dead dormant ways of doing things and take wings of eagles and soar anew to a new and great renewal and restoration of America, for and by the people. The people do know what's best.

It was a point in time for the future of America. It would make a difference as to the full quality status it would or would not retain for a robust, fruitful Unites States of America. The clock was ticking for its future of greatness.

Billy was essentially a lover of history, world history. He could see and fathom the movement of the world regarding affecting world markets as well as local ways of change. He enjoyed history, it was like a thermometer stuck into a glove taking its temperature. There were "hot spots" the world over. Ever changing, but nonetheless sending rippling waves outward from wherever they originated to across the planet.

In talking with his friend Eddy, they decided the real problem the world over was "enlightenment." People were uninformed, uneducated some barely knowing the history of their own tribe. Knowledge they surmised was power, and power of some measurement was affording one or a group to grow, gain or change things or places with and through actions. This would improve, or upgrade places or conditions thus creating healthier personal improvement or societal betterment.

Those that had God oriented hearts and thoughts, were certainly best oriented in society and able to lift the hearts and quality of life in a nation or the world. The more Billy thought on these things the more he saw the difference between those who saw the light and those who preferred the darkness of life. A mindset of negativity, being better than or put downs of other people. The more control the better.

It wasn't just his lifestyle, so far of success, both in the physical realm of this world, but also in the arena of the mind that the world desired to corrupt for personal means and desires. It too, was a corruption outlook in need of destruction. Destructiveness was in fact a pursuit that fed corrupt mindsets. It was its food of choice to faux success.

Each side of the good/bad scenario had beliefs that they possessed the right belief or action, because their goals were different and opposite making each correctly right in a perverse manner of speaking.

You couldn't teach history without versing oneself of governments, philosophies and heart. Yes, heart. Man's heart is evil without the influence of God himself intervening. Outcomes of anything are spawned by this equation. It was the beginning of having difficulty in discerning just what is the truth and what is not. The spirit of corruption of the mind was what played against America. The first line of defense, the US Government, was so far to the left that they almost aligned themselves with the desire-nots in philosophy of thinking.

America needed the wellspring of stable, God-fearing, conservative and creative thought producing men and women to rise up and say, "Enough is enough" – no more deceitfulness; return to the land of promise and work of the American way, that was established through the Constitution, and championing that the red, white and blue flag – that star-filled corner of the flag, which represented the hard working, dedicated American people. For the people and by the people.

The present leadership was heading toward socialism which is a pre-amble to communism and tyranny when played out. Totally not the American way.
America seeks to be like no other country but itself. Independent, strong and generous. America gets sidelined by smooth talkers, based in deceit, to further their own gains. America presently was being inundated by such people world-wide and our government was in "co-dependency" with these people for fear of offending them. There is nothing positive in that position. In fact, it is a traitor-ish tendency in its nature.

The landscape of America was being painted differently during the years Billy was in high school and at West Point. A new presidency and Congress were being positioned for governing the flock. The time, if ever in its history, there was a total need of real and realistic change, it was at the 2016 election booth. People with strong American tradition, and sense of American history, needed to be in charge of the America they loved and sought better for. The poor and middle class needed to release the strings that has tied them up over decades, from being the free people they needed to become and all the faux speaking promises by party past that promised for 75 years, and has yet to produce class upward mobility, but instead producing definite class instability and downward economic trajectory.

Today offers the hope for tomorrow and the hope for a new era way of life changed by new thought and a desperate need for action by Americans of a revolution kind. New blood is needed, new foresight of the dedicated American "Land of Lincoln" type folk whose heart would be steeped in the history and growth of the American ways of life. Not anyone else's ways, but the foundational ways that made America the greatest nation on the planet.

The America, the place where all seemed to want to come to – to work, to live and call home. Free to worship in their own way, free to speak out, free to bear arms against all those in America, or elsewhere, that wish to subvert it and change it into another fashion with perversion of the constitution and laws established by and for the people of the United States of America. It was an ever-present time or danger to 300 million plus American citizens, that vote for representatives to their government, who keep going to Washington and immediately subservient themselves to the status quo of the Washington insiders and the old ways of not doing the real business of the folks that sent them there in the first place.

They call those folks "spineless" politicians and they should be hung out to dry and tethered to shorter terms of endearment and service, their salaries rolled back, and their perks remodeled. The public, the people, are not being served and represented as they properly should be but are deceived in representation after they attain office. It is not right and there needs to be a big change in the name of fairness and honesty - that would be a new concept.

A new revolution of 2016 is in the making, hopefully it will be retaken by true Americans with core American values, for Americans by American citizens.

These were the times Billy was growing up in. It was dangerous corrupting, but with the good fight by good people, America would hold its own and return to its greatness again. Young men like Billy and Eddy would rise to the forefront on the American scene if not corrupted by the sly societal pull by those wishing to subtly subvert and convert the nation on a hill, that shining world star called America.

In Billy and Eddy's view and all the people rolled up in that All-American small-city of York, believed the fight was worth the battle – that to have America remain and be restored to its potential greatness. York had restored its lot and corruptness.

Apathy was not the core American way of life. Action was, and action would be the direction taken over the next 15 to 20 years once again lift the stars and stripes high – waving in the winds of the world. Billy and Eddy were in the forefront of the new life energy needed and available that America had on deposit in its' people bank.

America, in the words of John the Baptist, paraphrased, was in need of drastic "Repentance." The good guys were in the apathy mode and not using their God given gifts of power. Vice was too nice an allure to those fallen to deceitfulness. It was becoming too much the easy way out of life. Back bones were bent, minds altered, and wills forgotten. The darkness was putting the people of America to sleep.

Billy being steeped in the joy of learning "history" for what it taught about life as it was certainly a recollection, put to paper, hopefully unbiased, about the chronological happenings across the world or a specific place like America from its founding.

Billy embraced the epitome of the American story taking opportunity to move forward, move up, better yourself while you contribute to bettering your surroundings, your town, county, state and country as best you can do, with doing your best for others. Those things mattered in the world order of peace and prosperity. The better quality of life you make while trying to help make it better for all. The level of man's transcendence on earth is determined by how well each individual contributes to the collective well-being of all.

It all depends on you and me, individually be, contributing a heart of love, a heart Godlike, for a world with difference making in everybody's life. It was essentially a "good over evil" thing. It starts with the individual and metastasizes to all the world. It is a dream of mankind, held in a world of darkness because it's so prevalent in everyday life and left to fester.

It was in a place like West Point, where spines were straightened, strengthened, and minds set toward positives that were good. People flourished under the safety of the military protection in a world cast asunder with violence and dark minds with evil intentions. Sad as it all was and is, there will be evil in the world 'til Jesus returns.

But Billy and Eddy were being trained up in the world to serve America wherever needed. Someone fortunately had to do it, and they were our youth among learned tutors with principles of the "God and philosophy, and protectors of assurance that it would be in "perpetuity" forever. It was the only country in the world that poured out its prosperity to others, without thought of receiving anything in return.

Coming out of World War II it was that way. Where else would enemies of the state conquered then flourish. So, in the present, without the helping rehabbing of America's grace. And why, 'cause it was a godly thing to do!

At West Point, Billy was taught that war was hell, but as long as you're in one the main objective - to win. Not all wars are justifiable or wise to participate or to initiate. Mistakes are made, information inexact, and hunger for engagement over abused. Men are not perfect, minds not minding reason, hearts hardened and of course "fear."

When men's hearts are hardened, we of the armed forces are called for engagement for most any cause. We are at the "beck and call" of the president of the United States and Congress, which represent the people. They determine the button of war. We prepare you cadets for. You are the best prepared armed services in the world. The words of General William Abrams, speaking to us during the first week of orientation at the Academy.

Leadership and training at the high-quality levels were the rule, and not the exception at West Point. Billy was now steeped in its midst and learning fast.

He felt most satisfied in his present situation of life. He was pursuing his high school dream, flying high with Eddy towards a goal in athletics, and pursuing a career where excellence is rewarded for effort and personal talents wherever it would take him. Billy thought he had what it takes to make good his dream. He was positive in a positive oriented atmosphere called West Point Academy, US Army style.

He would receive a second lieutenant commission as an officer in the United States Regular Army with benefits. He was currently happy and satisfied with himself. Although he missed his love contacts of his parents and Anita.

Sacrifice was the game, if it was a game, that was it. All of life is a choice, you sacrifice one thing for another. Some things require a great amount, others not so much. It's one day at a time, breath by breath. That's every person's private journey.

Listen hard to Billy's journey. It's a hard duty absorbed by determination, responsibility, love and perseverance and excellence. What Billy does and accomplishes during his lifetime is an exemplifying human endeavor. His story continues like this. It is unlike any average lifetime story.

CHAPTER TEN

There are eight million stories in New York, so says an old television show. Where the human form is on this earth, there is a story attached. Anybody who peeks an interest of others. For uniqueness in their life, become sometimes center stage. Sometimes, and some things people do in life, such as peculiar and unusual occupations or they exert outstanding performances, daring do's or heroic actions drawing attention. People love those kinds of stories because these actions do things admirable that they themselves wouldn't dare do. But, they can vicariously live it through seeing or reading about accounts of other's actions. It's indeed, kind of a vicarious experience self-induced through the media of movies, pictures, reading and word of mouth.

In days of old, it was the repeating of stories about the tribe, its heroes and outstanding citizenry. The Bible times and earlier were prime examples of this, before the written word. Now, presently, there are literally hundreds of ways to pass on remembrances, in story, individual achievements, group acclamations, and national and co-collaborative international projects and grandiose achievements through joint participations.

In America, the people are clamoring for people that represent the values and strengths and weaknesses they wish they had or that others should have to promote peace, prosperity and integrity they themselves purport to emulate. People admire people that show leadership, that live the lives that relate somewhere, sometime, somehow to themselves. There are 300 million personal preferences available in the USA.

Rarely does one anything suit all. People are forgiving when love and care as well as passion is rightly exampled in whoever is the subject of scrutiny by the public or group who are related in some way. It is then when some feat or individual achievement attains greater proportion than it actually is, that promotes the following of others because it is spotlighted. The

American public are looking for real and truthful individual integrity which matters and captures the following of others.

On the Army West Point Academy campus, Eddy and Billy now were taking on her status, because the Army football team was finally and once again attaining greatness and notoriety. West Point was becoming an "in" word in the fall sports vocabulary among all other sports being played. The vintage heroes of "Davis and Blanchard" in the present form of "Brewer and Brandon" the daring duo of the Black Knights 2016 version.

The priming of their so-called time was in some respect due to the hope laid upon them because they had two more years potential as tandem teammates together.

This bode well in the minds and prospects of all West Point cadets and staff. It certainly was in their high hopes that Army would shine and have their due time again, in the spotlight of greatness.

The apparent facts of this hope by all West Point were to be realized as the next several years went by. It not only was the talent that Head Coach Monkin had assembled, but the dedicated and hard work of a team all on the same page. Their efforts and enthusiasm were spot on directed to becoming the greased aggressive machine needed to produce football game winners.

The West Point glory days of 1944 to 1946, with the noted Stars of Blanchard and Davis, both Heisman Trophy winners, was not showcasing their new and modern duo of Eddy Brandon and Billy Brewer. Quarterback and tight end. As with any team, the Stars if talented and really good are, that way because everybody else is doing their job with precision and perfection. That truly was the case to be made for the 2016-2018 Army football season's teams. Two National Championship seasons had been produced.

It was the fourth season for Billy that Army began faltering. Eddy had graduated the year before and many of the senior stalwart players had moved on into the regular Army located somewhere, some place, for some time, around the world.

Billy found life without his dear friend, Eddy, a lonely time. He was always busy but good friendships are dear to the heart. Eddy had done his ultimate best when in senior year at the

Academy. He received the coveted Heisman Trophy honor. True to form and dream prospect with Eddy, Billy received the Heisman Trophy his Junior year as he was a year behind Eddy. Both also received many honors for their outstanding performances on the national platform for college level football.

Billy's and Eddy's home trophy case were becoming lined with awards. Billy's showcase included many other fields of sports awards, like the martial arts and track and field events. All the accolades and awards started at York High School and were accumulating. High levels of excellence begat being honored in a society appreciative of such efforts, especially found in America. The crème does still rise to the top. There were many great athletes, Billy was an exceptional one. Billy and Eddy were both well-rounded, down to earth types from the heartland of the Midwest, hard workers of tradition. Indeed, hard work, responsibility, and perseverance. Both were excellent students, but Billy if compared, was a better student academically.

As a new graduated cadet with honors from West Point, carrying now a Bachelor of Science degree in history, with a political science minor and sub-minor degree in math, he also sported a second lieutenant commission in the regular Army. Billy was, his senior year, a true leader attaining high status in all three pillars of performance in academics, physical and military. His status in the cadet apparatus and ranking found himself at the top of his class as a Brigade Commander which traditional translates a "First Captain." Senior class cadets at West Point were known as "firsties." Billy was first among many, a born leader, an imposing leader at that! He wasn't just a jock at West Point but a military student athlete, matured to the West Point apex of its designed program and the fullness of the Army training experience that the US Army could generate.

You were now ready for duty full time in the regular Army, the US Army world-wide in scope. With his background of excellence, his future would be his choosing, his work ethic and "smarts" would take him high and far. He was now a part of the Academy's long, gray line" as a graduate. He was very proud of himself, having accomplished all, even more than what he had expected and planned for himself and with his friend Eddy.

The experiences had been humbling, hard and yet exhilarating. It was sad that there was so little personal time spent anymore with family, friends and Anita. That bothered him, and he pondered heavily over the thought.

Like high school, he had received both athletic and scholastic honors beyond his wildest dreams. His cadet chest of medals was many, more than most. Once again, he was prepared for the next rung in the ladder of his life. This time as a soldier in the US Army, regular. He would be assigned to a job or if he desired a future venue, he more than likely would be assigned it.

Billy being in superb shape, wanted to get into the Special Forces or Green Berets as it was better known. This would be hard duty attaining this goal, as it was only for the special survivors, a few only accepted and lasted the intense training. It would be another time in this life that family and loved ones would not see him for months. Choices were very difficult.

Again, he was not thrilled at all at missing time with his family and Anita, but he had a plan and a desire to become the best of the best. He had attained that in football, and on duty at West Point, and now desiring more as a full-time US Army Regular soldier, where he would again try to direct his life direction. He would choose entering the training program to become a Green Beret. Some would say it's the equivalent to becoming a Senior VP or President of a corporation as its responsibilities for which he would be charged. It was transferable to civilian life.

Number one, he entertained the responsibility and daunting task and excitement of being one of a chosen few, a special operations forces Green Beret. Only a few knew the intensity it took to actually become one of a few selected and be a soldier of such a highly esteemed organization. He weighed heavily the options and consequences of the different and difficult opportunities ahead for him. Life would not be easy in the route he was taking, but he was confident and proud of himself.

He presently was 21 years-old, heading to 22. He owed the Army five years of his life which would place him at 27 years of age. He then had a three-year inactive reserve status obligation tacked on, but he could leave the service after age 27 and retreat back into civilian life or further his career in the Army.

It would be his choice. Presently he was a second Lieutenant in the US Army with no assignment at the present. Billy talked it all over with Eddy, who now was attending JAG Law School, eventually desiring to practice law in the civilian life. They were desirous of different things and well-schooled and prepared for any choices they made for their future.

Eddy had gotten several lucrative offers from professional football teams, but he was tied to furthering his desired career as a lawyer by staying in the Army and being educated by JAG school educators and practicing in the Army.

Because of his career services he could marry his girlfriend, Penny, and live on an Army salary and benefits. He would avoid military active duty in harm's way but might be stationed most any place across the world. For a young man from a small town-city, it was education at its best, at the least personal cost financially, but it was restricted to Army life for the duration of time in his life. He had enjoyed his time at West Point and his choice to become a lawyer at the Army's expense., It would not be the freedom expected of a civilian track to lawyering, but it had its advantages.

Billy on the other hand, was a big husky hunk of young man used to heavy lifting and use of his body. He was agile for a large person, quick of motion and mind. Always a fast learner and desirous to be the best at whatever he did. He was nobody's fool and his decision making was rather acute and rewarding to him. High in ethic values, and order taking pursuits, highly regarded as trustworthy and responsible in whatever venue he participated in. He always seemed to be in charge, cool in demeanor and in action, when others were in chaos. He was a born leader, a fearless opponent of anything confronting him. He exuded confidence of an underrated demeanor. IN person he was bigger than life, and his strength was far greater than even a generous person might attach to him. The three Amigos had trained their mentored pupil well. They were ecstatically proud of his life, his personhood and lifestyle. They kept up and in touch with Billy wherever he went It was a debt Billy would not forget.

CHAPTER ELEVEN

It would be a rather agonizing determination of what challenge line his future would take. He was young enough for any physical challenge and smart enough to manage all the mind stuff required. He was leaning in the direction of action as opposed to administration detail or desk job.

His learning would require a really tough road to hoe, it would not include family or friends especially girlfriends up close. It would be a hardship. He had five years active obligation to the Army. He wanted an experience unlike any ordinary man would have. Very few men traveled where he was thinking of going The Special Forces' route, alias the Green Berets. He would be schooled in the ways and for the very best of warfare. He desired the best for himself to defend his country. He felt a certain pull, a duty to fulfill on behalf of America. Even a sense of urgency, a need for him to defend the American way.

America was weakening, from the inside out, and was being pummeled by outside forces destined to spread their way of thinking to consume us and conquer America, with its haughty and sinful ways. Excuses and delusionary thinking were always attacking America seeking its destruction.

America has a lot of fringe folk with lurid thinking, with subtle and toxic motives towards its disembowelment, especially philosophically and financially. The "Soros" and Alinsky's kind and obvious ISIS-type sinister folk. America had need of backbone and "cool" hand Luke-types able and willing to defend the basic American way of life. The stuff the founders talked about and fought for. The freedom fighters of yesteryear that made America the best "hope" in the world, for people, families and prosperity.

Nowhere else but America has the prosperity level exceeded itself for so many, that the world of suffering and damaged, has a friend who cares and shares its resources and wealth in rebuilding new and prosperous lives. That's America at its best.

Dastardly people come here to further their hate for their conditions or personal state of being. They're here to stir up trouble and destination, outrage and false propaganda and idea, usually long ago and antiquated or foreign and imposing their will on American culture.

In America certain things work others don't. Sharia law for instance, a venom to our society. Billy being a student of history, world history, and being from a small town-city in America, and having the opportunity to enjoy its benefits, saw the handwriting on the wall that America's very foundations were being attacked both from within its lands and from outside as well. Within America the silence of Apathy was increasing American weakness and vulnerability.

Someone, somewhere in America, had to rise up out of our great soil and stand in the "gap" and stand down the imposing stench of opportunistic infringement by so many others so desirous of spreading their ideologic disorders, the worms and adders of the world who were bombarding us with poisons. It was not a pretty picture if you were a true American countryman, a person of democracy. American, for the most part, were home spun folks, family loving, hard- working, tax paying inhabitants who like the America freedoms and opportunities they had, and its lifestyles afforded as benefit accrued through their hard labors of work; family superseded race and philosophical or cultural differences. When democracy worked everyone benefitted in every way. Nobody was held back or restricted. Each individual had the responsibility to work hard and produce for themselves with benefits spillover to the families and neighbors and other worlds beyond around the globe.

War was generally the prime example of serious overload of self-aggrandizement in one form or another, usually by some charismatic lunatic leader with an exceptionally narrow-minded outlook who sells someone else a bill of goods with fictitious facts of words as their patter on behalf of others.

Deceitfulness is the Satanic Culture behind it all. If God is for it, then Satan is against it and destines himself to the duty of destruction and opposition to "everything" that God does on earth. Everything is game. People, places and words. Bullets kill, so do words. Apathy kills, as well as finger-pointing. White lies are the biggest killer of all, throughout the world over.

CHAPTER TWELVE

Billy was caught in a culture of gloom and doom. Too many were catching it. He knew there were plenty of so-called good guys out there who knew how to get things done. He had participated with them in school, on the field, in the arena of competition and at Military College.

He knew there were good men and women older, before him, that were the epitome of what America was all about. He was developing a culture of mind and mindset of courage and purpose some of which he could see in his doing. He felt a direction, a pull if you will, towards a destiny for himself.

He felt like he was in training for his future unknown, whatever that was, or whenever. He felt that his life had a purpose and he was supposed to submit his all to fulfill his destiny. He increasingly thought and felt like God had his hand on him and was directing his ways. He felt a certain urgency now and then to God's promptings in his choices in whatever he did, and whenever he could, he sought to read the bible and attend church or pastoral service in his busy schedule. He felt a recharging whenever he came into the presence of God's teaching in a house of worship. He thought a lot about "Michael," God's chief warrior, he hoped he'd meet him sometime. He envisioned him his "hero."

The tug to choose; Billy put the choice clearly on God's front porch. The Special Forces or the regular Army offerings. There was a difference in experiential difficulties one most consequential and the other less so. His life was on the line. He wanted the very best for himself and that's why he chose joining the special forces experience and direction. The Special Forces experience was not for the fainthearted but for the rough and rugged and smart.

It was not what his family or girlfriend would want, but there was a bigger lot to be cast that was in charge of his decision making.

Billy had many times discussed at length his beliefs with Anita, of his feeling a "call" on his life by God. His history with the

3 Amigos through grade and high school, his association and friendship with Eddy and West Point enticement, and his success academically and physically in the manner it was, drew him into the beliefs and choices he'd made so far.

He had no fear in his choices, as he thought he was indeed in God's perfect will, it was "spooky" but true. Whenever he had a moment of time, he tried to dwell on these things and weigh them. He so far, felt "wholeness" in his choices and the way he was going. He was fully conscious on most of all that was going on around him. He would take advantage of it to learn about as much as he could and store it in his mental vault.

Anita was lonely and disappointed that Billy was seemingly drifting away from her. She realized those were selfish thoughts and she felt that their love was strong for the other, there was no competition dangling magnetic forces around them. No outside forces pulling them in the human form.

She was about to spend two years abroad in Paris at the "Ecole du Paris de Art" in a graduate course study program of the highest level for those with real painting power talent. She definitely would be full time busy for a while. This study would cover several years while Billy tortured his body and mind with basic survival and kill tactics with a vast quantity of weaponry the Special Forces used.

There was no holding Billy back from succeeding his training, being who he was and the shape he was in as well as the brain power he possessed. The old saying of "different strokes for different folks" were well penned for Billy and Anita's future lifestyles. The glue to their mutual attraction was their genuine love and caring for each other.

A strong mutual attraction at a very young emotional teenage year that was vested and knit in the eyes and hand of God. There was no question as they lived their separate and present ways. Nobody wanted but, in fact, they constantly encouraged one another to hold on, continue their way through schooling and study, perfecting their ways in their desired field of study and talents. So far so good was their financial survivability. She was basically cruising on scholarships and he was financed by the government. Because he had a few expenses, he, now on a salary of 2nd lieutenant with around $3300 incoming a month, which he tried to pack away in an account for future benefit for the both of them i.e. a savings account. He was trying to be a conservative and frugal person.

Long distance phone calls over "skype" through their computers kept them apprised of each other each week. They were able to create the "clean air" of communication between them necessary for a healthy survival. Each of them was in the loop with the other and were able to cushion the bumps that they sustained along the way and they had each other's shoulder to lean on. In their closeness, as much as possible, they added the cement necessary for their survival mode together. Love was in action. Love never fails. God had them in tow.

Anita resigned herself as she took her place in Paris. She was now embarked on what might be called the "final" round of personal professional painting instruction and tutorial study. She would be studying under the very best that the world had to offer. Paris was known as the world capital for painting and painters. Her specialty was fulfilling the art of painting "realist" paintings of all kinds, like those kinds and types where "pots on a shelf" looked so real you were enticed to come close up to feel, touch, the clay pots, painted with such clear clarity they appeared REAL. There was a whole school invested in realist-type painting, and the "Tromp l'oeil"-style was new and most complicated.

The term "Realism" was adopted by the great French artist Gustave Courbet around 1819-1877. It emerged in France after the French Revolution in 1848. There were many and are many who have followed this artistic school and style several Canadian and American artists to name a few; like Ken Darby 1940-2007, Winslow Homer, Thomas Eakins early 1870, a most important artist Andrew Wyeth 1917-2009, one of America's best known and famous artist.

Ken Davies, 1925-present, followed the likeness of Wyeth, excellence in still life. He transitioned from pure realism into the trompe l'oeil painting technique which is the visual illusion in art, especially used to trick the eye into perceiving a painted detail as a three-dimensional object. Visual renderings of these paintings were stunning in many cases, depending on the subject matter. Davies usage of sable brushes were labor intensive, but his results frequently appeared almost as photographs, but with trompe l'oeil and surrealistic effects.

Anita was in her ecstatic heyday learning time of her life. She was excited, and in love with being an artist and with her work. She was beginning to attract a following as her instructors were most enthusiastic with her talent and production pieces.

The word was getting out about her reputation in the Paris art culture and social circles. She became the young darling pretty American girl with a future greatness in early bloom. She found herself suddenly in another world and had a new set of worries and concerns facing her. She was establishing notoriety, a following and credibility of talent. She was no fluke, no sudden shining star, she worked and learned and practiced her God-given talent to the point of close perfection as a human can achieve.

She communicated all these recent events to Billy who was excited for her and responded with how proud of her he was and encouraged her onward to both enjoy her achievements and new friendships and a warning her to those looking to take advantage of her "Freshmaness" of success. There was genuine emotional tearing of her soul and spirit in not being around where he was to celebrate in person with her, hug her and talk with her in person. There were pangs of pain in their distance and lack of ever-present closeness.

He had a second thought of his chosen plan for his future. She was seeking life through her realm and he was seeking a pathway that would secure her safety and way of life, yet vulnerable to sudden death occurrence. It romantically didn't make any sense. The odds on that they would make it were slim. Their hopes were not so much that they desired each other, but that they put their trust and faith in God to keep and prosper each other for their good. They were in agreement and pledged their trust in God through prayer for their benefit, and long life together. It would be a hardship with dedication to their causes renewed every day. This would become their bond and troth, with each other. A taste of faith, hope and love in outreach.

Billy was currently preparing to enter into serious Special Forces training. It would be some time before that training would be finished. In addition, the on-the-job training extended beyond the formal training and it was critical survival in certain life situations.

The Green Berets were a special lot. Sometimes known as the "quiet professionals." They were self-contained persons who in much humility quietly went about doing their job, avoiding any kind of showmanship nature! Their work ethic, versatility, training usually defied what conventional wisdom would say was possible. These soldiers operated in some of the most austere conditions on earth.

Green Berets were trained to operate autonomously, to be self-sufficient and empowered to make mission critical decisions at any time. They are trained in decision-making processes typically used by their civilian peers and utilize the training to in times of resource constrained environments.

Green Berets special operation forces were often used in training, advising and assisting foreign forces abroad. Their success often depended on their ability to work closely with other cultures and nationalities. Continuous training in foreign languages plus their ability to teach military skills were essential to their effectiveness in preparing allies. Some of their effectiveness was in their versatility.

Green Beret candidates were chosen for their ability to be self-starters, self-motivators. Course curriculum training specialized in small unit tactics, vocational training, and survival and resistance training. Much of these things were practiced in the jungles of North Viet Nam against the Viet Cong.

Green Berets were not rapid deployment people. They operated out of secret and intense preparation. They studied with intense preparation. They studied areas assigned like a PhD student researching. They were to suck up every available open source and classified assessment of demographics, tribal class culture, local politics, religious leaders and schisms, history, terrain, the infrastructure, road maps, power grids, water supplies, crops and the local economy. IN addition, they plan, debate and rehearse both combat and follow-up on a plan of operations. They are attuned to absorbing and making a quick analysis of geographical problems or nuance diplomatic issues re(solve.)

Teams of Green Berets are given the firepower of an organization four times their size, and expected in combat to enable an indigenous force of up to a battalion (400).

They are looking for adoptability, and flexibility to solve things using good entrepreneurial skills and risks, calculate those risks, and use creative thinking. All this training had usable skills in civilian life and quite attuned to preparation for a CEO (chief executive officer). Green Berets are always pushed to the limit in whatever. Their cross training in many fields like medicine or as medics gave them uniqueness of versatility in use in mission accomplishments. Certainly you find in the Special Forces' menu, not the Navy way, Air Force way or even the Army way, but definitely the Special Forces adopted and unique way; usually those other ways were but a good start for their special way of training. It was the difference that made them the unique Special Forces that they were. Selection of participant personnel was critical in maintaining the narrow high quality needed in their membership. Narrow was the way. Special Forces people were highest quality recruits selected for their tribal units. They are a unique, unconventional combat organization. Indeed, they are the most versatile special operations soldiers in the world, an elite multi-purpose force for high priority targets.

These operatives essentially are tasked with primary missions of unconventional warfare – sometimes their original assigned task of helping foreign internal defenses and special reconnaissance. Many small governments just didn't have the wherewithal to remain stable or valid. They were in need of help.

Other branches of service had their elite troops, detachments or small armies with particular type tasks. Each had their particular talents and specialty contributions for the right need and task at hand to tip the united states favorably for whatever social, political or needful necessary mission so determined by our government.

The ability to be free citizens of a democracy as created by our forefathers who delivered us from tyranny and subjugation by others. The armed services served America well and has kept and made the difference in holding our freedoms we have determined for ourselves these last 200 plus years.

Billy Brewer was at your service, how as a critical professional soldier and unique in a specific curriculum as a person of high honor, dedicating his young vulnerable life in the protection of America and its interests worldwide. He essentially was an expert and highly trained foot soldier of the Army special operations forces, USA. They were ready to go anywhere, in any condition and serve America's interest as a best front-line, keeping it and its citizens safe and attuned to its way of life.

Billy's life would take him around the world, through jungles, desserts and deep into enemy territory. His training both physically and mentally were the finest that was presently available. Billy rose to those many crossroads and dangers the likes of Green Beret life and times. Nothing was easy in his life and duties. Billy was but one of many (the few) who were selected to serve his country in such a specific capacity. Much like a trained electrician, he learned which wires were hot and knew how to deal and manipulate through the maze of multi-layered, multi-colored sprawl of human political and combat scenarios. He had to learn several very foreign languages, Arabic and Farsi in particular, a scattering of Russian and some Chinese.

Billy's background of training, tasking, and determination plied him well to becoming a Green Beret and serving in such a capacity with them. His talents and strengths, both physically and mentally were to his blessing.

It all added up to man tethering with God, serving and surviving a young and dangerous lifestyle only but a few are a part of. Indeed, the few and the mighty. That little ant can do big and mighty things when loyal and determined trained citizenry takes charge in a world of followers. Lord knows, you need followers, but the world also needs leaders with integrity and honesty of the Soul. America did, and young Billy certainly personified such character. He certifiably believed in God and country and he was active in pursuing his first loves which he espoused as God, country and family.

Billy's lifestyle set him apart from most folks his age. Frankly, most folks his age were expressing their anger, rage, and anti-social behaviors as young free students and citizenry across the American landscape and around the world because people like Billy in his capacity, were protecting their freedoms to do just what they were doing.

Freedoms of expression do not come easy in most of the world. There is a price, sometimes a heavy price, to pay for being eligible to express anything but what the government dictates. People are put down by guns, tanks, wicked human beings caught in Satan's web, promoted by superlative ego-maniacs with a desire with sometimes indescribable and inhumane actions.

It was at this time in Billy's life that the public arena in America was under multi-attack from within and outside. Outside was trying to implode America by attacking it on all fronts. The strong America that was well known, was springing leaks all over. The will of the people was evaporating into a new and uneducated conglomerate, and citizens of the young, who had never been taught history, especially American history. Many couldn't name more than two of its presidents, and had no idea who were the enemies of World War II or who their state Governor was and what party. Disrespect and ignorance were a disease in motion, and vileness was a way of life. Everybody seemed to deplore violence, but nobody did anything to avoid or stop it. When it occurred, the good guys got booed and attacked and the bad guys got assuaged and lifted up as righteous and virtuous. America was losing its high on the hill status because things were not right in the land of the free and the home of the brave. The youth, without knowledge (other than electronics) and without integrity of leadership, was blowing in the winds, the hurricane winds, of unknown influences unawares, and downright onslaught of persons out to destroy America for personal and world-wide power desires. Conspiracies were developing sporadically but left alone would one day, coagulate together in a one world authority, the like no one has yet ever seen or been a part of. The seeds were being planted everywhere, indeed Satan was having a field day. "Without knowledge, the people will perish" is a known scripture of the Bible. How wise was that little tidbit of information? How little was it absorbed.

What was once of importance and purpose to Americans is being lost to youth without knowledge and men without spines. Paper and talk hardly are the materials to protect much of anything. Knowledge, spirit and determined backbone greatly enhance the future good health of this country. "Help, we're going down!"

In the Bible, Paul on his journey to Rome on a ship that went down as a result of a storm (among other things), but he was assured by God that he and the crew would all make it safe to shore and on to Rome.

America needed God would be a logical empirical thought to assume at this point. Billy was deep in thought about these things, as he returned from an assignment rescuing some American citizens in Somalia. It had been a harrowing rescue, but his military co-assignees were spot on in their mission and they were not to be denied their targets. A few of the hostage-takers were eliminated but all of his team was safely returned to Base and another day was completed in the life of the Green Berets.

Billy was always a fast learner as the 3 Amigos were to find out while he was under their tutelage. His experience at West Point was additional trial for his innate talents, yet fully not disclosed. He was truly a "sponge" of a human being and his mind unusually so. His record of life history was well documented with accolades of positive and rewards for his diversity of his daily lifestyle and attitude. He took on responsibility and jobs others backed away from. Indeed, in the military, he had experienced teaching that there was a time to retreat as a tactical maneuver that he might attack another time.

He was a proponent of General George Patton, but a hell of a lot smarter and more practical.

So much of modern warfare fared on the side on modern high technologies which were good to great, but as always it took manpower to do and place the technology where they were needed the most. Then there were the type of combat jobs requiring only a few highly talented and knowledgeable good men to perform. Danger was their mission, and knowledge and training were their most valuable assets. Green Berets and Special Forces never rested on their current assets but were ever in them advanced instructional and learning curves. Like a fine piano tuner, they trained to the fine line of perfection, that were in tune, and ready to go where duty called.

If ever there were "Intense" status of all the services, Special Forces were the epitome of the word. These military folks literally gave and give their lives every day. They do not wave their banners high but quietly carry out lifesaving and strategic missions for the retaining aid preserving the American way of life, and its people. There is no other service like it. Others do mimic it and are specifically talented in certain fields of endeavor, but the crème de la crème initials begin and end with G. B.

Billy was not yet seasoned to lead any special assignments at this time, but was apprenticing the leaders of those who were. Rest assured those leaders enjoyed having him participate in whatever the mission was.

CHAPTER THIRTEEN

The days and nights were filled with training. Both of mind and body. Maps were read and reviewed, equipment was being apprised for proper usage and deployment. Back-up plans were framed and assessment of man power were being determined. Complete knowledge of every facet of an operation was put on the table. Safety of men was critical, they were the best and most valuable of all assets. Thoroughness was their game. Once all the assets were placed, runs and reruns were the games of assuredness to success in their missions. These were just part of the Green Beret routine for specific mission operations.

In preparation for a stage play on Broadway typically and all important were the many rehearsals, to get the productions right and become like a second nature expended. Indeed, it was much the same, however, the danger quotient was astronomically higher. Death by incompetence or wrong doing.

The world lives in a vacuum of fantasyland, it is relegated to civilian forms of living – non-violent primarily. Sometimes the inner cities approximate war zones, but the Green Beret world and the civilian world are in a world apart.

Billy certainly realized this after his first and very dangerous mission assigned him in Somalia. And he entered into that other world of causing death to others. It, of course, was new to him, the actual partaking of death was a real, social and personal shock to him. He would never get used to such violence of "man's inhumanity to man."

It was not the reality of the infantry point man charging the machine gun nest, but it was small military groups infiltrating and penetrating sometimes protecting depending on the mission de complir.

After specific duties of participation on mission assignments, he was debriefed and given time off to recoup – the short time allotted. These times found Billy communicating with Anita in France from his headquarter location. Sometimes he had the availability of Skype, so that they could see one another as they talked over their computers.

All the more and once again Billy realized the importance of his job. Somebody had to do what he did. It had "essential" written all over it. He shared all his feelings and emotions with Anita as he so joyously talked with her. He greatly missed her and assured her he was where he needed to be. Such a "high" after saving American civilians from the clutches of the nasty and barbarous hostage purveyors and extortionists.

She didn't like it one bit, no matter what he said, it just wouldn't convince her to be away and doing the things he did. She understood all the reasons etc. for the need for somebody to perform those tasks, but why him, being so far away from her. She said to herself a prayer of resignation and a prayer for him and his safety.

She said she loved him also besides missing him nearby. They reassured each other of their fidelity to one another and once again departed from contact.

Billy returned his thinking and body to where he was. A Special Forces encampment on the Maldives Islands in the Arabian Sea. It was indeed a hideaway area for American deployment and Middle East base planning for the CIA and the likes. It bristled with electronics of all kinds, especially akin to snooping the airwaves. It was a spot in the ocean big enough to house several parallel 5000 foot plus runways. It had a natural formed harbor and small islands nearby full of American top secret and special supplies depots. It was a place kept out of the news world. It was an undercover and stealth part of the world. It was under the protection of one of America's battle fleets who kept an eye over that territory of the world.

Right now, Billy was hanging his hat on that main island as they were planning another strike to extract or kill a very high positioned Isis mullah who was calling the shots and directing its Isis operations. He was a crucial and critical player big time whom all the Isis movement seemed to flow around. He was the "big cheese" of 'Fatwahs.' His military name by the American forces was 'Mullahmoo.' He presented himself as the "Caliphate King Tut." He was a blustery bag of dessert wind, much like

"Babbling Bob" of the early Iraq administration of the Dessert Storm days. This guy was deceivingly cunning and exceptional smart besides.

The details and tracking of this "Mullah dude" were humongous. He was obsessed with hiding himself wherever, like Hussain had. Thus, he sometimes was difficult to locate, much less forecast his movements. However, he was establishing a pattern in his movements, that the CIA and its people noticed and was working on documenting details. There was only so much space and territory he wanted, or could, move around in. He was not exactly popular with the ruling Mullah in Iran and there were other lesser Mullahs either jealous of him or themselves didn't approve of his boisterous ways.

In this scenario could possibly lay the key to infiltrating knowledge of locating and creating a plan to capture or kill him. The CIA preferred to capture. Everybody else for killing the "bastard." The CIA surmised a weakness in the "tribe," might provide an opportunity to seize or strike him. The big plan was on, and the Green Berets attached to the Island were right in the middle of the planning – they were killers or extractors – as the plan played out.

Data and contacts the world over were essential to the CIA no matter what was needed from them. They were running wide open now in resourcing all of them to "pin point" code word "MOO" and his traveling circus of killers.

Moo was dangerous even in his bruha showmanship directorates. He was cagey, sly like a fox, but he had personal traits he took with him all along the way. He was kind of like a skunk who left a trail behind him. It stuck and those in his path got out of his way or were terminated. He was vicious in his bravado. Recently his army of Virgin Hunters, was taking a beating. They had to give ground in several areas, but still remained spread out and strong. However, many of the strongholds were indeed weakening and folding down. They had lost territory in the north to the Kurds, and got their gold standard oil butts bombed out in the north. Their Syrian hideouts and cozy lairs of iniquity were being missiled and bombed at every opportune time by the Americans, Russians and French. The Iranians avoided them like cancer carriers, which to them, they were.

The silent airways of the CIA and the small little islands of the Maldives was humming like a million bumble bees on the loose. This was a big King Tut strike about to let the cobra loose. The coils were tightening.

Billy felt the tension of the people involved where he was. And again, he was in all the high-level meetings and planning of the strike force and coordinating CIA teams. They had not yet determined the "hit" spot to tie Moo up, but they had multi-plan scenarios aligned for snatching him wherever he showed up.

While there would be a vacuum to his absence on the scene, there would be others to fill his gap. However, he would be hard to replace for a long time because Moo was privy to all the who, why, where's of the Isis movement, and the "King Pin" of all their involvement. He was not just a spiritual leader but King Evil in charge. There was nothing peaceful about him. He was cunnings, deceitful, revengeful and a killer. He definitely had not friends; those he had were afraid of him too. Everyone kept their distance and like "Old Joe" Stalin of Russia, all kept a distance from him, for fear of losing their head or life. He had an army of "yes" men under him, an eventual killer disease.

Mullah Moo was definitely planning his "Caliphate," his earthly space and a place where he would reign and be recognized as the Supreme Commander in chief, the Caliphate, the head of the serpent, called the Islamic State.

Billy was given privilege to attend all the planning and strategic inside knowledge of "Operation Moo. It was here he was familiarized with the history of the Moo Movement. It was much like a cobra rising up out of earth, an active volcano erupting on a specific spot on planet earth. The Sulphur smell was horrific and had a white stripe down its black suit of killer warriors. This was no rose garden; nothing pretty was visible came from these renegades on planet earth. Killer locusts if you will. They literally rose out of hell upon the world scene, out of the sink holes of the old Saddam Hussein regime.

It all got started on the throes of the defeat of the remnants of Saddam Hussein's resistant fighters who retreated to the sink holes of Iraq and just inside of the Iranian border.

The creation for the beginning of the current Isis movement began with a street thug by the name of Abu Musab AL Zarqawi, a Mujahideen wannabee who set up camps for training terrorists. He was looking to free agent and set up his own terrorist organization, which would be a party to "Monotheism" and "Jihad." These soldiers were mostly non-Iraqis and his enemy at first were the Muslim Shiite sect. Bin Laden and Al Qaeda regarded them as heretics.

The movement was taken over and rebranded as the Islamic State of Iraq, or Isis. It was taken over by a new leader by the name of Abu Mazeri Banditi. These soldiers of Islam's aggressive movement were mostly former Saddam's military group, an aire of an army, rather than just a ragtag military assembled outfit. There was order amongst.

Suddenly thousands of armed men now opened a second front against the Shiites in Syria. Assad, president of Syria, and his commanders were "Alawites," a Shiite sub set group, thus these new thugs from hell, were not part of the secular Syrians in uprising fighting against Assad.

Soon Banditi renamed his terrorist group the "Islamic State" both in Iraq and Syria, reflecting his greater ambitions. Isis is based on a government structure, to rule its terrorist conquerings. They have a cabinet, governors, financial and legislative bodies. Its hierarchy resembles some western countries, it values they reject.

What is it that Isis wants? To erase borders of the Mideast and establish and create a regional Islamic Caliphate (state) similar to the form of government that ended nearly 100 years ago with the fall of the "Ottoman Empire" in the Mideast.

The beginning of this is seen in Raqqa, where Isis runs social welfare programs, provides food and fuel to the poor and even operates its own food standard board. All this comes at a high price, and must observe their very strict personal observances of conduct or receive heavy rebukes and penalties.

Isis currently controls a land size area the size of Massachusetts. It is basically an extremist group which feeds on the disparity of innocent people spreading fear and death conquest over those who do not agree with them.

Here is an anatomy of Isis, its leaders and control:
Leaders and Control of Isis Government

Abu Bakr al Baghdadi
(Commander-in-Chief of Caliphate)

Cabinet
Baghdadi's Advisors

Abu Muslim al Turkmani
Deputy – Iraq

Abu Ali Ambari
Deputy – Syria

Governors of Iraq
12

Governors of Syria
11

Financial Council
Weapons and Sales

Leadership Council
Drafting Laws,
Key Policies

Military Council
Islamic State

Legal Council
Decision on
Executions,
Recruitment

Fighter Assistance Council
Foreign Fighter Aid

Security Council
Internal policing,
Executions

Intelligence Council
Information on Isis Enemies

Media Council
Regulates Media
and /Social Media

Inquiry of how they are funded can be found through organized crime and government activity. They extort business men, and collect ransom and loot state assets. It is known they stole 425 million from the Mosul's State Bank. In addition to this theft, they impose taxes on locals, and steal oil from the fields producing.

Isis is believed to hold some 2 billion in cash and assets. You can see they have a monopoly of one at their beck and call. Their entire Caliphate is trying hard to stay their course and to expand it where they can – ambition – world-wide through intimidation, fear and aggression.

Ignorance and apathy are the real enemy and we freedom fighters are in consignment to kill off these cancers of societies a little or as big a bit as we can.

"This concludes to days info presentation for today," said Major Allen Allistar, the Commandant of the Military Section of the Island Compound. Tomorrow we will spell out our game plan to you all, for the plotting and planning to extract the "Big Moo" from his moorings. Agent John Steelman of the CIA. Will apprise you with our current game plan for "Operation Moo." Please be here promptly. Thank you all for being here. Dismissed!"

CHAPTER FOURTEEN

At 0 8 hundred the next morning all the personnel necessary to the knowledge of "Operation (Mullah) Moo" was assembled!

"My name is John Steelman. I am the project director from the CIA, your friendly covert protection agency. Today we will continue the overall plan and description of our target and surroundings, their operation mojo and mind set.

First off, these people of evil are determined conquering bound for their cause. They are cold killers of humanity that in their estimation are on their way of progress towards their goal – the attainment of as big a regional Caliphate as they can generate and secure it through intimidation and fear – all terror oriented.

This was tried and defeated some 100 years ago – it was called the "Ottoman Empire." Once again, it's being resurrected by the chaos and disenfranchisement of a section of the Mid-East – it's tribes and sect-oriented clusters of volatile humanity. These are not your usual civilized Western European and Asian Communities. They are tribesmen of many stripes and narrow beliefs, each conflicting with another with variations of the same genesis. We are dealing with a philosophy of living based on false teachings and beliefs in a God they have created for their expansive and nomadic way of life. They that are extremists are very dark, oriented people. They are not happy campers – as we would say.

I am here to bring you along with my team a treatise plan of attack and the intentional removal, extraction or killing, of the head "Mullah" in charge of the extremist movement. He is the central leader, shaker and strategist for the Isis Movement. Remember Isis is not a religion as the world knows, but in fact, an extreme state movement to establish their dogmatic form of Islam as a state. It is a bunch of fanatics bent on making themselves a Caliphate state and established leaders/government for all Islamic rule.

These are not civilized people, they are a form of dictatorship under the guise of a religious covering. They are religious zealots on the loose. They are loose cannons on the march to conquer territory and subject people through the "sword" – by the sword. It is not a religion of peace as they would have you think – certainly not as the extremist think.

One might associate the fiction character "Darth Vader" as our present "target" Mullah Moo. He is cunning extremely dangerous and an active proponent of his mentor the late Al-Qaeda viral leader Osama Bin Laden; but he is currently a huge operations mover and shaker for the spirit of Radicalism by an Islam proponent. He has gathered and founded an Islamic Army of radicals bent on the subjection of any others to bow down before them and kowtow to their very dark way of life. It's a form of Satanism at best. They are an army of thugs among nations legitimate. They are an infectious disease let loose upon the world.

The present Mullah Moo presently resides in a compound, undisclosed but to a few. He is much like a salamander living among civilian people, acting low key, as he manipulates his army across the Middle East territories – little by little scorching the earth, surprises by surprises – murdering and pillaging all in their way. It's their way or the high way. Death or subjugation.

We have location of his whereabouts. He is indeed slipping, sleeping a different place nightly. However, he is a regular at his office of operations daily.

While Moo sleeps everywhere among the townspeople at night, he always appears at his headquarters office and compound of militia nearby the everyday public square farmers market, which is brimming with food produce for sale. It is located here because it is so close to the citizen townspeople who mass there to buy their daily. It offers him public protection and covering, and the office compound is quite inconspicuous and stealth-like. It was located where it is so that the enemy air attacks would not bomb or strafe them – with so many citizens mulling and congregating in one space so nearby his headquarters.

The compound is stealth-like in its structure by physical make-up, that it wouldn't appear like any government or military stronghold or structure and draw an eye specifically looking for such a hiding place. There are four outside guards dressed in civilian street clothes of local look-a-likes-with AK's under their shawls and Arab coverings.

These people also carry hand grenade-type explosives, but to the casual eye they look like part of the nearby crowd – shoppers all. Inside are many offices with doors and hallways going everywhere within. It is a two-story facility in some areas with staircases guarded by top and bottom steel doors. There are two routes to the top floor, or second tier, for escape purposes mainly.

The inner walls are fortified as well as the roof, and if you look closely you could see electronic antennas on the corners of the main building rooftop. Those are for their coded communications to their associates in terror, across the Caliphate territories.

Every hallway has a guard at each end armed with AK 47s and bandoliers of bullets. The top floor contains an elaborate suite of electronics rooms, maps and an open table room, also an executive luxurious type office with easy chairs, couches and propaganda all over the walls.

The whole "Mullah" compound lacked normal military security semblance as they are a mobile military hardcore group. Their preparations militarily were to fight and flee to fight again They weren't militarily astute enough to hold a particular area in a fort-like assembly. Anywhere a large assembly of terrorists gathered the allies would attack them mercilessly. So, their strength was in small groups, sometimes many small groups, mobile with an occasional small version of the "tank" small artillery pieces are used whenever could be found a vehicle to pull them around. The mobile vehicles were Toyota trucks with machine guns mounted on the truck bed.

They were essentially like nomads, "Genghis Khan's of the deserts mounted on their pick-up trucks were 50-calibre machine guns, - those were their desert camel horse on half-tracks attack vehicles of choice.

Isis is noted for their using human shields, the citizenry, to hide behind knowing the Western mindset of humane care and concern for the innocent and defenseless public populace. Their rules of war carried no concern for others, but only what advantages can be executed to fulfill their battle cry "Allah Akbar." The God they served knows no mercy or love, no kindness or care. The enemy is anybody that gets in their way. They have never heard of the word compromise or peace. Peace to the proponents of war or terrorism was to them but an opportunity to reload and strike out more fiercely. Their philosophy is to bury any and all enemies of the state no matter what circumstances are presented. Winning by any endeavor, using any means they can think of is prime resourcefulness on their part. It usually was standardized by propaganda in the fullness as they could spread it.

Agreements and understandings solely belong to their advantage because they held no such beliefs in their thinking, using them to, as I said before, to reload, relocate and attack mercilessly. Treaties, peace, promises, care, love, concerns, have nothing to do with other people not like them. Their own society was derelict of these Western values, because their religion wasn't one – its was a state enforced movement of terror and its presentation and the spread of fear as an enforcement and coercion asset tool to be exploited.

The CIA were developing a specific plan of attack. The battle plans were being planned. It was being hatched on a small group of islands located just southwest of India and Sri Lanka. Some 3600 miles from the snatch/or kill zoned destination. It was an assembly of the best covert planners the CIA had to offer. It also was surrounded by Americas top elite Special Forces personnel. Billy Brewer was one of the Green Berets special operations forces group located there. It was their duty to physically carry out the game plan on the ground, hatched by the CIA to secure or kill "Big Moo," bring him back dead or alive for intelligence interrogation. It would be another waterboarding event – as he was a prime person of vast knowledge of all Isis planning and movement. Information he had definitely or need to know situation – a special recruit suite for the "waterboarding" exemption law most recently voted upon by Congress. The senator from New York would cast a definite "Yea" on this one. It was equivalent to a Bin Laden capture/kill scenario a top-secret stuff.

The whole Operation "Moo" scenario and planning came out of the executive CIA discussion on the Middle East crisis. They needed also to just disengage the body Isis from its over aggressive leadership – who they passionately followed unto death. The purported virgins to be had and eternal <u>martyrdom</u> for killing infidels (which is everybody but them) was all the reason they needed to point an AK-47 in the air expending rounds of fire and gleefully shouting their conquering war whoop "Allah Akbar." Blood was happily running from their mouths as further darkness lined their hearts. Satan was alive and well in Isis-land. His plan was to kill and destroy any and all good that God created on this earth. Why? Because he wanted to be God – pure and simple.

Christian Westerners were soulful people with high guilt quotients and lots of Rules and Regs as to their behavior toward others and their enemies. To Isis, they were too civil to be effective human beings on this earth. Isis' God said, "Infidels are to be eliminated, one way or another, that resistance to Islam and its bent cause by God decree, made "Allah Akbar" the battle cry and 72 virgins the goal for every "cause" warrior. Blood spilled was territory gained and less to deal with in the future. The Islamic terrorists' goal of complete submission and subjugation of the world unto a universally Mullah dominated led Caliphate would be their goal for total peace on earth. Death by the sword was their way to strength and dominion of Earth.

The Caliphate society of subversive death and destruction was perpetrated upon the earth much like cancer inundates the world. Unlike Hitler, Stalin, Hirohito and Mao Zedong, dictators all, who annihilated literally millions of human beings, many their own people. The new kids on the block, Isis, their lineage Islam going back to 500 A.D. for its roots have bred the cancer cells of today's Middle East's black open sores in pockets large and small across planet earth. Fear is their strategy, death is their modus operandi, and subjugation their goal.

There are two kinds of living in the minds of men. Reality and fiction. The cancer-oriented death provoking very old(new) kids of earth's societal destruction gang are reality provoking fiction as a means to suppressing their enemies by means of deceitfulness, cunning, and an AK-47 mindset. They make up all the rules, based upon a bent religion.

The Chinese, Russians, Iranians are too formidable opponents and don't have central religions to overcome and devoutly disagree with. They are too well armed and close, and know they would throw their central state led forces at them in numbers that they could not possibly win against. They weren't controlled by sentimentalists, weak character and cumbersome decision layered like government bureaucracy that the western world presented, especially America.

America had lost its boldness, assuredness, its pillars of strength through attraction of its policies, policymakers, direction and a feel-good society. Bickering for insanity through the halls of once 1776 greatness and foundational granite – now withering within and through outside chiseling away who see opportunity and advantage to steal America's greatness away from them.

Societies fall when termites enter in. Backboned solid leadership would be a precursor to a renewed nation. The night people are among the trees of the forest, they must come out of the woodwork to the forefront, they must be God fearing – they must be found through prayer. World peace needs direction and circling of the wagons.

CHAPTER FIFTEEN

~ THE COVERT WAR ~

The waters were calm off the Lebanon coast, and the sky exceptionally clear. The carrier S.S. Nimitz was on active alert and its 5,000 crew were hustling about. The F-18s and F-16s were fully loaded for strike, the cruisers and destroyer escorts were on full alert – submarines were surrounding them with silent aplomb. The clock was ticking down, "Operation Moo" was approaching "zero" hour.

The CIA had ready their secret base rendezvous location. Their forces checking weapons and position details that each man had been practicing for months. Codes were learned by all of the strike force – each one having meaning as to prescribed duty operation, abort or secure, in progress positive, resistance – light heavy, none. These one-word combat information code words were designed for instant recognition of current operations that were being carried out. Time always was of the essence, strategically and humanly.

The seals had established a precedent in its covert operation of imploding and extracting Osama Bin Laden. Much refinement had been learned from that operation – from the planning, rehearsing, details and experience of fulfilling the mission.

One of the newest of military favored and critical gadgets "Moo" team had now was the wrist watch computer – connected to a military based satellite – connected to operations central.

Another current military tool was the lapel held TV camera as used by many police officers in the US. These things were the latest and most improved version of technical knowhow.

Other special weapons were issued to some of the Special Forces involved such as the new arm held 50-calibre machine gun – light, deadly and reasonably accurate to a trained combat man. These men had to be quite strong in order to carry and fire these new field man-held artillery pieces. They could penetrate most anything but very heavy gage steel, a quarter-inch thick or more. Some quarter inch steel of inferior quality it would penetrate. It was a devastating form of armament in the Special Forces arsenal.

The CIA's covert army unit, had stocked 25 helicopters at their covert base. Several were troop carriers and others were heavy gunships with Gatling type machine guns, while others had mounted 20 mm cannons on them. These were handy for blowing tanks away and heavy door type fortifications – to ground troop invasion breeching.

As "zero" hour drew near, cloud puffs began to form occasionally over the target area. Due to the landscape and placement of land masses, rainy weather was hardly likely.

The usual normal every day activity was going on in the greater enemy compound area. The comings and goings of town folk mixed with the Isis solders here and there. The "barnyard" area of the military compound was looking normal with the obvious Isis fanatical Jihadist protecting the military facility.

The area the CIA called the "Cow Palace" where "Mullah Moo" was presumed to be, was surrounded on one side by a large designated area reserved for the market place, out of doors. Hundreds of civilian folks mulled in the area touching, feeling their way along in the 'produce' of all kinds. IN spite of being at war, it was a lively place with an abundance of goods. Thus, the area was fully busy most all day.

To the careful trained eye observer overlooking from a high location, one could, if trained, discern separate persons hugging the edges, all male, along the nearest perimeter of the "Moo" compound building. To the general observer it all was quite innocent looking. Special eyes were tuned to the specific man-types that were definitely not busy lookers of the produce. They were there for certain, and under civilian clothing, shawls and loose coverings of color. It was as innocent a scene as the Isis stage crew could paint it.

The CIA appointed "barnyard" area there resided a facility compound central area, which looked much like that known in the "Old" American West as a fort-looking group of buildings. Isis-style military had to have its regional headquarters somewhere. This particular one was akin to Major Domo make up. Isis senior military personnel kept a low profile at this facility and only small groups of personnel were admitted and hung around, the guards were civilian looking from a distance.

This compound housed three squads of their hardest loyal combat Jihadists, along with a ton of fire power and ammunition. They were there essentially to provide protection for the "Senior Caliphate" Mullah in charge of everything. He was not a titular head, but an active dictator in high Islamic robes. He was known as one smart and cunning cookie by all, including his enemies.

The atmosphere of the town was about as normal as everyday could be. Inside of all the Isis operations militarily and strategically and politically things were humming along normally as their grip locally was strong and fierce.

The first cruise missile found its target in a decapitation strike, having arrived in a low trajectory precisely on the building for storing ammunition next to the military headquarters. It was one of two that were planned to be targeted within 5 minutes of each other. The first one was delivered to scatter all the Isis remaining soldiers nearby protecting the facility and military leadership.

The second cruise missile found its destination and detonated above ground to take out ever body standing nearby the military facility. They precisely did their job.

There were no incoming missiles anywhere near where the "Mullah Moo" was incubated. Thus, once again, the "Moo" felt he was inherently removed from any knowledge that the head "mucky-muck" was anywhere around town, or in fact in any danger, and his troops didn't attempt to bring to public knowledge "Moo's" location by rushing to surround the place, leaving his office facility space seemingly innocuous, unimportant and safe.

At about the ten-minute timeframe a force of F-16s arrived, followed by a small fleet of Huey gunship helicopters, followed by Special Forces troopships. They came in on the opposite side of Moo's office – away from the bombed compound area across the large open area. It was right in the midst of the market/food assembly of the town folk looking for produce. Everyone scattered except for the guards, who revealed themselves and were quickly disposed of. The CIA, Green Berets were in full observance and preparedness for battle and for the extraction or killing of the "Grand Mullah" and securing any files or computers laying around his central office.

Billy was about the fifth man out of the whirlybird. He was assigned a brand-new weapon called the Pb-50. It was the latest out of research and into select production for the CIA. It was a lighter weight (by 30%) and weighed 60 pounds, a 50-calibre special ammo, hand held machine gun. It could fire up to 500 rounds a minute on special models. The ammo was for hard penetrating demolition.

Billy was one of two who were issued this particular weapon. He was selected primarily because of his very sturdy size – 6'6" and 280 pounds.

The sky birds arrived, touched down and troops stormed the doors of Moo's main building, with "booby-bombs" to blow the doors, resistance was low as intruder Isis guards were taken out almost without a shot of resistance. Interior doors were blown apart by Billy's 50-calibre bullets in seconds, allowing storm troopers to rush in and take out any interior hallway resistance.

The first floor and entrance door were breached easily. The Moo was up the stairs through another steel door. Billy and his squad ascended the stairs in the seconds and Billy dispensed into the handle lock area about ten rounds around the lock. Two heavy lifters used a ram and broke the door down, it opened quickly.

The "Grab" team was lucky, it was lunch hour and the Moo bodyguards were at a table, or heading for their AK-47s several feet away. They were cut down in their tracks. Big Moo was stunned, handcuffed and mouth taped shut. He was snuffed silent, picked up by an assigned crew and hustled out and down the stairs and into a fast and light helicopter along with highly trained CIA large commando Green Berets.

The "A" team scanned and filled their special made satchel bags with papers, computers and anything else small but maybe important. It was vacuumized with precision. It all took less than 20 minutes before total lift off of the Moo-assigned bird and all the strike force protective gunships.

Meanwhile between the two compounds, a large open area, appeared a squad of F-16s were busy cutting down any and all Isis Jihadists left firing on them with AK-47s. The gunships with 20 mm cannons took out any nearby vehicular opposition armament. The vast open area between the "barnyard" compound and the "Cow Palace," was essentially empty as all civilian life was fleeing for cover. The Isis brotherhood lay strewn across the open area.

In half an hour all action was over. Everybody evacuated successfully. No body killed, two injured, but would survive. The operation "Moo" was totally successful and all returned to basecamp of the CIA encampments.

Operation "Moo" and its CIA planners with CIA Covert Chief John Steelman at the helm, reached into an iced container and pulled out some cold beers to share with the warriors surrounding him. All plans were still in motion as the remaining "Main Target" was being boxed, so to speak, and would be transported by special CIA jet to CIA headquarters in Langley, Virginia for interrogation.

Soon the brass of the operations would return to their assigned headquarters, the aircrafts and submarines would resume normal dormant-like service and maintenance. It was another call for America, its uniqueness at being great and resourceful.

Time, patience, practice, knowhow, technologies and hard, long work were the keys that unlocked success in any endeavor. It was another, this time a positive notch in the CIAs quiver, as a resourceful American government agency.

Many such agencies were beleaguered bureaucracies of fundamental famished reputations. This time, they scored a big "gold" feather in their cap. America would be proud, it's new leader ecstatic.

CHAPTER SIXTEEN

~ THE AFTERMATH ~

The transfer of Mullah Moo to Langley was smooth and without any mess or trouble. He was sedated enough to remain comfortable, calm and not much need of anything while on the CIA plane expressed from the Middle East. There were but six other people on the plane. Chief Steelman, Billy and two other Green Beret guards and a doctor and nurse and invited CIA associates of Steelman, plus the pilots and navigator. It was a nighttime flight and it was a covert and highly top-secret agenda.

All Langley CIA personnel and medical specialists were ready to move at transporting "The Prize" package to a special holding facility at the CIA designation home field airport.

The whole of the operation being a covert war effort was under wraps news wise and unknown to the government and public. The President was in on it signing off on all of the operations. He was well pleased with the results and had congratulated Director of Operations Steelman for his distinguished and outstanding accomplishment and duty.

Billy was on board with the inner circle, once again, for his personal strength and verbal general skill and his familiarization of the Arabic language. They all took turns sleeping during the flight. There would be a refueling time in Maine before the final leg on to Langley.

At the special area assigned to CIA activities at the Langley airport facility, they landed without measure of any difficulties during the flight. The aircraft was directed into a closed-door hanger where the CIA hid all the needed vehicles and personnel for security for taking the prisoner to his destination swiftly. It was early morning and the sun barely was curving around the sphere of the globe. It was essentially pre-dawn.

The cavalcade of black SUVs was ready for the motorcade to deliver and secure the prisoner to a lockdown and high security facility the CIA designated. Only a handful of persons were in on the reason for all the secure fuss going on, they did what they were told and with precision. It was their job. Again, the trip to the lockdown was uneventful as "Mullah Moo" had begun to come into aliveness, but hardly knowing where he was, or any understandings of his circumstances. It would be a couple of hours hence before his head would clear of the drugs administered and discover his bonding shackles about him. His helplessness would be a complete shock to him – he indeed, was in capture and subjugation to some other force. They were not friendly forces, in fact, they were the infidels he so hated and persecuted.

The following week in Langley was busy at the CIA. Most of the high need to know personnel at the bureau knew something "big" had happened. The bureau or Agency was and had been buzzing for months during the "snatch" preparations period prior to touchdown Moo. Lines of directives, information and instructions were compartmentalized, so highly sensitive, that information would not be leaked or disseminated.

Field Director John Steelman and agency Head Chief, Bill Cannon, were commiserating together with their team. One for the debriefing, the shakedown of Mullah Moo. It may take months. They were prepared as they had been planning extensively for just this moment in time. It would not be fun or easy. Patience of Job would be needed. Checks and balances would be essential in the administration of extracting all they could get out of Mullah Moo. The proverbial water from a stone trickle.

He would be an elephant in a small room, yet cunning like a fox, would rather be martyred than spill the beans. The task before the CIA interrogation process was huge and daunting an experience as could ever be realized. It would be a monumental task dislodging any information. Under present law and with the subject person in custody, maximum interrogation procedures would be available for use. Billy would be a very useful tool in the process they had prepared.

He would be stationed until further notice, in Washington/Virginia area. He would have to find lodging through the agency. He needed to contact Anita to reestablish touch, as his regular contact with her had been interrupted by all the covert action and planning of it. She would highly welcome the new news that he was out of the danger zone and would for the most part be newly located in the Washington DC area still assigned by Special Forces to a branch of government. He would not be telling her that branch was the CIA. He could tell her he would not be in any active combat zone. That would suffice her concern somewhat.

He would also tell her of his promotion to Captain and its accompanied pay raise. IN addition, on that subject, he would still be putting more money into their joint account towards their future. Surely that would help their pending conversation along a good pathway. Still his workdays and assignments were strictly under "top secret" category of information. So, he had to be careful what he said to her, or to anybody for that matter.

CHAPTER SEVENTEEN

As Anita entered into her Paris apartment, she heard her cellphone in her pocketbook go off. She quickly put down her valise of canvasses she had and retracted the cellphone after quickly rummaging for it.

"Hello," she quickly said, not having looked at where the phone call originated from. If she had, it would have shown a number she was not familiar with.

Again, she said, "Hello," as their connection had a dead space on it for a few seconds. This time she heard a voice – it sounded familiar. Her mind and body came to alert. She said, "Billy? Billy, is that you?"

"Yes." said Billy in his strong voice, "How wonderful to hear your voice. It's been too long."

"Yes, yes" replied Anita, "Are you alright?"

Billy sounded off, "I'm fine, a little tired but fine."

"Oh, good," said Anita enthusiastically. "Where are you? The connection is better now, in fact, good."

"Yes, it does," Billy said, "I'm in Washington DC. I will be here for the foreseeable future. I'm now out of harm's way and any battle action, and I'm glad of that for our sake."

"Yes, me too. How wonderful. Maybe I can sleep better now. Though I'm so exhausted when I get home from my daily activities, I really nod off pretty quickly."

"I'm glad you're keeping so busy. How is your progress in the art world going?" Billy responded.

"Well, I gotta say in that realm it couldn't get any better. I'm still learning a lot under several tutorials by really well-known established painters. They seem to like my work and kind of have taken me under their wing. I'm learning a lot from the very best there is in Paris."

"Super," said Billy, "How are you feeling? Healthwise?" "Oh, I'm doing well. I'm trying to do all I can, yet keep some balance to exercise and have sparingly free time. My time schedule is complex and grueling, but I've scrambled to maintain a semblance of order."

"God, it's good to hear your voice, and that you're happy. Praise the Lord!" said Billy enthusiastically. Continuing on he said, "Have you heard from any of the old gang?"

"Yes, as a matter of fact, I heard from Penny this week. Eddy is now relocated to the Pentagon Army Central. Seems he's assigned to JAG duties there. Hey, maybe you can contact him there through Army Services Corp. He'd love to hear from you, and I know you'd love to talk with him."

"Yeah, you're right about that, I'll try to reach him. Hey, sorry my job presently prevents me from disclosing anything about it except that I'm in Washington. I'll be calling my parents and others I know and say hello and update them as much as I'm able and cleared to."

Anita said, "Billy when do you think we can ever get together, for a dinner and lots of talking, a few wines, oh, I've developed a huge varied taste for wines here in Paris. No, I'm not hooked on wine. Maybe someday we can own a vineyard and you can operate it and I can paint grapes – Ha, Ha, Ha! She laughed., It was a good chuckle and food for thought for the both of them.

Billy, chuckling said, "Not as funny as you might think. Might dwell on that thought between crisis in my life."

The thoughts Billy conjured up of a nice home, kids, beautiful wife, lots of land nourishing good grapes and profits created a nice picture in his mind. It lowered his heart rate a bit and calmed his psyche. It oft-hand was a revolutionary good thought Anita casually thought out loud on.

"Well, I gotta get back to the dregs of protecting this nation, and our way of life." He thought "these terrorists have got to be stopped or our life as we know it, and have come to love, will forever be in the past and we will have become subjected to a passive, surrendered society in leg irons, those of us not tortured or killed first.

Billy sat down on his new easy chair in front of his TV in his new temporary home in the DC area. Though government owned, it was essentially nice, home like.

His thoughts rambled along in the lines of Mullah Moo's capture and the necessity of curtailing the Isis movement. These people are barbarians and they are at our gate. Billy continued to deliberate over the societal mess the USA was in. AS a history proponent, he could see clearly that the socialistic-like policies espoused by presidents and members of Congress were playing right into the hands of our enemies. Our enemies were many and on different fronts and degrees of wanting to storm our gates. Isis, Russia, China, North Korea, Iran and others on the outside and a bunch of loose cannon groups and individuals metastasized throughout America itself.

Billy grew tired as he sat in his cool now chaise lounge having a sweet glass of wine. He shoved the lounger handle to as far back as possible, raising up his feet as his head rested on the pillow section. He was sleepy and dozed off soon, once he found his comfort level.

He awoke at midnight and got up and went to his bedroom to strip and sleep some more. His body and mind were well enjoying his new present lifestyle. It would be all too short.

Anita just sat there after Billy had called. She needed to do that! Just sit. She really didn't do much of that daily. She was an on the go girl, standing frequently as she painted. Her talents and subject matters, plus her tutorial instructors were all over greater Paris. She marveled at her new-found ability to get around in her mini-cooper throughout Paris' roadways. Traffic was crazy is about the only way one could describe it. A flat-out mess.

She swore everybody drove with their horn, didn't have steering wheels! Your only hope was that the other "bloke" was only on wine and nothing more. A cheer on that thought. Her hopes and dreams were once again renewed, and she jammed her mental pep pills into her system for recharging her body and mind. She folded and went to bed. Tomorrow was another day. "C'est la vie."

The days ahead for Billy would be filled with extractions of information, painful, grueling, long boring time frames. It was the proverbial "cat and mouse" game. It was piece by piece. Moo would throw us a tidbit and then shelter inward with silence. The drill team would pursue often and with vigor questions, scenarios and bluffs trying to entice beneficial information extractions of any kind. The team would keep at him, constantly, continuously, bombarding his mind with hardships, one way or another. Depriving him of food, drink, warmth, cold and hard rock music which he hated. He hated Western music of any kind his research dossier had shown. He especially hated the music of the Grateful Dead. They played it often.

The cell in which Mullah Moo was held in contained a plethora of listening devices, highly sensitive to even whispers. There were speakers and microphones imbedded in the walls, and ceiling and absolutely nothing was penetrating or sharp in his cell.

Television cameras were focused not only on his bed place but on all the cell area including the toilet area. The recent escape by the Mexican drug lord behind walls of the toilet area through a tunnel taught the CIA not to ignore this area of coverage. The agency needed him surveyed 24/7.

When Billy was on guard duty, interrogating their captive he would talk Arabic to the Mullah. He had head knowledge of all the questions the CIA wanted to ask him – in one way or another. He worked his own psyche inquiry with "prisoner number one." All conversations were recorded and videoed. It would be a hard and difficult time breaking this "God of Islam" down. They had to do it. The world of sanity needed the information.

This "Jim Jones" Caliphate of Islam, was killing people at random, his own, others. Their enemies were infidels all people in the world on the wrong track. Elimination was the surest way to any future through the barriers they faced of endless infidels in order to conquer and hold ground in the name of Islam.

Islam terrorist brand of religion was dubious at best – a bent, crucified extrapolation of its perceived intention, it had its cunning side of interpretation. The leaders and followers of the Jihadist were practicing "Hunda" - the art of Lying – to deceive, lie, for the purpose of getting a better strategic position for Islam was a practical measure to be taken when dealing with all infidels. They felt no guilt in pursuing such verbal gymnastics for their case. It wasn't just boldness but a way of life.

Billy was well versed not only in the middle east complexity of the region's history, but also in the culture of those people in the countries and down to the tribes throughout that area. It was a different in many areas and aspects that one tribe was different in beliefs and traditions than another. Civilized or western cultures were quite different and an anomaly to the Islamic general way of life and beliefs.

The stakes were high for America. They, in spite of all other issues of international dissentions, were looked at as the power greatest with the ability to "fix" what's wrong where ever on this planet. Islam people even come to mother home, America, for peace and protection. Their way of life where they had lived, was essentially unsafe and way too violent and explosive.

Extremist were actively plying havoc everywhere – why? For their way of conquest through fear and death, by the sword. They have a penchant for death, a love of darkness. Their minds reflect this way of life. It is satanic in nature, and by parameters a circle of death.

America was and is becoming an Island of last hope. It still has a Soul attached to a living loving God. We most recently have been flaunting him, turning our back on him the one who gave us liberty or a choice of death. Choices. We seem to have a good case of the measles or chicken pox mixed together. It is easily seen and diagnosed! A case of cancer here and there interspersed.

The cure of course, is found in each individual's desire for life and peace and dispensing the proper internal anecdote to find the courage to say "No," that's not right and I'm going to do something positive to change it. Courage to change, willingness to action, and a heart generous to your neighbor, all contribute to a united joining of the American diversified populace – to vote or implement old Constitutional and ten commandment values and stand united for peace through strength.

CHAPTER EIGHTEEN

New life was emerging, spring was in the air. The CIA was bursting with success in Jihadist revelations springing forth from "Mullah Moo." The revelations attained through information gathered from all the captured materials, both verbally from Mullah Moo himself and combined with all the data secured by the agency from his computers and office papers when captured on the raid. It was slow in disseminating and putting all the pieces of the giant puzzle together. It was a monumental task assembling all the various loose ends of information and creating an understandable scenario map. The CIA was good at this type of task.

The information of Isis planning by Mullah Moo and his cohorts, indeed revealed the Caliphates future plans and planned attack points, propaganda outreach targets, troop deployments, and surprisingly discovered were "cell Jihadists," individuals and couples inundated throughout the United States. This data and information in of itself, was a treasure trove secured on the raid and worth the cost and the danger expended. It, in fact, would save many American lives by its capture. The CIA in conjunction with the FBI would be on top of ferreting out these gofers in the ground Jihadists among us, before they get active at bombing and killing American infidels.

Timing sometimes was everything, and apparently Mullah Moo was preparing to hold an interactive council assembly of all high-up Isis personnel in the region to discuss expansion planning of the Caliphate territory and need of having everybody on the same page. This was a big "If" for Mullah Moo to achieve, as no two Arabs ever agreed on anything about anything. One of the most revealing aspects of the captured papers and data was the discovery of specific state, sponsored backing financial and otherwise filtered to their cause – names and former deeds of assistance were documented. It had been a "gold Mine" of disclosure data. The CIA was almost feeling "giddy" in their discovery. It was a diplomatic "gold mine" also.

Mullah Moo's operational personnel were still remaining untouched, but they were now exposed as to where they were based, and who they were. What had happened with the 'head honcho's' head being removed – figuratively. The engine of the Caliphate movement had been dislodged from the train. It was now running along a track to nowhere. Mullah Moo had made himself so essential to the Jihadist terrorist movement that without his vigor, mindset, cunning ways, the juice of power began draining out of the whole of Isis engine. Isis was still dangerous as a venomous snake head severed from its long, slithery body, mouth and fangs still visible looking to strike – still knee jerking its ferocity. Other would be leaders of its killing machine soldiers were out there but none had the "Chutzpah" of Mullah Moo. He was a form of the Anti-Christ, but he was not to last. He was but for a time

Eventually the American people, discovered the war with Isis was drying up. Things were looking somewhat improved from the dregs of yesteryear.

The new American president could detail more effort into generating economic prosperity to a beleaguered and depressed society. Nothing seemed to be going right under the previous administration. New Hope was now an option the people could climb aboard on. They felt change in the air – positive change – which charges the hearts of individuals. Isis and the economy weren't the only serious problems America faced. America had people problems – heart and soul, values and direction. There had been no change for the American citizen for the last 12 years or so. Indeed, people were discouraged, depressed, losing hope that anything good would happen. Our government policies, outside world pressures and influences were pressing the delete button on the America's future. New and improved people power and spiritual mindsets, its values and getting things done in the name of cooperation for America by concerned and caring new revolutionists of the 1776 genre. Hope was pending.

A feeling was generated throughout the land that a right cog had fallen in place, a hope, had sprung anew. America would bond again and face reality with strength and fortitude. Things were evolving, slowly, but the sun was rising on a new beginning.

CHAPTER NINETEEN

Billy was sitting on his balcony, resting and thinking. His balcony was on the sixth floor and overlooked much of Washington DC and many of its familiar monuments. These were for the most part, dedicated to the founding fathers of what was then a new nation. It would take years of adjustment of its people and self-governing politicians ever so self-oriented, to move the new republic into a solid united force for good in the world, a world now headed south.

With one foot in the grave of the American revolution and a population growth spurt everywhere, people power, economic power, and scientific power was birthed along the way. Useful discoveries such as "electricity" and the widespread generality of its use promoted the Industrial American Revolution. Jobs and people prosperity reigned throughout the land. America was becoming the new power country on earth – the new kid on the block with revolutionary ideas developed in a new land of liberty and freedom to become. Restrictions were not words used. Opportunities were unleashed - prosperity would reign clear across America and fast trickle down elsewhere across the globe. America was on its way.

The doorbell rang loud in its sing-song manner. Billy got up to answer the door. He was expecting Eddy, his long-time friend and cohort of life. His shining face was a delight to see, likewise his. A huge big hug was displayed, as Eddy was ushered in. The short reunion began, it was indeed a high-time of good relationship renewed. It was about noon hour and Billy had stored in some fresh hamburger meat and hash brown potatoes for a short-order cooked meal.

Eddy sat in the kitchenette area on a stool at the counter, while Billy fired up the stove to cook the juicy burgers and prepare the hash browns. It was a meal
Billy and Eddy were fond of often downing several burgers at one time during the football season. While the chow was cooking, Billy got some maple syrup out to douse on the potatoes

at the table. It was something he'd grown accustomed to, and had sold its taste pleasure to Eddy's enjoyment.

Between bites and a few hours together their lives in absence were exchanged and updated. It was a wonderful time; old acquaintance be not forgotten. Joy would be a good word for their time together. Much laughter and many stories were told their doings and duties in the Army Corp. Billy couldn't disclose his activities with the CIA except to say he'd been assigned to a them for a while.

Billy and Eddie got talking about their sweethearts, Anita and Penny and the conversation got on to the possibility of marriage. Of course, such an event would not be considered until they got out of the service, at least the active duty time frame of it. They both agreed on that and it turned out both active duty tours were about to expire about the same time.

All that talk turned on a light bulb as they pursued their conversation. Billy said to Eddy, "You know what? I just had a thought which is that maybe, if you'd like to, we could have a double wedding ceremony together. Just a thought, and it sounds like a cool and fun thing to do."

Eddie responded, "Just as you led into that thought, I had the same thought too. Yeah, I would take that under consideration seriously I get out in six months and will probably go into private practice of law somewhere, or I may stay in the service as a JAG Adjutant. It's not bad duty. The experience is terrific.

Billy followed Eddy's spiel by saying, "My active tour duty is up in six months also and I'm going to get out of the military service and take a job, I think with the CIA or FBI, maybe the US Marshall's Service, I don't know yet, but in any event a civilian job, though government oriented. Let's give this some serious thought. Both of us need to present this idea to our intended, but neither of us is yet engaged. Anita will be returning to the states soon. She's fulfilled her art work training and apprenticeship in Paris and though she loves Paris, she wants to come home to the States. I need to find that out, ask her for her hand and "plop" a ring on her finger along with a "Yes, I'll marry you" response.

Also, I need to clear it all with her father. That shouldn't be a problem.

"Yeah," said Eddy, "Me too. I hadn't thought of that part. I don't foresee a problem there either."

The two of them continued to talk about that knowing that probably their wedding would be in York and not an Army Service extravaganza. Everybody, for the most part, was from there – all their old friends. It made good sense to the both of them – it served everybody's convenience and comfort level.

Eddy and Billy hugged each other at Billy's door, looking directly into each other's eyes. A certain joy was hanging in the air before they departed. They discovered they didn't live very far apart in the Washington area. They gave each other their address, phone numbers info, and turned as the door on their reunion closed. It had been a great time and together. No problems or time and distance tours of duty had interfered with their deep friendship. It was a good and solid.

Billy quieted down in his apartment looking out over his balcony view of greater Washington area. The Washington Monument was projecting its lighted projectile form into the darkness of the night. It was beautiful.

Old George reminded him of what he was doing, who he was protecting and fighting for – his bride to be – and all their families and the American way of life. It all was tenuous even more so if America showed apathy and weakness. Too many were out to decimate our country and its way of life. We were a valuable prize to conquer and own. Our government policies were thoughtless and weak. Our representatives throughout from top down were citizens of apathy and spineless souls. We were potentially naked in a forest of predators.

Billy dwelt in thought how he was in deep duty with the CIA and its attempt to dislodge information from Mullah Moo held in security from the world. The world at the present hadn't a clue as to his whereabouts, but speculation was that the US had snatched him before everyone's eyes. All assumed he was hidden somewhere in the Middle East. Spies were searching everywhere by Isis and its affiliation co-conspirators. The wires and airwaves were filled with buzz.

Billy was a student of history, world history, and small nuances in the political landscape on the global scene were easily explosive and noticed by followers of global data. What with the media's ability to know and show a lighted match burning anywhere around the world. The world was watching and waiting for the next hotspot to ignite. The world was vulnerable to its nuclear weaponry wherever hidden. Covert information was essential to attain, process and assemble honestly for the judgement and implications of their use and development. The CIA was our frontline of defense in the protection racket of the US arsenal. Knowing the answer to many questions was essential across the board for American security and safety for and to its citizens. It was the planning and bravery of dedicated men and women in the forefront and frontline duties of risking their lives for the benefit and safety of our people.

The world was full of skullduggery, hate, predators, and cunning manipulators who were out to get us one way or another. We were the new kids on the blocks but our naivete was tempered with practical caution and security measures sufficient to protect our interests. Therein lies one of our problems, what, indeed, was our interest?

We couldn't protect the world, even if we were sufficiently strong to do so. Policies and backbone of leaders would be necessary, a congress so immersed and maligned to stand tall in its deliberations on behalf of our interest, that the world would see us generating right choices among ourselves, which if metastasized world-wide would produce positive ramifications towards world peace on this planet. We had to be a strong democracy or dictators would surface again in their vile ways, strike us with their venom wherever they could at our weak spots – our president, congress and media alike. All weak spots in our spinal column.

The world vultures' quiver was full of deceit, testing our boarders, storming our gates that made us a powerful and good society in a world of chaos. Decimating evil inflammation into our veins would be to promote their intentions to conquer us wholly without regard to saving anyone. We are considered infidels by all tribes of this world who are looking to obliterating other nations and territories.

Billy saw the world stage made up of those wanting control of other territory for so-called religious inoculation, while others subscribing to dividing and destroying in behalf of the fatherland playing smaller bad guys-type predators. Kind of a mosquito warfare. Highly annoying.

Russia and China have great forces to work their diversified evil outreaches. Other smaller countries play the role of obnoxious irritants wherever they can churn the waters. It keeps Iran, North Korea, and jungle tribes on the move constantly. The little Caesars running some of these irrational and high internationally irritating regimes are worldwide. They bristle with malignant pride of their cancerous ways.

Billy finally got tired and headed for bed. He had a long day ahead back in the CIA holding cell of Mullah Moo! This dude would continue to hold off telling his story if it killed him. Some kind of break was needed for the "spilling of the beans" as the saying goes.

CHAPTER TWENTY

Six months from now would put the calendar at June 1st. On June 6th Billy would be 26-years-old, his life so far gave him the feeling of being much older and more mature than that. Army life had a way of maturing early the young men that came through the training and the service. It was exactly the need and experience he felt he needed to prepare himself for facing the world. Indeed, it was.

So to it was for Eddy. He confessed to Billy his thankfulness for the life and experiences he had availed himself. He had told Billy, and Billy agreed, that had he gone to college instead, he probably would have frittered away his time partying and romancing Penny, even getting married early, probably had kids and being tied down. Worse, he would have been relishing his glory from his rah-rah college notoriety and his head would have been bloated from publicity. He would have been a different animal as a civilian – no responsibility or social directions intact. Yes, he would have had the simplistic mindset of the average college student and his mindsets easily had been corrupted – again through his football talents.

Both he and Eddy were thankful for their choices in going deep within themselves, taking the high road of military life. It had been and was a blessing. They both knew it and had absolutely no regrets. It was a straight forward shot for what would be their new worldly choices for their future.

Billy made contact again with Anita. She was excited to hear his voice. She sounded so near, appealing and warm. He warmed to seeing her on Skype. It was humanly better in all regards. She looked so pretty, vibrant, and a matured young woman. His heart was touched.

They got right to their call and talk in developing plans on when she would be coming home in about 6 months. Exact dates were not yet available as they talked but their excitement loomed large in their craw. The time would go fast.

He explained to Anita that they would have to live and exist on faith in their relationship and order of life. What he needed to do for the near future was be in her presence for a few days that they could talk intimately together. He wasn't thinking in sexual terms but necessity for normal pre-marriage activity talk. He needed to ask her hand in marriage and slip that engagement ring on. He remined himself that he needed to buy one, actually pick one out, and ask her dad for permission and blessing of marriage to his daughter. What would he say – What would he say to dad? Billy pondered these thoughts and his future. Planning, more and more had begun his protocol of ways. It was not currently a thing he would get to but a way of life in dealing with most everything of the future. Future plans usually got changed. Contingencies were part of moving forward into the future. They were not to be dreaded but, in fact, looked at as challenges to improve current plans. He was pleased and got quiet for a few moments and prayed to God for favor in whatever was currently to come before him. Billy asked for wisdom to make good choices and blessings on his everyday living, health, safety and daily bread. He then thanked the Lord for his covering, counsel and safety in his daily life – for watching over him in his daily work activity.

He even said a prayer that he might get Mulla Moo's tongue unglued and provoke it to wagging. Billy laughed at his little prayer for that, as he closed up with thanking God for hearing his prayers. Amen.

The next day, Billy got on Skype to talk with Anita. She was really excited and related to Billy that last night was a juried show of young and new painters work at the National Gallery of Art where her work was displayed.

It was sponsored by a foundation created by a famous heiress of France, a woman by the name of Countess Liliane Bettencourt. Anita further explained that this woman is a family member of the founders of the legendary famous cosmetic company by the name of L'Oreal, almost a household name. She is purported to be the richest woman in history. According to someone, she is ranked number 11 in the world of richest persons. Now – today!

"Wow, terrific. How'd it go?" replied Billy enthusiastically lifting his excitement and spirits.

"Well, the two best parts of the whole evening, and it was a formal gathering at the Gallery, was that I won 1st place for my realist work and portrait work. Secondly, privately, Dame Bettencourt took me aside and commissioned me to do her portrait. She asked me what I'd charge to do that and I said I have no idea! Then I heard myself say to her, 'You judge what you think of my portrait work, and pay me whatever you think it's worth.' I paused and then said to her, in any event I would like a documentary comment by you in writing as to your opinion of it, good, bad or indifferent.

"Dame Bettencourt agreed, shook my hand, the deal was sealed. I will start next week. That project should take me till the time to come home. Billy, I'm so excited," exclaimed Anita.

"Wow," said Billy loudly, "That's absolutely terrific. What a coup for you. Winning that juried show was a real accomplishment. I love you! Oh, by the way, I got a call last night from my current boss, who wants me to go with him on a special assignment duty, and you won't believe this, yes, to Paris for 3 days. I can't disclose the why's of it all, but he guaranteed me time to see you while I'm there. This, Anita, answered prayer for me right now. I will learn more detail as to the timing of the trip today at the office when I report in."

Anita responded, "Wow, how absolutely wonderful. I'm totally recharged after that news. I know you can't tell me anything classified but you've told me enough to last 6 more months with my batteries fully recharged. I hope you'll get enough time off with me to see my collection of works I've done. I'm really proud, I think it's all actually good! I hope maybe we could have a dinner together. I know the quaintest, nicest little French restaurant in all of Paris – unbelievable good food with dessert. You'll be full, yes, even you!"

Billy spoke saying, "Well, I've got to go, I'm pumped and excited about being with and seeing you so soon, I think I taste it already. I'll get back to you with specific details on the timing. It'll be soon. Love you. I gotta go. Bye!"

"Bye, Billy, stay safe," admonished Anita.

The sound of Anita's voice brought calmness and peace to his soul. Loved ones sometimes have that quality surrounding them – in-person or even over the airwaves. It was a God thing.

Billy made a quick call to Eddy and related his conversation with Anita to him. He said he'd get back to him with details on the time he'd be gone. Nothing was said about the business he was gone for. On a scale of 1 to 10 this current stuff was an 11. Off the wall top, top classified information. Eddy had no clue as to Billy's doing, his goings or comings. It was as it should be. It was all covert CIA secret stuff.

CHAPTER TWENTY-ONE

Billy stepped out of his CIA loaned Chevy. It was a plain wrap version of fleet cars. It was basic transportation. He crossed the CIA parking area after having shown his credentials at the guarded entranceway on the backside of the headquarters facility. He went to a special elevator, looked into an eye verification peep-hole, pressed his thumb on a pad for finger verification and the door opened and he got on. He pushed 10 and waited. A few seconds later the 10th floor door opened. He stepped out between two armed guards and flashed his personal ID card. They nodded go ahead and he proceeded toward the director's office where he was told to go.

On the front of the door was a single name, Donovan, he went in. Inside, were two men, one being his boss, John Steelman, the mission's director for the Operation "Mullah Moo."

Steelman said, "Billy, this is director head, Frank Donovan. I've been telling him about you, shared your background, and the most recent "Moo" efforts you performed. I've shared with him your many and diverse qualities, your record at West Point, your duty assignment in Somalia. Your name keeps popping up to keep an eye on for assignments of special nature. You are reliable, more than physically able, highly intelligent, you are our kind of guy." Steelman continued, "I've got to meet some folks concerning company business which will take about 3 days. We will base out of our office in Paris and the people I need to see will meet us. You will be on assignment to be my bodyguard and sounding post. I can talk with you and get straight answers. I won't need you all the time, and one evening while there. There should be time for you to meet with Anita and enjoy her. We will return on the 3rd day to Langley.

As they all were sitting comfortably in the Donovan's rather plush office, the conversation turned basically to Donovan asking questions of Billy about his life. As Billy reminisced his past with them, Donovan in the middle of them pulled his seat a little closer to Billy. He seemed fascinated by his story and autobiographical rendition. John Steelman also moved his chair a little closer, he too was totally enmeshed in Billy's story. They both looked at each other often as they sat listening and encouraged Billy to continue.

Later, Billy was dismissed to again go to where the Mullah was being interrogated and get informed of the progress that the specially trained personnel that were trying to ply information out of Mullah Moo.

When Billy departed Donovan's office, Donovan turned to Steelman and said, "Where in the world did you find this gold mine?"

Steelman replied, "He was assigned as part of the Special Forces attached to me on the Maldives Island Agency facility. They were the hard-core battle group preparing to carry out the raid on the ground. Billy was a part of it as a squad leader. He was one of two who carried the big new PB 50 Caliber hand held machine gun. He led the way into the "Moo" compound. Blew two doors open immediately.

"Damn!" said Donovan, "sometimes we get lucky. Our country will survive the slings and arrows ahead of us, with men like this in leadership. We've got to promote him along, get and keep him in the Agency. I'll get word out subtly throughout our executive level directors. He is a must to be trained and kept. I bet he even gets that damned "Moo" creep unglued and willingly spouting state secrets of Caliphate size.

Steelman laughed at the image Donovan painted with his colorful talk. They respected each other and trusted one another to the point of good friendship. They both were enamored by Billy's presence and good sensed high and mighty things from Billy's future.

CHAPTER TWENTY-TWO

The three-day journey, in the Agency's jet craft to Paris was upon Billy. He had packed a uniform replacement to the one he had on, plus some civilian duds for when he was off-duty and with Anita.

The Agency had given him trip money, the amount surprised him, very generous. The two of them talked about some of the business that Steelman would be conducting with those he had come to see.

Steelman told Billy he could have the evening free on the second night they were there, but that he wanted him nearby to him all the times he was talking to these other persons he was to meet with, and that he not only wanted him near as a bodyguard, but as a sounding board – who listened in and had any positive thoughts he might add to the conversation.

Billy said to him "Are these talks pertinent to Operation Mullah?"

"Yes, I'm informing some of our Iraqi and battle leaders the most recent information we've gleaned from our "guest," and all the stuff we absconded with from his headquarters. It is quite a lot actually. You were there on the ground, and they will be impressed and take what I say more seriously, hopefully. I will possibly ask you something time to time for one reason or another. So, keep listening to our talks and if you have something to add without revealing our procedures or where Mullahs' located, please do so.

"OK," said Billy, "I think I get the gist of my being here, my job. And thank you for giving me some time with my girl. I have some serious business to talk with her about."

"I hope it's positive?" said Steelman.

"Oh, yes, I'm going to ask her to marry me and ring her in!" responded Billy.

"Oh, that's terrific. Congratulations beforehand. Do you know when you might marry her?" replied Steelman.

"Well, that's part of the time spent here – figuring it out. She has 6 more months commitment at the art academic training here before she can return to the states. My best buddy, who is in the Army JAG Service gets out then too. We're going to try to double connect up and hitch up together. We, our girlfriends from high school, go back many years. I plan to matriculate out of the service too, and am considering applying for a job with the CIA. It's at the forefront of American protective services. I feel like I need to be there contributing."

"Well said," his boss replied. "We desperately need good young men to follow in our footsteps. It's not a 'cool' thing to do in this era of thinking. May I pass your thinking and thoughts along to others in the Agency?"

"Yes, that would be very nice. Thank you, Sir," replied Billy.

"OK, good. Now I need to review a few things before we land. It's in the middle of the night in Paris. So, grab a few Z's for a while. You'll probably need them. Our talks will be during regular hours at our main agency in Paris."

Billy was quite satisfied with his talk with John Steelman. He liked him a lot. He was a man's man, a tough dude, who was a dedicated soldier in the American Services. America would be in good hands under his tutelage and direction. Billy thought proud that he himself was who he was, and in the service of his country, doing the things he was doing, making a difference. He was indeed privileged. He also was clear of conscience and at peace with the world and himself.

The three days sped by. All the business things went smoothly as John Steelman laid out his information succinctly and clearly to those battlefield leaders in the Isis campaign. Hopefully it would make a difference and help turn the scattered, battered Middle East Caliphate war around and push the "Mugwumps" back into oblivion. They would have to be found in their snake holes and flushed out, one at a time, much like the hidden Japanese leftovers hiding in caves and in the hills after WWII was over. Creepy crawler moles still dangerous to others.

Billy went to Anita's apartment in the suburbs of Paris. It was very nice and spacious. She had a whole room dedicated to herself as a studio where she painted. It had a large windowed area overlooking northward toward the city and Eifel Tower. It was ideal light for painters to work – with preferred evenness of indirect sunlight.

Anita was expecting him around 5:00 pm that evening She had dressed in her finest fashionable French dress and accessories. She opened the door with her grand smile, she took one look at Billy and leapt into his big arms, threw her arms around his thick neck and planted a huge kiss. They kissed long.

Billy was stunned at her beauty. This was a new Anita, a Sabrina moment in time. She said to Billy, "You're the biggest 'bad' bear I've seen, since I last saw you. Come in, come in." The smiles on their faces would have done Hollywood publicists proud.

He entered in then Anita showed him around her several roomed apartment. It was simple, but femininely attractively done. It seemed perfect for her needs. Billy stopped and said to her, "You look beautiful. Am I glad to be here, if but, such a short time. We've got a lot to talk about – quickly. What time do we have to go to dinner?" said Anita.

He replied, "My boss, Steelman, set up a dinner with dancing at the 'Boulevard Enchante' at 8:00 pm. I hope it's close. I'm to put the bill on the Agency's tab card. Now that was a surprise and wonderful thing for Steelman to have done."

"I think he likes you!" erupted Anita excitedly. It surely is nice. The restaurant is not far from my pad here. I know it. Been there. Out of this world good food.

Anita got them both some ice tea and they sat down together on the couch. There was a coffee like table in front of them. They turned and faced each other, then Billy said to her.

"I've come here for a specific reason and that is – he reached his hand into his blazer pocket and pulled out a little brown cloth covered box. He opened it displaying his choice of American beauty engagement "rock." He said to her, "I've come to ask you to marry me. Will you? I have your dad's permission and blessing to do so."

Anita was flabbergasted, almost out of breath, she most obviously was not expecting this now, maybe when she got home.

Billy had traditionally kneeled down off the couch on one knee as he presented his love offering and himself to her as a life partner in Love. As a big man as he was, his face was at the same level as hers while on his knees, and she sitting on the couch.

Anita looked stunned at Billy's face, heard his proposal, didn't faint, as she was sitting and he took the ring out of the box. He took it and reached for her hand. She spread her fingers as she loudly and lovingly said, "Yes, I will marry you. I have always wanted to marry you. You are the one and only love of my life."

Billy slipped the ring on her finger. It fit without a problem for size. His mind said "Whew, good luck." Anita threw her outstretched arms in the air displaying her "diamond" to the angels surrounding her. She could hear them singing "Glory Alleluia!" All ten thousand of them.

The two of them proceeded to discuss wedding plans and what he and Eddy had talked about, a double wedding. She thought that was an absolutely wonderful idea. Then Billy turned the conversation to his future thoughts, on leaving the Special Forces brigade, the Green Berets, when his service time was up in the months ahead. He further shared his desire, as a civilian to join the CIA as a career choice. He said he thought he'd be good at it, and be on the forefront of America's finest defenders of its lifestyles and democratic ways.

After a short discussion of that subject, they discussed where they might live. Her active career as a professional artist painter, portrait painter and her freedoms to do so, needed a good central and populated people of means. It was a circle of love around them as they quickly discovered the joy of new negotiating relationship of pre-marriage. They knew their times in this day and age would be short. Their activities in life in peak age movement of life – they had had time apart to think many things through. And now when the door was opening, they found themselves ready to make decisions to the both of them it felt very right, and the evening was just starting – a looming dinner and dancing time yet before them. It would be a wonderful and grand evening of Romance.

The grand evening between Anita and Billy was a rebuilding and cementing of time for them. Assuredness prevailed as their time quickly expired for that evening. They pledged to work and think of a time slot when they could get married together. Eddy and Billy would have to do most of the planning as the exact timing of the double-wedding vows. No, they would not honeymoon together at the same place. Everybody agreed on that.

Anita and Penny would gather their forces to work out wedding procedures and decorating. Eddy and Billy would talk about where they would hold ceremony – most likely the first Presbyterian Church in York. Everybody would contribute names to invite. Eddy and Billy would plan their honeymoon destinations with agreements of their brides to be, but not together. The intricacies would be thought about between now and six weeks before the wedding date. New life was giving birth to their lives. New jobs, careers, responsibilities and relationships.

The Army life would be put behind them, at least for Billy, and new routines and dedication of everyday duties planning and home life would become their new beginnings of a coupled lifestyle. New wine skins in the making of their future. The good vintage was just starting. They were excited.

Anita was allowed to see Billy get aboard the CIA jet. She got to meet John Steelman and immediately saw in him the things Billy had described. She loved that man. He was taking care of her boyfriend and future husband.

Billy and Anita kissed the kiss that lover's merger fare – well kisses make, and she watched and waved as Billy and Steelman proceeded to the covert CIA aircraft. It was early evening and the dark SUV that brought them all to the airport whisked her away after the plane departed into the sky. She was under safety and covering of her husband-to-be next boss and current one. She felt happy, secure and special – not everyone got to enjoy such an escort service as this. It was comforting thought to Billy as he sat back in comfort after 3 days of great goodness and accomplishment. He peeked out of his porthole window seeing a full white moon illuminating the darkness of the heavens, then adjusted his head pillow and seat and said goodnight to Agent Steelman and closed his eyes.

CHAPTER TWENTY-THREE

The Grumman Agency jet craft silently pulled up to the CIA hanger. A couple of SUV vans pulled up alongside and agency personnel unloaded their luggage and they sped off to their headquarters offices. They would spend half a day debriefing with a committee with the need to know basis people. They in turn were updated on any progress with Mullah Moo disclosures of any more dribbling's he might have belched up while they were gone. Nothing new had come forth. Mullah Moo was not tongue loosed as yet, if ever. He was a tough-minded nut to crack. They expected that.

It was wonderful being back home in the states. There, indeed, was no place like home! Billy thought thoughts of his real home back in York, Illinois, that little mini-city southwest of Chicago.

He picked up his land phone from his apartment and called his folks. It was a Saturday and they would be home. The phone rang a couple of times and he heard his Mother's voice in her sing song manner say, "Hello." He answered that with a "Hi, Mom, tis me Billy!"

Well, Mom melted on the spot and hollered at Dad to get on the phone. "It's Billy!" It was a long conversation for the both of them. Everyone was excited in talking to each other. Billy quickly took them through the last several months they hadn't heard from him. They knew he was going to "pop" the question to Anita because Anita's parents had phoned them after Billy had asked Dad Cantina for permission to ask for Anita's hand in marriage.

Mom was full of questions, the first one being, "How are you feeling, well?" You could hear his dad and mom release exhale of air when he told them he was leaving the armed services at his military release time. He told them he was applying for a job with the CIA, which would keep him in the Sates for the most part. It was an entry level job.

He further explained that Eddy was possibly leaving the Army, but wasn't sure of it. He then proceeded to tell them that

Eddy and he had agreed with Anita and Penny to have a double wedding in York when it can be worked out.

Mom pointed out that the whole town has been keeping a following eye out on his goings and comings of his life ever since he left high school – the both of you. "You know, the hometown hero stuff. What better else does York have to do, the news is thin here since you and Eddy have left town. I've been keeping a scrapbook on you and your career. Dad and I go through it all the time. Dad and I miss so your being away. Your dad takes good care of me. We try to take care of each other. So far so good.

"Great to hear that. I miss being with you all and the warmth of York and its folks. So many good friends. So many good times and remembrances by all. He had a warm, positive feeling go through him.

Billy and his folks wrapped up the conversation with Billy saying "It would be another 4-5 months left in his Army contract before he would become a civilian again. He told them he and Anita had lots to talk about and decisions to be made as to how they should live, where, for how long, all while we plan our wedding. We'll keep you and the Cantina's abreast in all that, as much as we can," spoke Billy.

"Well, said Billy to his folks, "great talking with you, you sound great, kudos to all you're doing to stay that way, keep it up! I love you both, and thank you for everything you've done for me over the years. You've been really good parents. I appreciate your love. They parted with their "bye's" and hung up.

Billy sat there for a few silent moments not thinking of anything. Then he thought he'd call Eddy and relate his talk with his folks. Maybe Eddy had talked with his parents. It was a Saturday and there was not time out in the grueling dual with trying to extract info from the "Grande" Mullah in confinement and all his other busyness in his life. He had the weekend off from his duties as he had time on his trip. That brought extra time off for special duty call. He sat back in his recliner and clicked on a football game. He hadn't done that or seen one in years. He found a game he would definitely watch – the Army/Navy game was just starting. He hadn't even had time to give his playing days any thought. The Army keeps you busy, really busy. And your life just isn't dull. The Army plans your life every day. He wondered what it would be like to be free of an active military life and the Green Beret Special Forces regimen. Maybe he'd actually have time to think. That would be novel.

The days ahead before the arrival of his severance with the Army was filled at the CIA basement headquarters, reviewing testimony personal responses to questions asked by CIA interrogators of Mullah Moo. Many hours he sat reviewing these tapes and documentations of what Mullah Moo had to say. A great deal of time was hashing with other interrogators how best to phrase questions and specific content to help loosen Mullah Moo's resistance to "spilling the beans." He definitely was a hard nut to crack. He seemed to speak most with Billy and Billy tried to develop a certain trust with him in their conversations.

Video viewing of all conversations by the interrogators was important. Mullah Moo's body posturing, face inflections and speech tonality all said volumes of information to the trained eye viewer. The CIA was leaving no stone unturned to extract information from their captured head honcho of Isis.

The battles with Isis were more frequent, more specific targets were targeted for destruction. The plethora of information retrieved from "the stash" taken from Operation Moo, was great and it translated into action on the frontlines of the battlefield. It was obvious by actions taken by Isis that they more frequently were disenfranchised and depleted in their efforts to gain or maintain their positions to wage battles. Human and auto bombs were now getting more frequent.

As the allies made headway on Isis' once gained territory, left behind hidden in tunnels and caves and vehicle IED producing plants were discovered and blown apart. More and more subterfuge production and storage areas were assembled in or under mosques or adjacent to populated area. These killers hid behind women's skirts for protection. They liked to be among people so that the allies wouldn't attack them. They used civilians to shield them from direct attack by the Allies. They used Allied restrictions of battle, to bring in supplies of ammo and food and military might. They were crafty people of deceit and bluster, always looking to slit your throat at the first sign of weakness. They were straight from the pits of hell. Satan's henchmen or minions around the world.

The problems of the world were nothing compared to being slaughtered and slaved into oblivion by these blood toothed sharks of the dessert, scorpions all.

The CIA knew the ilk of these people. They were not like others in the world except followers of the scorpion tribe from hell. The term "scorched earth" for the Caliphate rang their bell of believers. They would joyfully die for their cause. These people were desperate of a home life. Their women were slaves for sex and reproducing male warriors. They were objects of no affection but lust. Men thought themselves superior to women and women were subject to them. Life in the fast lane of Isis, for women, was to ride in the back of a bus dressed in a sheet of isolation.

Women's rights, freedoms, choices belonged to the men. The hearts of Isis men were fixed on darkness. No humanity shone its head else it would be cut off. Friendly fire was all too well known within the encampment of the Isis world. Freedom in their world is you do what we say you can do. You have that freedom or you are an infidel and absent from earth.

Billy had studied the history of these people. He realized it wasn't a religion but a state edict of social dictatorial mindset operating in "religious overtones" and public relations manipulation. It stressed outreach worldwide with the philosophy of the "corrupted phrase," you can fool all the people, all the time, over time!"

Billy knew why his life had direction that it did. It was the antitheses and desirability of hearts that loved God and other people. People of light. His source and life giving for the freedom enjoyed by the democratic way of life. So many in the world like to restrict others, make themselves clones and dictators of other lives. That is not freedom, it's slavery – death. There are two kinds of people in this world: those that like life and those that like death. In this country we have the choice to choose life.

Billy sat and pondered these things and he resolved and resumed to give his life to the cause of Godliness, life, positive thought, and help shed light in the world. He vowed to become a defender of those rights and desires of the heart. He desired to generate an enlightened way of life.

Happiness through love. He would bring as many with him that he could. His life must exemplify and showcase his beliefs through not only believing that way, but in showing his life as an example of light, as a "beacon on a hill" as a famous saying goes. He found Peace as he sat there. The world was desperately in need of it!

CHAPTER TWENTY-FOUR

Anita found herself immersed in her new contract portrait painting of Countess Lili Bettendorf. She momentarily thought if the Countess really liked it, she would have enough to buy she and Billy a home in the States. She vowed to do her best work, carefully and skillfully. She had recently of course, won the 1st prize at the Museum gallery major juried show. Dame Bettendorf and herself donated the funds to support the show and donating a first-place prize and money for best of show by jury judging three pieces of art by the artist painter. Anita had submitted three pieces, one, a portrait of the curator of the Louvre Museum and another of a scene along the River Seine. The third piece was a beach scene on the Mediterranean seacoast with some yachts anchored off shore. Anyone who enjoyed looking at these pieces of art were fascinated by the realist creativity shown by the artist – the piping plovers running on the shoreline were incredibly real. You wanted to touch their feathers. The scene along the River Seine with the sidewalk kiosks serving snacks and onion soup with the people were bright in the light of the day. Her artist touch was touchably touchable, realistic.

Anita was holding her breath as time went by before the announcement of the juries' decision. Dame Bettendorf was the jury. Solely in charge. It was her very prestigious show in Paris.

The winning of first place in it, ensured Anita of instant notoriety of accomplishment in the art world of Paris. Her winning would splash across the society pages with every art critic waxing poetic anthems of French in big print. Across the spectrum of daily newsprint would be seen, "Madame Grande" artist Ms. Anita Cantina, American, covets first place. All sorts of headline twists filled the French plethora of tabloids and dailies. Her name was now ensconced in the halls of ivy hierarchy designating supreme renown on the art world, a new premier accolade for the juried show winner. Headlines beamed out phrases like "exceptional talent," "realistic work you want to touch." Magnificent likeness portrait work.

Anita bought all the papers she could gather that had any mention of the world famous French Open Juried Show at the Museum of Art in Paris. It indeed, was the most prestigious show for excellence in artists new to the art world. Winning this show, put you on the map.

Anita wore her proud shawl hidden within her heart. She emailed her folks in York who got the word out through the owner of the York Patter, Ed Martin, who'd pass it on to the Editor-in-Chief, Carl T. Anderson. Soon all of York would know and subsequently it would be picked up by the Chicago Tribune which monitors sub suburban papers in Illinois that would cover another 4-5 million people. Because it was international news to America, who knows, it might be picked up by the Associated Press or Reuters worldwide service. For a flash in time, Anita was a shooting star. All this was now on her resume.

In her search for articles in the French venue of papers media, she found a lot of news about the juried show. She had won first grand prize in that year. Of course, along with the news, the financial remuneration of the prize money and benefits were detailed. This was not good. Too many in the world were out there that would now deliberate the separation of it from her. Anita first thought if you only knew who my boyfriend fiancé was you wouldn't even think of any shenanigans. She reminded herself to talk to Billy about these things. She was to say nothing about where or who he worked for. She could be generalizing by saying he works for the government. That was it.

As Anita completed the contract of Dame Bettendorf, she proceeded to go on track to begin assembling all her possessions she had in Paris, plus all her painting collection, which were many and ship them back to the States insured. This ending of a living time was much more complicated than the settling in part. Her reward was that she was going home to her Native Country, getting married to her lifelong boyfriend, and starting up a new life in her adopted career and becoming a wife living in a new home with her husband. Life at this point seemed beautiful, though getting there rather daunting. It all had to be done in such a short time.

Anita had all her windows open, airing her place out. It was a beautiful sunshine and warm day around 74 degrees, the smell of the air flowed through her nostrils and the freshness seemed like the smell of L'Oréal perfume, which smelled like new green money, or so you thought.

As she sat looking out her balcony window, she enjoyed the view through the wide space opening as the door windows were thrown back. She pondered about her near-term life before her. When assembled in one-time frame, it seemed overwhelming a task, but Anita since being and living in Paris had learned the "art" of partitioning time segment off so that life functioned more normal and realistically. She got out her large legal yellow pad and started writing lists and times – only action or lack of, would determine if she would meet her goal or not. She hadn't yet made her mind up on the exact date and time she would venture home. She had to plan that too and how traveled. Her list grew quickly, then she reorganized it as to priority need. Even the little she did at that time, helped her adjust her psyche and attitude into an attitude she could deal with. There were others that could help her in Paris, and contact with Billy now helped relieve her of what had to be done back in the States. She'd have to remember that he too was new in settlement into a new life and lifestyle.

Indeed, Billy was switching from a military lifestyle into a more civilian mode and career change. Anita and Billy spent almost an hour Skyping every day. Making lists, talking about their future. Time was filling up fast. Space was needed to secure it and to be wisely filled. They both had matured considerably over the last years in their life, busy yes, and most profitable in both their personal lives.

From the outside looking in they had prepared themselves with good foundation to build their future. The one thing they both decided needed shoring up in their lives was their spiritual lives. The career life they had been living choked out most of the spiritual overtones and times available for those matters. They fully agreed to rectify that deficiency in their lives, for they knew it was essential to strengthening their future marriage as well as individually for their future well-being and lasting power and survivability. Indeed, it would be their necessity.

As the days flew by the both of them more and more demanded satisfaction. In terms of progress towards leaving Paris and for Billy transitioning into applying to the CIA for admission and employment.

Billy had filled out all the papers and documents needed from his past. There was much written about him over the years past as he had indeed acclimated himself well, educationally and in the sports world and in his Army life. "His personal life was indeed a dedication to excellence. His record was clean as an eagle scout. His accomplishments were many as were his rewards. He was a person of high integrity and trust. While his 26 years were short in one's lifetime, it was filled fully with a life most average Americans never know, and some wished not to have.

While his life showed as a bright light spotlighted with success and daring accomplishment, it had been a hardship road of determined effort and denying himself a normal kids' growing up ways and freedoms. He danced to a different drum beat. He didn't feel denied of any so-called normal life. He, instead, felt privileged to be who he had become in the way that he had.

The college life of partying, freedoms of travel for pleasure, lack of responsibility were things he could have missed, but didn't. He felt no loss in his life for having missed those things.

What satisfaction would there have been in missing "panty raids" at college, missing the "booty" scored from some damsels throwing their "bra" out the window. Billy's rewards were fleeting and harrowing only to come home with American hostages in one piece. Certainly, more heartwarming than having a 38B bra hanging from your college cork board.

His experiences monitored more your great-or-grandfather's hard life of yesteryear, the entrepreneurial spirit of era's gone by. They had it hard, suffered, grunt out a living, saw a need, filled it, and many prospered beyond belief after a time. All said, it took a rough passage of time, but to them their life held hope and prosperity paved a way for them and their children to come, because of what they had gone through and done. There was truth in the memories of old. Work hard and reap what you sow.

CHAPTER TWENTY-FIVE

The matriculation out of the military was official. He did not re-up. He had a distinguished service time while in military employment and had the medals to prove it. One medal he did not have was the purple heart, achieved only by having been wounded in battle. He'd been in two military serious skirmishes and fortunately had not been killed or wounded. It was a medal he'd do without, thank you!

Billy reported into the office of the CIA director of operations, personnel, and budget, Director Edward Shannon. "Sit down please, Mr. Brewer."

"Thank you, sir, I've gotten notice to report to you directly from Director John Brennan."

"Yes, that's right," stated Director Shannon. "We have all your paperwork ever shed for public view and more than enough from your private life. We are nosey people. We snoop all over the world and under it when possible. Mr. Brennan has assured me we need to locate you in an advanced program headed by our European and Middle East director, Jonathon Columbo. He has been notified that you will report to him tomorrow morning, your official first day in our employment. We officially welcome you. Your record in your short young years on this planet is quite amazing in the light of what and who American youth seems to regurgitate up these days. It is refreshing, believe me, to be so pleased at your choosing our service with our agency. We choose, we think, good people, smart, strong and motivated to help protect and keep America secure in this world of unstable times. I will spend the rest of the day with you outlining our agency under the different directorships and their responsibilities. Hopefully it will give you the feeling and understanding of how we mobilize our "troops" in preparation for defense of all American interests worldwide. We'll be interrupted time to time, by someone bringing us drinks or snack food. Pit stops are anytime.

Before you are some materials already prepared by our sources. Also, some hardcover note books for any notes or thoughts you might like make. These, of course, cannot be taken off campus – ever. Other than a CIA issue sidearm, you will receive no papers of any kind relating to our agency, it's operations or transmittals. Your head is the storage place for any and all information outside of the agency walls of Langley.

By signing up with us, your statement of personal agreement with our rules and regs has been approved by you as submitted along with the bureaucratic legal stuff we had you sign. As the mafia says "we know where to find you." He laughed an agency laugh, thinking we're not too much different than that crowd – we rip off budget committees of Congress. He laughed again.

He hadn't had a good laugh that day yet, but he was glad he hadn't verbalized it to Billy. They'd string him up if it was ever revealed. He'd been with the agency long enough to know protocol and keep a "Midas Muffler" on his words spoken.

Billy got to enjoy his day with the director Shannon. He was a bit old-timey hard-nosed sleuth. He had a plethora of stories, some fascinating, some funny, all with a point to them. He was close to retiring and it was obvious to Billy he would welcome it sooner than later.

This was a place Billy thought that he wanted to be, it was current all the time. How could anyone possibly find this life ever boring or dull. The prospect after hearing the director's phalange of diatribe on the agency, he thought himself at attention and ready to appear and start tomorrow. Indeed, he was a lucky young man, his credentials, work, effort and labors apparently were more than sufficient to promote him to where he today was to be. In his country's service.

As he once again, talked with Anita, he confirmed to her his having had an intro and pre-appraisal session with the incoming director of personnel and management for the agency. He related how the director laid out an overlook of the entire agency and its management structure and line of personnel from top to bottom. He told her how much he enjoyed the day with the personnel director and the way he related to himself. He, the director, was of long in service and great knowledge with superb overview of the agency and the world with many stories. He was somebody Billy wanted to get to know and befriend. His experiences were worth a great weight in gold, plus they hit it off together personality-wise.

Billy told the "funny" gleaned from the director about him saying, "We know everything going on even under the covers. We even know what the bedbugs are thinking." Don't ask me how we know, but, trust me!"

Billy laughed at hearing himself saying the words to Anita. The story had a "hook" of truth in it. Anita laughed too, seemingly understanding the innuendoes hidden within it. She was happy for Billy and that he was happy and relieved to have made his new career decisions, to pledge his life to the CIA agency.

It was an agency dedicated to the protection of America through means overt and covert, whichever worked. Yes, it was an agency of the US government that helped people, or countries in their protection and desire to be independent or to their defense from outside influences too great for their capacity or capability to defend against. The many problems within a government's management or operations, i.e. subversions from within a government's favoring Western values or freedoms, we indeed, needed to help from time to time for they often didn't have the resources they needed to rebuff or defend against outside or internal coup forces. CIA was a resource available for such delicate transition work on/or in America's best interest worldwide. It also was an agency or interdiction to rescue or extract good guys from bad guys hands one way or another. Operation Mullah Moo being an instance of record. It also extracted its own people.

Operation Mullah Moo was still greatly under wraps, held close to the chest confidentially by the CIA. "Moo" was still held "incognito" from all overt knowledge of his whereabouts or aliveness in fact. The completed time of his interrogation was ongoing in the strong confines of the CIA internment facility. Billy was still on the case and fairly frequently was called on or scheduled into a special time talking and interrogating "Mullah Moo" himself.

With the starting up of classes and teachings by the CIA director of the Middle East and European countries, Jonathan

Columbo, Billy quickly had little time to himself. While Billy enjoyed being busy, he also at this time needed some personal time to work out his other life he was coming into. He was now engaged to Anita, with a marriage date in the near future, some 3 months away.

He was told by his employer, to schedule in the times ahead he needed to set aside from his new duties with the CIA. He was new, but they foresaw a gung-ho young careerist in Billy and wanted him. He was indeed potentially their kind of guy. He thought so too, and was looking forward to a good relationship with the agency. For all intense purposes, he to the public, was an employee of homeland security department of the government. His affiliation with the CIA would remain secret as it could get without public knowledge.

Billy turned his present direction toward his wedding. He and Anita decided that they would marry October 10, 2016 at 4:00 pm. It would be held at York Presbyterian church, York, Illinois. Both parents were made aware of that. Next the two of them needed to gather a list of the groomsmen and bridesmaids. That probably wouldn't take long to figure that out. The problem would seem to be who to invite to the wedding itself, and who to the reception after. The bigger problem was the latter one, as the two of them, Billy and Eddy were essentially "folk" heroes to the people of York. They had a following through their lives after high school via the "Patter" following their life and lifestyle through college and into their career choices. They were prominent persons of interest in York and the "Patter" kept their readers current and ever-present with following their careers, comings and goings which included both Penny and Anita.

Obviously, they were family celebrity amongst the citizens of York. It was a small town-city that neighbors knew neighbors and had their backs. The nature and in the makeup of York's people and city development over the years bode well for its new-found strength of fortitude that converted it into a model city for the times present. It was a converted city of progress inundated with new values designed to promote family life and good business practices and development. It generated moral value and good attitudes.

It had become a city of hope and prosperity. Young folk graduating felt drawn to stay or return and raise families in York. The old "dusty" corrupt ways were bridged by new life, determination and hope and the attitude of altitude bode York's future to be with favor and prosperous ways. The younger generations were not fleeing elsewhere. York was on the name list of being an "All American Small City," a prestigious accolade and honor among esteemed selected cities and communities across the country. These cities took to honor such designations seriously. York was proud of itself and of the progress it had made over the years. Everyone in York felt that way, and worked hard to maintain and hold tight to its accomplishment.

CHAPTER TWENTY-SIX

Life as Billy had known it was in full swing of change. Everyday seemed new, busy and usually pretty exciting. Anita was due into Dulles airport in Washington, where Billy would be waiting for her arrival with a borrowed agency black SUV van. She was bringing with her as much as she could get on a regularly scheduled commercial aircraft.

Her arrival was pre-planned so he was given time off to gather her up and deposit her to their new pad. It was a now his expanded pad, having secured the adjacent condo-apartment to his in her name. The agency was good securing whatever they wanted or needed. They were a good help in this time of need.

Billy watched her come down the hallway from the airplane into the terminal. The plane was full and pretty close to on time. His eyes lit up when her eyes met his when she finally looked up after watching where she was stepping. They both raised their hands in a "Hallelujah" gesture and stepped into each other's arms in solid embrace. Kisses were good and long before they turned to head for the baggage claim area back in the main terminal downstairs.

It was 11:00 am Washington time. The sun was shining, the air crispy fall in nature. Anita had just her overhead baggage and purse with her at the time. They clasped their hands together and somewhat swung their arms as they walked along the corridors to the main terminal. The smiles were big, their eyes bright, and the chatter flowed like two newlyweds in love.

Anita said," Thanks for meeting me, it's lonely when you singly have to arrive and not have someone meet and greet you!"

"Yeah, the boss gave me the rest of the day off to settle you in. I brought one of your favorite dark black SUV agency vans to carry any amount of checked luggage on this trip. Did the agency pick up your furniture and all your paintings?"

Anita replied, "Yeah, said they'd be there and they efficiently loaded up everything and took the stuff to their facility at the Paris International. It should be here in a couple of days."

"Good," I've stocked your place with some temporary necessities and furniture and a bed at your new pad until all your stuff arrives. There should be plenty of room for you to set up a home painting studio until you get yourself situated with a store front commercial studio somewhere."

"For a while anyway, you won't be eating French Cuisine that you're accustomed to. May have to survive on good ol' American junk food. "Big MacLand" type stuff. Actually, we can go out or I can cook in 'til we figure it out."

"Sounds all good to me," said Anita. "I'm sure glad to be back home in America and so grateful to be with you, to have you near and available by my side. I have been very worried about all your secret missions and doings with the Green Berets and combined with the CIA, I really got worried, so alone. I'm grateful to have us again together when I can see and touch you, and especially, kiss you." She smiled and her face lit up.

"My sentiments exactly," responded Billy, "My world had been rough and rugged, male-type human necessity in a world mean and ugly. I'm so grateful myself, to be home to where there is a soft side of life where meaning is healthy, whole and life a semblance of normal. My life has been anything but normal, however in this day and age, it has become one of those necessities in life that our country has had to create in order to preserve our way of life, frontline defenders of freedom. Someone has to offer up the task of subscribing to such duties. I can assure you, none of us particularly likes or enjoys what we do, but the greater act of being on the team to preserve the sanctity of our way of life and liberty is enough to generate a satisfaction of a job well done through sacrificing one's self to the cause.

"Most of what I did was plain hard work in training for what was a short time period of active duty, which was the time frame of the most potential danger. Someone has to be those people.

America needs people to be in the gap and repel this so-called evil. That was my job.

Civilians really don't have a clue as to what we do and the amount of specific training we go through to be ready to perform our maximum destination of service. When we meet our maximum requirement destination, we are max, prepared for maximum predicaments for the task. None of it is pretty or normal. I have been fortunate in my duties performed to return safely to home base, for another Motherload in the future. Training and mental skills are key garments of armor necessary to ably get through it all. Both physically and mentally we have to be the best in the world.

So far, I've dodged the bullet and am home by your side, "praise the Lord!" I'm not out of the danger woods yet with the type work the agency sometimes does, but my odds of staying healthy are now less dangerous and that hopefully we can count on."

"Golly, I hope so," said Anita realizing Billy had been through much she did not know about. Maybe someday she would 'bequaint' those living memories Billy had under his Green Beret.

They settled what little they could of Anita's into her condo apartment and since it was a nice fall day they decided to take a break and take a walk in the local park and relax together.

Evening fell early as the sun fell off of the earth's surface. Billy asked her if she had enough energy still to go out for nice dinner at a local Italian 5-star restaurant. She enthusiastically endorsed his suggestion and they returned first to their condos to shower and for Anita to put on the one dress she had brought with her on the plane trip.

The dinner was scrumptiously good and they were even serenaded by a couple of so-called wandering gypsy's playing violins. People weren't dancing, but she and Billy got up and danced anyway. Sometimes being big can have its advantages. No one was about to ask them not too.

CHAPTER TWENTY-SEVEN

As Billy reported in to his official office at the agency, the receptionist at the front desk said to Billy, "Mr. Brewer," he started by her not recognizing his last name as she had called out. He turned to her and said, "Did you call me?"

"Yes, sir, I did. You have a rather large package that arrived. We sent it to your office." "Thank you," and wondered at the smile she had on her face.

Immediately he couldn't figure out what in the world would that package be? As he opened his office door, there stood a "Lazy lounger chair wrapped in heavy plastic wrap. It was a garish purple color. Instantly he brought to his memory of ordering that exact chair. He kind of chuckled to himself as he stood there gazing at it and said out loud to himself, "Well, there it is, we shall see?"

Billy had a plan. He had no idea if it would work, but he was going to try it, because not much else had precipitated "Mullah Moo" to give out with much of any knowledge worthwhile. Billy brought his boss into the loop on his potential plan and Jonathon Columbo thought why not, it was certainly legal and human. The CIA specialized in motivation.

Billy called CIA maintenance to take the chaise-chair down to the Mullah-Moo's cell room and deposit it outside the cell, but in full view of Mullah Moo himself. The chair was stripped of all its wrappings and field tested by himself. He found it most comfortable and pleasing for his long big body. The longer he resided in the chair, the more his mind circulated a psychological plan for its use.

His synopsis of his plan was to build a desire of Mullah Moo to want to sit in the chair. It would become an incentive chair of opportunity. Mullah could gain points towards the chair time use by spilling some "beans." The plan worked on the theory of the parking meter for cars. The more quarters (information) you feed it the longer time you get to keep your car there. Same principle.

Billy remained in the chaise-lounger chair in his office pondering on all these matters, praying that maybe, just maybe, his new trial attempt at prying lose some information might actually work, certainly a new twist on human torture routine attempts.

After a half hour ensconced in his high comfort level talented chair, he arose and reupped the maintenance moving squad to now come and take the chair down to cell block #9 and place it visible before Mullah Moo's cell – outside. He'd let Moo think about it a few days. He wondered what would go through Mullah's mind, an Arab mindset that only the Mullah class might know of such comfort levels in their offices or homes.

Certainly, his cell accoutrements of furniture were sparse hard, totally uncomfortable, and downright unattractively ugly looking. This chair had the color of "Royalty" in the Middle East – purple. That would not go unnoticed by the "Mullah of Mullahs" of the Isis Caliphate.

If there was any humbling attached to his high Mullahship, was that he had been found., Snatched from his so-called "stealth" hideaway, without any major injuries to anybody, on the ally-American side, and almost all of his computers, electronics and papers were absconded with and in the hands of the infidels - his hated enemy He could rightly assume that his compound and adjoining encampments would have been decimated by many sorties of bombing and strafing that filled the air during the relatively short timeframe for the operation.

The plan for maximum damage and containment of forces both nearby and within the Mullah's secret hideaway fortress, was planned for speed.

Speed of procedure, accuracy and maximum attempt at securing documents of information and plans of operations of Isis. The CIA was in a high priority movement discerning every scrap of information that they'd dumped into their escape trash bags designed to carry without tearing from the loads of extractions found in Mullah's office headquarters.

Billy and the team of interrogators realized "Big Moo" as he had become known, was in total shock from all that had gone on. It had been an elaborate, precise and thorough – and total surprise strike. Mullah was stunned and his proverbial mind "blown."

Billy spent the day in his new office trying to establish a madness of method for his management and getting a grip on his two new areas of responsibilities. His assigned secretary would be greatly busy. He was not panicked but was trying hard to keep his composure over the sudden enormity of the assignment thrown into his bailiwick.

Billy had never once shirked his duties, his responsibilities or his job, as he knew it. His past, as it was, had contributed greatly towards his preparations for his duties newly assigned. They say, "to those responsible, go, opportunity for more responsibilities" knowing those that can, will.

Billy wasn't yet very young among those he worked with. He wasn't always the most talented, experienced, but he was a willing subject that literally sucked up information and fortified himself with it for future use. His mind was almost photogenic. He was an exceptional human being. He had a future unknown with flags of greatness awaiting his participation.

Billy's thought returned to the nearing time of his wedding He would get a 10-day vacation for his wedding and honeymoon time. He let out a sigh of relief thinking about that. That would be really good, he thought.

CHAPTER TWENTY-EIGHT

The wedding was scheduled for October 10, 2016, weeks away. Much had been done since Anita had returned home to America. Between she and her folks and his, the church was secured and the local "Yorkshire" Country Club for the reception.

The "York Patter" headed by Ed Martin, along with Editor-in-Chief, Carl Anderson, spear-heading this particular story along with sports editor, Stan Zalinski. They all were in a cahoots together promoting and reporting on the "Big Wedding of York." Every little detail was reported, updated, as they kept in touch with Billy and Anita and Eddy and Penny's parents and gave it their "Patter" spin for all of York citizenry. Excitement was brewing and they were hot on the trail.

While it was known to all of York that not everyone was invited to the Wedding and the reception, the York media, radio station, paper and now, since Anita and Billy were gone, a new TV station (local) had emerged into life, WYRK-TV. They were a new and fledgling media outlet and were gaining popularity quite quickly. They, too, were on the story seeing it and treating it as a "celebrity clambake."

The computer airwaves were a humming hotwire between the wedding party and the parents and the media and the public. A solid sneeze by anybody got reported one way or another. Once again York was coming alive with its new living and lifestyle. It was indeed, an exciting little city-town place to live. The city was growing and maturing into a fine community – an all American, small city. It's reputation every day on the line.

The days ahead were speeding by as all the participants pulled together to co-ordinate the wedding. Weddings are not simple occasions. They somehow magically arrange themselves and happen. This was no different, just two separate wedding ceremonies coming off at the same time. You know, "I do, I do, I do, I do – Kiss the bride – No, No, Yours!"

Of course, the wedding week was massively busy. All the parties among the past state championship teams. The re-runs of the good times had by all during the high school years, reminiscing the special times had with particular friends. The memories of great times spent with the 3 Amigos, Max and many others. It would be a time to remember after more than 10 years ago, or so.

The young adults felt young, and the parental aged folk felt their years weigh upon them. Everybody seemed in pretty good shape for the shape they were in. So much was relative to maturing the length of time since they had left high school. Time stood still for many of all that were in attendance of the wedding, and anywhere the excitement drifted.

Those that had gone on to college seemed to enjoy their cocktails and drinking more than Eddy and Billy who had to deny themselves of such partaking as their jobs were so competitive and demanding of concentrative attention. Libation luxury had to be limited to survive living the lifestyles they did. Being in shape and alertness was critical to people like Billy, less for Eddy, but it was an essential part of living for survival. Especially for Billy it could mean the difference between life and death. They couldn't afford to have a wondering or dismissal brain drain.

The wedding day came and went. Very well. It was a chili day, but clear. No snow – too early in York. The expectations on all sides and measures were successfully met. The brides each got kissed by the right spouse and all the "I do's – did." The reception was indeed a blast had by all. From max's gym to the state championship players all, to a few Army buddies that showed up, but no current sleuths from the CIA were among the crowd (or at least not known of.)

The TV cameras were rolling, the radio station and "Patter" folk were interviewing everybody including a few lamp posts after the evening wore on, but nobody got out of hand or order or misbehaved too much.

The Charlie Klingbeil Orchestra fired up the dance floor was well used by all that liked to dance. The ladies entirely looked their stunning best and in such beautiful dresses. It was fun to see Max out dancing with long-time bride, and so too, the 3

Amigos, still looking like they were getting ready for the Olympics or the Mr. America contest.

So many seemed not to change much at all. Baldness and excess fat were not being shown yet on Eddy and Billy's friends. It was a holding pattern and pending.

The chauffer got the brides and grooms swiftly out of the bon voyage crowd throwing rice and on time to the O'Hare Airport where the pair of them boarded the same plane to Miami, where they then would separate and later see each other back in Washington where they both now lived.

Time had flown by, Billy hadn't had so much fun since high school. It would be nice to have a week of downtime peace and share intimate time with his bride, Anita, and love on her awhile without interference. It would be a mutual thing.

Eddy and Penny hugged Billy and Anita at Miami International saying they'd see each other back in Washington. They separated and each went their different ways for their honeymoon.

They each thoroughly enjoyed a week free of anything but loving on each other, lazing in the sun, swimming, and touring the area they were in. Honeymoons were perfect for relaxing and having fun together, laughing and making love. Sleep was optional.

Where Billy and Anita had gone, the Cayman Island was known for driving on the wrong side of the road, scuba and snorkel diving, next to the grand earth canyon fall off, just off its coastline and Pina Coladas for tasty libations during relaxing times anywhere.

They visited the "turtle sanctuary" where life studies were done and toured the island stopping anywhere it looked interesting. They spent most days on the beach, the 7-mile beach where everybody hung out. People watching, was the thing to do there. Most people on shore enjoyed the tour ships arriving, big and small, pull into the harbor for disembarking side trips to all the tourist trap shops.

Tourists were fascinating to see, with their camera's strung around their neck, and rhinestone hats, shoes blouses, and gobby gold belts were usually the dress of the day. American's waived its Glory Gobby to the world. McDonalds Big Macs and shiny glitzy rhinestones for show. No wonder foreigners shed wonder about us?

CHAPTER TWENTY-NINE

As the Boeing 737 approached the Washington National Billy leaned over to Anita beside him and they kissed, the kiss of united togetherness, solidarity, one. Each smiled knowing the assuredness that their life would be cemented together, and they were both under God's providential covering, separated no longer. It was a good feeling and their faces radiated the joy of the time they had together.

They booked a limo from the airport to their condo, now gathered together as one and all their honeymoon luggage and various souvenirs acquired along the way. Their favorite one was a brass statue of a boy and girl dancing in native attire, rather naked, jubilantly expressing themselves. That went on the mantle of their fake fireplace. A wind-up music box with island songs accompanied it by its side It was cranked up often, each time with flashback memories being joyfully generated.

Life again took on a new life, more serious in nature. Anita pursued her search for a sidewalk-type studio to practice her wares, while Billy returned to his duties at the CIA pursuing information from Mullah Moo and learning the intricacies of the CIA operations across the board and summarily reporting on them to Congress. Both were high priority CIA directives necessary to carry out the work and priorities delegated by Congress to the CIA agency. To Billy, his locker of duties was full.

After appearing at his office, he walked down the hall to a large meeting room. There he was a part of the CIA community that was required to listen to the morning synopsis of news, and inner CIA information that pertained in any way to their need to know requirement. Most of the morning was taken by this timeframe. His first one was most interesting, not only the subject matter, but the explanations and directives resulting from what matters were introduced.

After noon and after lunch time, was his first time back, negotiating information extraction from Mullah Moo at this cell side. Billy entered into Moo's cell area and greeted the Mullah with a spirited "Hello, Shalom and have you missed me?" Billy spoke nothing about his personal life or recent marriage, nor where he'd been or what he had been doing. This was information that only shored up Mullah's stealth plans he might use somehow against him. These people were of the Devil himself, and they didn't need any food for thought to provide nefarious skullduggery planning. These people were nasty, stealthful and demon determined to skillfully play out their dark ways to perpetrate death on any and all infidels. They were immersed in corrupt thinking for their benefit and detriment to all others.

Death was a glory for them and death to infidels boasted glory days in their heavenly realm and with benefits of sexual gratification by many. These guys took their so-called religion and its bent, to the extreme bending of it. As it became not a personal religion but a state religion movement. Love and tenderness were not in their vocabularies. Their hearts were devoid of peace and joy or happiness. Only victories over others provoked the sick joy and happiness expressed in shooting AK-47s in the air repeatedly and shouting "Allah Akbar" (God is Good). Smiles and laughter of the devil were inspired by victory and slaughter of the infidels, wherever! They were falsely inspired by too much spare time to preying on the poor, and expounding the language of Revenge, hate, and prejudice of anybody but them, as people to be eliminated on this earth. All were infidels, American Russians, Chinese, Europeans – anyone not embracing Islam and their specific brand of it. No exceptions allowed.

Billy spoke his greeting words in Arabic. Mullah would understand them as he was an educated Cleric who wanted to be the Calafate High Mullah" in charge of Islamic State movement. "Fear" was his avenue of traveling, AK-47s were his spoken weapons of choice.

The Mullah spoke some words in Arabic to Billy saying, "That damn chair has been sitting there for a week, what's that for?"

Billy replied, "It's for me, Mullah, it's for me having to waste my time with you while we hold nefarious conversations on dead space while I'm here. The longtime sitting and shooting the breeze with you. I find pleasure of little sitting in some comfort while awaiting your freedom to speak up. I'm sure you'd find it a lot more comfortable if you filled us in with your sullen plans as you have mapped them out. I know we can make your stay with us infinitely more comfortable, even enjoyable, but we need to hear some truths as you know them to come forth with joyous delight in your sharing." Billy laughed.

"Oh, yeah, right," stated the Cleric in English. "Til hell freezes over," he gave Billy his best evil look. It was a look that said I don't think I can intimidate you with them, but I'm going to try.

Billy acknowledged his thought by remaining calm and still, measuring his words carefully as he dallied with Moo verbally. He (Billy) was now sitting in his chaise chair, often lifting the heavy mass without difficulty and replacing it closer and more strategically located so that the overhead lighting shone onto Mullah from the fancy looking spotlights like those at art galleries.

Billy watched Mullah Moo as he lifted the chair and replaced it where he wanted it. He noticed a raised eyebrow when he first lifted the chair without measure of any stress. He then sat down and wiggled himself to a point of feeling comfortable. He pushed a button and leg platform went out carrying his legs to extended comfort and his back reclined to a pleasurable distance back where he thereby stopped it from further recline. Billy purposely didn't kick in any of the vibrators anywhere. He'd do that another day.

When the chair was set, he let out a noticeable "sigh" of comfort and relief and looked some more at this captive prisoner.

He said to Moo, "Pretty nice and very comfortable chair. Not much on the color, but it's sure designed well. I think I'm going to enjoy my time spent with you. Whatta you think? Billy spoke directly to Moo, looking specifically at him, questionably furrowing his face. It was lead-in talk.

"It looks too comfortable for the mind to work properly," he spoke to the Mullah. That was a deviation of mind and spirit issued from the norm of his speaking so far. "Ah, said Billy," I think we're going to get along, just fine!"

Both knew "not" was closer to that answer and later than sooner would any change be made. Hatred is not easily broken by men. Only God moves inward on the heart when God is allowed into those spaces made for accommodating propositions of change. Billy would wait and listen for God's unction and words. It would come. He knew all things were possible with those that loved the Lord and were called by His name. After all, God had the keys to hell already in His hand. Billy thought, "Be patient!"

Billy thought he would wait. He would be patient. He would direct the times and choices of what to ask. When to listen. Billy could see that the Mullah was and had been sizing him up since his capture, for he was a devil of deceit and manipulation and that was his platform of verbal dueling. Moo viewed all other sub-cultured and inferior to his intellect and station in life. He was the leader of his world order according to his way of thinking. He would not be intimidated by anyone, from anywhere, especially an infidel from America.

What the Mullah did not know just how much information was gleaned from the raid on his headquarters. His first thought was that they wanted him dead or alive and that was pretty much it. His ego was so big it was difficult to get past it without the thought the infidels would dare take time to retrieve anything else beside Him. Apparently, he didn't learn from the bin-Laden snatch. The fact was and the plan was, to secure any and all things in his office that would be information.

Besides the Mullah, a special squad was attached to the raiding party of gunmen to "suck" up any and all paper information items in the Mullah office – maps, codes, pictures, files, doodle pads, etc. The gunmen were there to kill, maim and destroy and protect each other. Planning and executing were the precursor to executing action. The plan was rehearsed and to be carried out. The raiders did not leave a stone unturned.

Billy daily since his return from his honeymoon, had been on the job of interrogating Mullah Moo. He continued to daily rest back in his easy, Lazy Boy chair while asking questions and talking with the prisoner.

Finally, in much disbelief to Billy, Mullah let go of some information concerning their religious determination to decimate the infidels of this world who were inferior of mind and spirit and in need of Islamic redemption – death or subjugation. Thrown in among all the Isis propaganda were tidbits of strategic agenda that were planned, regionally and in France and America.

Billy was cautious in his interrogation, pursuit, not to be blunt and direct in his search for immediate answers to questions he had. He'd use diversionary questioning that hopefully prompted attempts at challenging the Arab manhood ego and its personal proudness within that "Allah" was on their side, therefore, their side as the right one, or right cause that the only way in the world to achieve fulfillment an individual human being needed.

Billy was practicing the "art" of brainwashing in a diversionary fashion of pursuit. He was using Peter to get to Paul tactics and it began to work.

Mullahs pride was so huge that to challenge it erupted a small volcanic flow to defend his on high dignity a superior dignity and world view as the only way of world existence and lifestyle. The only trouble was he and his kinspeople have never been off their slum reservation and to them propaganda input by other leaders driving inerrant and dyspeptic thinking into their people's heads and others, providing incendiary potential that "everyone" else had to be eliminated. Hate drove the dialogue as the Mullahs and leaders spewed their brand of truths and facts irrelevant to reality. Facts were fictionalized whenever circumstances provided opportunity for their use in conversations of the mind.

Deceit was essential to subjugation by Islam Jihadists in particular. It was an appropriate and useful tool in dealing with infidels wherever they were. It was preferred verbal contact with all enemies which were all those not of Islamic belief- especially the off-brand kind of those associated with the Jihadist terrorist movement.

Billy was an historian at heart. Historians learn the culture of people, the mindsets and significant adhering cultural ways of religions, habits, and daily flow of everyday life of countries. Even regional lifestyles and mores. Billy was long in the knowledge of European and Arabic cultures as well as the topography of these areas of the world. Green Berets were trained in these areas of knowledge not just in Special Forces combat preparation.

Billy was a student of people learning the psychology and thinking of cultures around the world. Each had their own world view and regional view of themselves – sometime others. Each held that theirs was best and all others needed to conform to theirs.

Obviously, on a global perspective, these ways were separate from a God of the Universe concept so indeed peoples made up their own gods, and most said they were him. Thus, the world now finds itself in the midst of chaos, and the tower of Babel dilemma – people are scattered into their own fragmented individualistic societies and mindsets divisible by death.

Billy's mindset and beliefs were held to Christian dogma of "Love thy neighbor as yourself." Surely a relational way of living and an abomination way too many who had such a narrow tunnel vision of the world, living in oppressive and intolerable conditions.

By such a lack of trust, love and pin prick knowledge of the world, the world's people were restricted in vision, much less understanding, of others across the road, over the mountain, two valleys over and regionally no clue. Integrating themselves with others was foreign to them. Others were considered foreigners at best.

The great American experiment started in 1776, has been trying to spread that freedom light of peace through love and assimilation and the appreciation of each other as pieces in a gigantic puzzle if melded together would bond together differences into a beautiful melting pot strengthened by its cultural differences joined as one. America's foundation precepts were unique and prosperity reigned in its great and good land. It was a land of opportunity to potential greatness. It features a land of choices to get along, to become successful or fail, but still be able to rise again and prosper.

The phalanx of opportunities to promote yourself to that which God set you free to become was fought hard for to become a land that provided individuals purpose in life to the fullest degree possible that an individual could raise himself up to. It was and is called the "noble experiment!"

Billy was working full-time in such an agency purposely formed to protect and best interests of the American way of life, it's freedoms and liberties. Your abilities and choices were the only prerequisites toward gaining those goals should you set them.

Billy in his young life had opportuned his choices so far, in successful and useful like directions that was positive in his growth and development as a human being. God had covered him well as he sought His will and direction for his life. It was a different and difficult choice for anyone including him with much disciplined oriented lifestyle engaged in every day. His lifestyle balance was blessing him fruitfully, so far, and benefitting many others through him. He knew he was blessed and often gave "thanks" for it. He enjoyed passing his blessings along.

It would take a while before the Mullah Moo would become gently involved in the verbal transactions they were having. Indeed, time provided and provoked the inclusiveness into mutually endorsing a certain participation together. The doors opened for trust, respect and verbal disclosures that slowly were disclosed by attaining a certain friendship level – one less adversarial.

CHAPTER THIRTY

It was a month into Billy's job of interrogating Mullah Moo. The job was tedious and tiring, boring and challenging. Mullah Moo was going nowhere fast. He didn't have a clue as to where he was. He was in a steel cell on hold and he was inaccessible to getting out. He was dealing with a man of enormous size and also superior intellect and in his estimation a counter infidel with American power. He had respect for him in every regard as he daily talked with him.

They talked daily on many levels and on many subject matters of interest and had not much diversification of experience in the world. His was desiring power through Islamic knowledge relationships, and learning the art of intimidation. Much like the US Mafia, competition was eliminated wherever enemies of Islam were to be found. Then you didn't have to deal with them.

Hostages were useful for bargaining for their lives – lives of human beings including theirs were on the line as martyrs for the cause – everybody is expendable. Even him. There was and were awards in Islam heaven giving your life for the "cause of Islam's Allah." Their search for Islamic manhood was found in the shouting of "Allah Akbar," "God is Good!"

Billy and Mullah Moo spent hours talking. Billy when asked about his background had shared his football part of life and mullah was not familiar with the sport and inquired about it, desiring to learn about it. Billy tried to enlighten Mullah generally about the game and shared his experiences in the sport knowing his verbal time talking to him was time "Moo" didn't have to talk. Billy measured these time allotments as he threw the towel back to Mullah to breach the subject matters Moo had gained in turning them into distractions for Billy actually learning anything positive from Mullah.

In all these exchanges of fireless-side chats, Billy kept pursuing the Mullah's background and lifestyle. Billy saw a pattern of places that Moo had lived and what he did in those places. As the timeframe of geographical places lived emerged, there was clearly a strong storyline of Islam religious study and training involved. As with Billy, a pattern of self-determination, directional choice and sacrifice of normal secular lifestyle ways to the greater purpose and choice of improving his life status and purposes for power. He desired power early on when he saw how he could get it, and that ruthless ways were necessary to get him there and to the zenith of absolute power in his world.

So, doing would elevate and metastasize his personal desire to achieve the greatest of Islamic prizes of his life, that is, to become the New Caliphate of Islam. Then he would be on a power level with all the kings and presidents of the world over.

Billy knew he was central to extrapolating a story amazing and hair raising in its hearing. He also knew that every word, whisper, was being recorded by high level sensitive microphones hidden in the walls and fixtures surrounding the cell he was in. The system was tested every day for its sensitivity and quality, by the CIA super technicians.

The friendly exchanges between Billy and Moo continued as each lessened their hard-nosed positions of resistance to talking with each other. One day, Billy arrived and said to Mullah Moo, I want to share my chair with you for a while. I think you will enjoy its comfort; despite any pre-conceived notions toward the chair and physically heisted it in where he wanted it. The guards retreated and, in a few moments, brought in a large living room comfort high-back cushioned chair for Billy.

Billy watched Moo's face specifically as all this musical chair bit took place, he saw the face of Mullah actually smile and relax in surprise! Billy was pleased, but cautiously aware of the slyness Mullah had tied up in his past. Caution was good, but right now the two of them were embarking on a new playing field in relationship, that would prove beneficial to everybody involved. Indeed, all time spent with the Mullah was recorded and filmed on tape and would be indelibly archived and retained by the CIA.

Billy sat down in his new living room easy chair and watched Mullah cautiously approach and sit down in the loaded lazy-boy chaise chair. He did so and reclined with his feet long out as he shown his pearly whites big time in thorough pleasure and enjoyment. He was obviously and genuinely thrilled at this sudden gesture of friendship from his ultimate enemy. Everybody's head was still connected. Hearts were temporarily warm.

CHAPTER THIRTY-ONE

Back in the suburbs of Langley, Billy's and Anita's home condo was taking on new dimensions and décor. They had punched a doorway into the second condo that had been Anita's sole abode before they got hitched. Now that the two were united in matrimony, they reassembled their home for joint use.

Anita fitted out a north-side window for her home studio, where she did most of her stills and landscape canvas works. Also depending on where her customers lived, if nearby, she'd do her finish work to her portraits at home. Most of her customer's sitting work was done at her new "Studio One" store front on Tyson's corner, a shopping mecca for the Washington metropolitan rich and famous. The "biggy" being the Tyson Galleria. Everyone that was anyone knew Tyson Corner for its upscale shopping. It was a distance of 6.1 miles or a 10-minute drive. Traffic, of course, was always a problem in the multi-plex of Washington DC and its surrounds.

Billy had a company vehicle which was specifically fit out with custom CIA stuff and gadgetry, weapons holders etc., and the outside looked typically normal standard like, nothing unusual looking, even white in color. It was new, an SUV with power under the hood. It had 4-wheel drive for winter or wherever, and it had Virginia plates, with a special code on it denoting CIA.

Anita also had a Buick SUV, a very nice-looking maroon red one, to be able to haul around her paintings and things. She loved it, and it served her well.

The Brewer family had located and settled in well. They were pleased each had less than a 10-minute ride to their workplace, though in opposite directions.

Anita had gotten her store studio and storefront appropriately appearing to her liking, the lettering, lighting and comfort level and décor best to serve her customers. As in any business, it was at first slow. It would take time for her reputation and location to become known. It was now for her talent along with Billy's help in creating a venue for reaching the public about her product and services.

Anita's first efforts were to assemble a showcase bulletin magazine like advertising pieces, slickly done in excellent color and quality. These were fashioned as mail outs to specific qualified potential customers as well as handouts or pick-ups at specific businesses.

Ads were carefully generated in specific oriented artist related publications and a few local paper publications popular to the McLean Area, pick-ups at grocery and drug emporiums.

Because Anita had quite a resume of paintings sold in Paris and many times winner of juried and judged shows there, plus her huge honor winning of the European show of shows judged last year as the Blue-Ribbon Grand winner of the Paris International Juried Show winner, winning the Bettendorf Grand First Prize. This itself propelled her to international prominence and reputation. Her accolades were impressive and preceded her new so-called "Virgin" status in the art world of America. IN the art world her reputation esteemed her highly and she was notably thought of as a "Primo artist."

Things were exciting, and each day grew the adventure for both their new lives in the Greater Washington area. They would be ensconced now and fill their passions in their appointed rounds of new careers.

~ SOMETIME LATER~

Back in Normal, Illinois, the congressman from the 12th district, the honorable Jonas Sterling had died. It had been sudden, a heart attack at the age of 83. He had been a notable Republican downstate public servant. He ran a good congressional district and was quite popular, thus continuing his place in congress for many a term. Billy got word of his death through his folks in York. York was some 25 miles northeast of Normal, Illinois, and situated pretty much in the middle of the 12th district which took in Urbana, Kankakee, Bloomington, Decatur, Ottawa/LaSalle to the northwest and straight across to the Illinois-Indiana border then down to just below Danville on the southwest district corner on the Indiana border. It wasn't much different type of territory than that which Abraham Lincoln first ran in out of Springfield. Jonas Sterling had run on Law and Order, moderate conservative agenda across the board of politics.

He was popular with the voters of his district and did its good tidings over his term years. The Republican party needed new, young blood to fill the term of Jonas' vacant congressional seat. They also needed some young live wire capable to go against any Democrat candidate. The Democrats would try hard to find a top candidate from their party ranks to challenge for the seat at election time a year ahead.

The Republican inner circle of the state of Illinois, quickly scanned all potential candidates they could find. They had a difficult time finding a candidate suitable to their status and need requirements. It was at that meeting when George Huff, a Central Committee member, and the sheriff of three counties in the district, suddenly came up with the idea and selection of Billy William Brewer as a candidate.

Well that name got tossed on the table and bantered verbally about. He certainly had some recognition in the area, and his background was impeccable and clean – he hadn't any political experience, but he had been and was a person respected for his service to his country; His academic credentials were impeccable and excellent and his career choices always found achievement and promotion. As far as they could find, he had no political enemies and his heart was strong for America, it's principles and a Conservative Moderate in thinking. He was honest, forthright and didn't blow his own horn. He was a law and order principled guy. He had great potential voter appeal all thought.

The question was then asked, did anyone know him personally? George upped a "yes" – noting they played on the state football championship team together – he knew him well.

Well that excited the Central Committee who went into deeper thought and talk about Billy as a candidate and by sessions end, George was selected and given leave of duty to seek out Billy Brewer and travel to Washington to pay him a visit and search to find their potential "right" candidate to step in as representative to fill the 12th district of Illinois for congressional vacant seat for two more years of his predecessors remaining term. It would be his job for two years to terms end, and election time for his seat to open again for public service rerun against a democratic opponent. Incumbents usually won, especially if they had some charisma and their record of job satisfaction was favorable with the districts' voters.

The Republican Central Committee then agreed to find, seek out and select Billy William Joseph Brewer, to the fill the vacant seat of Senior Congressman Jonas Sterling, deceased. They appointed liaison duty to George Huff the task of summitting this opportunity to become the districts most public servant. It would be a hard choice for anyone of Billy's caliber and ambition to turn down, no matter his rather recent attachment and career choice with the CIA. It would appeal to the base of Billy's craw to serve the greater societal level of people, to fight for them and participate in forming America through voting on laws and measures brought before the 2nd highest legal house in the land. It would place him where he could help America become great again. It needed such help. Men unafraid and patriotic.

George prepared for his trip to see his friend Billy Brewer and present him with this huge opportunity. It would be a humble and an incredible meeting.

In Washington: -

It was a Friday, the day of the renown Black Friday, the day of insanity spending by most of America. The shops everywhere would be crowded.

Anita had gotten up early to head to her new store studio. She hoped it would attract many people to look at her wares and buy or maybe make appointments to do commission work or a portrait for Christmas. She kissed Billy goodbye not knowing what plans Billy had for the day.

Billy's plans for the day were to sleep in some, arise and drive to Tyson's Corner and spend a day with Anita in her shop, maybe even, help her. She would be surprised, hopefully pleased.

As Billy approached the Galleria parking area, he viewed the mall itself and noticed many people running out of the mall, fleeing in hurried scattered manner.

Just then his cell phone rang. It was Anita in a troubled fearful voice saying," Billy, they're shooting at us in the mall. Where are you?"

Billy responded," Can you see any of them? Lock your door and get down."

Anita said, "I've already locked the door and no, I don't see any of them. They may be on the first floor. I don't know how many shooters, but everybody is running past my store. I'll get down behind something."

At that moment Billy's APB CIA Box started squawking about the shooting, the police and SWAT squads were on the way.

Anita said, "Where are you?" Billy said, "I'm in the parking lot of the Galleria putting on my armor and loading up my weaponry. "I'll be with you shortly."

"Oh, my God, how....be careful!"
Billy said to her," It may take me a while to reach you, but he'd knock on her door two short and one extra loud to get in. OK?"

"OK," said Anita. "Gotta go, sweetheart, don't worry. I'll be alright. Keep praying for me, bye!"

Billy strapped on a second pistol, and grabbed his custom M-16, slipped on his blue CIA windbreaker and ran toward the mall doors. He grabbed a young man, who seemed terrified, looked at him with a rifle, Billy flashed his CIA badge to him and calmed him down some. He asked him, "How many gunmen? Where had he last seen them? Were they together or apart? What were they wearing? Did they speak English or other?"

The young man stammered out all he could remember and then said they were shouting Allah Akbar" and shooting everywhere. He hadn't seen anyone hit yet, but they moved together were on the first floor going west slowly almost causally."

Billy thanked him, got on the police band/CIA band and said he was on the scene and ready to enter in and fully prepared. He repeated I have my CIA jacket and armor on. 10/4."

He turned and raced into the lobby, hugging the edges as people streamed by, he grabbed a loose cannon escaping and asked where were the gunmen? The man turned and pointed and said "They were headed slowly that away along the bottom first floor, The floor we're on." I let him go and got into a better position to see the entire first floor cavern, which was long. I heard another couple of rounds go off, then screams, I saw them in their dark clothes with AK-47's shoot people and shooting in the air at the hanging chandeliers, watching them shatter, then shouting "Allah Akbar." They were traveling slowly knowing the police would be there soon, and then they would be martyred, so there was no hurry. Meanwhile, I quickly set my scope to their distance. They had not carefully looked behind them. They were too interested in what surprises might lay before them.

I assumed a flat on the floor firing position. My sight aligned up quickly and I got off a round on one of them and waited a second and as the other gunman leaned over to look closer at his buddy, my sight fell cleanly on his head. I squeezed the trigger and instantly he fell over. I jumped up and ran toward them with my "Jackhammer" on full ready to right bullets in their direction.

They did not move. I nudged them both, and kicked their weapons free of their reach and frisked and relieved them of any other weapons in case they miraculously came to. They didn't.

Suddenly I heard a bull horn saying, "Hands up. Don't move!" As a good smart gesture, I did as they said. Any police officer with a gun pointed at you, if he says, "Drop it," drop it pronto!

Momentarily he was surrounded by 20 highly armed SWAT team officers followed by medical personnel running around everywhere looking for the wounded.

The head SWAT captain with everybody pointing their AR-15s at me, saw my CIA jacket and armor and the weaponry I was carrying, he turned and commanded everyone to stand down with their weapons. Everybody did and were looking at each other then back to the two dead. Who were they?

And unbelievably to the man, all pumped their fist in the air. They all inspected the bodies and searched them thoroughly, finding cell phones and notes of different kinds. The captain and those nearest the bodies noticed that the bullet hits were direct to the head – no second penetrations. The Captain said softly to the team nearest him, "We got us a professional hit man. Wonder what the distance was?"

Billy heard him say that and he said to the captain, "Specifically 289.1 feet." The captain took me aside, looking at my CIA credentials and said, "Who are you?"

I said, "I am in he in that CIA ID. Sorry I can't give you any more personal information than that."

"Well, how did you know they were here and beat us?" the Captain said.

"Well, I was coming to get some presents on Black Friday, pulled up to the mall, saw everybody running and panicked, I grabbed a runner and he told me what was going on. I had my agency battlewagon so I quickly put on my "stuff" and entered into the fray. The rest is history. Now that's my story, sorry you missed the fun. I gotta put my toys to bed and get on with my plans for the day. "Bye!"   He looked stunned and puzzled and wondered what'd he'd say to the media. I headed upstairs to Anita's shop. The police searched the entire building and parking lot, finding their car.

The media got a story unsatisfactory to them. I knocked two short and one extra hard on her shop door. Anita peeked over the counter and came to the door running and gratefully let me in and sunk a huge hug around my neck. It felt wonderful and I sucked it in with pleasure.

She said, "Where have you been. I've been worried about you?"

I said, "Thanks for your prayers they helped a lot." I kissed her and sat her down on one of the posing lounge chairs and said, "Do you have a Pepsi?"

Her eyebrows raised up in wonderment not having a clue as to what had gone on, what went down.

She said, "I heard the vast shooting, the screaming of 'Allah Akbar.' I knew it was the bad guys and wondered where you were. All I could do was pray. What has happened? I heard two loud distinctive shots, maybe a few seconds apart, then nothing. Just quiet, real quiet! Then I heard a bull horn sound."

"That was me lowering the boom. They are in paradise now and we are in good riddance of them. Safe for the time being. Oh, the bull horn was the SWAT team arriving on the scene."

Anita came over and embraced me again, saying, "Oh, you big bear. I love you. Why were you so near the mall?" So, it was, I replayed my plans for the day and it obviously wasn't a surprise any longer.

I stayed with her through the day as the Mall returned to a semblance of Black Friday spending normalcy. A half dozen were wounded, one critical, no one dead. It was a miracle that I arrived when I did. I thanked the Lord for his kindness and timing. It was indeed a blessed miracle.

I got to meet and greet with several customers who were enthusiastic about her work and tell others. They took her card.

The following day the Washington and American papers and airwaves were headlining the mystery hero that saved multitudes shootings or deaths from happening. This person appeared suddenly and took down the gunmen from 290 feet – bang, bang. The hero remains a mystery and his company or affiliation does not allow its personnel any disclosure or ID. Sources unnamed named the CIA as the hero's business affiliation. The paper's articles just gave thanks in worldly vernacular the best they could. There were, certain protesters, not knowing anything, declared the gunmen were shot down in cold blood. 99% of the readers and hearers could be heard to say, "Yeah, Right!!" Not!

Billy helped Anita to close up shop, and take a few paintings home along with my arsenal and protection gear I hid in some of her cloth material and bags. We made our way to our cars in the parking lot to head home. It had been a busy and long day at the office. Before escorting Anita into her car, she threw herself against Billy and hugged him again thanking him for all he had done. What he had done was just part of what was in his line of duty as a CIA agent. Indeed, he was blessed with God's covering for that day.

They returned home, and went out to dinner, even dancing and enjoyed the passions of living at home.

A night of rest to see the tomorrow and head off to work.

Work for Anita was quite a normal day. However, work at the CIA that day was extra busy for Billy. Head director John Brennan summoned Billy's boss, Director John Columbo, to quickly get to his desk a report on Billy's day involvement with the Tyson Corner Jihadist incident. Billy was told to spend his morning, in his office preparing a full report on his involvement in the "shooting" incident at the Mall in Tyson's Corner, Virginia.

Once again, he repeated his full day doings on a day off, detailing his travel and thinking and all actions taken until his feet left the Mall and for home with Anita. He included anyone he spoke to, his talks with Anita prior to any action being taken the outgoing messages he sent and the incoming as well, and the APB message that he was going in to confront the enemy. Time was of the essence for offensive measure to possibly reduce anymore potential deaths by murder by these thugs. He related his advising his superiors of his abilities in times of gun-slinging action during his previous career in the Green Berets. He was no neophyte that went in there. He was a seasoned vet.

Billy finished up his report and gave it to his assigned secretary to type up. It would be quite a coup for the agency another reason for its existence, a favorable one.

Hell, it was his duty as an American agency sworn to protect its citizens. He only did his duty and job. He reported then to director Columbo, who personally thanked him for his bravery and quick action in the face of fire. They both looked at their watches and director Columbo said, "I'm going to go down to the commissary for lunch. Do you care to join me?"

Billy replied, "Sure, I could go for a snack or two." They finished their meal and time together and headed back up the private elevation to the 7th floor executive director's suite. All the directors and associate directors, secretaries and armed guards dwelt among the floors' rooms and very large specialty room. Most rooms bristled with high tech communication equipment for hearing and viewing information. The floor below, the sixth was one huge information gathering facility with a plethora of technicians for running and operating all the various equipment in the CIA electronics arsenal.

Billy hadn't been through all the CIA facility and asked Director Columbo if he could get someone to tour him through the building. Director Columbo made a call and up popped a tour guide. Billy found the tour entirely fascinating and informative. Little did he know, the range and extensiveness of reach that the CIA had at their disposal. When the guide returned him back to his office around 4 o'clock, he realized he'd put on a lot of miles walking in buildings – through seven floors of CIA facility headquarters located at that spot in Langley, Virginia. No mention on the "house" tour of any detention area or facility where "Mullah Moo" and he rendezvoused most every day. It was the "hole" nobody talked about. Few knew of it. Even less had been there. Those that had were known as "The Hole in the Wall Gang." The privileged few.

His week was spent assembling information of the CIA that the congress needed to hear. Especially the house intelligence committee. He daily reported to the European and Middle East area briefing rooms for current and updated status and news of those areas important to USA interests. Those things came under his new job management. They would be interesting areas of introduction to the CIA Jungle of divested pursuits. But little did Billy know his life would soon change again, he would soon be leaving the CIA for a bigger, more important job, in the service of his country.

NEW BEGINNINGS:

About 4:45 pm on Thursday of that week his personal cell phone hummed in his pocket. He pulled it out, looked at the number and name and hesitated a second in answering it as it was a name well known to him from the past. He clicked the "on" button and said, "Hey George, how you doin'? Long time no see or hear!"

George responded, "That's for sure Billy. I know you're very busy, but I need some time with you about some important business. I'm coming in town tomorrow. I hope you can give me a few hours to hear me out. This is "BIG" and major and I've been chosen to deliver you the message. Can you make time for me tomorrow afternoon late or in the evening? I'm planning to stay another day should you need time with me. It may weigh heavy, but positive on you and Anita, I think I have a plan you could live with should you accept my offer. Whatta ya say!"

George, if it were possibly anyone else but you, I'd say no, I'm not interested, whatever it is, but I'm intrigued by your phrasing and mystery and besides I'd love to see you and spend some time joining Anita and me. In fact, stay with us the night as long as you need. Save some bucks too. OK? Meanwhile I'll satisfy my curiosity when you get here tomorrow. It sounds rather urgent!"

George broke in, "It is or I wouldn't bother you – OK! That would be great, I'll be on ground around noon – one o'clock and I'll meet you at your office or after work at home."

Billy re-upped the conversation with "That's good for me. Say, why don't you bring Marcy with you. Stay with us, it would be super great. We could rouse up old times and fill in spaces. Whatta ya say? Stay a couple days, we could do our business and Marcy could hang out with Anita."

"All right, I accept your invite, we'll be there Friday noon-time. OK, that's great! I love it." They said their good-bye's and hung up. Billy called Anita and related his talk with George and informed her that he and his wife Marcy would be staying with them for two days. He and George had business to talk about. Can you handle it?"

Anita answered his call, and replied, 'That's great, I remember George and Marcy back in high school. They were good friends of ours. This will be fun, I wonder what he's so anxious to talk with you about? Oh, well, we'll find out soon enough. I'll prepare my old bedroom for them so they'll be comfortable. I'll have to make a couple of adjustments but, no problem. I wonder what's on his mind? Anyway, it'll be fun. We could tour some monuments, show them sights."

"You're the best. Thanks. It will be fun to see them again. We had such a short time with them at our wedding reception. I'm looking forward to it. OK, see you tonight when I get home. Hope the Mall was quiet today?"

"Yeah, it was thanks to you. Love you. See ya!" They hung up.

At 5:30 pm Billy folded up his desk work and proceeded to head home. His secretary had left at 5:00 pm as had most of the office help.

He slipped into the 7th floor only private elevator to the ground floor across from where the regular elevator doors opened. There he walked through the lobby and history museum displays for visitors.

The first floor had many armed guards and a few roaming CIA sleuths under cover watching and peering at folks. It was open to the public, but security was tight.

It was but a very short travel to home. Again, he was in his agency's vehicle the white SUV. He arrived home and found a space in front of his condo. They would enjoy a time at home this evening. Quiet – just them. The Huff's would be with them the next few days. Quiet times were pretty precious to the both of them.

Billy spent the next morning with Mullah Moo in the "hole." He was lookin' good and sittin' in his E-Z chair waiting for me. The guards had told him I'd be there today.

When I first entered the "hole" area, he was grinning, actually smiling. I was instantly tuned into extra sensory perception. "What's he up to?" To my surprise he was actually glad to see me. We had become chummy, as Satan and Jesus were in the desert. In fact, our relationship was much similar. The only difference being he thought I was Satan, and I suspected he was, well at least he most often acted like him.

He blurted out in English, "Good Morning 'big bull' and I responded "Good morning Mullah Moo. How are you?" He liked his newly given name and laughed as I said it. Our relationship was growing to the point we were only enemies - not arch enemies.

I said to Moo, "I see you are enjoying the new E-Z boy lounge chair again. Have you enjoyed the vibrator relaxer yet?"

"Oh, yeah, this thing is terrific. I really appreciate you sharing the seat of luxury. It's a little too decadent for me, but I sleep good in it!"

"Well, I wouldn't want you to be uncomfortable, now would I?" I laughed an uncertain laugh of "if you don't give me some more information to chew on, I'll yank it!" Moo seemed to get the drift and I could see the wheels spinning searching for ways to evade my desires. He knew he couldn't fool me, at least not for long. I knew his crafty kind. I made it a point to study the Arab Jihadist mind set as dark as it was and as evil as deception could take it.

Deception was a main characteristic of the Jihadist mindset, especially with infidels, much less among themselves, where the pot calls the pot black, and they know it. Among themselves nobody fools anyone else. They all lie to each other. It's a form of sport. They live by the gun and die by the gun. Without a gun they are neutered and left to slick talking.

The session was revealing that how Isis actually curried money from one area to another and basically who was funding them. He bragged that the world dollars would always fund groups opposed to the American greed mongers. He was developing an attitude that their side would always win even if the infidels knew what they were doing, thus he was disclosing so-called inside information to me – realizing it, bid him Lazy Boy time in his windowless cell.

The only thing was, I'd quote back the rest of the story from information we had gathered from computers and paper trials gathered from his headquarters during the raid. Mullah soon realized his surface disclosures were old information and he was peddling backward towards chair time. Moo started paddling newer information and more details on defenses they'd set up and were preparing for. He even revealed the whereabouts of some secret bombmaking facilities and improvised rocket and IED manufacturing locations, several of which were found in the latest round of Allied Forces attacks. Maybe old Mullah Moo had done some soul searching and realized he was just another human being desiring peace in the world.

Being nice and pleasant as Billy, his infidel new friend was to him, had a certain merit and desirability in the midst of all the world violence. Moo had known nothing but violence to achieve his cause since his earthling beginnings.

His thought of being interned in a cell somewhere in the world unknown and without any chance of escaping or returning to power, gave him a certain "space" in time and life of peace of mind. The "Chair" was fodder to feed the body some level of comfort and rest. Death was every Jihadists ultimate goal and 72 virgins to chase down in heaven were among his vast martyred benefits program his religion proposed to him.

Billy slowly and methodically interjected Christian beliefs and attitudes into their conversations. Actual discussions of religious beliefs were avoided. There needed to be actual demonstrations in the living now to show conviction of faith discussion vying to impose by theoretical verbal manipulation talk was imperfect and ill-gotten gain way of converting any mindset of a position different of their heritage. The two divisions of world religions were butting heads on the world scene.

The trouble was one religion had as its proponent and evangelistic outreach conversion by force of the gun. Deceit was imbedded in the liturgy and arguments for the "cause." To those that see black all their life, don't appreciate gray or white and reject them.

When there are 101 dialects in China alone, no wonder one area of China can't understand another. The world's people were scattered at Balim and they raised up united in one mind or spirit since. Men have become their own God and are convinced in their own calling in life, that everything revolves around them and so under their control or in their bailiwick. The world has become full of "niches" and people like Mulla Moo who like power of being a head "niche," but then either you have to control all your vineyard or somebody will take it away. So, it's me against you. What peace and comfort level is that?

Billy and Moo were exploring exactly that. They were moving together, not apart. Like human beings, things were allowed to merge and mingle, as they were removed from the trappings of other and violent influences.

CHAPTER THIRTY-TWO

George and Marcy arrived at the Washington National Airport. They called Billy to let him know they were in town. Billy told them to head for his condo home that he would call Anita. It was shorter for Anita to get home than for the Huff's to get there from the airport. So, Billy told George he'd be along in a little while as he needed to tidy up a few things before he headed home. He said he'd be home by 3 PM. It was currently 1 PM eastern time.

Billy unlocked his condo door and there were Anita, Marcy and George having some ice tea and cookies. They all arose and excitedly greeted Billy with hugs. All the girls loved anywhere to hug Anita's big bear husband. Even Marcy whose hubby was a "bear" himself, but shorter. Billy, at 6 foot 6, 280 lbs. in superb shape, was a formidable human being. Plus, some of the ladies said of him "swooning" – "He's so good looking!" Smiles and chatter ensued immediately as they all sat back down to seriously "schmooze."

They all spent the late afternoon catching up with the last years gone by and even dwelled in some reminiscing of the York Raiders grand days of championship football teams. Like proverbial Bridge Players, and golfers they could remember every play of the championship games. It was like yesterday. They were indeed joyful and full of laughter.

Soon it was six o'clock and all the energy output, needed renegotiating and re-upping with some food. Billy suggested they all go to one of he and Anita's favorite places called "The General's Steak and Lobster House." Right away that sounded like a hit, and they headed to their rooms to freshen up before going out to dinner.

They assembled and shipped out in Billy's CIA SUV, not the most comfortable but certainly accommodating for the four of them. Two large sized men, as George was still maintaining his football playing days at center weighing in a 270 lbs., a frame somewhat expanded since those days. It was helpful being in shape for his career job as a county Mounty Sheriff.

Together with their rather petite brides, were a rather fearsome twosome - viewing them as they walked together. They indeed, reminded folks that they might be "secret service" agents for the president.

Billy and George didn't talk business the whole evening. The ladies were delighted., The ladies felt themselves well protected knowing that Billy was a CIA agent, who usually always carried a weapon and George was a "County-Mounty" Sheriff in Illinois. They ordered this time a couple Wild Turkey bourbon drinks as the ladies partook of some lighter rum infected cocktail. The men had big size servings of custom selected steaks and the girls enjoyed the buttery battered flavor of Maine lobster.

They enjoyed their evening feast for about two hours and headed home – stuffed! Once home Anita checked on the coffeemaker to finish off the evening in front of their electric fireplace. It didn't put out much heat, but it was delightful to look at.

The next day was Saturday and they lingered around the kitchen table putting together flap jacks, bacon and OJ stuff. By 9:45 am, Anita and Marcy headed out the door to Anita's car to head to Anita's studio store for most of the day while Billy and George settled in to talk business stuff.

Billy opened after they were settled in, with "Ok George, what's the big scoop you got for me? By the way, I'm really glad you and Marcy came to visit us. I know Anita is thrilled to see you both again.

"Us, too," replied George, "Billy, there has come to the people of Illinois a new challenge. Jonas Sterling has died recently leaving his congressional seat temporarily vacant. We, being on the Republican Central Committee, have the duty of replacing him with somebody. It will not require being elected to the office at this time. As usual when a death or leaving causes a vacancy, mid-term, we must fill it with a temporary person, who preferably will be an able and a voter-pleasing candidate as we can find. To be upfront and candid, many names were thrown on the table, none of which peeked much interest for one reason or another, until I thought of your name. I don't know why, it just came out, but the more I've been thinking about it, the better and brighter you appear.

Now first of all, by passing your background, personality and talent for a moment, I got thinking about the logistics of it and how it would work for you and Anita. Let me explain my thinking.

"Of course, you will have to resign your current job if should you embark on the civil representation as a United States Congressman from the 12th district of Illinois. That means you will have to own a residence from and in the district, anywhere in the district, even York.

My extended thinking is you can keep this place as your Washington place to stay, unless you like flying a lot.

Continuing, George stated, "You will currently fill the term Jonas has left, almost a year-and-half left before a re-up run for re-election. You being the sitting incumbent, are re-elected almost 90% of the time. Though you are a new face on the political scene, you do have name recognition in the district because of your publicity in our aggressive York "Patter" readership and Ed Martins leadership and sports editor Stan Zaleski hype on you, and his so enthusiastically enamored with York High School sports. Your past has superseded your presence in York. They follow you and Eddy Brandon's careers like celebrities' groupies. Name recognition, career validation, war heroes, and government service are outstanding pluses with voters. You are a fresh face to politics, with a clean slate background, my guess, and I've been on the team a long time, you would be a natural candidate. I see a candidate, much like Jonas Sterling, different, that would be a US Congressman long in the making of a great career.

I can assure you our team Committee Republican Party is very adept at managing a campaign of impressive measures. The opposition party will have a hard time coming up with a candidate with the virgin background you have. I see nothing they can throw at us, from their corrupt, far left-leaning party. They have a large corruption problem in their Illinois party line. Chicago politics is steeped in corruption. They are old-fashioned in their approaches to things. Patronage is still a disease with these people and they just don't get it with a public who are dying for some honesty, genuineness and fresh air. You, my friend, should you accept my offer as Senior Representative of our Republican Party delegation, which I can almost assure you with the person you are, your values and accomplishments, that your government congressional life, will be long, successful, fruitful and joyful. Oh, by the way, the salary is $165,000 a year – free stuff and office."

"While you are in office, you will have immunity from arrest, they have a great and generous retirement plan and lenient "Franking" privileges with your constituents. With your background you will probably follow Senator/Congressman Richard Burr onto the Intelligence Committee. You may even know more now than he does, he's an outsider, you're an insider."

"Anyway, we can help you with seeking a home place in the district or any matters related to your office. Well, my friend, that's it, why I'm here. I told you it would be exciting and big. You need to talk it over, all of it, with Anita. As I can see it, you needn't move at all, just add one more home on back in District 12. Most of your time will be spent in Washington executing your duties as a US Representative from the 12 District of Illinois. It all has far-reaching possibilities, in a world like it is today. Jonas was nearing his retirement from office and his energy was diminishing and the time at this post growing old and faded. It's a new era, new young minds are needed. Give it some thought you two. I'll be here another day if you have questions, I can help.

"George, this is stunning and certainly as juicy a subject to chew on imaginable. This will be my biggest choice ever, I feel. It will take serious consideration. I must talk with Anita. This is really BIG."

George interdicted, saying, "I'm just glad I happened to be on the committee and the one sent to you to deliver our message of appeal. I gotta say, I'm honored to do this, as well as to be your long-time friend."

"Yeah George, that you are, my good friend indeed. I know this was hard to do, but you're a responsible guy, you gotta be, doing the work you do – law enforcement. Hey, let's go and get some lunch somewhere. I need to get out of here for a while."

"Good idea, let's go!" Spoke George.

Billy's mind was whirling now – speed dial. Light miles seemed slow at the moment. He definitely needed to sit down with Anita and go through all this new stuff. Accepting a new career change would take him out of a lot of potentially dangerous involvement the world over.

Though he never shunned such dangers, his getting older and newly married carried new responsibilities his way. It meant a total reboot of his life, their life. He felt an emotion of "yes" in his entirety of his being, it was a sense of destiny that invaded him. It was a definite surprise, all this, it had big repercussions. Should he accept this immense responsibility? But now he, had to operate his life for two. He had known Anita since high school Freshman year. They were indeed, now one, a team. He wanted her in on all of it.

Anita was coming home with Marcy around 4 o'clock that day, both of them were in the dark about the contact subject George had come to discuss with Billy. Both would be shocked to some extent. All Anita wanted was a certain comfort place in Billy's life. She knew he was an accomplished "A-type" personality that worked hard for everything he achieved. All she needed was his consideration and love and being included in everything that had to do with their life and its living.

Honesty was no problem, nor truthfulness. She would be by his side, discuss the problem and solve it the best they could, together. But little did she know the complexity of this decision They both relied on God's help in all matters and would heavily lean on Him for seeking His counsel, direction and nudging on this one. After all He knew the past and future of all the universe.

So again, they would face tomorrow not as one but as three. They would work through it all.

When Anita and Marcy returned home and came through the door, there were their two husbands looking like they had talked about surgery or something. They were pensive and temporarily resolute, silent in talking.

Anita said, "What's going on?" having an uneasy tinge run through her. Billy spoke up saying, "This is really a 'biggy' subject matter that's hard to start at the beginning. You all sit down. I'll talk."

I suppose I'll start at the start. Why George is here, which is to relate to me and you a proposition appointment as the new Illinois, District 12 replacement for Jonas Sterling as slated by the state Republican Party. They are offering me his seat, a future in politics for the long haul. They are officially offering me to replace Congressman Jonas and take his seat, a remainder term and then run a re-election campaign to keep the seat Republican as long as possible. This in the face of a very democratic state, but in the light of Able Lincoln's partisan help.

Of course, there are pros and cons on this immense decision for us to make, considering where we are and what we are now personally doing. Apparently, we have 30 days to fill the seat, so we have a few days to generate talk about making this decision.

Anita and I need some quiet time on this matter plus time for us to delve into the complexity affecting our future current living style."

Marcy kept to herself. She was stunned that Billy was possibly to be the new United States Congressman from their district. It was a huge and demanding job, especially on the heels of the illustrious Jonas Sterling. Her thoughts were that indeed Billy would be absolutely the perfect choice. She hoped he would take it and spoke up saying, "I think you'd be absolutely perfect for the job, Billy, we need you, the State of Illinois needs someone with creative statesmanlike, honest, quality that you'd bring to the table. You'd be the next best thing since Lincoln in my estimation. Our state has something like Seven governors behind bars now, or still, over the years; Let's bring back integrity as an integral part of civil society politics. It can be done."

Her words struck a chord with Billy and he thanked her for her thoughts. This would be a huge decision not to be taken lightly.

George and Billy, Anita and Marcy sat around with some ice tea and took on the subject trying to help and clarify the complexities of the decision on the general front and not delving into the Brewer's personal things much at all. They would have to sift those things out together, on their own time.

They all decided to terminate the talk on the pollical arena and reverted back to reminiscing old times and current events. They all went out to dinner for the last time on George and Marcy's visit as they were to leave the next morning back to Springfield, Illinois. There was sadness as the evening rolled shut, but jubilation of being together again in friendship renewed. George would not be returning with a "Nay" or "Yea" verdict on Billy's acceptance for the job. He would have to wait a few days. George understood the enormity of the decision. They hugged before boarding for the trip back home. There was much to talk about now in Billy's and Anita's young married life. Life was getting full. Were they ready? So much was suddenly served on their plate. They needed digesting time.

CHAPTER THIRTY-THREE

Billy and Anita watched their friends get on board their flight for home. They were heavy with heart and would be missing their old friends and friendships. They looked at each other and hugged and kissed then turned and headed back through the terminal to their car. They held hands and didn't say much of anything while they walked.

Finally, after they had gotten into their seats of the SUV, Anita stated to Billy, "I will work with you whatever you decide to do. This is a huge decision on your part -less so for me. We have no children yet. You have a new career-type job, secure, I have myself now oriented for a commercial painting career, but flexible. You and I are relatively young in this worldly world and so far our life has been a big positive piece of work. We have been blessed and we have each other. I'm wonderfully happy, you seem to be too. Now is now with a new turning of the proverbial page just ahead."

Billy jumped into the conversation as they headed home, stating, "Anita, I love you - always will. I want to be a good husband, friend, lover and a daddy someday. We have approached our first mountain in our life. We shall overcome it with prayer and us talking between us. We will sift until we think we have it right. Again, God will keep us in the right path. I hope He loudly lets us know.

"Yes, I hope so too, Billy," said Anita. "I want the very best for you." She continued, "Do you know what you want? Can you see beyond this mountain any? I can't because I don't know what your dreams are for our future. We haven't really talked the talk about that since barely settling into our new home and current employment. Now this, at least you aren't positioned to head off to "Mosul" or somewhere where bullets are flying."

"You're right about that, I don't want that either, not now with family rearing its head for us. I'm with you, and our need to wend our way through all this. Part of the problem is our lifestyle is about to be changed, from war and active duty possibilities to now fighting for peace through civilian democratic means and ways. I'd have to resign from the CIA and return to a civilian life and lifestyle, but this time I could be talking American policy for peace and its positive posturing on the world scene. A different style of war. It would involve paper pushing, legislation of ideas, and laws designed to stabilize America, and protect her. I would represent a constituency of people and how they see and desire America to become, and help clarify and design ways to make that happen through policy and persuasion, debate and communication. I've always been an action guy, thrive on it, and as the years pass by I must help America grow into the future and present the best ideas and challenges America has to offer. We must speak to its future in faith and belief that God will show us the way. This is too big for just us to solve. America has a destiny since 1776. We must follow it! We must protect it from worldly airborne flagrant human diseases.

"You've got that right Billy, I'm with you. Where shall we start?" said Anita. They arrived at home and went into their condo. It was quiet and peaceful, they were alone. They had the rest of Sunday to sit and think and talk. The bears were playing Washington in Washington and Billy noted that in his mind to catch at least part of it.

Well the two of them started in to the what ifs, shoulds, and shouldn'ts, maybes and definite nots. They posted all this in a loose-leaf binder notebook and labeled it "DECISION ONE!" Anita took notes. Later Billy did. The book filled fast and by late evening they were spent racking their brain and sapping their energy, discussing all they could think of. They would sleep on it and try to conclude a decision the next day, after a day of work.

The concluding diagram page looked like something Billy would have come up with for a Green Beret planned attack on something. Billy was good at such planning he'd been in on a lot of them.

As Billy saw it, the goal was not the taking of Jonas' seat, but deciding if at such a young age he wanted to get into politics and the political arena of living your life. It was a different and mainly fish bowl style of living, not much was private. But on the other hand, the United States needed to go somewhere, it needed someone or someone's to take the helm and move the country into the 21st century.

Big problems were bursting world-wide like Chicken Pox or cancer. The American landscape was dead in the waters. The politicians, need to get some fresh air, new oxygen sources, clearer heads and develop new and better ways to steer America through the storm fronts facing her. The cross-nation sections of foul weather were battering the gates of all its world citizens. But most specifically the stars and stripes of American lifestyles, freedoms need new opportunity to spread its wings of potential greatness once again.

The inhouse partisan bickering and social unconscionable party sickness of corrupting ways for upping voter registration to re-vote policies and platforms unwanted, unamerican and unequal to all its citizens. All in the name of propagating one party or another.

Useful policies, laws, directives were reflected for highly partisan agenda to get votes. People, the actual people of America were being discarded, and used for political gain against one another in the name of insanity. Votes and control in order to dictate were the objective.

"The races of America don't have a chance in hell of commiserating together when a party doesn't want that to happen. Special interests, special exceptionally wealthy individuals with very dubious political and philosophical backgrounds plot and manipulate their cancerous ways into the societal landscape unknown to the average "Joe" voter. Most special groups or interests have one thing in common - each has an agenda they want perpetrated on America for their own business interest of personal or philosophical gain. Altruistic motivations. Corruption has a jillion tentacles, each poisonous when touched. The tentacles are growing and our political people are succumbing to the overwhelmingness of their reach and power."

Anita jumped in "Who will stop them? How can it be turned around? Who even thinks anymore about the future? We're the only country around the globe with potential to change things for the good of mankind. The world is going 'dark' quickly, we need water on our plant life – new thinking, brave and aggressive new ways of doing and seeing things. Backbone of steel is needed and excitement in the world about new ideas – risk takers – America still has those people."

Billy entered in saying "You're absolutely right, the people must be led back into the international game, they need to be heard, they need to see things happen in their own backyard that they feel more fulfilled in their soul and in their pocketbooks."

"I really have been looking at America through the eyes of protecting her, the real need is to get some new parts within her that lead to return her to the original founders' intentions of turning up the necessities within, re-oiling the parts, finding captains of courage to take hold of the rudder, and steer the ship with authority through the storms of tomorrow. The waves part when ships sail with purpose. And the people will follow when they believe. It's not happening now. The faster America goes now the behinder it gets. We are becoming a paper tiger despite the average American's neutering by those in our political systems. People make a difference; common sense policies are the rudder. We need some good steerers who don't turn and run when the ship splits a large wave and it washes over the ship."

Anita's book of thoughts and talk was filling fast. She was getting excited for them and for her country. America needed strong backboned change – 'damn the torpedoes' – men and women. It was getting late and she said to Billy, "Let's quit, regroup tomorrow after a day of work and thinking. We're making headway!"

Good idea, I'm kind of spent too. Yeah, I'm getting nudgings and visions while we are talking," Billy said.

"Good," said Anita. "We need His help!"

The following day they got up and had breakfast and headed to work. Anita's store at the mall didn't open until 10:00 am, so she lagged behind.

"Any revelations from sleep last night?" said Anita.

"Nope, not yet. I'm still grinding the whole thing out. On balance I'm tilting forward to jumping on the political bandwagon. Things of worldly matters get determined in legislative government not in local or state territories. Those matters affect our back yards only. The big picture is in congress and the Senate. The minor corrections are subject to the state and local governments. IN the tradition of America, the people speak the government does their bidding, except when too many outside soirees and intrusions interdict and poison the wells of the public mindset.

America is weak in its seams and its walls are turning to cardboard. Somebody has to grab the rope before insurrectionists burn it, cut it or tie it off. The will of the people needs resetting in steel and cement. Somebody and somebodies need to put down the slings and arrows being hurled at us from inside and outside., As it is, they know not what they do to themselves and others. They are thinking past their neighbor and they don't have a clue either. Well I've got to go," said Billy, "See you later this afternoon, evening. Have a great day love – bye." Billy headed out the door to the CIA not knowing how much longer he'd be there.

Anita left for work, thinking the same thing. A bit disturbed as to their future in the coming months and year ahead. She was confident they would come out on top of things, but it might be a rocky road.

The world was turbulent, unsettled, and the populace uninformed and riding the waves of emotions, bias of the lost and misdirected souls who were subject to other's influences and mis-directions, deceitfulness and threats.

Where Billy was, they put out local fires, did it well, but the world needed leadership in the larger realm, like peace through power – American style. Billy needed to be in a place where he could promote common sense, individual greatness, and opportunity for everyone to rise up to their God given destiny and potentials, not others telling them what they are to do, say, act or believe. America was and is the greatest land of immigrants in the world. Individual opportunity is nowhere else the likeness found in the USA. It's been that way because of beliefs in God, relying on him and working His freedoms hard.

Anita was beginning to see the obvious for Billy and she and Billy honed in for a time such as this. She needed to support him, stand by his side, help indulge him in wise choices and love him at every turn. They were in Love, it had slowly but consistently grown to where they were today. They were at this point in their life, a timeframe, that it was now a time to think about starting a family. They'd have to consider this seriously and probably quickly. Time was fleeting. Anita was strongly favoring his taking the new challenge as a congressman. Based on the longevity potential, if successfully re-elected providing the voters liked him and his job performance. He was perfect for the job, and there was nothing Billy couldn't do if he put his large shoulders to the task. Anita knew that was par for the course, to heave ho at his best, no matter what! She would tell Billy of her persuasion for his choice tonight.

Billy's day at the agency was busy. Again, he had duty with another session interrogating Mullah Moo and was in on apprising congress of all the goings on by the CIA in addition. He thought often and hard about what he wanted in life, its opportunities and where did he fit to accomplish and impact the world with his influence, where best could he realize his potential.

He saw the limitations if he stayed with the CIA. Yes, he could be good at the Agency and work his way up the ladder to the top, but his near-term influence would be nothing like it might be if he were in congress, where he could influence many, many people, even 'round the world in outreach.

By the time he got home, his thoughts were pretty clear. He would go with it., The opportunity looked really appealing to him, and a lifestyle the both of them could enjoy and master.

His new arena would put him right in the middle of having outreach to America as well as worldwide. It was a coliseum of prima donnas, left and right political thinking talk-a-thons, and few, if any, seemingly true American statesmen with any common sense. He could make a solid difference in this world of chaos and ignorance and on coming valueless society worldwide. Nobody was accountable anymore. Leaders were so beholden to voter block, that decisions were hung in effigy before ever getting debated. His decision was made to take the new job as congressman. Tonight, the two of them would commiserate together and make their decision. Finalize it.

Anita got home first and was waiting for Billy with a big hug. He was totally ready for that, and held her tight. She was so precious in his sight. Love was a many splendored thing.

"Well, how'd it go today?" said Billy. "Did you come up with a thought or decision on your part?"

"How about you, Billy? Any decision?" Billy nodded affirmatively, and said, "Yes" clearly.

"OK," said Billy, "On three we say yes or no to taking the congressional job."

"OK," replied Anita. "One, two, three!"

The room echoed "Yes, yes." They again hugged each other, and kissed. Then looked up beaming delight. They had just made their first huge, big decision as a married couple. They would go out to dinner and celebrate.

Oh, what a relief it was to have that behind them. They could adjust and get on with their new life. They would not have to move, but expand their home front back to Illinois.

Anita hesitated and said "Billy where do think you'll like to live in Illinois?" They both knew and he said, "York, of course!" They'd be returning to their birthplace and first home love, at least off and on for hopefully a long, long time.

In the back of Anita's mind, she was thinking of a future family and maybe, just maybe, they could now plan for it. She gently mentioned her feeling on this to Billy. He concurred. She was delighted. They prepared the way.

They spent the night exchanging their thoughts on making their decision about Billy's new job. It had been a hard one to do. Nothing is simple in the human arena of life. Options aren't like a light switch on or off. Click. They are more like incandescent tube lights that linger slowly illuminating before they get fully bright.

The two of them enjoyed and lingered over dinner at one of their favorite steak houses. The onion rings were excellent. They tasted great on the heels of a successful decision making. They were on their way, a team and married couple. God knew what he was doing. They felt they were following His lead – the star was bright in the East!

BOOK 3

CHAPTER ONE

It was early evening and they put in a call to Billy's friend George Huff. They would inform him of their decision. He would be very pleased with their call and decision.

The conversation proceeded along these lines.

"George, this is Billy. After Anita and my serious thoughts and prayers we have decided to accept your job offer. This is a huge undertaking for the both of us. We have weighted in as much on our scale as we could think of plus all of our emotions. Based on love of country. I'm throwing in with a battle front unlike the one I presently serve. The battle for public self-determination for what this country is all about, was founded on and is losing.

"I believe I have something to offer my country, the people who love it, and what it used to stand for – good values, fairness, honesty, truth and statesmanship among nations. I want to help America become 'Worthy again,' admired and even followed. To do that will take a Herculean effort and backbone of God's grace. But I want to try. George, what's next for me to do to fill statesman Jonas' seat?"

"Congratulations Billy and Anita. I know it was a tough decision. Our election committee needs to reconvene and affirm our vote and confirm you as our living candidate to replace Representative Jonas Sterling, 12th District Illinois. You need our confirmation vote by our republican committee., Next you will have to come to the district, find a dwelling place, purchase it and meet and greet some of the public folks, that have backed Jonas and love him. Then you need to show up at Jonas' office here and then back in Washington DC meet the staff, then go sit in his chair (or get your own) and begin work for your district 12 legislating matters."

"Knowing you it won't be long before you're influencing those you need to – on the road to get America back on track again."

"Let me know when you and Anita can come here. Meanwhile, I'll get things hummin' and in motion with the committee to prompt progress in moving you and things of transition along. We need not lose momentum of a republican vacancy in the halls of Congress. Your vote is needed and does count.

Just call me when you can soon be here. We'll take care of the transportation and dwelling locations until you pick something out. Jonas' office here is alive and well. They will help you in anyway. Just ask.

I'll email you his office personnel and job descriptions, who to grab hold of in his office? That would be his and your no. 1 assistant there. So, call me or email me. I'll call Jonas' office immediately and let them know all we've talked about and that they can expect a visit anytime soon from you and use his office as yours as you like after tomorrow. I'm sure it will be delayed possibly by the time needed to back out of your present job at the Agency. They won't necessarily be happy with your decision, but it's your life, not theirs."

"Right on, George, I'll speak with Anita and arrange a time to come there. I must let the Agency know tomorrow and give notice. As you know bureaucracies take time to change, do anything, even the CIA., So, I'll keep you apprised on the timing of things going on here. Thanks for everything George. You're a good friend I can count on. Blessings on you and Marcy. See ya – bye."

After he hung up, he looked on his computer email and saw a note from George. He read it. "Just saying to soon stop into Jonas' office in DC and introduce himself to the staff. Might call first. – George."

Billy made note of that in his weekly planner, a book he was filling fast. It would get worse soon.

The following morning, he made an appointment to see John Columbo, Mideast/Europe Director at the CIA to terminate and offer his resignation. He asked if they could meet together in the bureau Chiefs office at 8:30 am. The office said they'd try to make that happen but couldn't guarantee it.

Billy huddled with Anita to plan their trip to Illinois to settle out the takeover of Jonas Sterling's seat. Billy would be there to receive formal installation by the Party as replacement congressman for the 12th District of Illinois. Also, the meeting and greeting of the district office personnel. It was important to get to know them and they him. A smooth transformation was the goal for replacement procedure. He would try hard to make it all work. It would show the solidarity of the Party and their ability to meet emergency obstacles.

The democrats of Illinois were ready to pounce on any replacement candidate as a lame duck temporary candidate for the job, while they looked for a good candidate to run against whomever the republicans would choose to fill Jonas' term. They knew they couldn't beat Jonas, he was popular and an excellent public representative servant for their district, and had been for decades.

His reputation was "gold" at the voting booth. The Republicans needed to find a high-quality candidate and they were told that Billy Brewer was "the up and coming" candidate they had.

They were excited as a Party that was involved in presenting "Billy." The more they heard about him, the more they were confident he would be a terrific candidate and dedicated public servant. It was all hearsay and talk at the moment. No one yet had met him outside of George Huff. It was all on paper and word of mouth. Starting with George and his team of folks. Soon things would change upon Anita's and Billy's sojourn to Springfield.

CHAPTER TWO

Anita and Billy arrived in Springfield, Illinois, the Illinois State Capitol. George and the 12th District Office Manager, Juanita Sanchez, met them at the airport and took them to the district headquarters office of Jonas Sterling in Bloomington, some 25 miles from York.

There he met all his new staff in the office, had some coffee and sat talked with them. This was an "intro" visit to get to personally meet and greet his upcoming staff members. They were certainly nice folks and very competent in their job duties. Old pro Jonas would have nothing less. Billy sensed the quality of his new office personnel and was glad to meet them all.

The visit to this satellite office at home base was most enjoyable and educational. He was in good hands in District 12, which included York nearby.

So far, his busyness had included his official resignation at the CIA and the new challenge currently acting as the 12th District of Illinois representative to the 114 Congress of the United States.

The official ceremony and installation by the Republican Party declaring him the new office replacement Congressman to that district took place. Now all he needed was to show up at this new/old office of Jonas Sterling in Washington, DC. His first official vote to be cast, would be held on the "House Floor" in a week. He would be there to cast his vote for his district. His vote was to declare the will of the people for the 12th District of Illinois. His reigning personal criteria was "Is it good for America, then it's good for our district."

It would be all new to Billy, no more strategic planning involving foreign lands, no more gunship diplomacy daily., The one Caveat he maintained was an un-official relationship with the CIA in the capacity of a negotiator interrogator with Mulla Moo once or twice a week for an hour or so. This duty would be under cover, private time matter. Really no conflict of interest involvement. The CIA was still believing Moo had some answers they needed or could use, thus the interrogation continuation.

Billy and Anita successfully concluded their Illinois trip with the purchase of an old Victorian-type home in York. It needed work and love, but now it was theirs., He established that as his permanent residence. Things were shaping up. It was a lot of work for the both of them. But the more they did now, the smoother things got on down the road.

Relatively speaking, it was worth doing it that way. They got to visit both their folks and spent an evening with a group of York citizens, a lot of whom they knew. It was a good political start. their trip home was uneventful and enjoyable for the both of them. They were well pleased with themselves and where life had them.

Many adjustments were on the way, that would be tomorrow, the day after. They put their seats back some and dared to snooze a little. This evening would see them in their own bed awaiting a restful night. Another day would roll around much too quickly. "Rest" was gold in their hectic and busy life. As Billy dozed off, he thought of how lucky he was to have Anita beside him, as his bride and partner of life, on that thought z -z-z-z.

They awoke about 15 minutes prior to their landing in DC and peered out the window as the stewardess (to those in Rio-Linda) flight attendants, got on the cabin microphone PA system to announce their DC approach. You could see the lights of the city, some monuments all lit up and, of course, the Capitol in all its glorious splendor. Indeed, it was beautiful.

The landing was uneventful and they pulled into the gate. As they searched for their car in the parking lot, Billy thought of his short days with the CIA interrogating Moo, the days seemed long. He was imbedded as a public servant now with the status of an American United States Congressman his name was William Joseph Brewer.

As they proceeded back to their DC pad, they chatted about their feelings of being back home in York, and talking with the people and friends. He was their man in Washington, there to represent them and their feeling and opinions about America and elsewhere., He was now part of the three major functions of government.

Because of their sleep time on the plane, they were pretty much awake now. Their luggage had traveled with them and arrived concurrently with them. Somebody had gotten that right. It was about a 40-minute drive to their condo, and they were happy to be back in their now familiar married home.

As they took their luggage into their condo, they sat for a while, turned on their gas fireplace, propped their feet up and faced each other while staring into the leaping flames of many colors. It was relaxing and they were happy and feeling good about themselves.

Billy was thinking about his talks of departing the CIA with Director Wm. Cannon, and remembered his close ties with field director John Steelman and his most current boss John Columbo, Director of Mid-East/European countries and territories. His thoughts even included Mullah Moo. He quickly reviewed the deal he cut with the Agency to continue his interrogation of Mullah Moo, his arch enemy, and Isis Chieftain, on an hourly basis periodically. He hoped that would work at three times a week visit. To him it was always an engaging time between the two of them, especially in these last days of visit. They were breaking ground and becoming "trusted" friends of the slightest kind. There was a loosening up of demeanor towards each other, a certain respect afforded each as head of state to another.

Mullah Moo had come to know and realize that Billy was a primary cog in his being where he was. He had straight out asked Billy if he'd been on the "raid" that resulted in him being here (in his cell). Billy never outwardly told him so, that he was, but let the assumption rest on its laurels and suspicions.

Mullah Moo, obviously getting bored in his cell, would always ask Billy when he saw him, "Where had he been, what have you been doing?" Billy picked up on the chatter as being informational, trying to get a handle on where he was, who had extracted him, what Billy did, how high a function did he have, anything to get an attaching string to something concrete. It was still the mindset of "if I ever get out or escape this confine, I want to know you and kill you before the world with it watching.' Mullah Moo while subsiding in his grandiose fashion, had not yet lost his hope of ever revenging his captor. His strategies were ever consistent and stealthfully pursued. His eventual fall and submission would be slow, but in some fashion would eventuate. Death of course, was an option. His guards and video watchers worked ever vigilant in his viewing. He would martyr himself if he could or really desired too. He'd rather go out with "guns blazing" and take some infidels down with him. He was yet still self-determined to victory for the Caliphate.

As Billy said to himself, "He's still "wired hot" and a formidable opponent, dangerous and cunning, somewhat charming, yet deadly. He was definitely not a fool or foolish. He did everything with a purpose. He met his match in Billy Brewer, American infidel. Physically he was putty in Billy's trained military hands and his personal size and strength – no match.

Billy sensed Moo, knowing this, and his ever probing of Billy to ferret out a weakness. It would be of the "mind," maybe emotions, Americans were feeling people, not thinking people. Billy was on the wrong side of "Allah" and would perish at some point. Then he would seize the moment and plant a sword deep within. Meanwhile, I will spar with the infidel 'till death I will employ. Mullah Moo fought being captured. He was humiliated.

At the moment the only thing Moo had going for him was life in a prison cell. With no way presently out. His captors would increase certain pleasures when he "coughed up" some informational treasures about Isis. He was right about those things.

One of the things Billy had asked Mullah Moo was "what the world of Islam thought of him and his Caliphate movement of Isis Jehad extremist?" He and Billy had long discussions on this subject with Billy avoiding getting his opinion included in on the matter. This annoyed Mullah that Billy wouldn't jump in and personally express his opinion. Billy stuck with the world view and tribal thoughts and feelings. Mullah didn't like to hear such verbiage. Billy tried to keep his opinions and knowledge at bey and only give up what might be necessary to exploit the conversation. Mullah Moo wasn't gaining converts where he was.

Anita brought Billy out of his dream thought land and back to earth where she was. She had her business and planning to do. She desired so to get producing paintings to sell, to get herself advertised around Washington and eventually open a branch shop back in York. Her desires were important too. Anita realized she had to keep Billy aware of her needs to apprise him she was a partner and half the marriage. She knew Billy wasn't and didn't turn his back on her, but that was his personality type A that occasionally got him on the narrow pathway to something in his head and in his inimitable style he took off running like the tight end he was, heading for the goal line of whatever current game he was playing.

Billy was capable of multi-tasking, of great thinking and had capabilities exceeding most people because of his past. He drew much respect even at first meeting him, then definitely thereafter.

CHAPTER THREE

~ BILLY'S NEW JOB ~

After their respite in front of the fireplace and an evening talk, they retired to their bedroom. Billy turned down the fire to a simmer then proceeded to the bedroom to get ready for bed and a welcomed good night's sleep.

A lot had been accomplished in their short life span – a lot worthwhile. Their life was not of leisure and frivolity it had been of purpose and determination to prepare a way of life for success through planning and doing. Good choices were their goal to be realized. Time was the essence of life best spent for themselves and that took character., For them, coming from their backgrounds and past, decision-making was training ground to what happened next in their life.

There had to be a plan, execution, and a certain joy in their life as the transition created the appearance of generating positive progress – growth. It wasn't simple or easy in the throes of life. They were honed and sharpened for their future.

As they approached their bed from the opposite sides, they looked at each other, their eyes met and they knew. Each stripped off their clothes and got under the covers, which wouldn't hold them for long. It was baby-making time. It was a tender explosive time for the both of them. The love-making was strong and something beautiful. There was a joy in their soul. God was good, they felt His presence in the midst of their finest hour.

Their enjoyment and ecstasy subsided into a peaceful cuddling tenderness, and drew them into a graceful slumber for the night.

New life would arrive in the morning. Billy would appear at his new job at the Cannon House building where congressmen had their offices in Washington, DC. It would be a whole new world and they truly hoped they would be alive for it and prepared to face it successfully. They looked forward to their future.

Billy arrived at the Cannon house office building at 8:00 am. He took the elevator to the third floor and proceeded to C-313, his house office, formerly belonging to Jonas Sterling, United States Congressman.

He would find his staff at work processing all inquiries to that office from lobbyists and constituents and others. As he opened his front office door and stepped inside, all his staff looked up and gave him their attention. They all came to surround him and welcome him warmly. He would be the new Jonas Sterling in charge. They were very happy to see him face to face and said among themselves "He's bigger and taller than I thought. Handsome dude too!" Staffs always need direction and are creatures of habit and repetition in doing things a certain way. Things would be now somewhat different.

Billy greeted each of his staff. There were presently four staffers on duty that day. His executive assistant was Marjorie Lawler, an attractive red head. She had been Jonas' right-hand gal. His report on her said she was totally sharp at all things. She managed his schedules, reviewed and researched invitations, handled his personal files, correspondence and any travel arrangements. She also handled legislation correspondence. She had a big job with Billy now, who needed her badly as he dug in to his new job. There was work to be done.

There is no formal job description for a member of congress. Each representative is expected to define his own priorities., The Constitution only sets forth the qualifications necessary for election. House/Senate rules only require that members be present and vote.

Ultimately, these votes decide if a member is living up to their expectations for the job determined at the next election by their constituents, approval or not.

"Time" for a congressman becomes an essential element in getting business and political matters done. There are lots of hats that congressmen must wear. Decisions as to time - consumption spent on each "hat" is sometimes critical.

Marjorie and the staff had assembled a brief synopsis of five services a congressman needs to perform at minimum, not necessarily in order of importance. Here's what her list looked like.

1. Must answer phone calls from constituents. Also, correspondence, emails.
2. Needs to hold town hall meetings and have open office hours to hear local views on issues and concerns and problems of his district people.
3. Meet and greet with as many citizens from the district who request appointments as possible.
4. Help get information from all the Federal government for inquiring citizens.
5. Help solve problems citizens have with government agencies.

These Marjorie directives were printed in large font for Billy's placement in his office for himself. Indeed, it was helpful for the new Congressman "Plebe" in office. Billy spent the early morning with Marjorie, as she familiarized him with the office - where things were. She also said that according to government allotment, congressmen could have up to 22 staff spread between the home office and Washington, DC. He made a mental note of that for future reference and need.

Marjorie gave Billy a summary pamphlet she had worked up especially for him on the job – descriptions a congressman does and needed to know. It was most helpful and precise - an excellent crib sheet. Billy browsed the headlines to find...

The pamphlet targeted seven learning areas of information for the "plebe" congressman.

1. On constituency service. 2. Making national policy. 3. Committee work. 4. Floor debate. 5. Leadership inside Congress. 6. Political leadership outside of Congress. 7. Education (a congressman's job to perform.)

While it is most essential that a US Congressman/Senator be familiarized with these tools of the trade for house members, the general public only looks at results by their local representative and if it was good overall for their general welfare and pocketbook. However, it is both Billy's and my (author) feeling, that knowledge is a best weapon to have about anything. Knowledge is power, for anybody. We think you need to know what your government representative does and how he functions, or is supposed to! Wisdom behooves all of us to higher ground. Here goes – knowledge matters, as does character, morals and judgement. How does your representative represent you and your views? Communication is essential.

On an overwide front a congressman must participate in debate on national and international issues. They contribute the perspective of their district or state into the debate. It is therefore, important to meet with national government officials to bring local perspective to their attention. These things bring to basis how you decide to vote on national legislation in order to benefit the whole nation. This requires you to spend time with experts to keep current on complex national issues.

Debate on the floor of the house chamber is where one gives statements for public record. Where arguments for or against a bill is made. It is where you offer amendments to change language of a bill to improve them before the house votes on them.

It is the duty to talk to other members about any issue to try to persuade them to vote your way. All leads the congressman to decide on how to vote, whether to pass the bill or to kill it.

Billy was interested in securing a spot on several of the congressional committees. It was important to obtain a membership on a committee and subcommittees which do preliminary work on issues for the house or senate. Lots of study is necessary to become as much an expert on the issue assigned to the committee, as is possible. This sometimes involves questioning expert witnesses to find ways to improve legislation. This then leads to possible corrections to offer amendments to change the language of a bill before a vote of "yea or nay." If the committee approves/or nays it, it is sent to the full house as recommended for the "yea or nay" full house vote.

Billy looked over the list of standing committees to see which ones he might be interested in, or asking to be on, hopefully selected for. Here are the present 18 standing house committees:

The Armed Services; Banking and Financial Services; Budget; Commerce; Education and Workforce; Government Reform; House Administration; International Relations; Judiciary; Resources; Rules; Science; Standards of Official Conduct; Transportation and Infrastructure; Veterans Affairs; Ways and Means; Agriculture; and Appropriations. These are not all inclusive.

Committees help to organize the most important work in Congress for considering, shaping, and passing laws to govern the nation. 8,000 bills go to committee annually. Fewer than 10% make it out for consideration on the floor. The standing committees usually continue with each congress. They conduct investigations. Select committees are formed for a special purpose, i.e. to study a particular issue. They usually do not draft legislation. Some long standing "select" committees eventually become "standing" committees, like for instance, the "small business committee," which recently has become an important one.

A couple of other committees are important. "The Joint committee" – i.e. the house and senate members. These help to focus public attention on major issues. One committee called the Conference Committee is specially created when house/senate need to reconcile different versions of a same bill.

If the nefarious mystery of being a congressman is enough, it sometimes is essential by some importance, or ego-oriented desire, to rise to prominence, and some congressmen strive to rise to leadership positions within their party. These leaders are those who meet with the president to discuss the legislation agenda of the nation and prioritizes what he and Congress agrees on.

Congressional leaders speak to the national press to explain what the House/Senate has done or is planning to do. Leaders co-ordinate discussions among its party members trying to reach a unified position. They count votes and try to encourage members to vote with the party. Leaders also negotiate and struggle with the other party on questions of procedure, when and whether to bring up a bill, and how to spend on it.

One of the most tedious and personal heavies being a congressman is that all members who run for re-election must maintain a campaign office and staff separate from their congressional office staff. They must raise money to fund their election, and campaign expenses. This means hitting the "Rubber duck" trail of banquets, conferences, giving speeches, asking for money. They must make important campaign decisions.

Members of congress are considered the top official of their party back home in their district or state. Therefore, they must maintain good relationships and cooperation with local political party officials. Also, they must provide leadership to encourage candidates from their party to run for local offices.

Once a congressman is ensconced in office, they become educators of the public in your district, town meetings, speeches, banquets, rallies parades and other events like TV, radio, public newsletters, write columns for local papers, etc. They encourage voters to vote and to participate in the political process including the young folk. All congressmen must account for all equipment and expenses of their offices – i.e. budget out spending.

Obviously, the wider the breadth of knowledge and experience helps greatly the case for being able to maintain and handle the job of being a congressman.

The people you select as staffers are the must "gold" in your "quiver" of seeking success. Your team congressman, Billy Wm. Brewer, must be first class, reputable, sharp. Your success can be determined by your competence. Your leader ship quality is essential to that end.

Billy had early desires to be on several committees. His first choice was to be member of the House Armed Services Committee. With his background, he thought he could contribute experience to the committee. He also thought he'd like to be on the Education and Workforce Committee as he held interest in education generally and specifically.

The congressmen that were new to congress were coming in much younger and less wealthy than their previous counterparts. Most house members were lawyers – maybe one half, many from the business world and education. Some from banking. Nearly all went to college, many with advanced degrees. However, those surrounding entry into congress around Billy's time were a greater flux of women and minority members.

A congressman's pay scale put them in to an elite income earners group of the top one percent. They are prohibited by law from supplanting their incomes through such things as honorariums or paid speaking engagements. It is to be remembered that they have a large expense account generous travel allowance and a very good pension and health care plans at low cost, and free postal service to constituents called "Franking Privilege." Some nice "perks."

One of a congressman's "arrow in the ribs are the watchdog groups," Common Cause groups, and less so these days, a dress code. Today's Reps are looser and more casual in their dress. Appropriate appearance is taken seriously but tempered towards casualness. Today's voters are more inclusive to their representative being like them than the Washington stuffed shirts of old.

Sometimes a new "plebe" congressman gets assigned to a committee the selecting committee desires them to be on. So, you serve if you're a Party follower and not an independent individualist. These type assignments have to do with connections, personalities, or even because of regional needs for representation.

Usually these congressional assignments were done so prior to taking their place in office, sometimes not, especially filling a vacancy, as Billy was.

Billy's first day was long, very busy, mostly basic learning about his new job, and being educated by Marjorie, the longtime assistant/office manager to Jonas Sterling. Now the business of the office of a United States Congressman was underway – on stream for the term left vacant by Jonas Sterling, a man of honor, integrity and wisdom. It would be a challenge to meet his talents and longevity of service, both to his constituents and to the nation as a whole. Billy took a deep breath, as he put his coat on, turned out the lights and headed out the house office Cannon building to go home. Anita would be waiting for him when he arrived. He looked forward to that, to hug her and kiss her. She was special in his heart. He loved her.

CHAPTER FOUR

Tyson's Corner Center was an extremely busy place. It contained over 300 specialty and department stores. It had celebrated restaurants and a Hyatt Regency Hotel, a vita apartment complex and a huge office complex building some 22 stories high glass, which served as a regional headquarters for prominent consulting, technology and many federal contracting firms, firms doing world business.

The 30 floor "Vita" apartment building had a sky lounge and a top floor sundeck. Tyson's was known for its world class shopping stores the likes of Apple, Bloomingdales, Gucci, L. L. Bean, Lord and Taylor, Macys, Michael Kors and Nordstrom.

Tucked in among the many specialty shops was Anita's Art Emporium. Across the front of her space read, "Cantina's Portraits, and Landscapes." Her front window space contained a show window in a theatre stage like presentation offering whatever paintings, show pieces she selected of hers to display for passersby to view. To the side was a marquee-like presentation board which she changed often, designating her works variety and talents.

It invited the world to enter in, into the world of Anita Cantina, and enjoy art work by her. The "Patter" was selling her talents, showing, displaying her prize-winning French productions she acclaimed while living in Paris and her art experiences. The window featured a copy of the "Grande" portrait of "Madame Bettencourt" and the winning of the Grand European prized treasure of $1,000,000 American dollars and receiving its prestigious award. There was a pictorial still photos of the celebrity presentation event in Paris in 2015.

Any person viewing the window would be entranced by the fine quality of the winning portrait of Madame Bettencourt in her finest French regalia, as well as, other still work Anita had produced. Her work depicted photo likenesses of her subject matters in living live photo-like presentations. Any one that had a "twit" of art appreciation could see the absolute talent Anita produced. Many potential customers filtered in to browse her studio and see her works.

Anita had comfortable seating viewing her display work with appropriate strong spotlights or custom lighting on her artwork, depending on the subject matter, be they landscape, stills or portrait. Her specialty involved special color highlighting in many of her still life photolike art paintings. It was a talent and skill she perfected, different from any other commercial artist. It was intriguing, interesting and inviting. Indeed, it invited you into the scene or to join her canvas work to the point that you (the viewer) injected yourself into the subject work and its production. Her works were inviting and intriguing and made you say to yourself "How'd she do that?" Such perfection!

Anita now had some time to do some serious planning. She needed to get people into her store studio. She needed to find ways of outreach to promote herself, her work. She thought she needed to entice people into her store and into her "live work viewing area" of her studio.

She thought she had located her store in the right venue for exposure. You go where the people are, where the wealthier clientele do their shopping. After all she was a vendor, with a product to sell. The trick would be to sell her service and products under her maiden name which would be different than her married name, Mrs. William "Billy" Brewer, wife of US Congressman of the same name.

As Anita sat in her small office to the side of her studio, she thought, it was time to step things up and get herself some organizational and creative thinking help in her store. Her thoughts turned to Penny Hunter, now Penny Brandon, her old high school and college friend. She would call her and share her plans with her. Yes, she would be a perfect helper, promoter and creative assistant to her future growth of her artwork. They got along well, and she would fit in well with her business plan of things as she saw them.

As Anita fleshed out her thoughts of how to grow her business it was imperative that she devote herself to painting, not other stuff which would congest her time and life into distractions and certainly dislodge herself from producing her true talents of producing quality portrait and artwork of various subject matters appealing to the public eye. Anita made a note to herself to contact Penny. She needed to talk serious business with her.

That evening Anita gave Penny a call at her home. Eddy answered her call. "Oh, hi Anita, How you doin'? Good! Yeah, Penny's right here. Hold on."

"Hi, Anita, good to talk with you again. What's happening?" said Penny joyfully. "Yeah, I've got some time right now to talk. So, what can I do for you?"

The two of them talked a good while as Anita briefed Penny of her needs for someone handling her store chores and free her up, giving her more time for painting. Penny expressed interest in her doing that and would like to come visit Anita's store to see the layout and get familiar with current procedures Anita had in place at the time. Yes, she was intrigued with the general proposition Anita spun for her and made an appointment to meet her at the store the next day at its opening at 10:00 am.

Anita thanked her, and said she was very glad that Penny would consider the job. She needed someone there full-time for the most part and she needed to get back to her painting. Anita related to Penny that she would be of help in marketing of her services and products, and that that would become more and more important a job, to solicit for customer's and scheduling customers for sittings.

Penny had been working at her husband's office of the military law section of the government at the Pentagon. She was getting tired of hanging around the Army legal -beagles all day and too much with her husband, Eddy. It was too family all day long. She needed a change. This would be good and new and fun with her longtime female best friend. They agreed to the time of their meeting the next day and parted ways on their cell.

Penny then turned to Eddy next to her, and proceeded to relay the conversation with Anita. Surprisingly Eddy thought that it was a good idea, the two of them indeed both of them, needn't be hanging around each other 24/7. Penny was surprised that Eddy gave her up so easily, maybe they were being practical, maybe even saving their marriage.

Personally, Penny already felt a certain relief in her decision to hook up with Anita and her studio. Change was inevitable, one only needed to deal with it. The challenge was on.

It was kind of like an old homecoming reunion as Anita met up with Penny at the store studio, in the Tyson Corner Center, a large mall, just outside of Washington, DC. The rich and famous of this greater Washington DC area did their shopping there. It was the place to go and to be seen. It was Anita's place of opportunity to make a name for herself and on the American scene. She would pitch her "tent" so to speak right here.

As they entered into Anita's store, Anita flipped on the light switch and the house lights shone brightly, vastly improving one's sight. She walked Penny over to the counter where she approached her handy-dandy coffeemaker and cranked it up to gettin' some Java hot.

Anita first showed Penny as they went back out front of her store, into the Mall walkway, and stood in front of the large window space, overlooking her space and display. She explained her thought process for the arrangement and use of word power inclined toward enticing people to seek further information by coming in or to peek their interest in seeing individual additional paintings by the artist. She didn't carry other artists works, just her own.

She carried a variety of pastels, watercolors and oils, shown in her variety of still and landscapes, portraits and a section relegated to "creative brain sparks," a corner devoted to different fusion of color and shapes. Anita called it her "Cantina creation Corner!" It was an explosion of colorama fusion mergers. It was a fun and unusual display of a variety of creative abstract works and style. It was totally unique.

Penny ooowed and ahhhed her way along looking at Anita's expressed talent! Indeed, Penny was highly impressed with the totality of Anita's talent. Her work was precision and astutely creative. She thought the public, when seeing these works, would love to own such paintings and show them in their home or office. The work was good, no, excellent!

As Anita laid out her store's reason for where things were, Penny got the picture and tapped into Anita's brand of thinking and philosophy of ideas and ways for her present way of doing business. Penny's expertise was in the theatre, the arts, more toward the performing arts. She kept the thoughts Anita had shared and tried to incorporate her own thoughts and background and integrate something new and exciting into Anita's business future! Their friendship was developing into a positive team effort, potential was rearing its head.

Penny spent the day with Anita in her studio shop and listened to Anita talk to any customers that came in. Some just wanted to browse. Some picked up a pamphlet extoling Anita's artistic background and training alone with her infusion of accolades of honors, shows and contests she'd contributed her works to for judging.

Penny picked up one of each of Anita's pamphlets on her different painting mediums, for oils, watercolors, pastels, and other genres. She saw in the main feature on Anita's background that it was mentioned that some of her works were being held in private collections, which she had declined to mention them for privacy reasons. However, Penny asked Anita about them and Anita went through the list with her of those holding her works. It was not a lot, but someday those people will find a value of them at least doubling as Anita extended her talents into the consumer and art world.

Penny would find herself busy, along with Anita attending art shows and invitationals for all kinds of artists, new and established. There were galleries all over America in medium size towns and cities and, of course, large cities. She and Anita would be hobnobbing with the affluent and art aficionados of the nation over the course of Anita's future exposure. It would be a whole new world to her, and somewhat so for Anita during the first years or so of their working friendship in the art world.

It was exciting for and to the both of them, their new adventure. Penny and Anita came up with the idea to not only promote Anita's art work, but bring in additional revenue by establishing a promotional theatre and special events ticket reservations office for procuring tickets to all kinds of opera, Broadway-type theatre productions, musical productions of all kinds, rock concerts, that were held in the Washington DC area. The two of them were excited and that night they booked themselves into a nice restaurant with Billy and Eddy to engage their future plans on them.

After all, they now had talent they could use, Eddy a lawyer, albeit an Army one, and Billy a rising United States Congressman, to both girls it all looked like a rich field to harvest in the future. The only sure thing at the moment was Anita's future – it was bristling with potential success. Penny could taste the style and grace Anita had and that could add to the beauty and joy of the world through her fine arts works. Anita needed exposure and publicity. That would come.

The evening at the restaurant together was fun and fruitful, but the girls received a warning that they should go slow and plan well. They thought their ideas were good and encouraged them to take the "helm" and charge on. It was good news to Anita and Penny. So, they established every Monday morning as a time to hold strategy meetings and plan out their growth and future.

CHAPTER FIVE

It was soon that Billy was noticed as a leader in the Freshman incoming new congressional members class. It was a younger crowd, who were quite personable and determined to change the way Washington worked, at least the legislation process and the cooperativeness between the two parties in the house. There was a mandate by the people for serious action to be taken, and that both aisles better get working together for the cause of America or they will be thrown out of office the next election time.

Washington was at its lowest peak of public approval it had ever been. Leadership was missing from the scene and leaders of old were being castigated out of office, and departed from being selected to new leadership positions. It was becoming ever slowly, a younger congressional scene, churning in among the old school and the new future and determination for solidarity of realistic legislation and the necessity of getting the American people moving to greatness again

Billy was a born leader behind his flaws of early youth. His intelligence and personal demeanor were most inviting to the establishment of confidence. People bought into his way of thinking. Billy was on his way, maturing and posting himself in ways to become meaningful and useful as a public servant. He wanted to speak and represent the people of America. They were wonderful people, hard workers, except for those cast aside by the present party's old ways, thoughts, discriminations, bad policies, and hateful really old idiocies of personal or political prejudices.

The basis for future headway and growth of a nation required new personal commitments and thought patterns and listening to the public who demanded a new nation under God, with people loving people, and treating them as they would want to be treated. This required new personal demands for bridging hatred and prejudices long established and cross over the bridge to nowhere to a new land of living. A future where the valleys are alive with lush vegetation and water.

We as People were given a brain by God, given choices and in cooperation with one another, given the opportunity to all participate in the welfare of a good planet.

Only our selfishness, deep seated prejudices and propensity to hang on to old ways, kills or killed the joy landscape of what could become the greatness on earth. America needed to lead.

Billy was maintaining steadfast determination that he would stand for the best of old values that served his constituency with respect and to perform his duties as a public servant with all his energy and talents, to do what was right and not just convenient or stringently correct to a few. Political correctness was a judgement and directive as prejudicial as race baiting. No good was its flavor, intentions or usefulness in promoting future wellbeing.

Billy would hold onto his values learned over his lifetime and career from the time he changed from the grade school drifter and truant preteen, to the growing up under the 3 Amigos tutoring and mentoring and his high school changes and West Point training. Add in his maturing factor, responsibilities, service and daring deeds performed between then and now, he found himself as prepared as anyone could possibly be to stand guard over the future and capable, if taken, to rise up and lead the way of people. Few, if any, of the old establishment and fewer of the new breed had such a background training to have knowledge he had been exposed to over his 33-year-old life.

Plus, he had the advantage not only of having the friendships he did, but a sweetheart wife that loved him and was a total independent being in her own right. They were a formidable twosome.

As Billy sat in his office chair behind an oversized old wooden desk, with the American flag draping behind him, he thought of his life; it had been fast and furious, Billy had brought many pictures he had of himself at West Point, with his two high school state football championship teams, his many doings in and as a Green Beret service member, then some in his first civilian suit of clothes as a CIA Agent. And finally, as the inauguration of induction as a United States Congressman – freshman class.

He needed to get someone to take his picture sitting at his congressional desk in the stead of the very honored longtime revered Jonas Sterling, server of the people from the 12th District of Illinois.

He was fully ready to go to work and serve the people of his district the American public, the people he loved. He would make it his lifetime work, so help him God. Little did he know of his influence to come. Indeed, it would be his time. God was in control, he picked the good, bad and ugly for times of His purpose, and promotion. Billy ruminated over his life as he had a quiet time. His life, indeed, had been a preparation, in this case, to do battle in behalf of a nation falling by its waysides, with leadership waning and draining.

Because of his training periods through life, he began in his mind to foresee a plan of gathering forces for good, good ideas, good legislation, good results – America reinstated as containing greatness in the world's eyes, because it was a great place to live, love and serve. In his heart, he felt a great tender place that he was an American, and had the opportunity to serve her, and help promote her to a world longing for wellness and health, riddled by naysayers, despots, evilness leashed, cunning behavior. Deceitfulness of a few in the world, metastasized worldwide in dark clouds floating through an atmosphere of human existence.

It generated bad seed and cruelty and dominion by a few. Darkness exposed to the light cannot function for long. People with a heart turned to God, spread butter on the bread of life and would eradicate the sources of evilness with good measure.

These things are a continued worldly fight of the specks of man on earth. Nothing is really new, but upgraded to a more modern set of toys and circumstances. Leadership was begging, and in need of men and women fully alive for modern times, that still maintained character values held humanly dear by the general people of the world.

Those that had room to love one another in their heart. Resistance breaks down when people treat you as they desire to be treated. They would face you not with hands out with a gun,

but arms out to hug you to unite you with them in peace –
Shalom!

Suddenly there was a knock on Billy's office door from the outer office room, he gave a yell to come in. Marjorie came into his office and said a congressman by the name of Paul Sherman, Senior Congressman of the Illinois delegation, was here to see him.

"Send him in Marjorie. My first visiting congressional guest." Billy rose all his 6-foot 6 large self up to greet his guest, as Congressman Sherman entered. They had met casually before, but this would be a more intimate time together, at least he thought so. The last time was a "hello" at a Republican state function recently.

"May I call you Billy? You call me Paul. OK?" stated the congressman.

"Just fine," said Billy. "Glad you came by. I've been so busy vacuuming up information of my new job, I've not reached out yet to others. Glad you came by. It will be good to talk with a senior congressman on the scene. I honestly can say, this is all new to me, having been in the military service for many years, then for a time in a para-military civil agency with the CIA."

They both sat down to the side sitting area of comfortable couches and chairs. Billy offered him a soft drink or water while he visited. He was a "Pepsi" person himself and got up to pour them the beverages. Sitting back down, they reignited their conversation as congressman Sherman said;

"Billy, I've come here on behalf of the Republican Standing Committee to be on. On the front side, we would like to see you on several committees. Because of your background we have chosen the Armed Services Committee. And because of your education interests and background, the Education and Workforce Committee. Those I know who have heard you speak or know you, say you're a natural for the beneficial promotion of what's good for education.

Your work ethic has been outstanding in your field and exemplary to all. I hope you will consider these committees. I think you not only would enjoy participating on those particular ones, but even flourish in serving on them." Paul let go of the conversation and threw the ball back into Billy's court.

"Very interesting assessments your committee made. Those were my top two choices I had made as I looked over the 18 standing committees. I would have asked to be placed on those two committees. So, I feel I'm off to a good start here. I haven't been here anywhere long enough to be on most of those other committees, but I know I can contribute to the two you suggested. Billy was confident and energized by their conversation.

The two of them sipped their beverages and talked generally about themselves to better get to know each other. Congressman Sherman was from the 16th District of Illinois, covering most of the southern part of the state south of the 12th district where Billy represented. The people had continued to re-elect Sherman, as he was "their" man on the job.

The two of them hit it off quite well, and although Paul was in his 70s, old to some, he was obviously wise in the ways of the halls of Congress – highly regarded and respected by his peers there. His longevity of life as a congressman hinged on his ability to share the spoils and mitigate positions of controversy. He was low self-serving, but high in a confidence level of assertiveness that would plow the "currents of congress."

Finally, Paul arose, and said to Billy, "It's been a pleasure to have personally met you. I've heard many fine things about you. I look forward to working with you and the new congressional membership of Republicans, as well as, the Democrats. Give me a call anytime, drop in, whatever. Thanks for seeing me, and I'll hear from you later."

Billy shook his hand and said to him, "Paul, I accept being on those two committees. Call that positive assignment will you!"

"OK," Billy I'll see you get those assignments, as they go out next week. Thanks for accepting to be on them. I know you'll not be disappointed, they seem to reflect your past experiences. The committees are important and you will find honor in your assignments."

Billy led the Congressman through his door and the Congressman said a parting "Goodbye" to his staff as he headed out the front office's door.

They all turned with smiles to Billy, and a question mark splattered all over their faces. "What was that all about?" Said Marjorie looking at Billy's big smile.

"Well, I was offered to be on two standing committees, which happened to be the exact ones I had selected myself. I, we, will hear next week when the assignments are handed out. I feel assured of my positions. Congressman Sherman is a really fine man, a man of high integrity and purpose. A true American icon of a public servant."

Billy went back into his office with a smile and warmth within. It was a good day. He would serve with honor and dignity and make his district proud of him. He would be their personal connection representative to the US Government Congress and make a difference in Washington. He would be a leader, a fighter for the American way and greatness again. Someday the world would look to America with confidence and envy that it had reaffirmed its stake and returned as the world power leader. The imagination center of the world. Truly the balance of power for good and truth. At this stage and time America's place and stature in the eyes of the world was nowhere very positive to where it should be.

World countries looked to America for strength but finding America so disheveled and coming apart from within and being pummeled by so many of its detractors. Many countries themselves were coming unglued because they attached themselves to the lead and leadership of the United States. They saw our armed forces being withdrawn and reduced, and cut back with weaponry and down-sized. America was a sanctuary for freedom, liberty, and prosperity. America needed to change for the better and soon. Outside evil was lurking and chasing it with a vengeance. America was vulnerable.

Between Isis, and the evil forces within, trying to spread its moral and philosophical poisoned tentacles across the land,

America needed a jumpstart of new leadership with guts and "Chutzpah." The likes of William Joseph Brewer, Billy, were the future hope of the young men of integrity and boldness for such a time as this.

Billy had the sense that he had a real stake in the future of his country, maybe make a difference in the lives of his fellow people. Little did he realize just to what a large extent his influence would make on far more than just American terra firma.

Indeed, God had a plan, and indeed, Billy was his happening catalyst to engage change and move America forward into the new future. The future is tomorrow and beyond. Too many were dwelling in their sorrow and problems of the now, and bickering and blaming one another with a vengeance and volatile loathing and could not see above the mire and quicksand they were sinking in.

The blame game, the feel-good cursing of others, the selfish and strategic self-inspiring narcissistic out reaches to others played havoc in the world. Pardon me, but it sounds like a plan old Slew-foot (Satan) would pull or cook up. You think? Darkness was the tone of the day during this era of the world history. It was hard to see through.

Would God let the world, succumb to its evilness, or would he bring forth another time of renewal and greatness in the country He founded where lives, all lives mattered. There were parameters, rules to live by, blessings to be had, seed to sow, and repercussions to things that were said and done. You know the "sow and reap" thing.

Words and action, still and always will have meaning. Lighting a wick to a dynamite stick, will reap what you sow. What are your intentions? Honorable or evil? Life is full of choices. We are born to make choices, right or wrong big or small. Impress a friend, or to world an end. Individual choice does matter, America needs to become part of the solution not part of the problem. Too many were finger-pointing at each other as the problem. No one was emphasizing any solutions, and America was losing its power to do so.

Jonah had a whale to save him and when he was beached, he finally did the right thing. America was now still in the belly of the whale at this time. Things had to change if she would survive and it was a matter of survival, no doubt about that!

Inspiration is an essential part of any plan, enthusiasm sometimes cements the deal. If impression is a factor of transacting a deal or creating a favorable air in negotiations, Billy was and had the personality and physical stature to swing the deal. People who know him already knew him to be a really smart and learned person. Some people said he reminded them of John Wayne. The ever-popular western movie star. Not so much in looks as in his voice sounding much like his deeper speaking baritone sound. Billy was a good deal larger than "Big John" looming in at six foot six and 280 pounds and in superb shape. He was still relatively young at 34, but in no ways succumbing to becoming an easy chair congressman, dining on the "rubber chicken speaking circuit" and getting fat.

His life was of exercise and determined mental awareness of the world around him. He had not been of leniency of living, to be lax in his training and pursuits on the jobs he had. Lax in his mindset could easily mean death by opposition. One on one confrontation – no one was a match to him. He was exceedingly strong and thoroughly and highly trained and agile of body. His size was intimidating, but his talents, abilities and smarts were stealthily hidden. Big was not slow, or dumb by any means.

As the world goes, as an individual goes, Billy stood tall in the saddle with wisdom beyond his young years. Since he was 12, he'd put in a lot of active searching and educational years including some on the job experiences second to none. It would be a long time coming that all of Billy's life would be upfront and known by the public. They might have to read about him in his memoirs or autobiography. Indeed, he still was presently engaged in a secret, covert military activity through the CIA, known only to the President, the CIA and his wife. Nobody else had a need to know.

CHAPTER SIX

It was Billy's new job, to show up and vote on bills before the congress on behalf of his constituents from the 12th District of Illinois. Always being interested in details he made it a personal educational adventure to know what was actually in the bills he had to vote on. He was what some would call a "speed reader" as he had more than just congressional bills to read for his job. It would serve him well. He indeed, had brainpower as well as retention power. Those had served him well also through his years in the military.

Billy came to work early and tried to get home by 6 o'clock to be with Anita. Sometimes Anita didn't get home until 9:00 – 9:15 at night. Mall hours would take her into the early evening. She thought of shortening her hours open to 5pm, but tried working the late hours to see what kind of traffic, if any, would come in. During quiet times she would work on "landscapes" and "still" or her new "abstract" style of painting. These didn't require the pure concentration that portrait painting demanded, and that she usually did at home.

Billy's day, a new on the job freshman congressman, was more demanding than he had thought. However, his style was work oriented and proved to be like any other of his past work-related days. Unfortunately, his new work required sitting most of the time, so he scheduled in every other day "exercises" at the Cannon house gym located in the basement next to the swimming pool room. Twice a week or more he was scheduled into the visiting and interrogation of "Mullah Moo" at the holding cell in the home office building in Langley, VA.

"Moo" hadn't yet spilled all the beans that they could determine. So, he still participated in grueling "Moo." They were now on a rather friendly side as opposition foes. Moo was still allowed to have the special chaise lounge recliner in his cell by Billy's order and directive. His innovative torture improvisation sat well with Moo who dropped a few bean gems more often.

Billy sat back in his own office chair and pondered his present life. It had been and was, very full. That was good. Things in life were settling down some degree. Their life was developing some repetition and business.

The life as a congressman took on its routine, and idiosyncrasies of what congressman and senators do. Most all had the same parameters and duties but the differences came in the personalities behind each representative. The hangers on, daily plodders, the super aggressive ego centrists, the "Slick Willy's" and cunning manipulators and those emerging front runners who stood out as natural leaders who work people in connection and negotiation to bring forth results to problems. Bargaining, giving and talking mixed with right and wrong by talking things through. Billy's motto was "If it's good for America, it's good for me!"

Billy would say to his fellow congressmen, "Look here are the points I like about this bill, here are some I don't. The bill needs to be tightened up, cleaned up, to have some teeth in it in order to work for everybody. Here are my thoughts, what are yours?" His meetings would be vacant of name calling, swearing, non-negotiable partisan politics and political correctness. In the meetings he attended, others came to know him as a true patriot, for America first, and that he was an experienced man to deal with regardless of the years as a congressman he had been chosen to replace the highly respected Senior Congressman Jonas Sterling. People dealing with Billy over the years ahead would find him a man with integrity of high moral standard, and abilities that were stealthily hidden and brought forth at proper times.

His views and presence to a meeting or group brought forth higher levels of courage to try to get things done. He held himself and others to high standards of the position and job descriptions they represented. Egotists, show-offs and elitist he had not much respect for. They were trying to be someone other than themselves. Some personality quirks just got in the way of meaningful progress needed and they set up barriers that made things more difficult to hurdle, and reason out. It was helpful to have had a psychology background to understand where some folks were coming from.

Having dealt with Mullah Moo for the time he had, actually prepared himself for negotiating with his congressional peers. Others found dealing with Billy had a whole new appreciation of his abilities far from being a civilian just off the street or from the business world. Billy was formidable as he sat in front of you, upright, solid and relaxingly intense on whatever was business at hand. He was twice formidable whenever he stood tall and large in front of you. He obviously carried a most favorable impression to anybody around him.

Billy was a kind man, gentle in spirit with the average civilian folk and treated everyone with due respect. He abhorred anyone who looked down on another, who was discourteous to women and used foul language. Such language exception was on the battlefield where some very foul language expressions expedited speed and intention of importance. Such language resulted in being very understood by some.

As the public back home in the 12th district got to know him, through his town hall meetings, and as his peers in Congress came to know him better in caucuses, committees, and one-on-one encounters, his public persona became well known and his public awareness grew. He was much like Congressman Sterling in many regards, younger, much more handsome, much larger in stature and pleasant but firm in his nature. He had a good, joyful laugh which he expressed often. He enjoyed a good joke – even on him. As a new congressman, his attributes of high morals, honesty and love of others would propel him successfully along in the future.

He was on his way to somewhere, bigger doings and was drawing closer every day to the inner circles of government. Right now, he would take it one day at a time, but as the days drew longer and the months whizzed by, his presence on the Washington scene was becoming known to all, the Congress and Senate, including those in the administration which included the President. His connection there had been ongoing through his knowledge and approval of Billy's work with Mullah Moo and the CIA duties attached to the "extraction plan" of Mullah. Obviously, the President had a "need to know" basis about the whole covert operation.

The President was in his first days of office, also 37 years older. He too, had a beautiful wife, a former model, with an intelligent mind and apparent talents. She was definitely the softer side of the relationship as he was so outwardly "rough" and ridges oriented. Actually, the President and Billy got along very well. The word was respect that held the glue to their relationship.

Billy's new job was beginning to become ever more satisfying. The scope and breadth of what he did, while not physically protecting the American people, it was helping to keep America informed and strengthened from within which is where the present-day problems were eroding the pillars and foundations of the American scene. People were wobbling and weaving and life was not looking as stable as it was or had been.

Outsiders and stealthful insiders were bent on imploding America and her foundations and in the business of undermining America's society at every turn – trying to destroy its values patriotic in nature. It was a planned uncoordinated attack on a country beginning to look dead in the water. In fact, it presented much like a pre-Pearl Harbor timeline in a new era. America was and had become quite vulnerable – politically, societally, and weak of mind – as it foundered in the wind for leadership stability and some super glue to patch back the strengths of a feisty and strong national democracy. America was on the verge of losing its moorings tethered in granite. Acid was flowing over and through its people.

One of the main problems was that people lost are attracted to the rumors and propaganda of some few who speak out and lead as a pied-piper who seems to attract the strays and weak-minded and spirit, that blows in the wind, whichever way the flavor of the moment takes them.

Weak people are easily suckered into directions that sound like anti-establishment normal ways of reacting. Yes, they will follow "Satan" right into hot hell, because it looks bright and warm and is a perceived alternate to drifting along as a national body into oblivion. Deceitfulness and corruption rise right in the face of non-orienting directions within a nation. The lie is spread. Truths are bent, the cunning lick their "chops."

Billy penned these sentiments into his new notebook of thought and ideas – entered into his diary as a congressman. This diary was kept to establish his thoughts and feelings to help consolidate them into meaningful dialogue for purposeful use at some time in the future. It would prove to be a very useful and helpful record to review as he drew down his time as a congressman. It was a point of satisfaction to him. It would give him reference to his thinking philosophy and variety to ides that crossed his mind, his opinions and strategies. It would be his "owner's manual" of operations.

Billy's life was changing from a covert mindset to a transparent oriented direction where his thoughts and feelings would be a reflection of his constituents of district 12, Illinois. Here on the "Hill" one opined openly in order to dialogue with others. Ideas were premium gold points scored when dealing with his peers. They had to be accompanied by facts, solid background, history and tactical use as practical and positive fodder before sharing it with others. Will the idea work, in practical terms? For whom will it benefit, what repercussions to whom if instituted. This life anew had and carried meaning. The innuendos of speaking also carried weight as to the speaker's sincerity, truth and tone of what was being said.

Billy had intimate knowledge of the nuances inferred in words people spoke, he honed in on their tone, use of words, mindset and delivery. Deceitfulness with professionals could be clever indeed. Billy had knowledge of many international mindsets, their history and cultures. He had studied these with purpose to catch the meanings and flavor of those speaking them. Everyone had tone and volume control Some had peculiar rhythm in their speaking. Others spoke slowly or fast and would give themselves time to think out what they were going to speak next. Being able to speak well, and on your feet had definite advantages in many situations. Occasionally a loud toned voice had advantage-like those in the pit of the floor of a stock exchange.

Being tall and large of stature and good looking also carried positive weight in advantage – disadvantage when discoursing on a personal basis, depending on whom you were with. Egos were forever interfering with progress in negotiations. Humbleness got things done and high active egos presented problems and usually slowed things down. Billy had developed a large repertoire of people's personal nuances of body language and speech, it was usually quite enlightening, and revealing. It has and was supporting him well in his life work. It was an ongoing learning experience. His talking abilities were a blessing to his wife, who like most women, fed on communication. Conversation for women was a life blood necessity. Many a marriage lacked such intimacy, and distance between couples would grow. Contrary, the enhancement of communication could well spark and enliven the intimacy levels both partners desperately desired. It kept many a bedroom alive and well.

Billy was always in his chair, in his congressional seat to vote on the pending issues brought before the chamber members. Most of these were bills in the "hopper" so he had to quickly bring himself up to speed on the "meat" of each bill. Frequently, he had to appear at the two standing committees on education and the Armed Services. He had lots of opinions about both subject matters. They threw you under the rug – raw – to hear your views and notice your demeanor and knowledge to assess and give you their personal grade of achievement and quality levels. Politics was alive and well in Washington DC. You were tested early on by your peers and house membership, daily.

Some congressmen were right off the bat trying to limelight themselves into prominence and power. Each were elected by their constituents back home some really tried to truly represent those home folks, others sought to "showtime" and stake out a career of being noticed whenever and however they could "showcase" themselves in public.

Billy was a flying personality, more stealth-type. Only his physical stature immediately drew your attention to him. However, when he spoke, in his John Wayne-like voice, he attracted hearing attention immediately people quieted and listened intently to what he had to say. Partly it was his tonal voice, partly his large sculptured physique and partly his facial attractiveness – especially to women. Men noticed it all too, but in terms of manliness in prime form. He appeared always confident and in charge of the moment. People and peers were immediately impressed whenever they got to hear him speak. He spoke well – with authority. People listened – people noticed – and liked what they heard.

Billy had no political background to be known in the public arena. Only those that lived in or near York, would have any idea of who he was or his history as a person. The York "Patter" public rag, a highly respected city paper with literary accolades and acknowledgements, a Pulitzer Prize winning small city paper who since his high school years had made it a point to follow his career. Many small towns in the 12th district were subscribers to the York Patter and they too might well have recognized his name over the years when he became their local congressman taking over from the deceased predecessor, Jonas Sterling. He, of course, was their champion congressman and well loved. Billy had a challenge in his chairing his seat as a Freshman new congressman.

The word was out from the local GOP 12th District Central Committee and gradually his name was recognizable and talked about. With the help of people like George Huff. Who kept plugging publicity in the district in any media he could find enlightening the public about Billy Brewer.

Upon the congressional seating of Billy in Jonas Sterling's place, the Patter under the owner's direction, Ed Martin, were running a full profile of Billy's background and career choices, along with family disclosure and including his wife, Anita. It was inclusive and well done with lots of pictures of his high school glory days, West Point achievements, and his duties in the service of the Green Berets and stint in the CIA. Indeed, the "dossier" on Billy was growing, and his talents were many. It was obvious that he was a man of accomplishment, quality, and integrity. News traveled fast and soon the public in the 12 district and outside of it was gaining knowledge about their new congressman in Washington, DC. He was new and different, a man to watch.

CHAPTER SEVEN

Billy's leadership qualities were everyday becoming noticed and visible. He always was a man with a plan and conducted himself in a manner of assuredness, confidence. He was a principled man of values who started with self-reflection. This helped him to guide himself in making choices that aligned up with his values, and focused on things that mattered the most.

Because of his personal history, and opportunities allowed him, he developed an uncanny ability to see situations from multiple perspectives, see different viewpoints and gain wholeness comprehension from all the parts to being able to see the whole in terms of the parts and determine the whole of the matter.

Billy was the essence, for the most part, and mastery of certain skills true confidence enables, an ability to recognize your strengths and weaknesses and being able to focus on continuous improvement and life building.

Billy had great balance in his life and carried in his craw a certain humility that was genuine., His make-up had influence on other folks in direct and/or subtle ways. He treated others as he would want to be treated. Such character idiosyncrasies had or could have profound influence on individuals, organizations or even the world. These were the ways in which Billy carried himself in dealing with others.

Leadership is, of course, the ability to influence others. Billy had a knack to get people to follow him. Any change had to be positive in nature. His value-based leadership was crucial American style. Too many of the old-line ensconced leaders had fallen short of maintaining a primary adherence to integrity; they'd waned in their human weaknesses, and lost their way, in their personal life, family life and career life.

It is imperative to do the right thing, not confusing activity with productivity and to make choices aligned with your core values. To be only who you are – making it clear to see easier and make choices easier.

Leaders who pursue balance realize that their perspective is just that, theirs. Other input is important, especially opposing opinions. When you take time to reflect issues and situations, holistically, the world becomes simpler and a plan of action becomes more obvious. Trying to be cute, sly, backhanded, stealthy, underhanded, or deceitful, not only causes vulnerability and opposition, but leaves others with a bad taste in their mouths and memories of untrustworthiness. Plus, in the long run, negotiations became a mountain range of obstructive progress. To be open and dependably honest upfront presented oneself in the best light – light has a way of shining bright in a spirit of darkness.

Enemies of the state often negotiated out of deceitfulness and ill will. To a seasoned negotiator, lies and subterfuge were all too obvious and didn't or wouldn't pass muster. That is why a thorough background in history is so important - it separates the repeating of bad history in a new era. Deceitful negotiating only works when innocence of knowledge takes place when weakness is detected. One good reason as past President Ronald Reagan had said, "Leadership through strength." America had to always be the strongest country on the planet – physically and mentally. At the present, we were advancing to the rear – on both counts. This was political suicide for a nation such as ours. The evil people were plenty to take advantage of it both within the nation and hungerly waiting around the world. Our enemies were by nature cunning and deceitful and ever-resourceful in piercing our weak armor areas. They searched our weak spots. They wanted us down and out!

We needed to be ever vigilant – daily. Billy was well aware of these things and was determined to help reinstate America to its prominence and keep it there. He would make it his life work and direction. He set his sights high and fiercely. Others near him realized Billy's strong stance for America and his determination to right what seemed to be so wrong and to improve the American way. America was lost and getting "worsely" so by the minute. History will follow a strong leader even if he be a bad or evil leader. However, there has to be a history in direction for those desiring to become true leaders.

If you're good, your record in the public eye needs to have some longevity showing positive directives. Billy's record of achievement for his lifetime was truly advanced positive thinking and direction. It didn't take anyone long reading and reviewing his dossier to determine the quantity and high quality of service to his country. The American heartland from shore to shore was again looking for a George Washington leadership type. The stalwart, fierce independent oriented true American type folk, who were willing to sacrifice for securing and saving their country from tyranny and political shenanigan's by stealthy and vicious plotting deviates, as well as self-serving dictators. America was inundated by much apathy and evil lurked behind its beautiful landscape and prickly rose bushes.

CHAPTER EIGHT

TEMPUS FUGIT! Time flies whether you're having fun or not. Bad, miserable times, conditions, oppressions and incredible man's inhumanity to man occasions fill time and space regardless. Years go by with nauseous political reactions generating nations and people's directions whether they want it or not. People follow the good and the bad for different reasons.

In a sense they are headed to heaven or hell – a little over simplified, but not too much. Many would say they're into alternative thinking and lifestyle. Really? Stealing gum from a candy store at age 5 – depending on what you do with that experience, may determine whether you become a "priest" or wind up in the big house on an island in San Francisco bay. In some cases, you may lose your hand, head, or worse, a lovely world!

Life is full of choices. In America we are losing our choices to those that would have you with limited choices, preferably those they grant you with, and they would be the ruling class – dictators in charge of your life. Never happen in America?

Do nothing and wait and see? Too many have caught the proverbial disease called "APATHY." Billy was worried about this aspect of American culture. It was not positive or good – certainly not healthy. Congress and the President needed to work together, not separately. Divided parties and party lines needed to repair and quickly. It was imperative that cross aisles of congress get to their jobs of unifying America, by doing what's right for America, and realizing that they will most certainly be re-elected by pulling together for all, and not bickering in the basement of darkness getting absolutely nothing done for their nation. Yes, the ones that last elected them to their "plush" confines of federal office to supposedly be representatives of their home constituency.

The "us" versus "them" idiocy perpetrated on the public by the elected. Is it any wonder how little liked or respected these bureaucrat representatives have become? Worse than a "skunk" in an outhouse carried the image of these public servants.

There used to be a saying in a fraternity that "a 'plebe' was so small, that if he could sit on a dime with his feet hanging over the edge, floating down the Mississippi River, he wouldn't get his feet wet." Well Congress has developed itself into that likeness. Hope springs eternal in God and in people who strike deep into the souls of men with their honesty, quality, integrity and direction of life and mindset. People still have heart even in the depths of discouragement and derelict, and look to and follow their heart regardless of bribes, false promises, and errant directions opposed to the center of values and core integrity to generate goodness, healthfulness and positive lifestyles in keeping with each person's established standards for an American way of life they had longed for and had dreams for. Politicians only fool some of the people some of the time but not all – all of the time. Americans have limitations, then they push back.

Billy's career as a congressman would span 26 years or so. He would become even speaker of the house for many years. His authority and integrity for accomplishment in directing the Congress to do its business in a timely manner serving the American people as well as he could get it to function. That was his purpose and goal.

The Nation would start to recover under his stewardship and influential direction. It would come out from under the divisiveness of the 'teens, 20's and 30's of the 21st century. Other leaders came forth from under the sway and the tutelage of the American fringe politic groups and joined alongside of the American patriot voters when they voted in a hard-starting determined class of public representatives, following Billy's popular leadership and laws, and repeal of laws adjustment of policies and institutions for new and common-sense laws, regulations, tax reform, spending monitoring and American asset protection and upgrading's.

It was a transition time for America under God's grace to get America in balance and on a righteous path to greatness. It could be done. There were many paths to solutions. The right ones had to be found, secured and set upon. The fringe politic thought they had the right ones, but usually it benefitted only a few. Too few. The people could smell that "skunk" in the outhouse and voted out the "skunks" and in with the patriots of common sense and reason. It was time to exert change.

There was the backroom boiler-room, Tammany hall politics of the early 19th Century and the patronage era of the Daley Chicago machine of the 50's through the early 2000's and the partisan politics of the mid-teen years of the 21st Century. These movements passed by but lingered here and there.

New times were the result of a survival need by those who had been shunted aside by both party fringes who aimed to do a takeover of the dictates of a few over the many and to run a nation into ruin, while thinking how wonderful (big pockets) they were.

Usually progress in America is slow. The fringe groups wait and plot together to seize their prey. Sometimes God throws a monkey wrench in the mix and things change quickly, such as the Trump presidential election results.

Since God also gave us the last 43 presidents, good or bad, or good and bad, resulting in a business man not a lawyer or politician gaining the helm of the American ship. The rioting in the streets is protesting God for His selection. Most people don't realize this real aspect. He alone assigns Royalty, good or bad. He has a plan, and He is not you or me. Protesting is in vain. God is not intimidated. Man will continue circling the mountain and die before they see the promised land.

CHAPTER NINE

Anita's life became more and more fulfilling. The Mall store studio began doing quite a business. Surprising to her, she was commissioned to paint specific subject matters which customers requested. This was a new direction artists came to embrace in their work. It was challenging and different, but profitable and enjoyable.

Anita reminisced for a moment their return to York with Billy to open and visit with what was the Congressional District GOP office. It had been a nice visit seeing so many old friends and meeting all the new flock of voters that had supported Jonas Sterling. As she was working in her store one day, she felt her body telling her something. She paused to assess that thought. She didn't feel sick in any way. What was happening? She sat down for a moment to think.

Suddenly it dawned on her. She had missed her last period, but had been too busy to clock that into her mind. Once again, suddenly she outburst with a "Oh, my, maybe I'm pregnant?" Anita quickly closed the store and headed to the drug store within the Mall. There she bought a test kit for pregnancy, and returned to the store where upon she tested herself in the store's restroom facility. "If these things are accurate," thought Anita after testing. She viewed the results and it showed a positive result. She was. She quickly called Billy at his new office and said, "Billy, Billy. Guess what?"

Billy hadn't a clue as to what she was talking about and said like a comedy team retort, "Guess what, what? What are you talking about?"

Anita responded, "Well, hold on. You're going to be a daddy! I think."

Billy engaged Anita with "Hold on wait. Start at the beginning. I'm getting excited at your potential news."

"Well, I was working doing things here at the store and suddenly I had a feeling of heavy funkiness, had no idea why the heaviness. So, I sat down to think. I suddenly realized I'd missed my last period. It went by unnoticed! I shut my store and headed for the drug store here in the Mall and came back and tested myself – twice! Voila! Big Daddy, we're on our way to having a family. I'm excited!"

"Me too!" responded Billy. "Wonderful. I guess there must have been something in the hometown York water when we were there."

"Maybe so," said Anita. "I'm thrilled."

"Now don't you be moving heavy stuff at the store. Do you hear me?" blatted out Billy. "Don't you worry, honey, I'll be careful and we'll have a family going' soon. No time like being really busy to start a family," stated Anita. "The busy keep the world moving – so c'est la vie. Another challenge worthwhile. I love you and remember that! Billy responded."

"I know you do," Anita cooed into the phone dramatically.

Fast forwarding history at the Brewer home. Anita had fraternal twins, a boy and a girl, in that order. Their life even more dramatically changed. They were aglow parents with double-down purpose in life. They sent their children to private schools the first eight grades, then sent Kevin to a public school while Nathalie continued in a private Charter School.

While the Washington DC public high schools were a mixed bag, Kevin was a very good student, a talented athlete – into basketball and football like his dad – who somehow made himself present to most of his games especially Junior and Senior year.

Nathalie turned out a sterling academic performance herself along her pathway and became a top high school seeded tennis player. It was something she really enjoyed and starred at. They both made application for enrollment at the University of Illinois. Kevin and Nathalie both received athletic scholarships, she for tennis and he for football.

Anita and Billy were very proud parents of their children and were there for them as much as possible. The kids absolutely loved their parents and gave them little troubles through their teen years. They were too busy and nobody fought with Daddy. Nobody.

Over the years of 20 or so, and because her husband was becoming a quoted congressman now a speaker of the house and was close in association with the President, her portrait business was flourishing. She had become known as the Portrait Painter of Choice by persons in the government that wanted to preserve their memory for the public square. The income significantly increased. Anita was excited and really happy during these years. She was so proud of her husband and his patriotic effort to turn America around bringing on board as many folks as he could to generate "spark and fire" to the revision and pathway for America.

The Congressional mindset indeed, had slowly turned from egocentric partisan representation to acting in closer union with the American citizen body politic and voting, what is best for America and find ways to pay for it. A pay as you go society. Future generations were now not saddled with humongous debt as earlier government membership had done and heaped upon them. As a result, everybody breathed easier. Government was now a vibrant entity and again, was becoming the leader worldwide in most every category imaginable.

Americans were again feeling good about themselves, and it reflected on congressional approval ratings in the highest numbers ever recorded. Future government candidates were happy to serve their country once again and be proud to be an American in a world that while still fighting bad guys, was winning the hearts and following of more and more nations that wanted to tailgate America, the prosperous!

New prosperity was the catch word. Work hard, work smart, and hop-on-board with the stars and stripes. Hatred in America had taken an aspirin and gone to bed to think and slumber itself into new awakening. Indeed, America was in a generation renewal of heart and Soul.

The transformation of repentance seemed to pierce the heart of the hatred of America, in wonderment and realization that it bred self-hatred more than other hatred, thus one at a time resumed resuscitation and change of heart about their neighbor. It seemed like the spirit of a living God was overflowing all the stars on our beautiful flag. Even a new law establishing a jail sentence to those desecrating the flag, especially burning it. It was no longer considered a freedom of speech or expression. It was a cherished representation of America now protected by common sense law and public opinion.

Once again, the Supreme Court was marching to a healthy body of America and not be the fringe America that had their interests in negativity and for but a few. Dictatorship, Socialism, and Communism were not consistent with American hard-fought ways and national struggles to relieve itself from such hamstrings and strictures. Americans were bound in strength to one another because everybody migrated the world over to come to this land of opportunity and freedoms unlike any other nation in the world. It was amazingly unique as a country of migrants, integrated to serve the world. No other nation of the world sacrificed for so many, feeding, clothing, rebuilding as the United States the proud and prosperous hard-working folk of America.

The body America, born and bred in humble beginnings, striving to become an independent nation, to rise and prosper on its own, integrated with the nations of the world, leading, so that that others might prosper also.

Billy was determined to hold himself accountable to the values and standards of what had been fought and bought for, independence, liberty for all. Indeed, he had broad shoulders, and stood tall in the days as he served his beloved country as a public servant in love with its diversity of people. America was and is a unique country and experiment on the world scene. The newest kid on the block. Anyone with a speck of vision could see that only God could have designed such a nation of internationals, founded on a shoe string of faith, guts and determination.

Ever since the tower of Babel, when God scattered the folks worldwide and gave them diverse tongues, languages, that they might be separated from one another, and that they would have to work and have faith together if ever a united world togetherness would ever be realized again., Rebellion is the call of evil intensions. Darkness is loved by many, for they are disengaged from others in the need for love and fellowship. It is easier to tear down than build up. Weakness creates a vacuum for evil.

Billy was a creative builder of things, enjoyed seeing good growth and happiness spread itself. Happiness generates hope, hope generates positive deliberation and meaningful outreach. Happiness established good mindset and good health. It helps establish positive wellbeing and positive societal results. The opposite is just plain detrimental to mankind in every regard. Misery is the devil's playground, and it is obvious the world is busy at its play. It looks for company.

America was on a roll again. People and nations were noticing. As countries following the lead of America, prosperity again took hold and envy of the populations of evil leaning nations were weakening. Evil was not the choice general populations wanted to follow. It was hollow living, hollow promises, and hollow prosperity to individual pocketbooks. Evil brought on misery, disparity, divisiveness and depression and the devil's workshop called "hate." Darkness brings on the loss for hope and no future improvement prospects. There was no flourishing grace, or happiness under evil dominated national leadership. Men died and were killed for naught and at a political expense, opposition was annihilated, one less irritating opponent for the regime to deal with.

Regimes were rising, people wanted change., They sought leadership responding to their new ways and desires for dignity, integrity and honest government. Good leadership was always hard to get. Positive results for the people became the norm – way demanded. People sought quality in their management of their nation. Good was indeed triumphing over evil, as the half century mark of the 21st Century passed by. 2056 found the world watching and not wanting for results. It was an actively seeking and searching for true valid, honest leadership with spine. The political cunning, self-seeking parties and politicos, were filtered through and out of the system. People were voting their heart, asserting their rights and wisely so.

Results were not won by the lying scoundrels of old-line politics, who decorated their halls with hollow nirvana promises. It was about people's best welfare – the policies best fitting progress in binding the wounds and celebrating liberty in wholeness of new and progressive political sponsored positive policies for the people. False talk was seen for what it was, deception, hollow and at the booth voted down. The old school politic was on its way out fast. People took charge at the voting booth. And heaved the unworthy out. Evil ones are always around, hiding and slinking in their "hole" waiting to kill and devour any that they can find to dominate. Evil is a social disease hard to eliminate but it is detoxed by people doing good. Opportunity is paramount, it must be provided by leadership – policies and general positive environments that are presented.

Leadership was, and is crucial to determining future happiness and welfare of the pocket book. Standards of living rise when good prevails over evil – evil prefers you live in poverty. Playing fields are leveled and people prosper as they work hard. It wasn't complicated. Evil folks want you to get so caught up in the details that it looks hopeless to head through the storm Confusion, controversy, hatred, class envy, personified evil thinking. Uphill battles find encouragement one battle at a time. When God is blowing at your back, you rise to the top of the mountain, no matter the steepness involved. The upward winds were blowing strong around the 2050's and beyond., As the old TV Soap said, "As the World Turns," God was breathing favor on the US of A. He was not ready to return to earth to set up His Kingdom. It was not yet Armageddon time.

CHAPTER TEN

Billy's life was very fulfilling and his enjoyment of it was not only more than he expected, but every day engaging his think tank to be vigilant and working its God-given talent. His days were always educational in nature and his stature as a congressman grew exponentially with time. As speaker of the house, his prominence grew having close association with the President. They worked together to get things done for the country. The will of the people about the worldly business.

It was soon to be his day to personally yield the chamber floor to himself, as it was his day as speaker of the house to use in bringing his message to the body concerning the two standing committees he was on. The education, and Armed Services committees. His day had come as he prepared for his two presentations before the full house of representatives, all 435 members. This, of course, did not include the senate of 100 members. His first-floor speech was on the education of the nation. Its hopes, prospects, and current status from his perspective. Here's the transcription of the speech.

SPEECH to House Membership on Education by Honorable William J. Brewer, Congressman, 12 District, Illinois, United States of America.

"Good day fellow house members. Today I bring to you my thoughts and experience in the field of Education. It is a big field, a big business and there are almost as many opinions about it as bee's in a honey farm.

Education is quickly emerging in experimentation. Our leadership among nations has placed our quality of education adrift in the fog of where it should be. We have today in the United States a plethora of experimental educational solutions going on.

Today for the student in Massachusetts, results and quality are being supported to a high degree of educational success. Places like New Mexico, Louisiana are at the same levels are at the greatest deficiency for 4th and 8th grades. Why is that/ There are many and various reasons. A one-size plan for all 50 states doesn't work.

We are a nation of innovators, entrepreneurs, problem solvers. We also are a nation that has special interests in everything. Money talks, favor talks, buying votes talks! Fringe policy adherers want it to influence innocent children into adult misbehaviors through certain progressive policy.

It is my belief that teachers not bureaucrats should reform education. Except for pay scales and making sure teachers are compensated fairly. The teachers' union is a hindrance to education.

I am of the belief, as are quite a few others, that the breadth of education is important to the wholeness of mankind. Reading, writing and arithmetic is just a small part of a child's mind development. These things, while necessary to function well in society, do little in the search for enjoyment in learning things needed on a daily basis. It is my experience and contention that, and a West Point education ignores, is what is called, 'creativity.' To the detriment of building not only enjoyment through learning, but expanding their worldly awareness around them and influence their possible appreciation of life and its potential for them to fit in. I'm in favor of including curriculums of K-grade through 12th grade opportunities for art, music and drama. Many of these type programs have been cut for the lack of funds over the years. I find that incredibly dumb. There can be great joy in learning these activities, essentially giving each child a great overall learning experience and the joy of learning greater worldly subject matters. We have been wasting half a brain by eliminating the lost opportunity to build wholeness of the mind and person. It is essential that our children not only learn certain basics but that they find a joy in learning period. Expand their life in basic necessities, and parameters.

Exciting things are happening in all fronts of education in America. Things positive are happening one student at a time. We need to find ways to increase that. Charter and Classical schools are increasing by unprecedented numbers and home schooling. Test scores are bearing this out – quality of education better benefitting our children.

Private schools, academics, are leading the way in innovation and successfully educating children, providing them with ancillary courses in the arts. They are increasingly being broadened in K-12 for being better qualified to face college successfully. They come out of the K-12 shoot loaded for bear. Too many are indeed being left behind. We bureaucrats are plugging the pipelines with old fashioned thinking and interference and meddling with false seniority experience with teachers failing our children because of heavy leaded unions and bureaucrats can't keep their greedy hands off their meddling and dinosaur ways of doing things. Seniority plugs the pipes, when that is the sole reason for hiring employment. It is dead wrong. WE need to unclog the pipes, so our children get on the learning paths quicker.

Today technology leads the way to new innovation. It's not a sure thing for success, but often it enhances better learning. Trial innovation is necessary, social cultures, state and local cultures can be obstacles sometimes. We must press on and get rid of the blame game and move on. Status quo is neutral, stagnant. We must be a body in motion. Stagnation and old ways get too comfortable and they are good for a time, but eventually most expire their usefulness.

We owe it to ourselves and our children, to throw off the shackles that bind us to any status quo, pop relativism, situation ethics and arrogant utopianism that pervades the university college life.

It is an air of toxic gases circulating the bastions of idealistic young people who still have their heads in a bag. This new "pop" culture is propaganda agenda by people with philosophy agenda in other directions than the American norm and basic patriot citizens. Things done or allowed to be done to our children are going unchallenged by the mainstream fringe fold. Toxic philosophies and cultures are quite often hoisted upon us (the children), slipped in as substitute sugar that'll be good for you stuff. Our young folk need the tools of learning history, art, music and drama to discern all the negative and deceitfulness perpetrated on them. They are vulnerable teen agers and grade school populations. Adults must be responsible for what is being taught. Parents have rights over their children. Outsiders do not know what's best. They are the foxes in the henhouse.

Everything we get outside of free gifts of nature, must in some way be paid for. The world is full of so-called economists scheming for getting something for nothing. The government loves to spend; thus, our debt continues to rise. These dreams have always led to national insolvency and runaway inflation, inflation, of course, is merely a form of vicious taxation.

We Americans are a hard-working people who create wealth better themselves. Excessive government threatens this process.

Certain portions of our society want to hoist their central power answers upon our children and public schools which is often sugar coated. To decentralize power is to reduce the absolute amount of power, and the competitive system is the only system designed to minimize the power exercised by man over man. Competition spurs variety of thinking.

Who can seriously doubt that the power which a millionaire, who may be my employer, or yours, has over me is very much less than that which the smallest bureaucrat possesses – who yields the coercive power of the state – and on whose discretion it depends how I am allowed to live and work.

Americans basically are idealistic people that attitude is reflected in instruction in schools and its political rhetoric. Parents must become involved with the choices that the public arena offers. There are usually many. Some of the public language falls into being too "idealistic" in nature, and the words "ring out" hollow or too saccharine like.

Many programs need revision, elimination, or promoting. School vouchers seem good in some instances. College loans are something to do away with. K-12 parents should choose where their child goes to school and be involved. Many realize the large savings when home schooled.

American innovation thrives in a free country, liberty for all, choices. Central planning, dictatorship, always limits choice and outcome of peoples and children.
Pell grants for K-12 works well for choice.

We as a nation are facing a secular socialist ideology that is alien to America's history and traditions. Traditional America values hard work, entrepreneurship, innovation and merit-based upward mobility. Free enterprise and competition sharpen everybody and raises standards to high values. We need not stand helplessly by and watch the incompetent bureaucracy destroy our children's lives.

We must rethink how we educate our children, especially in math and science. We need to groom young ones to new levels and challenges and delete the force-feeding numbers and theories and line up some excitement through solid, innovative leadership.

It is an object reality that we are NOT producing enough 18-year-olds capable of sustaining this society into the 21st Century. It is our need to be bold in challenging this problem. One helpful probability is waiving interest on student loans for undergraduates that major in science and math.

Our society today holds little consequences for poor shows, misdemeanors, serious harmful to the public crimes to which we lightly bruise their wrists with a wet noodle. Accountability in the American scene is virtually inactive. Courts need to tighten up not loosen up. Judges need to get real.

So much of the failing in our present child through college population is that we are under assault by multiculturalism, situation ethics, and new values. We have not been teaching American history or its values. They are being ignored or ridiculed. Unless we act to reverse this trend, our next generations will grow up with no understanding of core American values. This will destroy America as we know it, as sure as if a foreign conqueror had overwhelmed us.

To know America, its core values, culture and mores and its exceptional greatness, if passed on and realizing our immigrant population came here to this great land for freedom and opportunity. If Americans don't appreciate America then how will they be willing to defend her? What backbone will they have/ God forbid.

From my perspective there is no attack on American culture more destructive or more historically dishonest than that perpetrated on our society by, the secular left and their relentless effort to drive God out of the American public square. Subversiveness is alive and well trying to penetrate all our core values and liberties and freedoms.

AS for me and my house, I for the record, will dwell in the house of the Lord and be confident in America to always rise to her best, through its lost ways and to her greatness. I will do all I can to keep the beautiful ship afloat and sailing well through all the seas. I will and do encourage the body America to climb on board and that we all sail together into our destined future. But it's going to take a shoulder to shoulder doing and separating the toxins from our society that won't or don't want us to succeed and refuse to pitch in to make a better United States of America.

Thank you, ladies and gentlemen of Congress. Have a good American day. SALUTE! (Billy salutes out!)

Those that were in the House Chamber, a full house, gave Billy a hand of applause in a slight and polite manner not too, effusive, but everybody participated. Yes, even the democrats. Many came up to him after and affirmed him, encouraged him that his talk was a good one. Billy appreciated those that personally spoke with him. He was not put off by all the others that didn't. This was body politic and the opposition party was not in the habit of expressing effusive applause for anything, a kind of partisan privilege they reserved for their own discretion and party members.

There was always opposition to any introduction of a talk into the House Chamber. It was a place to vote and debate. Everything needed tweaking or changing. Sometimes the presentation or tone and emphasis by a speaker was appealing and impressionable. Looks or stature of body was rarely a plus point thing. However, Billy was such an impressionable viewing due to his size and good looks, he right away was formidable and got your attention with his John Wayne sounding voice or just standing there did it for some.

It was a beginning for Billy in that freshman year as speaker of the house. He would again repeat this appearance again the next day speaking to the Chamber, this time as a member of the Armed Services Committee. Here he would carry more weight as a he spoke having his military background experience he had been through, behind him.

He no longer was interrogating Mullah Moo! That had long ago finished as his usefulness was no longer profitable or current.

Isis had for all intense and purposes been neutered, sent into the hills and caves of Iran and Iraq again settling into the serious task of trying to unite itself into a coalition government. Isis of Syria had been flushed out and basically slaughtered as they fled to escape eastward, but being caught in a pincher military trap by the Allied forces all, who had finally gotten their act together in a united and coordinated front.

Much of the intel came from all the gatherings of "Operation Moo" and the resultant information from the raid, and some from the interrogation of Mullah Moo himself, in which Billy was the prime interrogator. The Middle East was no longer in total chaos with a large Cadre of outlaw bandit killers perpetrating their brand on society but now the tasks were to get Russia out of Syria and keeping Iran from shooting "Nukes" all over the place against any and all infidels opposed to Iran. Iran was a cancer upon the world, spreading terrorism whenever and wherever it could. It felt enhanced as a power every time they could inflict injury or embarrassment to the Western infidels.

This was, of course, spurred on by the "Mullahs Chieftains" and their military control over whom they wished. The people of Iran were essentially good world citizens but as usual under dictatorial control they became rogue rebels on earth. Their chief exporting policy was and is irritating everybody it could, especially the Western world, while fearfully threatening those all around them, especially Israel.

Iran is a Persian country. It is the second largest country in the Middle East and the 18th largest in the world. It is a country of 82.8 million inhabitants, and is the 17th most populous country.

Iran is not an Arabic state, and its language is called Farsi, an off-brand of Arabic. It contains large reserves of fossil fuels and has the largest natural gas supply in the world. Most inhabitants are Shia Muslims. They are ruled by a political system which is based on a 1979 constitution which contains elements of parliamentary democracy with a theocracy governed by Islamic Jurists (Mullahs) under the concept of a supreme leadership, who presently is Ali Khamenei. The country goes back to 678 BC. About the only thing they have in common with the US of America, is they drive on the right side of the road. In case we invade Iran, we won't be stopped by a cop for driving on the wrong side. I'm sure our military cares. Right!

CHAPTER ELEVEN

As Billy and Anita returned from church, they fixed up a noon brunch spread. Billy handled the grill and Anita fixed a delicious salad. They sat down on their porch and enjoyed themselves to the fullest.

It was a rare time together. The both of them were busy people now with two kids under their wing. They were now getting old enough to help do things and chipped in on lunch preparations.

Several of the Washington monuments were viewed from their now large condo. Kevin was doing well at school and in sports and Nathalie was thoroughly enjoying her school experience. Anita was pleased with her progress at their studio and the assistance of Penny and their new ticket agency thing.

Anita's art career was flourishing and expanding its customer base. Many government officials of the past administrations, as well as in the present one, were contacting her for sittings for their preservation and legacy for future generations. All in all, their life was called successful and prosperous and maybe too busy. But they were yet relatively young and capable people, every day with making new connections and friends and voluminous associations of new people.

As speaker of the house, Billy was forever playing political pundit, and, in the limelight, which seemed quite often. The public and government now waited for his up and coming speech in the House Chamber as a committee member on the House Armed Services Committee.

This coming Thursday was his day again in the chamber to pontificate his views on the status of the Armed Forces of America. It was of course, a subject matter near and dear to his heart and mind, and concern. After having been given the experience of presenting his views on Education to the chamber earlier, he felt less uptight about his upcoming presentation before the House.

It was during the early part of the week before his speaking engagement that Mullah Moo had died of a hemorrhage to the brain.

Suddenly and quickly. Moo was buried quietly and in an undisclosed place the CIA chose. Billy attended the brief ceremony and actually said a few positive words he had for their growth and closer relationship that produced a certain respect and friendship they gained during the interrogation process in the CIA confines. He made note of this Lazy Boy chair hair brain enticement torture to get Moo talking. To some extent, it worked. Billy had no idea it would ever again be used in priming the pump for spilling the beans of a prisoner of war. This case had special characters involved, he and Mullah Moo.

Thursday came. It would be a big day. He was feeling well and healthy, and pumped himself up for the presentation time on the floor of the house before all of his peers. He was proud to be an American. Proud to be a United States Congressman representing American People from a section of the country the 12th District of Illinois. He was actually representing far more American people throughout the entirety of America and its many states and territories. The world would be following closely his presentation and his thought for America's military. America needed a reality check and boost. If anybody in government was expected to promote improvement, it would be he. The veterans and military personnel and the public wanted to hear him recommend and strengthen the armed forces to the max. Sentiment said let us be the best military on the earth. Peace through strength. Billy was ready to give them the good news they were ready to hear.

The left and the apathetic weak weeds of America were shouting and marching down the proverbial highways to the evil sinkholes they loved. It was dark there and they all could wring their hands and moan together – save the trees, flying ants, and those peckerwood fly eaters, the Chinese coal burners and the New York Times. The fringe America on the loose. America, the core patriots of America had the knowledge that "A" came before

"B" or "C." Priorities were essential and essentials were to become a priority.

When the democratic operated American way Prospered, then the horse was in front of the cart as any sane person could recognizes as productive activity. Americans worked hard to prosper, competition promoted the better welfare of everybody.

America is an entrepreneurial capitalistic society from the git-go. It's what made it so great an international achievement. America is a world class leader that has taken a left hand turn into dark places. Its people are optimistic souls who have confidence in themselves to produce through hard work to provide for themselves and their families, even through generosity to the outside world. Their finest by-product. They are inclusive folks. If you're hurting, they will take care of you. Liberals keep insisting that extreme wealth is obscene, as if the economy were a zero-sum game in which people get richer only if poor people get poorer. That, of course, is not true. "Wealth" is good and the more people who can create and earn it, the better.

The left in America seem to abhor the rich. Funny how many of them are and how often they complain about just everything. And we know who they blame it on – you got it. They have a deep jealousy desire to be so, but they want everybody else to be supporting those who don't work, or those who more often than not, who won't work. They see themselves wanting to switch places, when in fact, if they did, the rich would be back on top within three years.

America, the land of milk and honey isn't so because everybody sits around navel gazing. The worlds eight richest men own as much wealth as the world's poorest 3. 7 billion people – half the planets population. It's called by some "the vast income gap" – expressing it as a "moral" and social calamity. "it is all a striking statistic, but it's also irrelevant." First of all, these eight richest persons aren't parasites exploiting the masses. Through hard work and ingenuity, they created enterprises that improve the lives of billions, moreover each gives massive amounts to charity. Meanwhile, thanks to the "C" word, Capitalism, the world's poor have been climbing out of poverty at the fastest rate in human history. Over the past 30 years, the number of people in extreme poverty has dropped by 75% or 1.2 billion people. Extreme wealth is not "obscene" when folks like the above eight spread it around. It's the lottery winner who hasn't a clue how to invest it, spend it wisely and benefit so many people. It's called the blame game, embarrass and point fingers at others – forgetting their thumb is pointing back at them.

The American attempt to move towards socialism is perpetrated by some fringe folks just plunders under the strength and prosperity of capitalism. When freedoms and liberty flow unobstructed and American dreams are fleshed out, goals are reached, people prosper, families and marriages flourish. When those things work together for good, America is flush with greatness again. Everybody says, "I am doing better," keep it going!

Tax bases increase as revenue pours in to do the business of America. It's roads, bridges, border fences, laws to relieve cities of gangs, enforcement mindsets to usher them to jail or out of the country. Good laws get made and, on the books, old antique ones are culled and deleted, and enforcement of all of them observed.

America is at a crossroads of returning to what God called us to be in the beginning. We have for a great part disregarded His callings to follow Him. He said, "I will be the God of all who do." If He is for us, then who can be against us. Let's bring Him back among us and working for us. He doesn't like to be an outsider, after all we are his children, and yes, we have a will of our own, and we certainly entertain and use it. And as Billy stated in his education speech to Congress, intellectual properties and capabilities are essential for making wise and wiser choices in life.

Life improves when one gets beyond the "feel good" basis for making decisions and is encompassed with facts and better balance of overall knowledge of what's going on in the world.

Two PM in the afternoon arrived for Billy, as he presided over the House Chamber, beneath the vice president. It was again, his duty to cast this opinion and personal take on the state of the Armed Forces, it's health in relation the world.

Billy took the podium with his prepared speech for the day. He was feeling good and ready to stand his 6 foot 6 inches tall frame before his fellow delegates of Congress. The speech would be carried on C-SPAN channel of TV carried the world over. The <u>antagonists</u> all would be listening.

House Chamber speech to Congress on Armed Services, USA.

"Good afternoon fellow delegates, I appreciate all your attendance and my opportunity to express my impressions of need, wants and must haves that I think America is calling for its military defenses.

While our country is a peaceful loving nation, we likewise face nations and people who are not. Some are directly hostile to us, others more subversive in nature.

Our policy basically is "Peace through strength." American strength is a strong guarantee for peace and stability among the nations of the world. We are in need of restoring health to our defense industry weakened by a combination of neglect and misguided policies. We must align our military power with strength of American society, which at present is not good. Our skilled people, advanced technology and proficiency at integrating fast-paced systems into potent networks, are things we must advance. We must also rejuvenate our foot soldiers to maximum peace status. Maximum peace is fulfilled by maximum readiness.

The US now faces the growing problems of readiness, moral and the ability to prepare for threats of the future. We are subject to blackmail and deceit in order to lower our guard from those who wish to do us harm.

Past administrations have cut defense spending to the lowest percentage of gross product since 1939. We are becoming more vulnerable every day we do nothing but talk and or retreat from our high calling as a world leader. Our military strength is waning, before our eyes at the expense of liberal political funding or lack of, for saving the blue-eyed rat population and the crooked trees in Marin County.

We must expand our building a stronger alliance with our Allied nation countries to improve united efforts in combat situations against enemies of mutual threatening groups and foreign alliances.

To be current with hostile nations on the move, we need immediate upgrading of all missile defense, missiles, silos and submarines – that our equipment is second to none. We must deploy missile defenses to the most strategic locations worldwide, in light of China, N. Korea and Russian aggressive behaviors and newer ordinances and locations.

We must develop better policy and planning to defend against the rogue nations, like N. Korea and Iran and its aerial deployment of ground to air missiles and their long-range planning of their advance missile technology.

On the positive side, we must work with all nuke missile countries to contain, remove any hair-trigger status – the high alert kind to reduce and prevent risks of accidental or unauthorized launches. We must quickly upgrade with modernizing all our strategic forces. In this fast-paced world, we must improve our assessment of conventional territorial aggressiveness by the Soviets, and China. We must help NATO in strategic regional confrontation affirmation that aggressive Russian and China pressures of bullying are presenting. Their operations outreach finds new ordinance coming out of their closet onto the front line. They lead with deception, lies and false cover their planned aggressions expanding their territorial pursuits. More recently advanced surface to air missiles.

Our strategies need to reduce Russia and China's temptation to use its non-strategic nuclear weapons, they're "inching" to this by posturing bullying fronts against everyone and practicing subversion extensively to gain territory for bases, influence and dominance. Recent coziness and intrusion in Syria, and Crimea are prime examples. The old world conquers for expansion –

they are flaunting their "oats" again. Communism propelling itself through dictatorship government despite what they call it.

Further, we must seek further reduction of our dependence of oil from others, increasing our own exploration to develop field and supply routes that will keep oil prices low and effectively reducing revenues for Russia and Iran, to pour into their defense-offense military expenditures. Ronald Reagan effectively did this. Likewise, China is on the move with huge military expenditures on their navy and missile programs, thus presently they are testing the waters expansively across the Far East, also bullying neighbors in behalf of the Communist leadership. It is becoming an attachment nation – anything it considers near them is subject to attachment threats by their "Mother Country." Thus, its navy building program has greatly expanded under its modern-day Communist Party expansion policy and financial direction. It is also viewing America as a weak and paper tiger.

Our past has forsaken us in the name of liberalism, socialism and apathy. We've become lethargic and apathetic and our soul is getting pushed into a hole these recent years gone by.

Peace through strength is, and always will be, our best policy. We need to move fast before we have not only no funds, but for environmental control, because Russia and China will have capitulated us into so much apathy and socialistic neutering, that we become no earthly good. There is no other nation on earth to stop these earthly evil doers, and we will at some time, earlier than later, succumb our way of living to the evil intensions of others who desire their brand of evil to toxify the world.

Believe me when I say, Revelation and Armageddon are just around the corner if we do nothing but listen to all the naysayers, and pillow pushers bent on crucifying us with lies, deception and their desire to capitulate us into oblivion or a political or military corner. We are in a world chess game of deceitful words and saber rattling with live ammo.

Our country needs thinkers, doers and men and women who will stand up to all our internal flak and damn the torpedoes. We are already in the throes of vulnerability these last years in this mid-21st Century. This time has moved us downriver heading for the falls, and a precipice for disaster. We must fight back, fight together and realize our potential and real strength and step forward into confronting the real world on this the battle of international survival. This planet is calling us to act to give people hope to succeed. America, it is time to give our best in today's world court. We must lead. The alternative is death by evil.

I am and will do what I can to strengthen our country. This is no play game; the stakes are monumentally high. America must win. "Give me liberty or give me death."

Give me your help, our generals and admirals have spoken "Help us, for God's sake," they say. It is an investment in your liberty, freedom, security and prosperity, not to mention our future wellbeing and way of life. Our first need is for "wisdom." Our second is for "Action." Let us not invite another Pearl Harbor.

Thank you all!

God is good and God bless America.

So, ended Billy Brewer's speech to the entire Congressional Chamber membership. His first standing committee Armed Forces report.

There was applause from the membership of the chamber and many congressmen sidled up to Billy to congratulate him and make a comment that they had. As noted earlier, the democrats and their left agenda were relatively quiet in their demeanor and response. Not surprising to Billy, but he was awaiting the public's response, and knew the left leaning media would be blasting its bias on the side of the democrats, a tradition as long newspapers and public communication had existed.

It really didn't take much viewing in the public and world arena to see that America was losing ground. The outside noise of the world was bombing us with their negativity and outright attacks. Get them while they're perceived weak.

The fear to Billy, the apathy of the nation – he was hoping it wouldn't take another World Trade Center episode to jar America to its senses and to action. It might be too late.

It was time for war with our enemies, not a time to coddle them. They would take advantage of every, weak flaw they could find and attack. We needed to get into a war positioning fast. Strength was respected in the eyes of bully nations. America needed to raise its level and modernize.

In other regards, increased spending on military rebuilding would put people back to work and with increased renewed work on American infrastructure and the 'pipeline' expansion for self-determination of America's supply of fossil fuels. America could be humming along pretty well in the next several years. It would put our enemies on the notice, and our allies in confident persuasion to their own folks.

Billy went back to his house office for a while to congregate with his staff and thank them for all their help. He couldn't have done his thing that day without them. They huddled around him and poured on accolades of praise. They were sincere when they said, "You did really well!"

Billy's office mail lit up like you wouldn't believe. They were coming in from all over the world. They were positive and encouraging for America to get rockin'. The rebel nations all continued to jab him as a war-monger, murderer and a Satan. Billy noted their tone of rebuff and made a mental note of their wicked stance toward America. His thought from a worldwide perspective diagramed a new evil axis of Russia, China, N. Korea, Iran, Syria plus a spattering of irritational bowel syndrome small covens, like Hezbollah, Al Qaeda, and Somalian area tribesmen scattered around. These were world trouble nations stirring volcano like.

As early evening wore on, Billy folded his office day and headed home to where real peace, comfort and love was in abundance. Whether Anita's day had been horrendous or ordinary, her demeanor and charm always melted his countenance down to near normal blood pressure. Needless to say, his work out sustained him immeasurably through the pressures of public office which were many. Her arms and charms were always warm in his embrace. They never faltered. He was enamored and in love with her.

Anita loved their openness and fed on the electricity it generated between them. Billy was her very stalwart lifelong companion/lover and she embraced all the good husbandship he offered, which was often, as it was tender.

Communication was their lifeblood, honesty their glue. It hadn't changed in their lifetime of knowing each other. Their marriage was still on high through it all. All the falderal and high profile of politics facing Billy, his moral compass was point on a due North on Anita. It never wavered.

Billy was a star among the dark caverns of the Washington splash and dash, all of its sidebars and enticements of money, power and sex. Billy had been, through earning his way, more was often too much for him. He had learned to live within his means. Extravagance was definitely not his style. He was generally low-key. He needn't be in the lime light, or forefront except when his presence called for it. Then he took total charge, which generally didn't take long to establish. Those that forgot his fortitude and strength soon retraced their thoughts of aggression as he did have an established reputation as a career Green Beret and CIA operative. In the words of a famous movie, he conducted himself as "an officer and a gentleman" until otherwise called for. Those that could remember the one time he had been talking to the President while in a public place, when a huge 300 lb. man burst through the protection ring of the Secret Service with a knife in his hand to attack the President, Billy assessed the problem instantly, and dislodge the knife from the assailant and picked him up over his head and slammed him on the ground whereby the Secret Service in entirely pounced on him and led him away in cuffs. It all happened so fast that few even witnessed it happening. The media, at least a few, had snapped away with video and flash. It, of course, made the 6:00 o'clock national news. You had to be an expert to have seen the moves Billy had put on the assailant, extraordinary! To the Secret Service guys, he was their hero. To the President, he was a hero already. He had known Billy's military story and briefings on Mullah Moo interrogations.

Billy was a rising star at the helm of the House of Representatives. It was an orderly body in action, actually, huddling together across the aisle and finding ways of pounding out solutions benefitting all Americans. Status of wealth or power, political persuasion, clout of not, he had his House Chamber doing their work. He led by example. He was envied and followed. Politicians knew when it came to re-election times, favorability numbers climbed when they signed on to the positive doing of the work of America. And both parties tended to be self-inclusive in being re-elected. Actual Congress's favorability numbers rose substantially. Even the democrats found that cooperating and negotiating America first worked well for them too. The public headline should realistically say, "America on the move." Both sides of the aisle were going the same directions.

Billy's service to his country was a history featured tale all by itself. His affection for and life blood companion Anita, the kids, Kevin and Nathalie, who were exemplary young talents of their own making, were profound on and in their remaking of America. That people can and do make a difference for good when God calls. Exceptionalism is captured in people who desire to serve others through using their talents no matter what those are.

Every field of endeavor has a few leaders out front. Billy's led to politics. He was a willing server and a born leader in behalf of others.

Billy noted in one of his latter interviews, that it was his "privilege" to serve not only his district 12 of Illinois, but the American people as a whole. When America puts its shoulders together, America works well. When America is strong, the world hums the song of the peace of Jerusalem. The world likes each other through "Respect." One only earns respect.

CHAPTER TWELVE

Once again it was time for Billy and his family to return to his home district and to his home town of York, Illinois. Here he would conduct a town hall meeting to charge up the constituents for another re-election. His popularity, respect and appealability were in the high numbers.

There was again no contest by the democrat machine to his re-election. The folks back home swamped his family on his return rejoicing in his presence. ON returning with his family to York, his followers all flooded the streets to meet and greet him. Kevin and Nathalie were thoroughly enjoying the attention. They were now at the University of Illinois.

Billy had given some thought to retiring from politics recently. It was a passing thought he hadn't put much interest in. His kids were active at college, Anita was busy and successfully growing her artistic career, he was at the head of his political career long established about 20 plus years now. He was still relatively young as a person, and as politician. His 52nd birthday was soon approaching. He felt very good.

The phone rang at Billy's home. Not many had his number. He offered a hearty, "Hello, Bill Brewer here!"

"Hi Billy, this is George Huff. Are you sitting down?"

"Yeah George, why?" responded Billy.

"Well, I'm on a 3-way call with Richard Ridenour, who as you know is the GOP National Party Chairman. And we, the local GOP state apparatus got a call from the National office in Washington. Presidential elections are coming up in two years and President Barnhart notified us he would not be running for re-upping his position and run again. That means we are all searching for a candidate to run in the 2052 general presidential election.

"Oh, really!" stated Billy, still listening.

"Yes, and we have for some time now been canvassing every Republican candidate that the party general could think of. You, my friend, are without a doubt number one on our list to run. According to our polls you are an impressive, way ahead of anyone else, including any potential Democratic candidate. This call is the call from our party to ask if you will consider and be our next GOP candidate for President of the United States. You are prime time for this time in America. You are credentialed to the max for the job. Dick and I are asking you in formal, official and as heads of our party, if you will seriously consider being our candidate for GOP president of the United States year 2052."

"Hey George, what do you and Dick do for a second act. Wow! I don't know. This is so sudden. I must talk to the family, have a conference – an inter-home pow-wow with them. This is serious stuff.

"Yeah, I, we, understand thoroughly." Spoke George continuing "As far as I, we, are concerned, we have looked but don't see any other GOP candidate's jollying up with any interest. Your credentialed life and present historic timing of your career pre-empts all others for being the best candidate around. It'll be you against the best DEM they can find. Personally, I think they'll be at a loss. I hope you do run, Billy, it sure would cap off your long and quality laden career. No one has your record. It's clean and successful.

"Well look, this has been a major surprise, a heavy thought-provoking moment in time. I need to family-size this whole matter. I'll get back with you in a week. Is that OK?"

"Sure Billy. We have time yet to determine prospect candidates, but for now you're it. You're the best damn presidential candidate either party has seen in a long time. Give us a call in a week. Dick and I look forward to again be working with you, closely. Our party is strong these days and four years with you in office as president would do America proud, and make America great again. Hear from you later. Blessings in your considerations."

"Thanks George and to you, Richard." George and Richard hung up – pleased.

Billy put the phone down. He sat there in his chair, looking out over the York countryside. He reminisced his life of beginning truancy as a kid and his life passage ensconcing him in his present job a speaker of the house of representatives. It was a sling-shot fast journey, one of great joy and love, for Anita, his kids and for his country. The joy of his kids and the opportunity to do the work God had destined him to do.

Indeed, he thought his face reflected the sunshine coming through the window. It looked like destiny was throwing him his last challenge in a life so full. His thoughts drifted up the sunrays penetrating his soul. He heard the "song of heaven" speaking "Yes, I will accept the challenge and honor of serving my country, the greatest country on earth.

Then a question invaded my mind, why do I want to be president? My response was and is, because I will not permit the country I love so much, the country I have sacrificed for, to continue down a road that would lead to possible economic or moral disaster. Things presently were quite positive and prosperous. Billy was convinced that America's finest hour was not in its past, but in the now and in its future. In God I will trust and be comforted.

Billy reminisced for a minute more and realized the love and honor York and the 12th district bestowed upon him the loyalty over the years of his life, the prayers from his hometown people during his service years and congressional years, they believed in me. I hope to continue to make them proud if I'm elected as President of the United states. I will serve them to the best of my ability, one last time. God help me – Amen.

~~~ THE END ~~~

THE WIND BENEATH MY WINGS

~~ Adopted song of Billy and Anita for one another ~~

Did you ever know that you're my hero
And everything I would like to be
I can fly higher than an eagle
For you are the wind beneath my wings

– Jeff Silbar and Larry Henley, 1982

ABOUT THE AUTHOR

I was adopted by loving parents and two older sisters, in 1935. I was raised in a northern Chicago suburb and attended not the Ivy League schools, but rather a small Missouri college and graduated with a degree in business administration and psychology minor.

Job life promoted me through the world as a brick salesman, stockbroker, investment advisor writer, farmer of sorts, and co-creator and founder (wife included) of a K-12 independent college preparatory school, just outside of Winston-Salem, North Carolina, and then worked in the land development business before retiring.

Health problems of my wife brought me to St. Louis to be closer to a son. Upon her death in 2007, I moved into a senior retirement community, where I reside – living today.